The Cydarions

Revelations

Adrian Cox

For my fiancée, who gave support and encouragement throughout my whole
writing process.

Prologue

"Thou didst cast me down to feed thine own vanity, deeming me
no better than the wretched works of thy hand. And yet-*behold!*–it
is by *their* ignorance that thy throne yet standeth-for had I ruled in
thy stead, mercy would not have stayed my hand."

Lucifer

Lucifer had vowed revenge on God, and this time he is prepared.

He produced more offspring, accelerating their growth, and sending them out younger than ever before. He needed to decimate, not just more worlds, but all worlds. More deaths meant more souls. More souls meant more power. And Lucifer needed all the power he could get, to take on God. Some of his offspring will take up the time of the Cydarions, while the majority will secure more souls for him to thrive and grow stronger. His well-conceived plans are starting to come to fruition.

The Cydarions are losing. Not only have their rules been rewritten and an academy formed, but some individuals are starting to feel a change. Old and new members join the fight against the spreading evil. More Callings are appearing, stretching the Cydarions to nearly breaking point. New information comes to light, which could bring about an end to the Cydarions. Unbeknown to them, they are walking right into another trap.

Xania having her palm re

Chapter 1

Xania was nervous. Her right hand was busy unclipping and reclipping a sai in its holster. Her left hand flicked through the menu on the table's data screen, but she wasn't even looking at it. She wasn't even hungry, she felt nauseous. Her attention was focused elsewhere. She sat in a bustling café on the planet Dusorf. The place was filled with all types of creatures and aliens, all lost in their own conversation. No one was paying her any attention. She had chosen a back-corner table on purpose; it was out of the way and had a good view of the customers. She had arrived early and was already on her third Stimi drink, when the waitress offered her a refill. Xania declined, waving away the server.

She had no idea what she was looking for, but her eyes never left the entrance. She glanced down once, to check her own data pad for any new messages. Nothing. Her knee started to shake; her heart raced. Was she prepared for this; she wondered?

The past twenty rotations had passed her by in a blur. Between the skirmish on Une and the long hike on Liatur, time had given her a chance to think about her future and what she wanted. She still missed her father, that wouldn't change, but since she had found out the truth about her real parents, there were more questions niggling at her. Questions she had come here to answer. Hopefully, anyway.

"Xania?" A soft voice said from her right, snapping her out of deep thought and making her jump, *where did this guy come from?* she thought to herself. She turned to see two beings: both with warm smiles on their faces. Xania's jaw dropped open, her mouth went dry, and she couldn't find any words. The first to speak was Kee Enclu, a twenty-one-decimetre tall skinny man, weathered, but not old looking. Large disc like eyes, glowing purple, beamed from his bald head. A bony beaked nose that hooked down to his top lip. His mouth was twisted in an enormous smile, his pointed teeth clearly visible. Dark brown robes covered his square frame, all the way down to his modest slip-on footwear. His arms were held wide open and welcoming. Xania thought he was actually glowing.

"Kee?" Xania asked. As she got out of her seat to greet him. Kee nodded warmly, and Xania fell into his outstretched arms, for a long overdue hug.

"I've been looking forward to this for a very long time, Xania." said Kee, "Jodrell has told us so much about you."

Xania closed her eyes trying to hide her tears as she gripped him tightly. This was the closest she'd ever get to meeting her real parents.

Kee released his grip and leant back, "This is Swift," he said, gesturing behind him. Xania edged passed Kee and stepped up to Swift.

"It's lovely to see you again, after all this time," he chirped. Swift was slightly taller than Xania, but his head was much bigger. His skull was covered in light blue fur, soft to the touch. A round face with small round ears on top. Dark brown eyes, set deep in the middle of his face. A dark blue snout and a mouth showing a huge smile, revealing massive canine teeth. His neck was the same thickness as his head. He had a slim body. Covered in dark blue fur. Two large feet kept a firm stance with four claws protruding from the dark fur. Strong dexterous paws reached forward to Xania and pulled her towards him, lightly squeezing her. His four digits gently stroked the small of her back.

All three of them settled into the booth around the table. Kee asked so many questions, Xania didn't know where to start.

"How is Jodrell? Still moaning his way through life?" asked Kee, a mischievous grin on his face.

Xania's smile slowly faded away and she moved uncomfortably. She didn't know what to say.

"He's passed on, hasn't he?" Kee said eventually, with sorrow in his voice. Xania nodded and explained the events of the last quarter cycle, and how everything in her life had been turned upside down. The two sat and listened, each holding one of her hands, nodding and asking more questions. Eventually they were all caught up and the conversation turned to themselves.

"So, what have you two been up to since leaving the Cydarions?" Xania asked.

"My dear girl," Swift said jovially, "just because we don't live in the citadel, does not mean we aren't Cydarions. We still live by their rules, well, I guess, their old rules." He chuckled softly to himself.

Kee took over talking, "We live here on Dusorf, there are no end of sinners passing through these parts. We just try and set them on the right path. It's not as rewarding as saving a whole planet, but it has its own merits. We are still sworn to help the unfortunate."

"Ah, well that's great news," Xania said, feeling happy for them. "Why don't you come back to El' Azar and carry on doing what you swore to do?"

"That's very kind of you, Xania, but it's not as simple as that. We were banished from the Cydarions, and we must abide by their decision," said Kee.

"We thought you'd say something like that, so, Master Pace has a message for you," Xania said, switching on her data pad. She tapped in a few commands and up flickered a hologram of Pace.

"Greetings Kee and Swift, I trust you are well? I am Pace Conor, Master of the Cydarions. By now Xania has told you about our current situation and asked you to return. Now it is my turn, Kee Enclu and Swift Obe, I am officially asking for *your* help. We appreciate the heartache that you have been through and I am willing to change the records to reflect a favourable outcome for yourselves. All of us here would extend a warm welcome to both of you. If that hasn't yet persuaded you, then let me be honest with you, kind sirs. *We* need your help, so many vulnerable beings need your help, and I believe God himself, needs your help. Lucifer is expanding his destructive trail into many more worlds. For us, fatigue and exhaustion are setting in."

Both Kee and Swift nodded, understanding Pace's situation.

"We now have an academy to train suitable candidates for the role of a Cydarion, but, as you know, it takes time. And time is what we don't have. We need your experience, your experience in battling these devils and to help show these new Storous' the correct path."

The hologram of Pace glitched and the image showed him getting down onto one knee and slightly bowing his head. "As the current Master of the Cydarions, I am not only asking for your help, but I am also begging you to re-join us." The image suddenly disappeared and there was a fraction of silence.

"Hmm, what do you think?" Kee said, his eyes glowing softly.

"Well, it does seem like they need us, and we did enjoy that life," said Swift.

"That's true, maybe we could give it another try? Pace did ask nicely," Kee said with a laugh, "besides, we will get to spend some more time with Xania." Kee smiled softly at Xania.

"Yes!" exclaimed Xania in excitement.

"But!" interrupted Swift, "first you must agree to something."

Xania kept the smile on her face, but her stomach twisted in knots as she thought about how the Cydarions had treated Kee and Swift nearly twenty cycles ago. They had given up everything for Xania, a child they never knew. Now here she is, asking for their help. She owed them so much, but how, how could she possibly repay a life, her life?

She nodded slowly; unaware her smile was fading.

Kee and Swift looked at each other.

Shit, they know what I'm thinking.

Swift gasped, "Oh my dear, no. We just want you meet our friend."

"Koách, yes Koách has a proposal for you," said Kee.

Xania frowned, "A proposal?"

Swift and Kee both nodded.

"What kind of proposal? She doesn't even know me."

"Not she," said Kee, "just Koách, and Koách knows as much about you as we do. We are always talking about you."

Xania blushed a little, "I'm sorry, but what kind of proposal?" she asked again.

"That my dear, you can find out tomorrow," said Kee.

"Okay, I can do that," agreed Xania, still feeling a little anxious.

"That's settled then," said Swift, "we're meeting Koách next rotation. If you care to stay with us until then, we will happily introduce you," he offered.

"That sounds great," Xania said, "I want to know more about you two anyway."

"That makes my heart happy," Swift announced gleefully.

For the rest of the rotation the three of them wandered around the busy market stalls, chatting and trying out the local food delicacies, while getting to know each other. Kee bought Xania a hand woven dark brown cloak, just like his own. A present to make up for all the birthdays they have missed. The street illuminations were just coming on and the sunlight was fading as they reached the end of the market street, suddenly a hand grabbed Xania's wrist, and she spun around. An old woman, in loose ill-fitting clothes, smiled at her.

"Tell your future?" the old woman croaked.

"No, it's okay," Xania said, trying to wriggle her arm free.

"Won't take long," said the old woman, insisting.

"Oh, we don't have the time," Xania said, trying to pull back, but the woman's grip on her wrist only tightened. Her eyes never left Xania's.

"Your aura is... clouded," the fortune teller murmured, tilting her head.

Xania froze, confused.

"Your future, now that could be interesting," Swift said, nearly bouncing with excitement.

Xania sighed, then gave a small smile, "Fine."

The old woman led her to a small table and gestured for her to sit. She took Xania's right hand turning it palm up.

Her eyes widened. Slowly, she traced a line with her thumb, then shook her head. "You shouldn't even be alive; your lifeline end here."

Xania smiled knowingly. "I know. But I was saved, with God's help." Kee touched her shoulder in quiet support, while Swift leaned closer.

Suddenly, the fortune teller seized Xania's other hand and spread it open. Her pupils dilated. She muttered in a language no one understood.

Xania tried to lighten the mood. "What is it? Too many children?" She laughed at Swift.

The woman's gaze snapped to hers, "My child," she whispered, "this mark says you should not be alive. But this…" she jabbed a crease in Xania's left palm, "this foretells your end. You will die… with a red one!"

Xania frowned. "A devil is going to kill me?"

"No. You will die *with* them," the woman said, clutching her hands tighter.

Xania shook her head. "You've mistaken me for someone else."

"*You* are working with the red one," the fortune teller pressed.

"No." Xania pulled free. "You're wrong. I would never do that."

Kee tugged her away from the table. "Come on, she's just a crazy old woman."

"Be prepared, child! Only you can change its course!"

"I will change things," shouted Xania over her shoulder, as she was led away, adding, "I promise." A statement she muttered more to herself than anyone else, and she meant it. The Cydarions were still going through the new changes that Pace had implemented nearly ninety rotations ago.

Swift placed a credit on the table, "She's just a girl, shame on you," he said, and walked off to catch up with Kee.

"Just forget about her," Kee said to Xania, "she's always been a strange one around here. Come on, I'll make you some delicious food," he offered, as they headed to their accommodation.

"Yes, that does sound nice," Xania said with a smile.

A quiet evening was spent in their apartment talking all about being a Cydarion. The warriors of God.

Xania spoke of her feelings when Gods light washed over her after she read the allegiance.

Kee smiled as he reminisced about his very own pledge, "It was on an unusually stormy night. The cove under the citadel where the sacred stone is, had water lapping onto the bottom steps. The others had to wade into the water to witness the ceremony. Well, just as I had finished the allegiance, a huge bolt of lightning hit the water, right at the entrance of the cove. It lit up the air so bright that I was blinded. I was amazed and thought it was all a part of the allegiance. But it wasn't, I had to be taken to the medical unit."

Swift stroked Kee's arm, "Poor thing, it must have been terrible for you."

"You've heard this story many times before," said Kee.

"I know, but I still can't imagine it."

Xania let out a little giggle, "So what happened?" she asked eagerly.

"Well," said Kee, "after a few rotations my sight came back, but I felt different."

"Different how?" Xania asked.

"Something inside me, here." He tapped the side of his head. "There was a feeling of energy behind my eyes. It wasn't painful or uncomfortable, but when I concentrated on it, a white beam shot out from my eyes. I blew the door out of the medical unit." He chuckled to himself as he remembered the image.

"Anyway, to cut a long story short, Jodrell trained me to harness that power and to control it."

Xania smiled at the mention of Jodrell's name. She was already feeling some kind of connection with these two ex Cydarions.

There was a comfortable silence as the three of them tucked into a hearty meal.

Xania cleared her throat, after she cleared her bowl, "Have you thought about Pace's offer?"

"We have spoken about that, at length, over the cycles," said Swift, "and we always came to the same conclusion."

Xania nodded.

"We agreed, that if the Cydarions ever sent us a message and asked us to come back, we would decline."

Xania's face dropped.

"But!" said Kee, holding up a finger. "We never expected, in a million cycles, that the messenger would be you, sweet girl."

Xania faked a smile.

"So," Swift cut in, "because you have made the trip all the way here, just for us, we would gladly go back with you."

Xania gasped, "So you'll come back to the Cydarions?" she confirmed.

Kee smiled. "Yes," he said.

"That's wonderful," said an excited Xania, "but, just for the record, I was coming to meet you anyway. Pace asked me for a favour."

"That warms my heart," said Swift.

During the evening, they spoke about many things and Xania told them of a diary she keeps. Ever since the records keeper had given her a journal for her tenth birthday, she would write in it, her private thoughts. She hoped to pass it down to her daughter, in time.

"I'm sure you will, precious Xania," said Swift, with a smile. Kee gave her another big hug.

Koách

Chapter 2

At first light, the three Cydarions meditated together. Xania experienced a spiritual connection with the two older males, making her feel their warmth. Soon they were on their way to meet Koách, passing back through the marketplace and down some narrow side streets.

Kee and Swift led Xania to a rundown part of the city, where tin and plastoid sheeting resembled a form of housing. A mere piece of cloth acted as a door for a tiny one roomed dwelling. Inside, a sweet sticky smell filled the air, as though some cooking had taken place.

Swift introduced Xania to Koách.

"I'm pleased to meet you, Xania," said a gravelly voice.

"Likewise," Xania answered, "I hear you have found God?"

"It was more like… he found me," said Koách, "please, sit down." Xania looked around for a place to sit, then felt a little embarrassed that there was only a rolled-up mattress and a small cooking burner in the tiny room. Kee and Swift settled onto the ground, Xania quickly joined them.

"Please, carry on," Xania said warmly.

Koách looked at Swift, who replied, "It's ok, you *can* trust her."

Koách was nineteen decimetres tall and nearly half as wide. Wearing only a wraparound sheet that covered the whole body, arms, legs and head. Koách's white skinned face had soft features, yellow eyes with blue pupils, a small nose and a large flat bill. A black scar ran down one whole side of the face, from the right eye socket to the corner of the bill.

Koách stepped forward, towards Xania, and into a ray of light streaming through a gap in the poorly constructed home. Koách lowered the hood, opened the wrap, letting it fall to the floor.

Xania gasped, clasping a hand to her mouth. Stood before her was a body that was covered in scars. Scars on top of scars. Healed welts that had turned into solid hard skin. Looking like the armoured skin of a crocodile. The scars were all black with the occasional hint of white natural skin underneath. Koách had large, six-digit hands, twice the size of Xania's, and two six toed feet, standing shoulder width apart. Xania saw a fighter's stance. The scars went from Koách's head to the soles of the feet and everywhere in between, making it look like a black and white camouflage skin.

"Please don't be afraid," Koách said softly.

"No, I'm not, it's just," Xania paused and pointed to the scars, "do they hurt?"

Koách grimaced, "It's not the physical scars that hurt."

Xania nodded solemnly as Koách took a deep breath and carried on. "I used to be a slave gladiator on the barbaric moon of Shentle. I was taken from my family at a young age. My species are known for their strength, but that is all I know. I have never been home; I don't even know what my home world is called." Koách looked directly at Xania. "I was beaten regularly by my masters. There were so many of us, but no other like me. We were kept below ground in an abandoned mineshaft. It was so deep, with no way to climb out. There was only daylight for one section per rotation, when the sun was directly overhead. The children were there to do chores, cleaning up the stadium and arenas, but when we were old enough, they put us into fighting pits.

Koách paused briefly, unsure whether to be totally honest or not. Swift nodded with a kind smile and urged Koách to continue.

Koách's gaze moved from Swift back to Xania. "We were forced to fight to the death. If we refused, the masters would kill eight of us, just to make an example. We all agreed to be sacrificed for the sake of each other. But that didn't mean we were close friends; we were just trying to stay alive. Everyone kept to themselves, so we didn't grow attachments."

Koách looked down, "It was a lonely existence. But, for some reason, I was befriended by an old Rodian. I don't know how long he was down there; he never discussed it. But our master's must have forgotten about him. He took me under his care and taught me how to fight properly. He was a God loving man and parted his ways onto me. He told me about a group of warriors called the Cydarions, and that if someone else is fighting for the righteousness of others, then the least I can do is fight for myself. So, I trained, I moved rocks all rotation and other exercises to build up my strength. All the while being beaten and whipped, fighting for my own life in that arena.

Xania wasn't sure what to say while Koách took another deep breath to steady their breathing. "I have tried my best to block those events out of my mind. But what I do remember the most, is being taught about God by the only person who cared for me. Eventually when I felt God in my heart, the darkness of that prison seemed to be bathed into light. I have never seen that darkness again. I fought for my freedom; I had no choice but to survive. By being undefeated in two hundred and fifty fights, I had earned my freedom. When I was released, I asked my only friend to come with me and escape that prison. He refused, saying it was his destiny to teach the young captives. He was too old to fight, so he was fighting the only way he could, by saving one child at a time.

"I was lost when I was finally free. I don't know where I came from, I don't even know my own name. Koách was the name my master's gave me. I thought about changing, but decided against it. My name is a reminder of who I was, and that's something I will never forget."

Koách sat down in front of Xania, taking one of her hands. Koách traced the outline of some scars with Xania's fingertips. "You see these scars? Each one of them represents someone I have killed, just so I can be here today. Every waking morning, I pray for all their souls. I have gotten used to the blackness of my scars, for death is blackness. But you see my white skin coming through between the scars? That represents me, and who I am now, the light shining through.

"I wandered the galaxy looking for work and answers. Work I found, security in a few places, but all of them were corrupt. That didn't sit well with me, so I moved on. I did think about revenge on my masters, I thought about it for cycles, but that isn't what my old friend had instilled in me. One day I heard a voice in my head, I thought I was going crazy, but it was a calming voice, it had warmth to it. The voice told me to follow my heart. So, I did, and it led me on a few adventures, but finally I ended up here. I met Kee and Swift, they gave me a lot of peace. They asked me to stay with them a while until I figured out what to do next." Koách looked at both Kee and Swift, "They are so generous, that they took in a complete stranger and wanted nothing in return."

"They have told me all about you and the Cydarions they used to be." Koách stood up and placed a large hand over their heart and took a bow. "Lady Xania, my body may appear broken, but my heart is pure light, and as strong as a nucleus."

"I don't doubt that," said Xania. "Koách, are you aware what a Cydarion does?"

"Defeat evil?" Koách replied.

Xania agreed, "Yes, but it's more than that. God sends us to a planet that is most in need of his help. While we are there, we learn about the different species and their rules. To understand their way of life. But also, what is happening to them and their planet. We follow the Calling..."

"The Calling," Koách interrupted, "that's a feeling, isn't it?"

Xania nodded, "Yes, you gain it after you pledge your allegiance. And if God deems you worthy."

"I believe God has already done that part," said Kee with a smile.

"But there is training first," Xania carried on, "there's a lot of history to learn about. Although, thanks to Drake, a retired Cydarion, who is now a school-teacher..."

"You can retire?" gasped Swift.

Xania turned to face Kee and Swift, "There's been a few changes recently, hopefully for the better. Thanks to Pace, the Cydarions all have a say on how things are done."

"That sounds very progressive," said Swift.

"And the evil?" Koách asked, getting back on subject.

"Oh, sorry," Xania apologised, "The evil is usually dealt with in a manner most suitable to them. Occasionally it is letting them return home. Sometimes they are sent to the Dark Realm, but mostly, we do have to eliminate their threat."

"By killing?" asked Koách.

"Yes," replied Xania earnestly. "I understand you may be against killing, given your background..."

"Lady Xania, I have vowed to God to kill all evil. Until my very last breath.

Xania smiled. "It sounds like you are nearly a Cydarion already."

"If you would have me, I will gladly serve you, lady Xania."

Xania was a little shocked at the statement but quickly got to her feet. "You have already served under a master and earned your own freedom. You shall not *serve* under another one. You have welcomed God into your heart, and we are all equals. You *shall* become a Cydarion. It is I who bow down before you, Koách." With that, Xania bowed down as Koách stood upright. Xania was now eye level with Koách's heart, and it seemed to be radiating pure light. Xania gasped again.

"I have never met anyone so pure of heart, even my Mast...., my father, Jodrell may not have been this pure." Xania took a breath, "We would be honoured to have you join us."

"Lady Xania, although I am done with fighting, this is a cause that I would gladly enter the arena again, for I know God is on my side." Koách beamed with pride.

"Tell me, do you believe heaven?" wondered Xania.

Koách paused for a snap, thinking about the question, before answering. "It's not that I don't want to go to heaven, I just don't believe in it."

"Oh, why is that?" asked Xania, curious.

"I believe in God and what he can do," said Koách, "I follow the way of God, but I can't believe he has a plan for every living creature in the universe. He just can't. Does a roach have as its destiny to be stepped on? Do younglings deserve to be born with an incurable disease? Should families be torn apart and brutalised for the pleasure of others? *I* don't think so. If God had a plan for every one of my fellow captives that I have buried, then he is as cruel as Lucifer himself. What

I believe, is that God is the light, and we should follow that light, to wherever it shall take us, whether it be heaven or just a muddy hole in the ground." Koách shrugged. "I don't know, I may feel differently after becoming a Cydarion."

"Thank you for being honest," said Xania. "Do you meditate?" she asked.

"Of course, lady Xania. Kee and Swift taught me," said Koách.

"Would you do me the honour of meditating with me?" Xania asked, as she sat back down.

"It would be my pleasure," said Koách, then sat down in front of the three visitors.

For over a section, the four of them meditated together in silence. When they were finished, Xania pulled out a commlink and proceeded to contact Nyk. He was to collect them all in his spaceship, the Starlady.

Māra

Chapter 3

Nyk and Pace stood before the devil's lair. They knew they were here to stop this devil's deadly impact on this world. Either by its own demise or banishment to the Dark Realm. The fires that flanked the entrance hissed and spat. eternal and unyielding. No devil had ever repented; none ever would. Tonight would be no different. With a nod, they stepped into the darkness. Cold wet stone closed in around them. Mildew choked the air. Their eyes adjusted just as a low cackle echoed from depths ahead. Moving on, Pace drew his yonca blade; Nyk levelled his blaster. The passage widened, spilling them into a cavernous chamber.

Three devils. Two whispering on a slab of stone, the third bent over a glowing datapad. The stench of rot rolled off them in waves.

Nyk gestured, and they split. Pace ghosting along the right wall, Nyk circling left. while he went left. Together, they raised their weapons.

"You're finished," Nyk barked, his blaster trained on the one with the data pad. "This ends here, by banishment, or by death."

The devil turned slowly, smiling with teeth too sharp. "Ah... so you've come at last."

Nyk advanced a step, aim steady, "Your reign of terror is over."

The devil tilted his head, gaze sliding past Nyk toward Pace. "You haven't told him?"

Confusion flickered across Nyk's face. He looked to Pace, only to see his partner grinning, the yonca blade hidden beneath his coat once more.

"Nyk," Pace said, voice low, almost reverent. "This is Māra... he's shown me what we could be, what we *should* be."

Nyk's face went blank with confusion, "Wha... what are you talking about?" he stammered.

Pace stepped closer, palms open like he meant no harm. "Nyk, listen, we've been Cydarions for cycles. It's exhausting. Everything we do, helping. risking our lives, what do we get? Nothing. No rotation dedicated to us, no thanks. They don't even ask for help. Have any of those animals out there ever come up to you and said 'thank you'? No. They're blind, or stupid. Why save stupid?" He jabbed a finger toward the mouth of the lair.

"Pace!" Nyk barked "This devil's got to you, don't listen."

Pace smiled, not the man Nyk knew. "No, my friend. He's shown me what we could be. Powerful. Rulers of worlds. An empire. Think of the planets obeying our command."

Nyk stepped in front of Pace and levelled his blaster at Māra. "This isn't you," he said. "Let him go. Cease your mind tricks."

Māra laughed low and col., "No trick, I simply opened his eyes to what he could achieve."

"Lucifer's words fill your mouth!" Nyk snapped and fired. The bolt struck the rock ceiling. Chunks rained down. Dust buried Māra.

Pace moved like a viper and wrenched the blaster from Nyk's hands. "What are you doing?" Nyk demanded.

"Protecting our future," Pace said. His voice as hard as a steel, the words as soft as velvet.

"No!" shouted Nyk. "This isn't you. It's not our way."

"It could be." Paces grin widened. " I've made my deal. Now it's your turn. Ask for anything. Anything and you shall have it."

Nyk drew his spare, careful to keep it beyond Pace's reach, and aimed at Māra. "Get out of his head!" he ordered.

The reply didn't come from Pace at all. The voice slid out of Māra like oil. *'I'm not in his head.' It paused, savouring, 'I'm in yours.'*

Nyk stared at Pace. His friend's face was utterly changed, calm and certain. Nyk forced a laugh that tasted like iron. *'Not him... me.'*

Māra nodded once, slow as a verdict. The gun fell from Nyk's hand as if it had burned him. He breathed hard; sweat beaded at his temples.

"Isn't it wonderful?" Pace asked Nyk, voice bright with triumph as if revealing a gift. Nyk's lungs tightened and the world narrowed to the thunder of his pulse.

Nyk's voice was raw. "Why are you doing this, Pace? We joined the Cydarions to stand up for every living thing, to fight the devils, not become them!"

Pace smiled like something broke behind his eyes. "We're losing Nyk, can't you see that? Why wouldn't you want to be on the winning side?"

"Winning?" Nyk's hands shook. "This isn't winning or losing. It's about right or wrong. Those devils are slaughtering millions. I couldn't live with myself if I stood by."

Pace shrugged, "Then don't!"

Nyk froze, "Don't what?"

"Don't live."

A breath like silk, and poison. *'I can help you with that,'* Māra whispered.

Nyk swallowed. "Pace... you're not yourself, I can hear him too."

Pace's lips didn't move. 'Pace can't help you. Only I can,' said Māra inside Nyk's head.

"Get out of my..." Nyk snapped. Pace stooped and picked up Nyk's dropped blaster as if nothing were wrong.

"Make a deal," Māra murmured into his bones. *"And I'll stop the thoughts'.*

Then the world tore. Images slammed into Nyk like a velocity bike into a concra wall. His old girlfriend, Devon kissing Cole Tsera; Pace exploding on a steel landing platform; Xania being raped, the whole citadel bowing to a master. None of it real, all of it real enough. Nyk dropped to his knees, vision shredded by scenes that belonged nowhere.

'You can stop it,' Māra promised, *'say the word.'*

Nyk rasped, teeth clenched. *"You'll never..."* He crashed to the floor, every muscle empty with refusal.

Pace slid an arm around him, warm and traitorous. "It's simple Nyk. Accept, and you'll be free."

"The Cydarions have fought for thousands of cycles," Nyk gasped, "We can't give up. We won't. Every living thing depends on us."

"It's exhausting," said Pace softly, as if confessing a sin. "Risking everything for those ungrateful creatures. This way we live. This way we have the life we wanted."

Nyk looked up through the blur of tears and bloodied pride. "No."

Pace's voice dropped to a memory. "Remember? We talked about having it all. This is our chance!"

Nyk forced himself to stand. His voice was small and Iron. "The universe needs us to be strong."

"It's over Nyk, we can help end it all." Pace shook his fist, "That's real power."

Nyk shook his head, "No!" The word crawled out of him like an insect. *How could Pace say this? We had sworn an oath to stand against Lucifer and his demons. The vow rang in Nyk's skull and shattered against Pace's calm. A sour breath of rot rose from Paces skin.*

"All or nothing, Nyk. All or nothing," he said, as if reciting Nyk's own words.

Tears blurred Nyk's vision. "How could you?" he sobbed. "You promised your life. For them. For everyone!" His chest heaved; each breath hitched and left him hollow. The world tilted. The demon's whisper wormed through his thoughts, soft and steady. *Maybe he's right, maybe I've been wrong all along.*

Pace eased the blaster back into Nyk's hand, like a priest handing over a sacrament. "Is that what you want?" He asked. "To die for strangers who don't even know your name?"

Nyk stared at the cold metal in his trembling fingers. Māra's voice crashed into his mind, wild and possessive, *'I will always be here. You can never kill me.'* The thought and the whisper braided into one unbearable thing. Nyk's resolve frayed; memory and doubt tangled until he could not find the seam between right and necessary.

"Go on," Pace breathed, almost gentle, and lifted Nyk's arm.

The muzzle slid into Nyk's mouth. Time narrowed to the steel and the taste of dust. Tears streamed down his cheeks; his face scrunched in a soundless prayer.

"It's the right thing," Pace whispered. "You'll save them. You'll save us all." He smirked to himself.

Nyk pulled the trigger.

Silence came like an explosion. Nyk's body toppled, ragged and limp. The room swallowed the sound. Pace flinched, then let out a slow, satisfied sigh. A smile crept upon his face, composed and untroubled.

Crown Claw

Chapter 4

Nyk awoke with a scream, sweat poured from his brow. He looked around, Pace turned over and carried on sleeping. *It was just a dream,* he thought to himself, as he reached for his water pouch and took a big swig. *It felt so real.* He closed his eyes and rubbed his face; the sweat stung his eyes. He got to his feet and wiped the sweat away with his shirt. He wandered to the edge of the woodland where they had made their camp for the night. The low crackle of their fire faded into the distance as he walked. Nyk inhaled deeply, the musky smell of bark and fresh vegetation seeped into his body. The glow from a Radon belt around this colourful planet gave off a yellow tinge to the accompanying moons hanging in the night sky. He could hear the scurrying of nocturnal animals coming from the trees behind him, occasionally he'd hear a voice, in the distance. He's learnt to ignore the voices since they started, so long ago, now they're just a part of him.

He sat down on the cool dirt and leant back against the trunk of a hollow tree. He stared out into space and shook his head, "What have you got in store for me, sky daddy?" he asked God. "I've given you everything. All I ask for is peaceful sleep. I'm exhausted, in here," he tapped his head, dislodging a tear that got lost in his stubble. He shifted and sighed, "No answer, huh?" He waved a finger to the sky, "You know, even though you never answer, you do make me feel better." With a smile, he threw his arms out wide, "I mean, just look at all this."

The black mountains to his right, twinkled and sparkled like a gemstone under a spotlight. The blue silica land in front of him looked so inviting, he wanted to dive into it. Suddenly, a squawk came from behind him and a gust of wind wafted his long-wet hair, as a bird flew up to him and landed on his outstretched arm. Its long talons gripped his arm, the bird had pure white feathers except for its head which was long black fur. A hooked beak and two large disc-like eyes looked at him, the purple pupils seemingly spinning.

"Whoa" whispered Nyk, a little shocked, but kept his arm perfectly still. "Who's this?" he said with a smile. It was then that he noticed the black fur on its head, and he laughed, "You've got a little Nyk going on." He pointed to his own hair with his free hand. The bird's gaze didn't waver, but a slight head tilt made Nyk think it was listening. Nyk decided to talk further to the bird and spoke about the dreams he'd been having and how it's affecting his sleep. At first, Nyk felt a little dumb talking to a wild bird, but the more he spoke, the more he felt the bird relax, it seemed to be listening. He even managed to bring his arm closer to himself without the bird taking flight. Nyk looked deep into those mesmerizing eyes and felt calmness washed over him.

He spoke about how he had met Pace, and together they set out to do some good in the universe. "Everything changed when I joined the Cydarions," he said, "I suppose I grew up." He chuckled to himself. Then something unexpected happened, the bird hoped off his arm and into his lap, settling down. The warmth of the bird was felt through his trousers. Nyk made small movements to bring his hand up and slowly started to stroke the bird's head. It didn't flinch. "Are you sure you're not domesticated?" Nyk asked, knowing full well it couldn't answer. Instead, it just closed its eyes and started to make a sound. Not with its mouth, but through its body. Almost as if its heartbeat was being amplified. Thump thump; thump thump; thump thump, and Nyk relaxed too. For the first time in as long as he could remember, his mind was clear.

***

"Nyk?" shouted Pace from within the trees. Nyk stirred awake slowly, trying not to startle the bird still on his lap. Looking down he noticed the birds head had rotated 180° and two ears had popped up, something he hadn't noticed before.

"Do you hear something?" Nyk whispered. The bird had stopped making the rhythmic beating sound and outstretched its wings, then with a powerful leap and a flap of its wings, it was away. Flying high into the sky, the early light having just broken over the horizon.

"Nyk," shouted Pace again.

"Out here," replied Nyk in a loud whisper. The bird, still in sight, flew around in circles, getting higher and higher.

"Are you ok?" Pace asked, as he saw Nyk getting to his feet.

"Look," said Nyk, pointing to the bird, now just a white smudge in the sky. Pace looked at the bird, not knowing what Nyk was talking about.

"Now!" Nyk exclaimed. And, as though it knew that command, the bird stopped circling and dove, straight down.

"Whoa," uttered Pace, "that thing's fast!"

The bird swooped down to the ground and straight back up again, not quite as high but then turned and headed back towards the woods. "I think it caught something," said Pace. Nyk nodded, a smile crept onto his face. The bird flew directly towards Nyk, and whooshed straight over his head, dropping something straight into Nyk's open arms. Nyk's head swivelled as the bird kept on flying. Pace picked the item from Nyk's arms, it was a small furry mammal, long ears with a small round body and four short legs. Both sides of its body had been punctured from the bird's talons, the blood was still warm and wet. The mammal had died immediately on attack, the body now flaccid. Pace smiled. "Looks like we've got a hearty breakfast," he said holding the mammal by its ears. Pace mumbled something about a tasty recipe, as he headed back to camp.

Nyk watched Pace walk away. He felt compelled to stay where he was, without knowing why. Until he heard a feint squawk, he smiled and held out his arm again for the returning bird to land on. Nyk already felt some kind of connection with this majestic animal. The bird arrived but it didn't land on his arm, instead it just hovered in front of him. Its talons stretched forwards, towards Nyk. He cupped both hands to his front and opened them, palms facing up. And, with the gentlest of manoeuvres, the bird came closer and opened its talons, placing something warm in Nyk's hands. He looked down; it was a small, speckled egg. Nyk was astounded, his mouth fell open. The bird's mesmerising eyes bored into him, before squawking twice. Nyk swore he heard two words come from the bird. He smiled at the bird and nodded, "I shall call him, Crown Claw." The bird took one last look at the egg in Nyk's hand, turned, and flew away.

Nyk watched that bird go, knowing that he'd never see his new friend again. He vowed to never forget the peaceful time they had shared together. He looked back at the egg. It was warm and he felt a little movement from within. He whispered, "Stay warm, Crown Claw." He ripped off a sleeve to his under shirt and wrapped it around the egg, slipping it safely into his pouch. As he headed back towards Pace and a cooked breakfast, the voices in his head returned, this time, louder than before.

After a filling meal of freshly cooked meat the two Cydarions set off towards the Calling. It was an unusually quiet walk; Pace was busy thinking about other Cydarion matters and Nyk flipped between talking to his new little passenger and talking to the voices in his head. It wasn't until they came upon the devil's lair with the two eternal fires burning on the outside, that either one of them spoke aloud.

"This looks familiar," said Nyk.

"Yep," agreed Pace, "they all start to look the same after a while."

"No, it's..." Nyk paused, "it's different this time."

"Yeah," agreed Pace again, his brow furrowed. The walls were cold and wet. He sniffed the air, "it smells of mould."

Nyk looked confused when a laughing cackle came from deep within the lair.

"I hate that sound," said Pace, pulling out his yonca fighting implement. He looked at Nyk, who nodded in return and brought up his blaster, his hand was visibly shaking and sweat started to run down his back in the cool air.

"Are you ok?" Pace whispered to Nyk.

Nyk swallowed hard and stared at his blaster.

"Nyk! What's wrong?" asked Pace again.

This time, Nyk shook his thoughts away, "I'm fine, just... indigestion," he replied

Pace nodded. "We'll be out of here soon enough," he replied with a smile. They went deeper into the cave and turned a corner. The room that lay out in front of them was circular. Two devils sat on a stone table conversing with one another, while a third was entering information onto a data pad. The smell of decay entered Nyks nostrils, and he froze, memories of his dream flashed through his mind. Pace, who was in front, crept around the walls, staying in the shadows.

Nyk scanned the scene in front of him, *this is too familiar*. Just then, Pace came out of the shadows and aimed his yonca fighting implement at the standing devil.

"You're finished here," Pace said to the devil. Nyk's training kicked in, and he too exited the shadows and waved his blaster at the other two devils sitting together. If they were startled, they didn't look it. Barely a glance was given in Nyks direction. The devil looked at Pace, a little confused.

"You're not..." the devil said, before scanning the room and setting his eyes on Nyk, "You're supposed to be here," the devil said pointing to Pace. Nyk's face filled with shock. Pace looked confused.

"What are you talking about?" Pace asked the devil. The devil didn't turn to look at Pace, but instead, kept his eyes fixed on Nyk, and smiled.

"You haven't told him yet?"

"Told me what?" asked Pace, glancing across at Nyk, "told me what, Nyk?"

The devils mouth never moved again, except for a smirk, but Nyk could hear its words clearly in his head.

I'm Māra, I'm the voice in your head. Nyk shook his head and whispered, "No, no."

What you saw, shall come to pass, Nyk heard the devil say. Nyks arm dropped, as he lowered his blaster, his breathing increased.

"Shut up! shut up!" Nyk shouted and started slapping a palm against his own head.

Pace didn't know what was going on, his eyes flickered between the devil and Nyk. "What's happening?" he asked, not sure of who the question was directed to.

You know it's true, said Māra in Nyk's head, *see!* Just then, images of Nyk's life flashed through his mind, most too quick to fully remember, until the last image. An image that was fuzzy around the edges, but the subject was clear. Nyk was sitting down, the muzzle of his blaster in his mouth and Pace in front of him. A muzzle flash jolted Nyk out of the image. He lifted his blaster, walked towards the devil and fired four times, shouting, "STOP IT!" for every single shot. Pace had to move quickly for fear of being shot, but all four blaster bolts ripped into the devil, exploding it apart. Pace saw a red glow from behind him and turned to see one of the other devils escaping through their own portal, one racing after the other. Pace fired and took down the last devil, as the portal closed.

Nyk and Pace were now alone in the devil's lair.

"What the hell was that Nyk?" Pace said.

Pace, still in shock, looked at Nyk. "He was in my head," Nyk said quietly.

"What do you mean, he was in your head?" asked Pace aggressively.

"I don't know," said Nyk, his own anger growing, "he was showing me images of..."

"Images of what?" asked Pace, annoyed that he was not getting the answers he wanted.

"I don't know, bad things. He was goading me."

"Goading you?" said Pace, "goading you how?"

Nyk snapped, "TO PULL THE TRIGGER, TO SHOOT AND DIE!" he shouted, then slumped to the floor, crying.

***

Pace gasped, "Why would he want you to kill him?" he asked. Nyk didn't answer, he just pulled out the egg and held it close to his chest. Pace sighed and thought.

He went up to Nyk and crouched down in front of him. Collecting the blaster that Nyk hadn't realised he'd dropped and handed it back to him, "Here."

Nyk took one look at the blaster and freaked out, he shoved Pace over and ran out of the lair.

Pace sighed heavily and stayed on the floor for some time trying to make sense of everything that had just happened. He knew the Calling had ceased but knew nothing else. Eventually, he got up and looked around the lair, not sure of what to look for, until he saw the blinking lights of the data pad Māra had been holding. Picking it up he examined it but was unable to read the devilish language.

"I'll take you back, see if we can decipher you," he said to the data pad. Gripping it tightly he made his way out of the lair into the bright sunlight. A green portal was just closing in front of him, "Nyk," Pace shouted through the haze, but it was no use. Pace opened his own portal and followed his friend home.

***

Nyk raced through the citadel, not fast enough to cause any alarm, but he did keep to the lesser used corridors and exited the building via a small back door that led into the gardens. Ignoring some of Drakes students practicing their combat techniques, he rushed past and out of the grounds, following the clifftops until he reached the old ruins. There he sat, his back against the wall, just like Xania had done over a cycle ago. He remembered the advice he gave her back then, 'Let it out,' he had said. So, he did, he shouted at the top of his voice, "Argh!" and then another, "Argh!" He tried to relax and slow his breathing. He reached into his pouch and pulled out the still wrapped egg. Carefully he unravelled it until the egg was in his palm. Placing his other hand over the egg to keep it warm, he leant back and meditated. First, he thought of how peaceful his mind was when Crown Claw's mother had been around, then he let his mind wander peacefully.

By the time he came out of his meditation, the sun was still warm but setting low on the horizon. He looked at the egg and smiled, "I've got a plan for you."

Nyk made his way down to the farmhouse where Beau's parents now reside and knocked on the door.

Elisha answered, a smile lighting up when she saw him.

"Nyk, what a surprise," she gave him a hug and ushered him into the cosy house, shouting to Petra.

"What can we help you with?" asked Petra, as he offered Nyk a spare seat by the small fire in the family room.

"Being farmers, I know you're good with the land, but have you ever looked after animals?" Nyk asked.

"But, of course," nodded Petra, "Before Beau arrived, we used to have a menagerie of farm animals," he answered.

"But it was a lot of work for just us two, we were much more suited to crops and vegetables," said Elisha.

"Why do you ask?" wondered Petra.

Nyk smiled as he dug into his pouch, "It's this guy, I want to rear him," he held the egg up for Elisha and Petra to see.

Petra leaned closer, taking a keen look at the egg. "What is it?" he asked.

"I don't know," replied Nyk, before realising his mistake, "Oh, it's a bird. I was offered it by its mother. Other than that, I don't know any more. But I want to raise it," he said eagerly.

"How would you do that?" asked Petra.

"That's what I'm here for, I'd like your help too," asked Nyk politely.

"I see," said Elisha with a smile, "once it's hatched, you would have to be around a lot of the time, if you want to form a bond with it."

"I do intend to," said Nyk, "at least I'll try. What with our commitments already…"

"I'm sure we can help you out," offered Petra.

For the next full section all three of them came up with a plan on how to look after the egg and later, the newly born chick. Nyk held the egg up in the light of the fire and for the first time, he could see inside the egg. A pink-yellow shadow was growing inside, barely moving except for a little twitch now and again.

"You'll be safe here, little one," Nyk said, handing over the egg to Petra and thanking them both for their help and hospitality.

After leaving he decided to have a good night's rest. He would talk to Pace and Bork the following rotation, when his mind was clearer... Hopefully

Lucifers home on Gehenna

Chapter 5

On the remote planet of Gehenna, somewhere in the universe, a foreboding figure sat atop a large chair, intricately carved from volcanic rock. One wall of the room was full of windows, its glass, stained red from the blood of the first slaves, bathed the room in a red and orange glow. Those first slaves built this monolithic mansion, into the volcanic mountainside. A beam of light streamed in and fell across his face. Lucifer sighed, got up from his chair and made his way down the stone steps before him, to his awaiting officers. This was his favourite room in the castle. Not the place where he dreamt up evil schemes, but here, in the war room, where his visions took on a reality. As every hooved footstep descended the hot worn steps, he looked at his officers, one at a time. Each one bowing their heads in respect of their almighty. Lucifer had gotten over the power that respect brought him, a long time ago. He knew it was more out of fear than respect, but he still made them bow, so that they would *never* forget their place. Lucifer reached Kokabiel, who had waited to be spoken to,

"What news do you have for me?" Lucifer asked.

"My Lord, project M.U.R.I.S. is working well. We have affected seven areas so far, with many more looking likely," Kokabiel said.

"Good, good," said Lucifer, "but I've had a change of mind."

"Yes, whatever you want," grovelled Lucifers subordinate. Lucifer walked up to the thick wooden framed desk behind Kokabiel and placed a clawed hand on the tabletop. The plexi screen surface used biometrics to read his unique code and opened a group of files on the screen. He flicked through them, like an old rolodex and selected the star maps. Again, selecting a further file, he tapped the show button, and a hologram appeared before him and the two overlaying files. A star map of the Dettant galaxy. He moved his hands up to the hologram and moved them apart a couple of times until the desired area had been zoomed in on.

"Here," he said, pointing to a cluster of planets, "I want to try project M.U. R.I.S. in this area." He then quickly turned to another demon officer, "Biffrons, you're the mathematician, what affect would it have?"

Biffrons looked surprised to be spoken to so soon, and he shuffled uncomfortably, "My Lord, I believe that would get the desired results you have been looking for; with minimal effort," he added.

"Excellent," Lucifer replied with a clap of his hands.

"My Lord," Kokabiel said, "It may take at least half a cycle to get there, from our current position."

"That's okay," said Lucifer, "we can make a few stops along the way." He smiled to himself, a smile that would look evil to anyone watching, but to him it was a smile, a wry smile. Something that he's rarely seen with. And that just suited him fine.

"Such an excellent plan, will you be overseeing this?" Biffrons asked.

"No, not yet. I shall decide at the time, although I must admit, it is very tempting to me," Lucifer replied.

Just then, another demon came bursting into the war room out of breath, "Sire, I have word!" the demon blurted out between heavy breaths. Lucifer raised his hand, instructing the messenger to say no more, then turned to his officers and barked at them,

"LEAVE US!"

The room fell silent, except for the light scraping of feet and hooves on the solid floor. All four of the demon officers hastily shuffled out of the room and waited in the corridor.

Lucifer waited for the door to shut and placed his hands behind his back.

"Procel, you bring me news?" Lucifer asked the messenger, in a soft tone.

"Yes, master," said Procel, "I have found it. Their location is on here." Procel handed over a small data card to Lucifer, who then studied it before responding.

"And you're sure you weren't noticed?" Lucifer asked.

"Positive, my Lord. I was like ash on a dark night," Procel beamed.

"Excellent!" Lucifer remarked. Then added, nearly under his breath, "You may carry on with your other duties," he said.

"Yes, my Lord," Procel answered in a bow, then turned and walked out the room.

Lucifer covered the data card in the palm of his hand as his officers re-entered the war room.

"Shall we begin again?" he said with a smile. His officers noting a change in his demeanour. He actually showed signs of happiness, although subtle.

For nearly five sections, Lucifer held discussions.

First with Mastema, the demon officer of planning, to go over Lucifers new idea. Then with Buer, the demon officer of logic, who ran through tactics, and how best to implement them.

Thirdly, it was Biffrons turn, the demon officer of the mathematical arts. He provided the probability of the plan and expected numbers. Lastly, it was Kokabiel, the demon officer of stars and space. He was the one to suggest the best space route to their intended target.

***

After dismissing his officers, Lucifer stared at the data card in his hand, thinking about the possibilities. He soon made up his mind.

"I'm going to pay a little visit," he told himself. He exited up the steps, behind the chair in which he sat earlier, through a small door and up some stairs. The small doorway was a shortcut to his private living quarters of his castle. There were many names of Lucifers castle, the mountain mansion, Lucifers lodge, the volcano villa, but the one he liked the most was simple, home.

Although the vast castle belonged to him, he only had a reasonable sized space in it. The rest of the volcanic building also housed his four army officers, some personal assistants, the chefs and some keepers. Oh, and a dungeon full of slaves, below the main rooms. He couldn't abide all their moaning throughout the night when he needed his rest. Sometimes he had to go down there and kill one or two slaves, just to shut them up. Their souls often left a bitter taste in his mouth. The unkept fresh innocent souls not only tasted the best but also gave him much more power than the feeble guests cramped down below. To be honest with himself, he doesn't even know why the slaves moan so much. After all, they got free accommodation, food and water, once a day, all in exchange for a little bit of hard work out of them. He's been to various worlds where, 'sentient beings' are forced into doing the same thing. Working hard all day to earn a pittance, just to live in squalor, all whilst their employers get rich and greedy.

What's the difference, he thought, at least here in the castle, it was always warm. That was thanks to the eternal flame that surrounded the castle, as a moat of fire. Lucifer had lived in various hovels, dwellings, shacks, hotels, houses, caves and lairs, throughout time, but this building was his favourite. Designed by him, for him. He knew exactly what he wanted, when the idea came to him. He was clearing one of the moons of Kentol, of its inhabitants. Sure, it wasn't easy for his offspring and slaves to work together, cutting the large building out of the volcanic rock. Often squabbles and death occurred, but that was a price he was willing to pay. Although, to be fair, he didn't actually pay his workers. He just let his offspring take their souls when the slaves collapsed. A win for everyone he thought.

So, off he went to his private portal room, the very top room in the north wing. A small square room, barely big enough to fit a torture device in. Windows on three sides looked out over the moat of flames, and across into the distant countryside. Devoid of all living things, a deathly haze lingered over the baron fields. He gazed out over his kingdom, savouring the happiness, he couldn't stand all that greenery on the other planets anymore, everything looked so... alive. He turned to a wall mounted data screen and inserted the data card. The computer scanned its contents before presenting a name on the screen. It seemed vaguely familiar to him; *Maybe I've been there before?* He looked to the centre of the room and summoned a portal, Lucifer changed to his human form and recited an ageless verse, he kept repeating the name that appeared on the screen and stepped through.

Immediately he grew a distaste for the place, rolling green hills, blue sky with a warm sun and a sweet smell of nectar in the air. He hated it! Looking far into the distance, on a hilltop, he saw it. The stone building, the one he had been waiting to visit for such a long time. He headed towards it. He managed to get to the front door without seeing or being seen by anyone. Holding his head high, he sniffed the air, filling his lungs with the aroma of what lay on the other side.

He smiled to himself, "This is the right place!" he said. Just as he was about to knock on the door, he heard footsteps on the other side, coming closer. Then, to Lucifers surprise, the door flung open inwards, and in a blur, someone or something, jumped on top of him knocking him to the ground. A large yellow-ish-orange figure crouched on his chest, its tail, as sharp as a dagger, pressed to Lucifers inside thigh. One huge, clawed hand wrapped around Lucifers throat, its palm applying pressure to his windpipe and its claws dug into his spine.

A voice, lighter than expected, for the size of the creature, spoke, "Who are you, and what do you want?" Its large mouth contorting with every word, its lips, pulled back to expose dagger like teeth. A forked tongue flicked in the air, tasting the visitors' scent. A wide flat nose, nostrils flaring with anger, and its eyes burning red with fire and hate.

Lucifer didn't struggle, even if he wanted to, he felt the weight of this creature may be difficult for him. Through laboured breathing, Lucifer managed to swallow, the wind that had been unexpectedly knocked out of him, slowly returned. A smile crept upon his face.

Lucifer spoke, "Hello Lucigon, I'm Lucifer. It's good to see you again, son!"

Lucigon

Chapter 6

With Lucifers words, Lucigon's eyes widened, and he loosened his grip a little. He let out a roar of anger and climbed off. With a hand still on Lucifers throat, he thrust him straight up into the air. Lucifers feet dangled a full metre off the ground.

"I don't care for the lies of a stranger!" Lucigon spat.

"Then kill me!" said Lucifer with a smile.

Lucigon paused before he squeezed as hard as he could. His claws dug through Lucifers flesh and scrapped on his vertebrae, his palm unable to move against a solid windpipe. He tried again and again, but Lucifers windpipe just would not crush.

After a while Lucifer had had enough. He inhaled a lung full of air and shouted, "My turn!" Lucifer pulled his legs up and kicked Lucigon in the abdomen, at the same time as sending two fireballs at his chest, as he fell to the floor. Lucigon flew backwards, his grip on Lucifer being ripped out. Lucifer got to his feet and morphed back to his natural state. Lucigon landed on his backside, as he slid across the dirt, a look of shock on his face from the surprise attack. Shock soon turned to anger, when he saw Lucifers true form. He scrambled to his feet and sprinted towards Lucifer.

Lucifer threw a couple of light fireballs at Lucigon, slowing him down to a stop.

"I am not here to fight you!" said Lucifer.

"Then you came to the wrong place," Lucigon stated, walking towards Lucifer again.

Lucifer sighed, "You cannot kill me, just like you cannot be killed," said Lucifer.

Lucigon stopped in his tracks, "What?" he asked.

"I am a god, Lucigon, and gods cannot be killed by any mortal methods. You are my natural son, which makes you an immortal too." Lucifer paused to let his words settle.

Lucigon was exasperated, he didn't know what to say, but managed to stumble a couple of words, "My mother..."

Lucifer cut in, "Your mother, Faigon, was a Dragunis. She and I were... We had a special relationship," he said.

"My mother is dead!" snapped Lucigon.

"Oh, I know! It nearly broke my heart when I killed her," Lucifer said, nonchalantly.

"WHAT?" shouted Lucigon, his anger quickly rose, "You killed my mother?" He questioned, then ran at Lucifer again, this time, too quickly for Lucifer to react. Lucigon threw an uppercut, Lucifers head shot backwards, and his body followed. Lucifer had to spread his wings to regain control, flapping slowly, to stay airborne. He winced a little as he reset his jaw.

"You're very strong," said Lucifer with a smile.

"You think you can escape me, by flying?" Lucigon said angrily, then, hidden inside his back, two large wings unfolded, he flexed his muscles and with one flap of his wings, he was already in the air, right in front of Lucifer.

Lucifer was impressed. "So, you've grown wings, do you have any more tricks?" he asked smugly.

"Let me show you!" said Lucigon and set off at speed towards Lucifer.

Lucifer had to quickly spin away from Lucigon's attack. He whipped his tail around and struck Lucigon on the back of his head. Lucigon didn't see it coming, and it knocked him off-balance. He was sent hurtling to the ground, landing on his head with a great thud. He slowly got to his feet and shook his mind clear, as Lucifer swooped down and kicked Lucigon in the chest with both feet, sending his boy back into the dirt. Lucifer then landed atop of the young demi-god, putting one foot on Lucigon's throat and summoned the weight of the earth into his body, pinning Lucigon to the ground. Lucigon struggled with all his might but could not free himself.

"How are you doing that?" Lucigon asked.

"I can teach you, my boy," said Lucifer, "but you have to stop fighting me!"

Lucigon struggled some more, underneath Lucifers weight, then let out a frustrated scream. "Argh! Fine!" he reluctantly said.

"That's better," said Lucifer, as he released his weight and climbed off.

Lucigon scrambled to his feet. "You killed my mother?" he asked, still angry but not yet ready to attack.

"Yes, I needed to," replied Lucifer.

"Don't think for one snap that I am letting you get away with that," snarled Lucigon.

"Oh, I really don't expect you to," answered Lucifer, "In fact, I want you to keep that fire inside you. Never let it smoulder, keep it stoked, let it burn with anger, fuel it with your loathing. Get rid of wasteful emotions, empathy is a blanket that smothers you!" Lucifer retorted.

"The empathy for my mother, fuels the hate for you!" snapped back Lucigon.

"That's a start," Lucifer agreed, "but, you should really have hate for Faigon too. For it was her idea to have you. She knew full well who you would become. *What*, you will become!" Lucifer said.

"More lies!" Lucigon shouted.

"You don't have to accept it," Lucifer agreed, "you don't even have to believe me. But that won't change the facts. You are my son, you are a demi-god, and you were born with one purpose only, revenge!"

"Revenge? Revenge for what?" barked Lucigon. He was becoming impatient with this monster in front of him. Not a monster in looks, but a monster for killing his beloved mother. Lucigon started to pace backwards and forwards.

"Let me tell you a story," said Lucifer, settling down onto a nearby rock.

Lucigon scoffed at his insolence. A snarl at every word. A growl for every sentence.

"Before all this," Lucifer gestured around him, "Before anything existed, there was nothing," he shrugged. "Time and Space, were separate entities. Eventually, they found each other and fell in love. They combined themselves as lovers, creating the universe. They wanted to fill that universe with natural wonders, just as they were. But they didn't want to spend all their time on frivolous projects, they only had time for each other. So, they created their sons God and Lucifer, to share their vision," explained Lucifer.

"You and God are brothers? Ha, ha, ha," boomed Lucigon, "More lies! At least these are entertaining ones," he scoffed.

"I haven't lied to you, Lucigon," said Lucifer, with a straight face, "God is the eldest, so he naturally took charge of everything. We both created endlessly, until there was enough matter in the universe, to create all the stars, planets, and moons. The celestial bodies all lived in harmony with each other, and we rested. We even played games. Our parents, pleased with our work, faded away and left everything to my brother and me. Their parting words were, 'This is empyrean,' and we both felt satisfied.

"After some time, God then took it upon himself to create beings. All beings, large and small, sentient or not. When I found out, I was against his idea, it wasn't what our parents had wanted! God actually said to me, 'They've gone, and now I'm in charge!'

"I wasn't happy, and I soon let him know! His response was to tell me to bow down before them, suggesting that I should worship all beings," Lucifer's anger boiled over and fire erupted from his skull, "ME! LUCIFER!"

"Weren't you equal brothers?" asked Lucigon quietly.

"Yes," huffed Lucifer, calming down a little, his flames extinguishing. "But he didn't see it that way. He was older, so he was in charge. I was just another one of his subjects, to him!"

"So, what happened?" asked Lucigon, genuinely interested.

Lucifer relaxed, he felt like he had just hooked a huge Sondöl fish, "I refused to bow down to anyone, let alone pathetic beings that should not even exist. So, he banished me. Banished me from my home in the heavens. He sent me to this mortal realm to live amongst these mortals." He raised his voice, "A god living with insects! I was once his little angel, then, just by questioning him, I had fallen. I meant nothing to him anymore," Lucifer paused to take a deep breath.

"*My* name is never repeated, unlike *his*. In the name of... For the glory of... Our Saviour..." Lucifer scoffed and shook his head. "I was betrayed by my own brother! I begged and pleaded with him, just to get back into heaven. But, by then, he relished being the only god, and denied me. He eventually stopped listening to me, such was his ego!" Lucifer paused in reflection; he could still feel the anger of betrayal burning inside.

"For thousands of cycles, I wandered the planets looking for recognition of what I helped to create, but all I saw were beings. Everywhere I went, there were species, his creations, and I hated them, I hated what they stood for! My planets were perfect. Only to be spoiled by those disgusting creatures. One such being tried to get me to worship God, just like they do, ha!"

He shook his head and pointed a finger, "It was then, that something awoke inside of me, the fire. The primordial and uncontrollable, fire. I sliced the throat of that being, in a rage. Suddenly, the soul from that slaughtered animal entered my body, and it was erotic. I craved more. So, I ended up slaughtering the whole village," he shrugged. "My desire was quenched, albeit for a short time. It gave me focus, a purpose, and strength. I dug up their dead, for more souls, but they tasted foul, like ash. I received no power, only more thirst. I soon realised that only fresh soul's work."

Lucifer paused again, watching Lucigon nod with interest, before carrying on, "I was only one person, and there was a whole universe out there to conquer. I could kill God's creatures and get stronger at the same time. That's when it dawned on me. These beings, the creatures that God had made, it was all to make himself more powerful. That's how he managed to banish me. It was greed!" Lucifer smirked, "How ironic, power is what he preaches against, yet it was the one thing that he couldn't help himself to. Some beings talk about the seven sins, and yet, God was the first one to commit the first four them in one go. He was saying, 'do as I say, not as I do.' Such a false god! So, I came up with a strategy, the more souls I took, the more powerful I became. The less beings there were, the less powerful God would be. This was my way to get back on a level field. Only then, could I face him. The universe is such a big place, and I was only one. But I worked hard, and started to succeed, my power grew exponentially. I was coming close to getting even! But then, God came to me, asking for a truce. He would stop creating if I would stop taking souls," Lucifer nodded, reminiscing.

"I agreed, thinking my brother had come to his senses, and that soon, he would accept me back into heaven. But I was betrayed again! Yes," he snarled, "he kept his promise to stop creating, but what he did was so much worse. Instead of creating each and every creature himself, he gave the ability for every one of them to reproduce themselves, increasing their numbers without God's interference. He had swindled me again. But it was to be for the last time!" Lucifer vowed.

"So, I asexually reproduced and bore offspring. I trained them in what to do and how to act. I expressed that innocent souls are the most powerful. But they should take all, at any cost. For God to keep his powers, the population must forever increase, or he risks losing everything."

"It was him that started this war. I am just trying to get back what our parents envisioned, serenity in the universe." His last words came out as a whisper, as Lucifer looked to the skies. His gaze returned to Lucigon, "Yet I am labelled the bad guy!" A long silence stretched between them.

"Where is heaven?" Lucigon finally asked.

"Heaven is up there," Lucifer nodded above him to the sky, "and over there," he gestured with a flick of a wrist. "It's everywhere, and nowhere. You can't see it from anywhere, yet whilst there, you can see everything below. Like a data pad, you can zoom in to anything, sound too. Any angle, any distance. A quick scan and you're across the galaxy and into another one." Lucifer laughed to himself. "We used to make galaxies by throwing stones across the universe, some now call them asteroids or falling stars, but the resulting ripples caused some planets and stars to form."

"How did you wander the planets? I cannot fly into space," asked Lucigon, "This was before space flight, am I right?" he wondered.

"Yes, it was before space flight. As a god, I can portal anywhere, or rather. I could. I'd just say the verse and picture the place I had created, and there opened a portal to it. But when the sentients started naming the planets, my powers decreased. I then had to recite the name of the planet I wanted to visit. If I don't know it, I couldn't go there," said Lucifer angrily.

"How do your offspring get around?" asked Lucigon.

"The same way," Lucifer nodded, "but Baraqijal, my demon officer of Astrology, selects which planets to infest and sends them there. I have very little to do with how they run things now, it's more of a committee," he admitted.

"What is it you want from me?" Lucigon asked eventually.

"So glad you asked," said Lucifer. "I want you to take your rightful place in heaven, with me!"

Lucigon looked startled, "Me, in heaven? Ha! I would cause so much destruction if I was there."

Lucifer smiled again, "That's what I'm counting on."

"So, how would you go about it?" asked Lucigon, a lot more intrigued now.

"Well," said Lucifer, "you must kill God. But to get to God, you must kill a group of his warriors first," he scoffed at his next words, "They call themselves, the Cydarions." He spat on the ground.

"Why should I kill God, why can't you do it?" Lucigon asked.

Lucifer hesitated; he had been hoping this question wouldn't come up. "Because, son, God and I can't kill each other. If either one did the deed, the universe would cease to exist. One of us has to rule," he lied.

"So how do I kill him, if he's all powerful?" asked Lucigon.

"Ah," exclaimed Lucifer, "have you ever noticed that no matter what you do, there are no repercussions, no feelings of guilt. That's because God cannot see you. You are a blank spot to him."

In reality, Lucifer was in fear of Gods acclaimed power. He was quite willing to sacrifice Lucigon in the pursuit of *his* peace. Until Lucifer had enough of his own power to take on God personally, he knew it was only a fifty percent chance of survival. But if Lucifer could find the Lahat Cherub artefact, then his self-proclaimed prophecy would come true. He would defeat his brother and rule the universe himself.

Lucigon was now a mere pawn in Lucifers game of powers.

There was a quiet stillness in the air, before Lucigon asked, "If I kill God, would that make you mortal?"

"Not quite," Lucifer answered.

"But I could kill you!" stated Lucigon, an anger still burning deep inside.

"Well, yes, but you wouldn't," answered Lucifer.

"With you and him gone, who would stop me ruling the universe?" asked Lucigon, his eyes growing larger.

Lucifer smiled so wide, it looked like a grimace, "So you accept your legacy?" he asked.

Lucigon just grunted, "Why can't I just kill you first and then leave God alone?"

"What does your gut tell you?" asked Lucifer.

Lucigon thought for a fraction. "To kill everyone," he answered with a snarl.

"Okay," Lucifer replied, a little shocked, "But you can't kill me, only God knows how, and he won't. But I could kill him, or rather, you can with my help."

"With him gone, how long would we live?" Lucigon wondered.

"We would still be immortal. And, with the amount of power that we would possess, no one would even dare to attack us. A swipe of my finger and a whole planet could be destroyed," said Lucifer with a laugh.

"And we can do this by ourselves?" queried Lucigon.

"I have an army, and I want you to lead them," said Lucifer.

"An army?" Lucigon replied, a little shocked. "You just want me to do the work for you," said Lucigon.

"Not for me, with me," replied Lucifer.

Lucigon thought before asking the next question, "What weapon can kill a god?"

"The Lahat Cherub artefact, and when the time is right, we shall use it together," said Lucifer.

"What is the Lahat Cherub artefact?" asked Lucigon.

"It's a weapon created by God, thousands of cycles ago. He offered it to the sentient creatures to keep me in line. But they are so stupid, they lost it and eventually, forgot about it. I am getting close to finding it again. That is the weapon that will finish God's reign."

"If I agree to help you kill God, you have to show me everything," offered Lucigon.

"I intend to," said Lucifer.

"But first, I want to know about my mother," said Lucigon.

"Okay," agreed Lucifer.

"And why you killed her!" Lucigon added.

Lucifer dropped his head, "Fine," he muttered. "I met Faigon nearly seven hundred cycles ago, when your mother was an adolescent dragon. She knew who I was straight away, and she accepted me. She didn't try to stop my thirst for power, but rather she encouraged it. She too, was angry at the world. She was the one who suggested having a child by natural conception. We both knew how powerful that child would be, half Dragunis, half god. A demi-god would be unstoppable." Lucifer's words lingered as he thought of what could be.

Lucigon cleared his throat, bringing Lucifer back to the conversation.

"Yes, but after you were born, she changed her mind. She didn't want you to grow up to be hateful. She wanted you to see love and acceptance, not war and violence. So, she packed up, took you with her, and escaped me. I looked for her everywhere, any trace I found, you had just moved on. I was incensed. Everyone I've ever had feelings for had betrayed me. I vowed, never again. I doubled down on my plan and carried on regardless."

"You gave up looking for me?" asked Lucigon.

Lucifer shook his head, "No, I sent scouts looking for you both. But Faigon knew me, she knew how I thought, what actions I would take. She always stayed two steps ahead." Lucifer closed his eyes and gave in to a warm smile. "She was always the smart one," he nodded. "This whole plan, project M.U.R.I.S, you overthrowing God, everything, they were all her ideas. She planned them all while pregnant with you." His smile soon faded. "Then she betrayed me and left. I carried on with the plan, thinking she would return when she saw it working." He drew a breath and held it.

"A hundred cycles ago, she did come to visit me. I thought she had changed her mind, but she hadn't. She came to ask if I would give everything up, to live together, just the three of us, in obscurity." He looked Lucigon directly in the eyes and raised his voice, "She asked me to give up on my heritage, my birth right, to give up what I'm owed, mostly my revenge on God. She expected me to let HIM keep it all. That will never happen!" Lucifer stated.

"She said I would never see my son again; she would keep you from me for eternity. I would never see you, my only son. So, I did what I had to do, I killed her. I had to Lucigon; don't you see? I wouldn't have found you otherwise," Lucifer explained.

"How do you figure that?" asked Lucigon, his nostrils starting to flare with the mention of his mothers' murder.

Lucifer held his palms out flat, "Faigon, your mother, had said that she hadn't told you the reasons you had kept moving all your life."

Lucigon grunted, but Lucifer carried on, "I used that to my advantage. I knew you would stay too long in one place, so I doubled my scouts." He shrugged. "And here we are."

A snort from Lucigon. "Mother came to you in peace, and you killed her!" Lucigon shouted as he stormed towards Lucifer.

Lucifer stood up, but he wasn't prepared for Lucigon's left hook. Lucifer flew sidewards, over a rock, and landed face first on the ground. Lucigon jumped high into the air, ready to come down hard onto Lucifer. Lucifer opened a portal in front of him and Lucigon disappeared through it. Lucifer stood up, dusted himself down, flapped his wings and followed his son through the red portal.

Lucifer stayed still in the air, his wings slowly flapping to keep aloft. The portal closed behind him.

Lucigon, who had landed onto scorched earth, got to his feet and looked around. "How did you do that? he asked in anger.

"There's a lot you need to learn Lucigon. Are you willing to join me and finally put an end to your agony of all beings?" asked Lucifer.

Lucigon huffed a few times before responding, "I will listen to your teachings but at this moment, I won't promise anything," he replied.

Lucifer smirked, "Fair enough, where would you like to start?"

Lucigon looked around, "Where are we?" he asked.

"Home," Lucifer said dryly. "Gehenna. This is where you were born. I created it in my own image, without Gods knowledge. I'm sure he did one for himself too," Lucifer added with distaste. "I came here and built this place. A place of refuge, my sanctuary,"

Lucigon took in all the scenery. Dark grey filled the sky, black mountains to his left and an empty wasteland to his right. No other colours, and nothing alive, as far as his eyes could see. Behind Lucifer stood the outline of a castle, set atop a lone volcano. a flaming moat surrounded the fortress. "I like it," he growled, "It doesn't smell like all the places mother took me to." Lucigon shuddered with the recollection of the stench.

Lucigon looked at Lucifer. "I remember the rotation mother left. She never told me where she was going. She made me promise to keep moving, if, she hadn't returned within four rotations. I was to leave everything and run. Every rotation she never came home I got angry. Then I was all alone, on the run. I didn't even know what or who I was running from, but I grew up quickly, becoming more and more angry. Mother never spoke about you or who you were. Whenever I asked about my father, she would just say, you were lost, and that she hoped you would find the right path, soon."

Lucigon looked down at the ground, slightly ashamed of what he was about to admit. "When I was little, I took that meaning literally, I thought we were constantly searching for you, moving from planet to planet in the hope of finding you. But, as I grew, I realised that we were the ones that were being sought. It didn't feel right to me, to be on the run, but I didn't know any better. After mother never came home, I kept her promise and moved every fifty rotations. But everywhere I went, reeked of life. I tried to stay in places that mother would have liked, but I started to hate all living things," he snarled at the thought.

"That's my side of you," Lucifer said with pleasure.

"So, we will kill God, and then all living things?" confirmed Lucigon.

"That is the plan. We get the universe back on track, the planets living in harmony with each other. The way it should always have been," said Lucifer.

"Yes, that does sound peaceful," Lucigon replied.

"Come on," said Lucifer, "let me show you around your new home. No more running for you," Lucifer offered. Then he turned to fly towards his castle.

"Temporary home," retorted Lucigon.

Lucifer gave him a sideways glance, "Temporary home?" he asked.

"Yes, until we get into heaven," answered Lucigon, then flapped his wings faster, and flew off in front of Lucifer.

A feeling of pride washed over Lucifer. He shook it off and raced after Lucigon.

Swift Obe

Chapter 7

Kee and Swift took in their surroundings as they exited the portal. They had stepped into some sort of corridor. Steel flooring with faded, white painted walls. The paint was cracking, even peeling away in places. The ceiling had one long, diffused light. There was no breeze, but a stale musty smell hung in the air. A slight vibration could be felt, along with a muffled hum, coming from beneath their feet. A noisy throng echoed from one end of the corridor.

"I don't feel the Calling," said Swift.

"I don't feel it either," said Kee, "but we should take a look around, nonetheless, see what we can learn," he suggested. Swift agreed, and they headed towards the noise. A densely packed crowd came into view, by the time they reached the end of the corridor. An assortment of aliens gathered in a large open area bordered by four curved walls, walking and talking amongst themselves. Small stalls selling various food and personal items lined two of the curved walls.

The ceiling is too low for this to be a conventional building, thought Kee. The ceiling was lit to represent a blue sky with cumulus clouds digitally drifting across. Kee and Swift made their way around the crowds, listening out for any clues as to why they were there.

"There must be a devil around here somewhere," wondered Kee.

"But where?" asked Swift, "Everything seems normal."

"I'm not sure, but we have to find it."

"How about walking around this marketplace, see if anything is out of the ordinary?" suggested Swift.

"Hopefully the Calling will start soon," said Kee.

After a full circuit of the marketplace, they decided to give it another go and walked around again.

"You know what this place reminds me of?" said Swift.

Kee glanced around, eventually he shook his head, "No, do tell!"

"The rotation we met our lovely Xania again," smiled Swift.

"Of course!" replied Kee, clapping his hands together, "That was such a wonderful time." He smiled.

"I can't believe it's been nearly a full cycle since then," said Swift.

"I know," said Kee, "It's gone by so quickly, but we have been very busy with all the Callings."

"That's true," agreed Swift, "How nice is it to be back home with the Cydarions? Being peace makers on Dusorf was satisfying, but it wasn't as fulfilling. This is where the real pleasure is," said Swift. "Helping innocent souls find themselves again."

"I couldn't agree more," replied Kee, "and we got to spend more time with Xania."

"That Calling was a special one," remarked Swift, "she really is the daughter of Jodrell. Even down to his little quirks," he said. His mind wandered to a memory of all three of them sitting around a campfire on the planet Toord, when Xania explained how she found out the names of her biological parents.

"I do hope she makes peace with Beau," said Kee, bringing Swift out of his thoughts. "It really wasn't her fault about Jodrell. He always followed his own path; we all knew it."

"Yes," nodded Swift.

"Well, it looks like we're back here again," said Swift, after completing two whole circuits of the market area. Concluding that they were none the wiser as to which way or corridor to go.

They had noticed many more corridors leading away from the indoor marketplace. Some corridors were empty and quiet, while others were bustling and loud. Each one of the corridors had been painted a different colour.

"Let's just pick one and see where it goes?" offered Swift.

"Agreed, and if it's nothing, we come back and try the next one," sait Kee.

They chose a not too busy corridor, blue. The further they walked the less populated the corridor became, until eventually, they were on their own. A mechanical whirring and clanking sound started to get louder as they made their way further down the end of the corridor. Reaching the end of the corridor, they were faced with a round steel door, the noises coming from within. Opening the door with caution, they took a step inside.

"Ah!" shouted a voice from out of the dark, "You're here."

Kee and Swift looked at each other and nodded solemnly, getting ready to fight the demon if necessary. But before they had time to move one step, he shouted again,

"The main valve is on the left there, it's stuck closed. I'm overriding it by operating this solenoid manually, but even this is temperamental. I have to keep hitting it with this broken pipe." A male alien, the same species as the tall beings in the marketplace appeared. A steel pipe in his hands and dirt all over his face. "You should see this place when the steam valve releases, it's like the murky world of Irondo." He laughed, holding out two of his four webbed hands, "I'm Troen, you must be the water engineers?" he said with a large lipless smile.

Kee and Swift stepped forward and took a hand each, shaking them in a greeting. "Erm, we're not the water engineers, I'm afraid," said Kee.

"Ah, that's a shame, I'm sure they'll be along soon. So, are you guys lost or just interested how this recycle plant works?" asked Troen with a chuckle.

"We are sorry to disturb you, but we've just arrived here and don't know our way around," said Swift honestly.

Troen looked disappointed, "Don't tell me another planet has gone? It breaks my hearts every time I hear that," he said.

"Another planet?" asked Kee.

"Isn't that why you're on this spaceship?" asked Troen.

Swift jumped in thinking quickly, "No, sorry, we were mistaken. We were passing by and saw you on our radar. We stopped by, for supplies," he said hoping to be convincing.

Troen nodded, "If you know where we are, maybe you should speak with our captain. I don't think he knows where we are. I swear we've been going in circles for three rotations now," he said.

"Why do you say that?" Kee asked.

"Well, three rotations ago we felt a violent change of direction, and it hasn't eased. We have just kind of gotten used to it, of course, that was before all the trouble started," Troen stated.

"What do you mean, trouble?" enquired Swift.

Troen looked around, as though to check they were alone, "Well, the lurch was the first thing. Then I heard rumours about the vegetation section going offline, next it was the food reproducers. Faulty equipment, they said, but no spare parts. Now this!" he pointed to the pipes behind him, "the water recycle section is on the blink. The devils at it, if you ask me?'

"Why do you say that?" asked Kee.

"Oh, sorry, it's just an expression, from my home planet," Troen said, then sighed, "well it was, but now..." he shook his head.

"What happened to your planet?" asked Kee.

"It was terrible, our twin moons started moving closer to the planet. It affected the oceans, doing all sorts of things to the gravity. Our scientists couldn't understand why they had changed their orbit. As the moons got closer and entered our atmosphere, they started to break up. Meteorites came hurtling down, hitting our towns. We were told, that when the main body of the moons hit our planet, it would throw up enough dust to block out the sun. Suffocating everyone and everything on the planet for at least seven cycles. After that it may be possible to live there again, albeit very differently. Everyone panicked, what would we do, what could we do? None of us had our own transport crafts. Then by some miracle, after nearly a full cycle, this large spaceship was passing by, and it hailed us, saying they had room for the survivors. How could we turn it down?" asked Troen.

"Who does this spaceship belong to?" asked Kee.

"We don't know. Well, I don't anyway. All I know is that our leaders went to meet with the captain, and we haven't seen them since. I figure they have better accommodation than me." He chuckled again.

"So, you still don't know?" asked Swift.

"No, we travelled for a while, then got another load of refugees, then another, and then a third. Each planet having the same problem, but fewer and fewer survivors. It's amazing that so many moons are crashing into the planets all at once," Troen said.

Kee turned to swift, "We need to find more answers," he said.

"And the flight deck," offered Swift, Kee nodded an agreement.

"If you do find the flight deck, can you send a water engineer down? I can't keep on top of this," asked Troen.

"Of course, my friend," said Swift, as they walked back out of the round door.

"Red!" shouted Troen from behind them, "the flight deck is on the red corridor!"

"Thank you!" they both shouted back, then headed off for the ships flight deck. The corridor wasn't easy to find, due to the number of beings in front of the access. The actual corridor was found to be empty, probably due to the repulsive smell that seemed to be getting stronger the more they walked down the corridor. As they turned the last corner, before them stood a barricade of heavy boxes, twisted, broken metal and parts of the collapsed ceiling. Evidence that an attempt to remove that blockage had been made.

"I think we've found the right place," Kee said.

"It's going to take both of us to move those metal girders," admitted Swift.

They both got to work, moving parts of the barricade that they could, but the main structure just wouldn't budge.

"I think you should use your power," said Swift, after exhausting all other possibilities.

"You know I don't like using it. Sometimes I can't control it," admitted Kee.

Swift took his hand and gently squeezed, "I know you can do it; I have faith."

Kee blushed a little, then concentrated. He slowly closed his eyes, and when he reopened them, his eyes were completely opaque. Invisible power surged from them, straight onto the metal beams, crumpling them in place. The girders folded in on themselves, buckling and twisting into a heap on one side of the access corridor.

The pungent smell that wafted from the corridor in front of them brought Kee back around, and he had to cover his beak-like nose. "That's foul," he remarked.

Swift placed a large paw on Kee's shoulder. "Thank you," he whispered.

Kee smiled, then nodded forward, "Let's keep going."

It wasn't long before they were nearly gagging at the smell, soon finding the protective blast doors, slightly opened. Scorched finger marks imbedded in the side, and an unbearable heat coming from within.

Swift gestured his head towards the finger marks, and Kee nodded an acknowledgement. They slowly entered the control room of the flight deck, expecting it to be busy and noisy. It was neither. Silence covered the floor, along with dried blood. Every single being sitting at their console, were dead. Their throats had been sliced; blood puddled all over the electronics. Dried blood had stopped dripping onto the floor and stained the consoles. And it was unbearably hot.

Kee rushed to check on a couple of beings, but there was nothing he could do, they were gone. And for some time. Their decaying bodies were the origin of the awful smell.

Swift found the flight deck temperature controls, and unsticking them from the dried blood, reduced the heat in the control room.

"How could this happen?" gasped Swift, his body temperature already raised.

"This is definitely the devils work," said Kee, looking toward the helm. A slaughtered body was slumped over the yoke, fully turning it to the left.

"Troen *was* right," said Swift, "they have been going around in circles!"

"We should put them back on course!" said Kee, looking across the control panel.

"To where?" asked Swift, "Troen didn't even know where they were headed."

"I'll have a look at the navigation terminal, see what that says," offered Kee. A few fractions later he had his answer, "they were heading to an unknown region, nowhere near any other planets," Kee said.

"Hmm, maybe we should set the ship in that direction?" suggested Swift, "There may be someone waiting for them," he shrugged.

"Or something," said Kee, solemnly.

Just as they finished setting for the original course, there was a click, and the distant humming stopped. All of a sudden, beeping and flashing lights lit up a terminal. Kee looked at it in a panic.

"The air has stopped circulating," he said, an urgency to his voice, "We'll start running out of oxygen soon."

"We need to get down there and see what's going on!" said Swift. He turned and started to walk towards the exit.

"Wait!" shouted Kee, "this may help." He smiled, holding up a small holograph data card in one hand, that he retrieved from around the neck of a crew member.

"What's that?" Swift wondered.

Kee raised his eyebrows, "A map of the ship!"

"Good work!" said Swift.

"Come on, follow me. There should be a shortcut to the oxygen chambers around here," Kee said, walking past Swift and back into the red corridor.

About five hundred decimetres along the corridor, Kee stopped and looked to his right. "There should be an access panel here," he said scanning the wall, "Ah!" Kee held the data card up to a small emblem on the wall. There was a click, and a green light illuminated behind the panel. Then, pulling on a flush fitting ring in the wall, Kee pulled the panel. It swung into the corridor via a double hinge. Behind the panel, was a small access corridor, dimly lit and with mesh grating as a walkway above various pipes, wires and conduits running in all directions. "This should take us to the green corridor, from there we can reach the oxygen chambers," said Kee.

"Sounds good, let's go," nodded Swift.

They made their way through the inside of the ship, turning left and turning right, following the map on the data card. Twice ascending ladders, to reach an upper corridor. When they arrived at the green corridor access panel, it was already open.

"It looks like someone has already been here," said Kee, taking the first to step into the corridor.

"Maybe it was maintenance?" questioned Swift.

"I'm not so sure," replied Kee, "they shouldn't have left the panels open for just anyone to step into."

They found their way into the oxygen chambers and took a look around.

"There's no one here," reported Kee, a little confused.

"Look, over here," said Swift, beckoning Kee to come and join him.

"What is it?" Kee asked, as he joined Swift by a large array of frozen piping and valves

"Some of the equipment is missing," said Swift, "Here, here and here, there should be valves and control switches," he said, pointing to different areas, "but they've been removed!"

"Why though, for what purpose?" questioned Kee.

"That's hard to say," replied Swift, "but, with the water issue, the terrible events on the bridge, and now this. There must be more..." Suddenly all the lights suddenly went out, plunging the whole area into darkness. All the motors stopped whirring and everything fell silent. Kee and Swift didn't move. Within a few snaps, the emergency lighting came on.

"We've just lost electrical power," said Kee, looking at the data card, "this is only the back-up generator lighting!"

"We need to figure this out, and quickly," said Swift, "Where's the electrical room?" he asked Kee.

Kee looked at the data card, "Corridor teal, let's go," Kee said with more urgency.

Rushing out of the oxygen chambers, they headed back into the maintenance corridors behind the hidden access panel. Running this time, they cut a swift path through the centre of the ship and arrived at the teal corridor. Its access hatch had already been opened too. Immediately they heard a high-pitched maniacal laugh.

"He's here!" whispered Kee in response. They both moved cautiously towards the electrical power room. Only the emergency lighting was on, but even those were growing dimmer by the fraction. Due to the air circulation having stopped, or rather sabotaged, the internal temperature of the ship started to rise. Sweat started collecting on Kee's forehead while Swift got very uncomfortable.

Again, they entered with caution. Hearing the mumblings of someone talking to themselves, they crept closer.

"These wires will be perfect, oh," it chuckled to itself, "a thermostat, lucky me!"

Kee and Swift emerged from the shadows, stepping into the glow from an emergency light. "Put them down, devil!" shouted Swift. The devil jumped in surprise, nearly dropping his collection of electronics. The devil turned around, a live electrical cable he had been holding, slipped from his grip, falling onto the rubber insulated floor.

"W-w-what are you doing here?" he asked. A higher pitched voice than the usual devils Kee and Swift had previously encountered.

This devil wasn't hideous or grotesque, as the Cydarions have come to expect, but rather mundane, even intelligent looking. Its body was more humanoid, with dark red skin, slightly skinny, but with obvious muscle definition. A belt hung around its waist, and two electronic boxes with coloured lights blinked softly and quietly. His face was oval shaped with wide deep-set yellow eyes, a small protruding mouth and a tall ridgeline running up the centre of its face, a nostril slot on either side of the ridge. Large black bushy eyebrows, with a matching beard and sideburns covered his face. Instead of horns on its head, he had large ears, like that of a Lynx. Its hands holding the electronics were long and spindly, very dexterous, with matching feet.

"We are here to stop you, devil," said Swift, with a wry smile.

"Are you, them?" it asked.

"We are Cydarions," answered Kee, feeling some pride.

The devil laughed again, "Excellent," he said with a grin, "I shall take you too." With that, the devil picked up the live electrical cable with his foot, and turning on the spot, jammed it into an electrical control box at the side of him. A small explosion and a shower of sparks exploded over the Cydarions. Kee and Swift closed their eyes to the brightness of the flash and covered themselves from the sparks. The devil slipped away quietly.

Kee Enclu

Chapter 8

Kee and Swift regained their eyesight after the flash had faded and searched for the devil.

"He's gone!" Kee stated.

"Hold on," said Swift, "I feel it, the Calling. It's returning."

"Yes," agreed Kee, feeling it in his body, "but why only start now?" he asked.

Swift shrugged, "Maybe because we saw him?" he guessed.

"We do need to move, now. He's up to something!" said Kee. They raced out of the electrical power room and down the teal corridor, following the Calling, towards the devil. Their body temperatures still rising.

No maintenance corridors this time, they were in hot pursuit. Running further down the corridor, the noise of a crowd grew louder, until they found themselves in the large open market area they first encountered. Except this time, it was much darker, and the temperature was increasing. Even more so, with the number of beings in one place. They soon realised it was chaos. Everyone was arguing, pushing and shoving each other. A few fights broke out, and some small beings or younglings were getting trampled in the frenzy. No one understood what was happening, they were all scared, which in turn, just escalated their panic. Lashing out at everyone and everything. Swift started to slow down due to the heat trapped in his fur. Kee spotted the devil in the middle of the crowd, riling them up and laughing in their faces. He also spotted the Cydarions coming towards him, so turned and fled.

"Come on, this way, I've seen him," said Kee, pointing towards the devil.

Swift, now panting, said, "You go on... I'll catch up." Kee gave Swift a look of concern. "I'll be ok... you go," repeated Swift. Kee squeezed Swift's arm once, before setting off after the devil. He had to push and shove his way through the throng of beings, systematically getting jostled from side to side with every step taken. He soon lost sight of the devil, but followed the Calling, which had only gotten stronger. He glanced back at Swift but was unable to see him in the ever-moving crowd. Kee pushed forward, eventually breaking free from the mass of beings. Each one of them covered in slimy red sweat, much of which had rubbed onto Kee's skin and clothing, making him look like he was bleeding everywhere. Without a pause, he followed the devil down a black painted corridor. The faint emergency lights barely casting any light along the dark non reflective walls. He slowed down, letting his eyes adjust to the dim light. Up ahead he could hear mechanical banging and clattering. Kee spotted a faded sign on the wall in front of him.

ENGINE ROOM

Glancing around once more, hoping Swift had caught up. He took a deep breath and carried on forward, into the engine room. Masses of pipes ran in every direction. Steam was released at various intervals via pressure valves; a small rattle could be heard before every release. Motors hummed and whirred. An overwhelming smell of grease hung in the air, exacerbated by the increasing heat filling up the spaceship. The steam and motors contributing to its intensity. Kee saw a sub-light engine near the middle of the room, except it wasn't glowing white, as normal sub-light engines do. It was glowing red and orange, like a fire raging inside a glass sphere. Then he noticed a second one, the same as the first.

He gasped, "The eternal fires!" he muttered to himself.

And there, in between the sub-light engines, with the red and orange glow lighting up his smiling face, stood the devil looking directly at him.

"Stay where you are devil, you shall not escape this time," shouted Kee over the increasingly louder and louder noises coming from within the engine room.

The devil's shoulders burst into flames with anger, "Do not call us devils, we hate that name! You people have called us that for more than eight millennia. That word is old and dated, it means weak. That is why you've been able to defeat us. But not now, we are strong and organised. We are educated and free thinkers. We choose our own names, and you shall address us as such!" said the devil.

"So, what would you like me to call you?" asked Kee a little perplexed.

"My name is Vapula!" said the devil.

"Well, Vapula, I am here to tell you to stop this mischief and help these people. They have lost their home and are seeking refuge," said Kee, not taking his eyes of Vapula.

The devil laughed. "You stupid Cydarion," almost spitting at the word Cydarion. "You know nothing, we didn't destroy their planet just to let a few thousand survive and start again. We're wiping them out, all of them!" Vapula's last words were filled with hatred, his head erupted into flames.

Kee was shocked. "You destroyed a whole planet?" he asked, nearly stuttering over his own words. He wished Swift was by his side right now.

"We did," gloated Vapula, "I volunteered for this mission, as a challenge to myself," he said gleefully.

Kee shook his head in disbelief, only managing to utter one word. "How?"

Vapula shrugged, "Physics, it's simple really. We created a nuclear electro-magnet, large and powerful enough to disrupt moons and planets, sending them off course to their doom," he laughed loudly.

Kee's knees started to buckle; the thought of millions of beings being wiped out in an instant made him feel weak. "Surely you can see that these beings are desperate, can't you just leave them be and let them mourn for their kin?" pleaded Kee.

Vapula laughed again, "The more terrified they are, the sweeter their soul tastes. Father will be pleased with my efforts here."

"NO! I will stop this," shouted Kee, his strength starting to return. His eyes turned opaque, and he reached out with his mind's eye at the bulkhead above Vapula.

"Ah, ah, ah," said Vapula, "You see these boxes?" he pointed at his belt, "If my life signs stop, they'll send a message to the control boxes on the sub-light engines and ka boom, this whole ship explodes immediately!"

Kee opened his eyes, wondering what he could do. He really wished Swift was here, *where is he?* he thought.

"But!" Vapula carried on, "I consider myself to be fair," he said with a laugh. "I want these beings to suffer, which means you have a choice. Either you kill me now and everyone including yourself dies. Or you can try and save them before they kill each other. Either way, this ship is going to explode, I can't stop the sub-light engines from overheating and imploding on themselves. It's just a matter of time." Vapula laughed, the laugh of a maniac.

Kee was stunned, *what can I do? The devil is right, if I end him, I doom everyone. Is there a way to save everyone? These beings are the last of their species. I must do whatever I can to save them.*

He turned and fled, but only one thought flashed across his mind, Swift. He stopped in his tracks. His life partner was all alone somewhere on this spaceship. Kee then made a selfish decision. There and then, he would save Swift, at all costs.

As he raced back, all sorts of emotions overwhelmed him, tears filled his eyes and blurred his vision, yet he didn't slow down. He had remembered the way he got to the engine room and retraced his steps. *Of course, I want to save everyone, but how? There was nowhere to go. Find Swift and, and... I don't know!* He was conflicted and confused. He rushed back into the market area to find an awful mess, bodies were strewn all over the floor, lying motionless. He couldn't be sure if they were sweating or bleeding. Nearly every other being in the area was now fighting, reaching for any implement they could find, to use as a weapon. Kee started shouting out Swifts name. He had to be careful making his way through the crowd, as to not get attacked from behind or stabbed from an unknown source. He searched and searched the area, ignoring the Calling that was trying to pull him in the opposite direction.

"Swift?" he shouted, "Swift!"

A soft and feint, but unmistakeable voice caught his attention.

"Kee?"

Kee spun to his left and looked down. Barely ten paces away was Swift, on the floor, scrambling to get to safety. Kee ran over, put his head under Swifts shoulder and lifted him up. Swift's legs could hardly take his own weight. Kee got them both to an empty orange corridor and slumped down. "What happened?" Kee asked.

Through laboured breaths Swift answered, "The heat... I collapsed... was... trampled. ...Body... broken... lungs... punctured. ...I came too... tried to... escape. ...Then you... the Calling... I still feel..."

Kee cut him off, explaining the conversation that had taken place with Vapula, "What do we do?" he finished off by asking.

"Go tell... Pace. ...Needs to... know," said Swift.

"What about everyone here?" asked Kee.

Kee looked down when Swift grabbed his hand. Swift's blue fur was turning a shade of green, as it mixed with the red sweat of the stranded passengers. Kee noticed a pool of blood underneath Swift and looked alarmed.

"You... can't... save... everyone!" said Swift.

"I know, but..." Kee was cut off by Swift pulling him closer.

"Kee... you already... saved... me," said Swift. Blue salty tears fell from his eyes as he gazed up at Kee.

"You're coming with me, we can get help," said Kee, his voice now quivering.

"No... my role... now... is to... guide these... souls... to the... light," said Swift, his breath getting shallower with every sentence. Under tremendous pain, Swift opened a portal back to the citadel. "Tell... Xania... goodbye... and I... am proud... of her."

Kee stood shaking his head, his face contracted in emotional pain. Tears and sweat intermingled on his chin. Swift raised a limp paw to wipe Kee's chin and licked the mixed liquid. He could taste Kee's pheromones. Swift smiled and whispered, "I... love you."

Kee couldn't say anything but wrapped his arms around the one being he had loved for so long. There was a loud explosion and the whole ship lurched to one side, quickly followed by another explosion. The ship could be heard creaking and being ripped open. With his last ounce of strength, Swift pushed Kee through the portal.

Kee landed on the stone floor in the portal room and quickly looked up. The vacuum of space tried to suck him back through the portal. The candles had all blown out, but he still managed to meet Swifts gaze. A white glowing light immersed Swift and, abruptly, the portal ceased, no fading away to a point. Kee knew, in that instant, Swift was gone.

"Arghhh!" His pain and anguish erupted to the surface, like a geyser. He flung his head back and opened his eyes wide, they were glowing white. He pushed all the feelings out in one big, long burst. Two white beams erupted from his eyes, straight up through the roof of the portal room, exploding the roof, up and outwards. Two of the walls were blown apart, wood and stone were catapulted through the air into the adjacent gardens. Kee slumped to the floor, curled up into a ball and gave in to himself. The portal frames stayed standing.

Qútú Un was the first one to arrive after hearing the explosion. Daylight poured into the portal room, something it had not seen for thousands of years. He saw Kee on the floor and went over to help.

"Kee, are you alright?" he asked.

Kee eventually looked up, "He's gone," he whispered.

Qútú wasn't sure what he meant at first, then realised exactly what Kee had said. "I am sorry," Qútú said mournfully, "he is with God now." Kee nodded. "What happened here?" Qútú asked.

Kee looked around, unaware of the damage he had caused.

"That was me?" he asked quietly. Qútú helped Kee to his feet, noticing he was covered in red liquid.

Qútú grunted, "You need medical attention!"

Kee looked down at himself, "It's not blood, I'm not injured. I just need to see Pace."

"He's not here at the moment, but I do think you should get checked over," said Qútú.

"The record keeper then," Kee said, ignoring Qútú's request.

"Kee!" Qútú snapped, bringing him out of a daze, "I'll take you to the medical bay to get checked over. I will personally bring Bork down to speak with you. You have my word," Qútú said.

Kee didn't answer, his head lolled forward and Qútú had to adjust his stance to stop Kee from falling over. He managed to carry Kee to the medical bay and lay him on a bed. The residents got to work, examining him and carrying out various tests.

Qútú nodded at Kee once he was comfortable, and although Kee had passed out, Qútú said, "I shall keep my promise." Then turned to fetch Bork.

Qútú Un

Chapter 9

Nyk followed the new Calling into the portal room and froze.

The roof was gone, two walls reduced to rubble.

"What the hell happened?" he whispered.

"It was Kee," said Qútú, stepping from behind the swirling green portal. "Something went wrong on his last Calling. He lost control."

Nyk's chest tightened. "Kee did this? How?"

"He was angry. Emotional. He let it out."

"But why?"

Qútú shook his head, "I don't know. But Swift didn't make it."

Nyk's heart stuttered. "Shit." He dropped his gaze, eyes squeezed shut. Swift. Gone. "This will hit Xania hard" he muttered. "She was close to both of them."

Qútú gave a grim nod, then pointed at the portal. "We should get move."

With a clenched jaw, Nyk stepped through.

***

They trudged across a barren wasteland, wordless. For Qútú, silence. For Nyk, only the noise inside his own skull-voices, whispers, none of them kind. This time, though, something new pushed through the static: a vision. Shapes moving across the horizon. A crowd, drawing closer.

Qútú gripped his arm, spinning him around. "Nyk! Are you even listening?"

"What... huh?" Nyk shook his head, forcing the haze away.

"I've been talking to you," said Qútú.

"Sorry. Just... thinking."

Qútú's forehead crinkled, "Are you alright?"

"Sure I..." Ny broke off. The vision returned, jagged echoes rippling at the back of his skull. He rubbed his eyes, trying to crush them down. "Looks like we've got company." He pointed toward the figures advancing across the wasteland.

"Probably just a welcoming party," Qútú said with a wry smile. The red liquid of his eyes sloshed from side to side.

Nyk frowned, "That's not what your eyes say."

Qútú only smiled wider, pupils swelling dark and round.

"You know something, don't you?"

He nodded, "Their march is too clean. Flankers keep sweeping the edges. The leader..." he gestured to the figure at the front, "hasn't taken his eyes off us, since he scented us."

Nyk blinked. "You can tell all that? I can barely make them out."

Qútú towered over him, broad shouldered and rooted in the dirt like an oak. His dark blue vest clung to a barrel chest, arms thick as tree trunks. And his eyes-black orbs filled with restless crimson fluid-shifted and focused with eerie precision. A Golthum's gift, Nyk knew, though the ritual that forged it was a story for another time.

"Two reasons," Qútú said evenly. "First, my eyes can zoom. Their step is military. Too rigid for peacekeepers. It's meant to intimidate. The flankers scan, the leader doesn't blink. That's focus, or stupidity. And the only way they'd be this precise?" He bared his teeth. "They smelled us. They've been tracking for three sections."

"Wow!" Nyk muttered. "So many questions." He glanced at his chronometer. "We've only been here four sections. How could they have smell us that long ago?"

Qútú's eyes narrowed. "When the portal opened, it disturbed the ions in the air. Carried our scent across the currents above us."

"Right," Nyk smirked. "Exactly what I was thinking."

Qútú almost laughed.

"And the other thing?" Nyk pressed.

"Huh?"

"You said two reasons. You've only given one... granted, a very long one."

"Oh." Qútú leaned in, smiling. "The other reason? I'm just that good."

Nyk chuckled "Anything else I should know about?"

Qútú shrugged. "Not really. Except they're nearly thirty-five decimetres tall."

"Thirty-five?" Nyk blinked. "That's not normal!"

The land stretched quiet around them, short blue grasses rippling in the breeze, insects buzzing over scattered wildflowers, rocky outcrops cutting the horizon. A green sun burned low, throwing long shadows that hadn't yet reached the pair. The alien colours played tricks on Nyk's eyes.

The warriors drew closer, fanning out, each keeping two paces of distance. Now Nyk could see their height clearly.

"Only thirty-five?" he muttered. "They look taller."

"I am not wrong," Qútú said. "Maybe your legs are too short." He barked a laugh.

The line of warriors stopped ten paces away. Their leader stepped forward; gaunt, towering, humanoid but stretched grotesque, with elongated limbs and ashen skin. Whisps of hair clung to some scalps. Their eye sockets gaped black and hollow.

The leaders voice rasped out. "What do you want, little man?"

Qútú stepped forward, unflinching. "We want to speak to your devil,"

"We are the Nephilim. No one talks to Purah without my permission," the leader growled.

"I just asked for your permission," Qútú replied flatly.

"You *need* to ask permission," the leader thundered. "My patience is limited."

"It's more limited than your intelligence," Qútú scoffed.

Nyk shoved forward, shaking his head at him. "Can we *please* have your permission to speak with Purah?" he asked carefully.

"NO!" the leader roared.

Nyk sighed. "Pretty please?"

"I SAID NO!" The stone club cracked against the ground, dust spraying from the impact.

"Okay, thanks for your help!" Qútú called out, voice dripping with sarcasm.

Nyk tried again, desperate. "If you'd just let us pass, we'll be on our way. No need for..."

"Fight!" someone bellowed.

"What? No!" Nyk protested.

"Fight, fight, fight," the warriors chanted, stamping their weapons.

"That wouldn't be fair," said Qútú calmly. "He's too small, you'd crush him in a heartbeat." He tilted his head at Nyk.

"Thanks, man,"Nyk muttered.

"We fight!" the leader declared. "We'll smash your body, Purah will feast on your souls, and then we'll ground your bones to dust."

"And then the wind will blow us away?" Qútú quipped.

"You shall not escape us on the wind!" the leader snapped.

Qútú sighed. The crimson liquid drained from his eyes, leaving two black voids. "We tried reasoning. Now there's no choice."

Two knives flashed into his hands: one forward, one reversed. In a blur he leapt, steel singing. The leader's head hit the dirt before Qútú's boots touched ground.

For a heatbeat, silence. Then the Niphilim howled, raising their weapons.

"They have two options now," Qútú said, eyes glinting as he smiled at Nyk. "That was one of them."

"There's a lot of them!" Nyk shouted, panic creeping into his voice.

"You've got blasters," Qútú snapped back. "Start blasting!"

Nyk didn't argue. He whipped out his twin blasters and opened fire. Four Nephilim dropped in quick succession.

"Not bad," Qútú said, almost impressed. "My turn."

He clicked his heels. Steel blades snapped from his boots. With knives in hand, he launched himself forward. In a blur of motion he carved through two necks, spun mid-air, and split two more on the second line before landing. His kick drove a boot-blade into a chest. Another leap, another pair of heads rolling.

One Nephilim swung a stone axe to intercept. Qútú dropped flat, letting the blade cleave through its comrade instead. Using the falling body as a springboard, he drovea foot into the attacker's torso, tore it open, and vaulted high. He came down on two more, boots severing spines, then bounded from shoulder to shoulder, decapitating as he went.

By the time the Nephilim realised what was happening, half their number were already down. They spread apart, giving Nyk clean shots. He fired wildly, dropping more, but even his fastest trigger work couldn't match Qútú's slaughter. Clubs and axes flew as limbs and heads hit the dirt. The enemy thinned fast. A handful broke ranks and locked together in a tight circle. Shields raised wall-to-wall, weapons jutting through the narrow gaps. Nyk's blaster bolts ricocheted harmlessly off the barrier. "Not working!" he shouted.

Qútú smirked. "Then I'll finish this." From his belt he drew a slim cylinder; the E-whip. With a flick, a glowing tether snapped out, ending in a pulsing orb of light. He whirled it overhead, faster and faster, until a burning halo spun around him. Then he flicked it, the whip lashing and crackling, creating a shifting curtain of yellow fire. Encased in the storm of light, Qútú charged straight at the circle of shields.

Qútú barrelled into the shield wall. Spears shattered, shields buckled, and stone clubs cracked as the Nephilim were blasted off their feet. He stopped the spinning E-whip and lashed out-one warrior split clean in two, dark ash pouring from the wounds.

Nyk didn't hesitate. His blasters lit the air, dropping four in rapid succession.

Qútú retracted the whip, clipped it to his belt and drew his knives again. Two blades flew-skulls pierced. He finished the last pair with his bare hands, tearing the arms off one soldier and ramming them down the throat of the other.

Covered in fine ash, Qútú turned with a grin. "Enjoy the show?"

"Remind me, never to piss you off!" Nyk muttered, then froze. "Although... one's still standing."

The leader was rising, head reattached as if it had never been severed. His was cry echoed across the wasteland. All around, ash and body parts slithered back together, Nephilim re-forming where they had fallen.

"This is unnatural," Qútú growled.

"We don't have time to keep doing this," Nyk snapped.

"Then the mountains," Qútú said. "High ground may give us an edge."

"Agreed."

They ran. By nightfall they reached the base of the jagged range. The army still marched in the distance, slower but relentless. After climbing three storeys of rock, they found a ledge beneath an overhang and slumped down to rest.

"So," said Nyk between bites of ration, "what were they?"

Qútú inhaled through his feeding tube, eyes dark. "They looked like they were dead."

"Or undead?" Nyk forced a nervous laugh.

Qútú's gaze didn't waver. "I haven't seen that in a long time."

Nyk's smile vanished. "Wait, you mean it's real?"

"Yes, on Veltag, the dead come back alive, but not more than once. Kill the dead and they stay dead."

"Huh!" said Nyk, "That's one place to stay away from, I hate ghosts."

"Ghosts can't hurt you!" said Qútú bluntly.

"They're creepy, they can float and walk through walls!" Nyk countered.

"They're just looking for their next life," Qútú said.

Nyk shook his head, "No, no, no, they're out to scare me, and that's it." Qútú laughed, unable to say anything else.

After settling down for the night, Nyk had a restless sleep, dreaming of ghosts and awakened at every sound.

The following morning Qútú was scanning the horizon, as Nyk joined him by the rocky edge.

"They're at the base of the mountain," said Qútú, nodding a welcome to Nyk.

"I guess we better get moving," Nyk said. "Hopefully we can get around this mountain from up here?" Nyk wondered out loud.

"Yes," Qútú agreed, his eyes pulsing bright red in the dim morning light, "we should move swiftly. I feel the demon on this planet isn't taking much rest."

"Oh, how so?" asked Nyk, as he gathered up his rations and blasters.

Qútú just shrugged, "I don't know, just a feeling."

Nyk just nodded, knowing that a Golthum's intuition is hardly wrong, then set off across the rocky ledge.

They had barely got fifty paces before Qútú quipped, "Have you stopped crying now?"

Nyk stopped walking and turned back, a quizzical look upon his face. "What are you talking about?"

"Last night, you were crying in your sleep," Qútú smirked.

"What? No, I wasn't," said Nyk defensively.

"Yes, you were, three times, just before you woke up, you were crying," stated Qútú.

Nyk pulled a face, "No I didn't. Well, I had night terrors, yes, but I wasn't crying."

"Yes, you were," said Qútú.

"No, I was... I..."

"Your heart rate elevated, tears rolled down your face, and you cried out, quote, 'No, no, stay away from me!'" Qútú's eyes bored into Nyk's.

Nyk's mouth dropped open, then slowly closed. He took a step closer to Qútú coming within a decimetre of his face.

"I'd appreciate it if you didn't tell the others," he said, shrugging like it was nothing.

Qútú smiled, "Your shame is safe with me," he said, then bowed his head in honour.

Nyk opened his mouth again, but he thought better of it, turned, and walked on.

"It was your fault anyway!" Nyk shouted behind him. Qútú smiled, his red pupils exploded like starlight, but he said nothing. "If you hadn't mentioned ghosts, I'd have been fine... just don't do that again, man. Not cool!"

Qútú just grunted a reply, but for him it was only stifling a laugh.

The rest of the morning passed in silence as they both carefully traversed the treacherous face of the mountain. Every now and then a foot would slip and send shards of slate sliding down the steep sides. Its noisy echo penetrating the cold mountain air.

Nyk paused, holding up his hand, gesturing for Qútú to stay still and listen. He sniffed the air, his head twitching in different directions. "I smell smoke," he sniffed some more, "it's coming from around that boulder," he said.

"Are you sure?" asked Qútú.

"Yes, can't you smell it?" Nyk asked, turning to look at Qútú.

Qútú blankly stared back.

"Oh, that's right," Nyk smirked, "you can't smell anything!"

Qútú faked a grin.

"We should be careful, it may be them again," Nyk whispered.

"It's not," replied Qútú.

Nyk stood up straight, "Oh yeah?" he said sarcastically, "those eyes of yours work around corners, do they?"

This time Qútú smiled. "No, they don't. But the dead don't need to keep warm."

"Well... maybe they're cooking something?"

Qútú shook his head. "Think about that."

Nyk did think about it, and quietly replied, "The dead don't eat."

"The dead don't eat!" Qútú repeated, emphasizing every word.

Nyk shrugged, "We should be careful though."

"Agreed."

Slowly, they both crept around the boulder, hoping not to surprise anyone, or even be attacked themselves. There, they came across another group of Nephilim. Every one of them holding a spear pointing directly at them. Like their previous predicament, except this time, these beings were alive. Living breathing flesh, bright green eyes and short hair. They all looked scared. Nyk immediately raised his hands above his head. Qútú lowered his arms, palms faced outwards and stepped forward.

"I am Qútú, this is my friend, Stongol," he said gesturing to Nyk. "We are Cydarions, we have come to help you."

The Nephilim all looked at each other.

"Psst," Nyk whispered.

The Nephilim mumbled amongst themselves, their piercing green eyes not leaving the Cydarions.

"Psst," said Nyk again, this time a little louder.

"Yes?" Qútú replied without moving his head.

"What's Stongol?" asked Nyk. The Nephilim stopped their mutterings.

"Shush, I'll tell you later," Qútú said.

"Have they followed you?" A Nephilim asked.

"We outran them on the plains, before making it to this mountain. We are not sure if they are on the mountain or not. I'm sorry," Qútú said.

"They will kill you, it's only a matter of time," the Nephilim said.

"Is that why you're hiding up here? Are you the only ones left?"

"I am Zolang'd," said the Nephilim stepping forward. He gestured towards the fire, "Please sit with us."

Qútú and Nyk both nodded and sat cross legged on the cold rock floor, positioning themselves on the opposite Zolang'd. The Nephilim sat down too, his long legs bent awkwardly in a triangle shape. He waved his hand at the rest of the group, and they all lowered their weapons. Some faded back into the darkness of the cave.

"I wish we could give you a traditional welcome, Qútú and Stongol, but our life is no longer the same." His gaze dropped to the floor; a sadness echoed his words.

Nyk quickly whispered to Qútú, "What is Stongol?"

Qútú nodded to Zolang'd, ignoring Nyks question, "Can you tell us what has occurred? Any information, will help us, help you."

"What can you do?" asked Zolang'd.

"Our... assignment, will be much clearer if you could tell us your problems first."

Zolang'd looked across at Nyk, then back at Qútú. "Nearly two cycles ago, a dust storm ravaged the land. It uncovered the resting places of our dead. We may be a race of warriors, but we respect our fallen. When we went to rebury the bodies, they started to squirm and move. Naturally, we ran away, not knowing what to make of it. Our Shaman put it down to the bodies drying out under the hot sun, and that they should be reburied in honour of their achievements. The deeper the grave, the higher in rank they were. We went back to carry out the Shamans request, but all the graves were empty, every one of them. Again, we consulted the Shaman, who found it wonderful, he thought they had been accepted into the great battle above the sky. It is a great honour to be chosen for eternal fighting," he explained.

Qútú's swishing pupils steadied. "But *you* don't think that's what happened?" he asked.

"At the time, I did," replied Zolang'd, "but since then, everything has changed. Ten rotations after that had happened, our village was attacked in the middle of the night and without warning," he leaned closer into the fire, the flames flickered light onto his pink skin, "by our own dead."

Nyk shuddered. Qútú's eyes blackened in thought. "So, what happened?" asked Nyk.

"What could we do?" Zolang'd asked rhetorically. "We fled. We are not allowed to fight with each other. We are peaceful to our own kind, to anyone. We are great warriors, but we only do it for payment."

"So, you think someone paid them to attack you?" asked Nyk.

Qútú's red pupils raised like a roller blind.

"Why would you think anyone had paid them to attack us?' asked Zolang'd.

"Well, you just said..."

"What do the dead need money for?" Qútú said quietly, leaning into Nyk. Nyk felt stupid again.

"We don't know why they attacked us, but our law dictates that we can't attack them back. We tried to defend ourselves as best we could, without killing. Not that you can kill that which is already dead. Many of us died that night, but the rest of us fled. We felt like cowards and not the warriors we are supposed to be. Our elders stayed behind to protect the camp, but they too were eventually slaughtered, unable to fight back. We have since crossed paths with other tribes who are all in the same predicament. We agree to stay out of each other's way, thinking a larger crowd is harder to hide and an easier target," Zolang'd stopped and looked at the Cydarions. "Qútú, Stongol, we are alone, without a Shaman and starving. There is no food up here in the mountains, and there is barely firewood at the base. We are not going to survive, and that scares us!"

"There's no point fighting back," said Qútú, "they just get back up again!"

The pink skin of Zolang'd drained of colour. "You have attacked our sacred warriors?" His voice wobbled with horror. Spears dropped low and pointed straight at the two Cydarions.

Qútú's eyes went black, and he froze.

Nyk slapped him on the back. "What my pal here means, is that he has encountered a similar thing before, and he would never desecrate your sacred oath." He squeezed Qútú's shoulder.

"Yes," Qútú said, his eyes telling a lie, "I would always respect your laws."

Zolang'd waved his hand, and again the spears lifted. "What is it you think you can do for us?"

Qútú's eyes went back to normal as Nyk spoke. "We are Cydarions. We have been sent by God, to find the devil responsible for this, and put a stop to it."

"You think a devil is behind this?" asked Zolang'd.

"A hundred percent," Nyk nodded, then sneezed.

The spears all came down and pointed at Nyk.

"You all look hungry, how long have you gone without food?" asked Nyk, trying to diffuse the situation.

"It's been four and a half rotations, but I'm not sure how much longer we can go on. We've even seen our relatives in those armies. How are we supposed to defend against the very ones that are supposed to be defending us? Most of us haven't even reached maturity yet," his voice started to rise, "They're just kids!" His fist slammed into the ground. Reminding Qútú of the first Nephilim he had spoken to.

"Zolang'd, we can track down this devil. We will find him and put a stop to all this, and..."

"We shall do what we can," interrupted Nyk.

"I may trust you, but remain doubtful of your capabilities, you look small and weak, like a mountain hound."

Qútú smiled. "I guess that's *our* problem." He looked at Nyk, "Stongol and I will deal with it."

Nyk muttered, "What does that mean?"

"It's my natural tongue, it..." said Qútú, before being interrupted by Zolang'd,

"How do you intend to do that?" he asked.

"We shall end his reign. Although it is uncommon for a devil to raise the dead," said Qútú.

"How uncommon?" asked Zolang'd.

"Well, erm," said Qútú, "I'm not sure, but it could happen."

"You've not had time to read many records!" said Nyk smugly.

"You know I can read two books at once?" countered Qútú.

"No, I didn't, but you've still not read as many as me," Nyk said smugly. He looked at Zolang'd, "Raising the dead has never happened!"

"Our fate is sealed," sighed Zolang'd.

"No, I have seen it before, just not with a devil, only magic. You cut off the source, and the tentacles die too," offered Qútú.

"Sounds like we've got a plan," said Nyk smiling. Zolang'd gave a nervous smile back.

As the sun started to set on the short rotation, the rest of the group congregated around the fire and chatted with the Cydarions. By the time everyone settled in for sleep, Nyk was still wide awake. Not because of the fear of ghosts, but for the fear of failure. He had never been so close to an extinction of a species, and it weighed heavily on his mind.

Can they even recover from this? What if we fail? How do we tell them? What would I tell them? How can I live with myself knowing we should have done more?

The questions repeated in his head as he slowly fell asleep, staring at the flickering embers in the dwindling fire.

The undead Nephilim army

Chapter 10

Nyk felt his body being gently shaken and he opened his eyes. Qútú was standing over him.

"Time to go, Stongol. The sun has been up for a while," he said.

Nyk rubbed his eyes and yawned, "I feel like I only just fell asleep."

Qútú looked at him quizzically, his eyes glowing bright red, "Something on your mind?" he asked.

"Something like that," Nyk answered as he looked around the cave.

Qútú caught his gaze. "Some have gone to collect firewood, others are looking for another place to hide and some food," Qútú said, answering Nyk's unasked question. "We should get going too," he said placing a hand on Nyk's shoulder. Nyk immediately felt how warm it was and relaxed his already tense body. Nyk nodded, fitted the belt pouch around his waist and assessed its items.

By high sun, they had descended the mountain and traversed across a vast dried-up seabed and entered a rocky outcrop.

"There must be a lair around here somewhere," said Nyk, referring to the strength of the Calling.

"I see no protruding structures," Qútú said, his fluid red pupils changing shape to resemble a horizontal line.

"There!" Nyk shouted, a finger pointing into the distance.

Qútú swivelled his head. "Good work, Stongol."

"What does that mean?" Nyk asked.

Immediately, a thunderous rumble echoed across the landscape, shaking the ground.

"I hope we're not too late," said Qútú.

"Let's go and find out."

"Right behind you, brother," Qútú said.

They found a cleft in the rock and exchanged a quick nod. Qútú went first, hand on the hilt of his E-whip; Nyk closed in behind, blasters raised.

The tunnel was cold and damp at the mouth, warming the deeper they went. Distant cries and a strange, tinkling enchantment drifted through the lair. Nyk's impatience frayed.

"Hurry up. It sounds like it's up to something," he hissed.

"You don't rush a surprise, Nyk!" Qútú replied, displeased. Nyk blew out a breath but fell into step.

Two stubby flames were stuck into the ground along the passage. Qútú glanced back and nodded towards them. "I've never seen the fire so small," Nyk murmured, puzzled. A hot gust rushed past, then the air switched to a cool, damp current.

"Ha, ha, ha, I know you're there, Cydarion!" a voice spat, laughter like stone scraping. "I can smell you!"

Nyk sniffed his armpit and shrugged, prodding the darkness with his blaster. "Come on then." A corner later they stepped into a wider cavern. A fire burned low in one alcove; a cluttered desk in another held unlabelled vials and odd apparatuses.

"Magic," Qútú breathed.

A devil stood in the centre of the room, arms spread as if welcoming guests. Scaly red skin, a thick torso, legs that bent the wrong way at the knee. Six short horns sprouted from a deceptively gentle face. Its grin was enormous, nostrils flaring, eyes like coals that somehow felt warm.

Nyk stared too long; Qútú elbowed him.

The devils smile didn't fade. "Welcome," it said, "I was expecting you."

"Your time is over," Qútú answered.

The devil's fiery eyes locked on Qútú, but then snapped a voice deep and harsh: "Not you. Him!" His gaze shifted, and the smile returned as he fixed on Nyk.

"Me?" Nyk asked.

"Yes, you, Cydarion. I've been waiting for this meeting. I've come to accept my fate."

"And what fate is that?" Nyk asked.

The devil bowed his head, shoulders trembling as though in grief. "Death. You kill all of us, don't you? Every demon you meet."

"You get what you deserve," Qútú said flatly.

"Do we?" the devil asked, voice silk over steel. "Do you ever stop to wonder if it's truly justice… or just habit?"

"That's not entirely true," Nyk countered. "We're willing to give you a chance."

Qútú stiffened. "This is a mistake."

"It's our way," Nyk whispered. Qútú didn't answer, but his respirator hissed louder, betraying his agitation.

Nyk steadied himself. "Stop what you're doing. Leave the dead to rest. Leave this place and never return."

He remembered why he'd re-joined the Cydarions, after walking away once before. This rule, the chance at redemption, mattered. He'd seen too much blood spilled, too many lives ended. Each death weighed on him now. Maybe it was his conscience, maybe exhaustion, but he couldn't let this one be just another execution.

The devil laughed softly, almost pitying. "You think I want this?" He tapped his chest, where a red amulet glowed faintly against his scaled skin. "This cursed stone is my master. Osiris forged it. Every sin I've committed, every life I've taken it wasn't me. It was this." His hand lingered on the amulet, stroking it almost lovingly. "I don't even know who I am anymore."

He sank to his knees, shoulders sagging. "I beg you, take it from me. Free me. Destroy it. Or kill me if you must, but end this torment." His voice cracked. A single tear slipped down his cheek, glinting in the firelight, too perfect, too theatrical.

Nyk turned to Qútú.

Qútú shrugged. "Can't hurt to try. Just... be careful."

"Me?" Nyk asked.

"He was talking to you," Qútú said grinning.

"Yeah, but still..."

"What's the matter, Stongol? Afraid?"

"No!" Nyk snapped. Then after a beat, "Fine. I'll do it."

Nyk stepped forward, blasters still trained on the devil. Qútú moved in closer, drawing his E-whip and holding it ready.

Nyk holstered one blaster and drew a knife. "This better not be a trick," he warned.

"No trick," Purah murmured, voice trembling with relief. "Please, take it. I cannot remove it. The burden weighs heavy. Oh, to be free..."

Nyk stepped closer and reached for the amulet. It was warm against his skin, unnaturally soothing, like a palm-smooth stone. He pinched the leather band beneath his fingers and slashed it. The band fell away. Purah collapsed, gasping, then sobbed, "Thank you. Thank you."

He crawled forward and latched onto Nyk's boots. Qútú's hand snapped to his E-whip; he threw his arm back, then froze. The devil did not lunge. He grovelled, licking the leather as if it were holy.

"Cydarion," Purah breathed, eyes wet and fervent. "My life is yours. You have freed me I am indebted. Name it; any service, any humiliation, I will accept."

Nyk slid the amulet into his pouch and edged away, uncomfortable. The devil followed on his knees, words pouring out like oil. "Beat me if you would, like my father did, I will take it. Send me into exile, I will go gladly. Tell my people of your mercy; let my repentance sing your praises."

A snigger escaped Qútú. Nyk shot him a look, then leveled his blaster at Purah's head. "Enough."

"Kill me if you must," Purah begged, voice high and urgent. "Kill me now, while I'm free, end it." His eyes glittered. He sounded desperate. He sounded eager.

"Purah?" Qútú's tone cut through the pleading. "If we spare you, what will you do?"

"I wll go home. I will right my wrongs. I will tell them of your justice, of your enlightenment." He bowed, forehead in the dirt, making every syllable an offering.

Qútú's lip curled. Nyk felt the new rule, mercy first, press against his ribs. He found his voice. "Stand up."

Purah rose, still on shaky legs. Nyk exhaled and forced the stern line into his face. "We'll let you go. But if we find you again..." He let the threat hang, cold and absolute. "I *will* shoot!"

Purah nodded so fiercely his shoulders shook. "You have my word." He bowed once more, then turned and crawled toward the darkness, every movement soaked with gratitude, or with calculation.

Nyk watched as the devil opened a portal and slunk through. Qútú's respirator hissed softly beside him, "You know, sometime, I wish to go through their portal too."

"And bring more destruction and death into our lives?" Nyk replied sharply.

"What's up?" asked Qútú, noticing some anguish in Nyks voice.

Nyk shrugged, "This, the whole Calling, it just felt... different," he said.

"I've not been on as many Callings as you, but they have all felt different to me," said Qútú.

"Yeah, but this didn't seem normal," said Nyk.

"It wasn't normal," said Qútú, a small smile on his face. Nyk didn't react, he just stood there, watching the flaming portal fizzle out.

Silence once again filled the air, until Qútú spoke softly, "I was wrong, I got caught up in my old ways. I shouldn't have wanted to bring death so quickly." He nodded without looking at Nyk, "You know, I could learn a thing or two from you." Qútú nudged Nyk with his shoulder, "You did the right thing," he said, sliding his E-whip back in its holster.

"Hmm," Nyk mused to himself. Qútú thought for a fraction then lay a hand on Nyk's shoulder.

"Let's meditate," he offered.

Nyk looked around the lair and let out a sigh. "Sure," he said eventually. His mind swimming with a thousand thoughts.

***

"Come on, Stongol," Qútú said, gently shaking Nyk awake again, "looks like you fell asleep."

"Huh? Oh yeah," Nyk smiled back, "I guess I'm just a little tired."

"Are you alright?" asked Qútú.

Nyk nodded, "I'll be fine," he replied. He stretched his muscles, as though he'd had a long, deep sleep, "I think we should check on our new friends, tell them what happened."

Qútú nodded, "We do need to check if the dead are active or not."

Exiting the lair, Qútú noticed one of the flames had completely extinguished, but the other, although flameless, still had glowing embers underneath. Not wanting to bring it to Nyk's attention, he let it go.

Retracing their steps, they came across Zolang'd near the base of the mountain and went on to explain what had occurred in the lair of Purah. Zolang'd rationalised why they had come down from the mountain.

"Our scouts saw the dead suddenly fall to the floor. They just crumpled into a heap, as though they had died again. We came down to check on them and it was true. Their bones were all in a pile. If what you say is true, then it is over. We shall rebury the dead and strive forward with our lives."

"That's the right thing to do," Qútú agreed.

"We promise to return in one cycle. To see how things are, and if we can help any further," Nyk said respectfully.

"We all appreciate your help, Cydarions," Zolang'd said, bowing down before them.

"There's no need for that," said Nyk, "but it is much appreciated."

"It's time we were going," said Qútú. He turned towards Nyk, "Do you still have it?"

Nyk nodded and tapped his pouch, "Right here, it'll be safe in the citadel," he said, opening a portal home.

Qútú stepped toward the portal.

"Just one thing," Nyk asked.

Qútú turned his head, "Yes?"

"What does Stongol mean?"

"Stongol," Qútú repeated, nodding his head and turning to walk through the portal, "Yes, in my language, it means..." Qútú stepped through the portal and disappeared.

"Argh!" Nyk exclaimed and flapped his arms, then ran after Qútú.

"Say again," said Nyk stepping onto the familiar stone floor of the portal room.

Qútú, who was halfway through the arched doorway stopped and turned around, a grin on his face.

"It means, The Scared One," Qútú said, chuckling to himself.

"I'm not scared," said Nyk, then paused. "Wait a fraction, are you talking about that one time, the other night?" Nyk asked.

Qútú just smiled.

"Cos that... that ain't true," Nyk said, waving a finger.

Qútú raised his eyebrows, his eyes flashed red like a warning sign.

"Well... I... you said you'd never mention it again," Nyk said, a little flustered.

"And I sharn't," countered Qútú.

"Well, quit calling me that!" scorned Nyk.

"Very well, Stongol," Qútú' said with a wink.

Nyk's face went red, "I told you..."

"That was the last time, I promise," said Qútú quietly.

Nyk's relief was obvious. "Okay, let's go and see Bork, see what he'll make of this amulet," Nyk said patting his pouch,

"Do we have to tell him everything?" Qútú asked.

"Of course," Nyk replied, until he realized what Qútú meant, "Well only that which pertains to the Calling, nothing else!"

"Sure," Qútú smirked.

***

It was a couple of sections before Bork was free to receive Nyk and Qútú. "I'm sorry," said Bork, apologising for the wait, "but it's been hectic around here lately."

"It sounds like you could do with some help," said Nyk, a concern for Bork.

"Oh, I do have some help," replied Bork happily, "Well, I think I do. Young master Holan, he spends all his spare time in here. He is so eager to learn everything. He is like a Crendle sponge, soaking up as much information as he can. He's quite a joy to have around, always asking questions. In fact, he would make an excellent journalist.

Qútú nodded. Nyk replied with a short sharp, "Huh!"

"Oh, I'm sorry," said Bork again, "I get carried away. Please, tell me all about your latest Calling."

"Caanan," said Qútú, "The planet was called Caanan."

"Caanan?" Bork repeated, as he started typing up a record, "Please tell me everything," Bork said.

Nyk shot a quick glance to Qútú.

"Why don't you start Nyk?" Qútú said. Nyk nodded and proceeded to tell the story of the Nephilim.

***

After explaining their whole Calling, the subject turned to the amulet, where Nyk retrieved it from his pouch. "It is pretty," said Nyk, gazing into the ruby red stone.

Bork nodded, "That's for sure, but how does it work?" he asked.

"We're not sure," said Qútú, "but it seemed to release Purah from something. A curse maybe?"

"Hmm, that is interesting," Bork replied, looking at the object. "I'll put it somewhere safe until I get time to look into it further," he offered. "Pace has got me looking into finances for this place and I..."

"Does this concern me?" asked Qútú interrupting Bork.

"Well, no, Master Un, but..."

"Good, then we're done here," responded Qútú, quickly standing up to leave.

Nyk stayed seated, his mouth open as Qútú walked out of the small room. "I'm sorry for..."

Bork stopped Nyk with a paw up, "It's quite alright it's just his way. He doesn't like frivolous things that don't concern him. I guess it's a good trait to have. In some ways," said Bork.

Nyk shrugged and turned his attention back to the amulet. "Do you think you can find out any information about it?" Nyk asked, running a finger over the smooth stone.

Bork went to pick the amulet up for further inspection, but Nyk closed his fist around the red stone.

"It's mine," he snapped. Bork was taken aback, a look of shock on his face. Nyk soon realized his mistake and dropped the amulet,

"I... I... I'm Sorry," he said, "I don't know what..." He saw Bork staring at the amulet.

"It's glowing!" Nyk said, his eyes widening.

Bork nodded, "But why, what did you do Nyk?" he asked.

"I didn't do anything."

"It wasn't glowing a fraction ago," replied Bork.

"I know! But it wasn't me," Nyk protested.

"Okay, I'm sorry," said Bork, "Is it starting to work again?"

"I don't know," answered Nyk, "I don't recall it being like that when Purah wore it!"

Bork's eyebrows furrowed, "What could you be?" he asked the amulet.

"Bork?" Nyk said.

Bork looked back to Nyk, smiling. "I shall have great interest in this. Of course, when I get around to it."

"Can you let me know if you find anything?" asked Nyk.

"Of course, master Kepler," replied Bork, "I shall let you know of anything I learn."

Nyk smiled back, arose from his seat and headed for the door, he paused before turning back around. "Can I take another look?" he asked Bork. Bork held the amulet up in his paw, its red glow enticing Nyk. "I could hold onto it for you," suggested Nyk.

Bork looked at Nyk and clenched his paw quickly, the amulet disappearing from view. "It will be safe here," Bork reassured Nyk.

"Of course," Nyk said, shaking his head, and walked out the door.

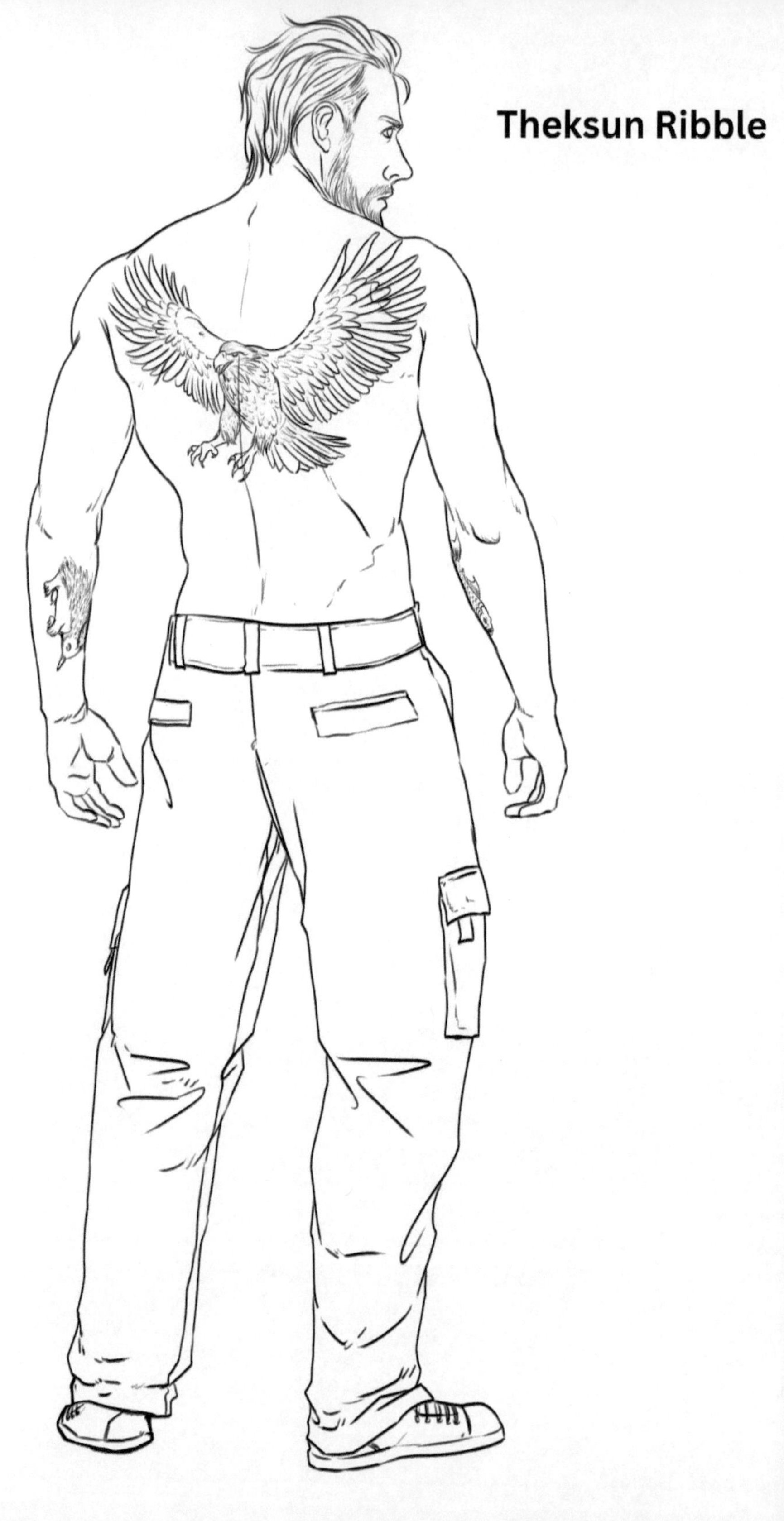

Theksun Ribble

Chapter 11

It had been a full rotation since Xania and Theksun had arrived on their latest Calling, and so far, they hadn't come across any sentient life. They had, however, seen endless amounts of various insects and small birds, all of them going about their business nonchalantly.

"This place seems quiet, too quiet," said Theksun.

Xania nodded, "Yeah, I don't like it," she admitted. "The gravity here feels twice the standard strength, my body feels so heavy!"

"I'm sure it has something to do with that," Theksun said, pointing up in the sky.

A large moon hung in the green sky, its size, reminiscent of the Versub sector, covered half the sky and blocked out nearly half of the natural light. Where green sky touched the horizon, it blended into the green foliage of the plains laid out before them. The air smelled sweet with nectar and left a sticky taste in the mouth.

Another arduous rotation of walking and they found themselves by a wooded area. At least, it used to be a wood, but all the branches had been broken off, tearing strips from the still standing trunks. The younger trees and saplings all wilted towards the ground. Suddenly, a crash came from within the woods, as another large limb broke under the strong gravity, and impacted the floor with enough force to make the ground tremble.

"It's probably best not to stay in there tonight," said Theksun, "but we should rest, it's already dark and we're both tired."

Xania nodded, "You're right," she said under a laboured breath, "could you check out what's ahead of us?" she asked, pointing at his back, referring to his tattoo of a Jayhawk.

Theksun shook his head, "No, unfortunately not. I tried before you awoke this morning, but it was a struggle due to the extra gravity. I don't think I could do it again."

Theksun was a Pogcite, similar to a human but, their internal organs moved around depending on their situation. His species lived for nearly five hundred cycles, due to the slow deterioration of their cells. They were a relative peaceful race that kept to themselves on their home planet and rarely ventured away from their own sun. Theksun had three tattoos on his body, all of which could come alive if he wished.

The pair started a small fire, the flames flickered like red and orange ribbons, the heat barely spreading out. They settled down and fell asleep easily. All around them, fields of glowing flowers, like fireflies, stood static in a breathless wind.

***

A violent earthquake awoke the Cydarions with a start. More tree trunks in the wooded area creaked and groaned before crashing down. Xania and Theksun were up and on their feet within a heartbeat. Xania yawned and wiped away some sleep from her eyes.

"What was that?" she asked.

"An earthquake, I think, but... shh," Theksun said, putting a finger to his lips.

Xania didn't reply but scanned the area trying to zone in to what Theksun could hear.

They both stood in silence for a few fractions before Xania whispered, "I hear it."

A feint sound was coming from over the hills, the sound of voices.

"We should investigate," said Theksun, stamping out the dwindling embers of the fire. Sunlight had just started to penetrate the early sky; a red glow gave of hues of orange before hitting the thick green sky above.

They followed the sound of the voices, getting louder as they got closer. Cresting over a grassy ridgeline, the Cydarions saw a caravan of beings. All heading in one direction. They noticed that the beings were all of the same build. Ten decimetres tall and green. Blending in with their background, both floor and sky. Thick individual bristles adhered their rounded backs. Pale faces, with deep set eyes and a black protruding nose. It wasn't until they got closer that they noticed a mouth underneath the little nose, small and round.

The beings all carried bags in their hands. Some pulled carts bearing possessions. Larger open carts were hovering above the ground, being pulled by a group of these small beings. None of them seemed to have a smile on their faces. Even the younglings were quiet, walking in line.

"We should stay back and observe them for a while," said Xania, "we don't know if they are a friendly species yet."

"They look approachable," said Theksun.

"A species can be quite unpredictable when faced with a lot of stress," said Xania.

"Like a devil influencing the world?"

"Exactly," agreed Xania. "I just hope we're not too late this time. Most of my recent Callings have been. Far too many species have suffered," she said remorseful. She wished she could have done something more, something different.

Theksun and Xania followed the caravan from a safe distance, acting like they were heading in the same direction, occasionally taking a step closer to the local beings. Until eventually they were close enough to speak with an adolescent.

"Greetings," Theksun said with a warm smile.

The young adolescent looked up at Theksun but didn't reply.

"Where are you headed?" asked Theksun, still keeping his smile.

"To the red man," replied the young local, its gaze not leaving Theksun.

"The red man?" Theksun questioned.

The local thought for a fraction before answering. "He will save us!"

Xania wasn't sure if that was a question or a statement. She stepped out from the side of Theksun, "What do you mean, save us?" she asked.

The adolescent's eyes darted to Xania, then quickly to the ground before running off to re-join its family.

Xania sighed a little and looked at Theksun, who just shrugged back. Then, from behind them, a voice spoke out to them, clear and mature.

"The moon, it's falling," the being said.

Both Xania, and Theksun stopped in their tracks and waited for an older being to approach.

"What do you mean by that?" Theksun asked.

The being gestured, "How have you not heard?"

"Oh, we've been... camping, for a while," Xania offered, giving a warm smile.

The being looked at the Cydarions quizzically but then proceeded to explain, "Our astronomers noticed our moon moving closer to us, slowly at first but then increasing in speed. It's heading straight towards us, it's unstoppable. It will cause the destruction of the planet!" the being said, a panic in his voice. He paused and caught his breath before starting again.

"Why are you even here, do you have a spaceship that can save us?" asked the small green being.

"Yes, can you take us?" asked another, turning around with excitement, "You can have all my possessions in exchange."

"I'm sorry, we came here to..." Xania paused, not sure what to say.

"To camp, and walk in the lush greenery," Theksun said, noticing Xania's pause "our transport isn't due for a while," he lied.

"Oh," replied the being, "maybe you need to join us."

"Where are you going?" Theksun asked again.

"As the young girl said, to see the red man. That is our only way off this planet. Those that could, have already left, either by private or public transport. We were told it would take seven rotations before it's too late!" the being explained.

"How did it happen?" asked Theksun.

"If you want to know any more, you'll have to walk with me. There's still quite a distance to cover and I'm not as quick as I used to be," the elderly local answered honestly.

"Of course," said Xania.

Theksun reached out for the handles of the travelling boxes the green being had been carrying. "If you don't mind, I can carry these for you," he offered.

The elderly male looked Theksun straight in the eyes and paused. A smile emerged from the round mouth, "Yes, that would be kind of you, thank you."

Theksun nodded and took the two box handles in each hand. "It's no problem," he said.

"Erm," Xania said, "so, what happened?"

"Please, call me Bastion," said the elder to Xania, "We don't know, is the real answer. About thirteen rotations ago we heard reports that our twin planet, Gomorrah, was being destroyed by its moon. Their moon started to fall out of orbit, just like ours is now, breaking up in the atmosphere. The debris came down onto the planet; its dust mixed with the air and turned it poisonous. Well, that's what we were last told, anyway."

Xania gazed off into the distance, thinking about Bastions words, even before he had finished.

"What happened after that?" Theksun asked.

Bastion shrugged, "We don't know, we lost all communications after the last broadcast."

Xania turned back to the local, "Bastion? If their twin planet was called Gomorrah; does that make this one," she paused and swallowed hard, "Sodom?"

"Of course," Bastion said with a smile, "But you knew that you came here to camp, didn't you?" he chuckled.

"You've heard of this place?" Theksun asked Xania.

"Mmm," Xania replied, "I'll tell you later."

Theksun furrowed his brow as Bastion spoke again, "Who are you really? You don't have enough equipment with you to be camping, what are you after?" Bastion asked.

Theksun shot a quick glance at Xania, who nodded, then he proceeded to explain who they were and their role on this planet. For the rest of the rotation the three of them talked about God, the Calling and devils.

"So, why didn't you get a Calling to Gomorrah?" Bastion asked after they had stopped to rest for the night, lit a small fire and had eaten a simple meal. The gracious hosts sharing some of their food supplies.

"Unfortunately, we can't answer that," said Theksun, "only God opens the portals, otherwise we wouldn't know about any of the events."

"It sounds like your God isn't all seeing, as you say," said Bastion. Xania and Theksun didn't know how to answer, instead, they bowed their heads.

Abruptly, Theksun stood up and looked at Xania. "We need to keep moving. We don't have time to stop!"

Xania looked up at him, "We have time to spend with our hosts," she said politely.

"Our job is to..."

"Find out the cause and do what we can," Xania cut in, throwing a stern look to Theksun.

Theksun's eyes shifted from side to side. He sighed and sat back down.

Bastion smiled, "The female is right, our problem is *our* problem, no one else's!"

Xania looked at Bastion, "We shall do what we can."

"Thank you," he replied.

"What can you tell us about this devil?" asked Theksun.

"You mean the red man?" said Bastion.

"Yes, it's surely the same?"

"Why?" questioned Bastion, "Do you judge beings on colour?"

"Of course not," Theksun protested.

Xania jumped in, "He's just asking about the red man, that's all," she said softly.

"We haven't seen him, not yet anyway," said Bastion. "But as soon as the last transmissions from Gomorrah came through, we had one from the red man, saying he could save us. He said he had just arrived in their orbit, when their moon was breaking apart. He rescued as many as he could but couldn't do much more. When he noticed our moon doing the same thing, he came to help us. He managed to organise a transport vessel for us. And that we should meet him at Koldek canyon. That's where we are heading!"

"And you believe these transmissions?" ask Theksun.

"I believe my own eyes, Theksun. Look up, our moon has never been so close, the gravity is getting stronger, the weather is wilder. I don't have to believe anyone, but I can hope this red man can help us. We have no choice!" Bastion said.

"How do you know he's red if you've never seen him?" wondered Theksun.

"Whispers," Bastion replied, "strong whispers, down our caravan. Everyone who has got to the canyon, sent whispers back, the red man can save us." He nodded.

"Maybe it's true?" offered Xania to Theksun.

"Mmm," replied Theksun before getting up and going to find a place to meditate.

Xania ignored her fellow Cydarion, and looked at Bastion "Please tell me everything you can."

Bastion nodded, "Of course, as long as you keep our records alive," he said.

"I promise," Xania responded eagerly, as Bastion explained to Xania, their way of life and heritage.

"We are peaceful beings and live a simple life. We never ventured for the stars, but the stars visited us. Many beings enjoyed visiting and spending their winters here. See, our climate is the same, all cycle, and we have perfect growing conditions for our wildflowers, as you can see. So much so, that they are our main export. Apparently, they are sought after on other worlds." Bastion laughed a little, "Can you imagine, something so insignificant to us is a luxury to others?"

"Have others ever tried to take advantage of your situation?" asked Xania.

"Yes," replied Bastion, "But our high council put forward a motion to the planetary commission. The motion was carried and now we are the only ones allowed to harvest our wildflowers. We have fields of them, all dedicated to production.

Because of this, our pollinators have thrived. With that, came our eco system, everything got healthier, and the air became cleaner. Can you smell how pure it is?" Bastion asked.

Xania had already noticed the fresh air on this planet and over-emphasized a deep inhale with her eyes closed. "I do, I smell vanilla, cocobolo and," she sniffed again, "Saffron?" she questioned with a smile.

"Yes," Bastion said, "with a hint of Boranthium. It's that which gives the flowers their glow. Apparently, we are the only planet that grows them. Or so I'm told..." Bastion paused, "Probably the last too," he said softly. Xania closed her eyes in anguish.

What can we do? she asked herself, then, with a thought formulating in her mind, she went to look for Theksun, whispering a plan.

"I don't know, Xania, we're probably better off staying together," he answered.

"We have to try something, to save them, we've lost so many others lately," Xania said, a little too loud.

Theksun took no notice, "If I did this, I wouldn't be able to come back and catch up with you."

"I know," Xania said, "but, as I said, we have to try."

Theksun sighed, "Okay, I'll go and ask him, but it may take some time."

"I know, that's why I'm telling you now, we've no time to waste!"

Theksun rubbed his face, and pulled out his locator and took a reading, then replaced it back in his pocket. He nodded and opened a portal home. Looking back at Xania, he said "Make sure you come back, too."

Xania nodded, "I will."

"No matter what happens," Theksun insisted.

Xania bit her lip and reluctantly nodded.

Theksun stepped through and the portal closed behind him.

"Can you take us anywhere?" asked Bastion, pointing at the empty space where the portal had been.

Xania jumped; she hadn't realised the small green being had walked up beside her. "Oh no, it only takes us back home," Xania said.

"Could we all go?" asked Bastion, "just until we can move on?" His question sounded more like a plea.

Xania's face went blank, she really didn't know what to say.

The official line was to say, *only* Cydarions can pass through the portal. But Xania knew that wasn't true. The rule was, 'No one, *other* than a Cydarion *should* pass through the portal.' *Under what circumstances? At the annihilation of a species? Were these questions even raised at the writing of the rules? Maybe the rules were out of date?*

With all these questions rushing through her head, she cleared her throat, "We'll do what we can." She even cringed at her own words. She felt conflicted.

Jodrell, her father, had taught her that only the majority matter, "A billion lives are worth more than a million lives." *But I just can't stand by and let that happen.*

The Cydarions had taught her, that they themselves need to survive, at all costs. *No, I can't place myself above anyone else.*

Pace, her first uncle and now Master of the Cydarions, would tell her, "All lives matter." *I agree with him, but how do I help everyone?*

Her second and favourite uncle, Nyk, would say to her, "Do what's right, no matter the outcome." *I agree with him too, but actions have consequences.*

Her head was in a mess. She apologised to Bastion and settled down for the night. Although she knew there would be no rest for her tonight, so she prayed.

Darkit marketplace

Chapter 12

Lucifer had given Lucigon a tour the castle, except for the dungeons, they would be a treat for later. Lucigon had been given four rooms to himself and a demon to serve him. When he was shown the war room and the plan for project M.U.R.I.S. Lucigon became very interested in the sciences, asking many questions.

Lucifer had eventually called for his officers and introduced his son to them. Every one of them were genuinely surprised, even more so when they were told that they all now reported to Lucigon, the General of Lucifers army.

Then there was Lucigon's portal training. With a lot of training and only a few errors, he soon managed to open a portal back to his last world and step through.

"You're a quick learner," said Lucifer, as he followed Lucigon through. "Tell me, son, have you ever killed?" asked Lucifer.

"Yes, I've killed many times," replied Lucigon.

"And what did it feel like?"

Lucigon was puzzled, "I was hungry and needed to eat. It was a necessity," Lucigon replied.

"No, I don't mean small pathetic creatures, I mean sentients. Have you killed for the sake of it?" asked Lucifer.

"You mean innocent lives?" Lucigon asked, "Mother wouldn't let me kill anything, except to eat."

"Ha!" Lucifer exclaimed, "Innocent lives? None of those lesser beings are innocent, they all play a part in God's selfish plan."

Lucigon nodded slowly, "Everything is all starting to make sense."

"You tried to kill me when we first met," said Lucifer.

Lucigon looked at Lucifer and snorted, "It was an urge, it just felt..."

"Natural?" Lucifer finished for him.

Lucigon looked down to the ground and nodded, feeling a little ashamed. "Mother wouldn't let me give in to my urges."

"Your mother isn't here anymore, Lucigon," said Lucifer.

Lucigon flicked his head up and glared at Lucifer, his yellow eyes glowing with hatred.

"That's better," said Lucifer, "use your hatred. Let that urge return! Tell me, where is your most hated place?" asked Lucifer, "The one that you just couldn't stand, where you..."

"Darkit," Lucigon interrupted quickly.

Lucifer was surprised, but didn't show it, "Let's go there," he said, nodding at Lucigon.

"Why?" asked Lucigon.

"You have to learn to kill properly, to kill without mercy. Kill efficiently and quickly. Where better than your most hated place?" offered Lucifer.

"But mother wouldn't..."

"Your mother is dead!" snapped Lucifer, then took a breath before calming down and continuing. "Your mother envisioned all of this. She was no innocent. When I first met Faigon she was on a killing spree. She had decimated three villages, before coming across me."

Lucigon looked stunned. "Why would she do that?" he asked.

"Because that's who she was, it was in *her* nature. She gave in to her natural desires. Faigon loved killing, it gave her a buzz, like she was in charge of her own destiny. But, when she had you, she became weak, thought she could change the world, with peace." Lucifer gave a sharp snort.

"Even then, she was a hypocrite. When she visited me, she confessed she still had the hunger. Sometimes she left you alone for a whole rotation, just to indulge herself. Lucigon, your mother never stopped killing, she just didn't want you to see it."

Lucigon's knees buckled, his tail lashed out to brace him. His voice came thin and broken. "She smelled of blood... of flesh... every time she returned."

Lucifer's smile curled wry and cruel. "It's true, isn't it."

"She lied to me?" Lucigon whispered. "My whole life?" For the first time, a tear traced his cheek.

Lucifer pounced. "She denied you your true nature while feeding her own. Tell me, Lucigon, how does that make you feel?"

"ANGRY!"

Lucifers eyes gleamed. "And how will you show that anger?"

Lucigon's nostrils flared, his body trembling, fire igniting in his veins. "I want to..."

"You want to what?" Lucifer pressed.

"I want to..." His body shook, a roar ripping from his throat.

"Faigon deceived you. Lied. Smothered you."

Lucigon screamed, a guttural roar of anguish.

"She wouldn't let you be yourself," Lucifer whispered like poison. "I will. Join me, Lucigon. Make your first kill."

Lucigon met Lucifers soulless eyes.

"If you don't enjoy it, you may walk away," Lucifer purred, tearing open a vortex of swirling red light.

Lucigon stepped forward, faltered, hesitant.

Lucifer leaned close, voice like a blade. "Your mother never hesitated."

Lucigon growled, frustrated, then hurled himself into the portal.

Lucifer smirked, savouring victory, and followed.

They found themselves amongst a crowd of sentient beings, all milling about a marketplace. Stalls selling various products, of all shape, size and colour.

"This place makes me wretch," said Lucigon, with a clear distaste.

"Yes, I can see why, everyone looks... happy. It's disgusting," admitted Lucifer. "Here, go down this alleyway," Lucifer pointed to a dark quiet place.

"Now what?" Lucigon asked, once they were out of sight.

"Patience Lucigon, you're immortal, you have all the time in space. Lucigon let out a sigh and leaned up against the durasteel wall. Lucifer stood for a fraction, admiring how well his son had turned out. "More impressive than we thought," muttered Lucifer, to the ghost of Faigon.

It wasn't long before a tall slender being wandered down the alleyway towards the two devils.

"I'll show you how easy it is," said Lucifer. As the being approached, Lucifer stepped out in front of it, but before it had a chance to say a word, Lucifer extended his elbow bone. A sharp, elbow spur moved in a bur, slicing the beings throat. Blood gushed out, all down the slain being as it collapsed. A black shadowy mist drifted out of the body and into Lucifer. He closed his eyes and bit his lip,

"Mmm, nothing beats that feeling," he said.

Lucigon looked on with interest, "What was that?" he asked, "the black thing?"

"That was his soul, I fed on it," explained Lucifer.

"What is it like?" wondered Lucigon.

"Why don't you try it for yourself? Look, another one is coming down here. You kill it!" suggested Lucifer as he quickly moved the slain body out view.

Lucigon nodded in reply and readied himself. The being walked past Lucifer and nodded an acknowledgement at Lucigon, who froze. The being carried on walking. Lucifer looked at Lucigon and pointed at the being passing him by, Lucigon look a deep breath and stepped out behind the slender alien.

"Excuse me," he growled. The being stopped and turned around with a smile, "What can..."

Lucigon swiped his claws at the being's throat and ripped out its windpipe. It reached for its own throat before collapsing Convulsing on the floor, a heartbeat it was dead. Its soul floated up and into Lucigon, who immediately let out a cry, "Urgh!"

"How did it feel?" asked Lucifer with a smile.

"Euphoric," Lucigon said, catching his breath. He looked up with a smirk, "and addictive!"

"Good, what do you think about doing it out there?" Lucifer asked, nodding towards the marketplace.

For the first time that lucifer had seen, Lucigon smiled.

"After to you, father," Lucigon said gesturing to the open space.

Lucifer's grin stretched unnaturally wide. With a thunderous flap of his wings, he launched into the sky and dropped into the bustling marketplace. His feet struck stone with bone-cracking force, crushing a being beneath him. The body split, ribs snapping through flesh, organs spilling out in a streaming mess.

Lucigon landed beside him, wings slicing outward like cleavers. Screams erupted as his blades carved through torsos, splitting bodies open in showers of blood. Limbs spun into the air, thudding wetly against stone.

Lucifer waded into the crowd, a storm of claws and jagged bone. He ripped a victim in half, the spine tearing free with a sickening crack. He gored another on a protruding spur, lifting the writhing body high before hurling it aside like refuse. Each kill fed him, souls dragged screaming into his blackening core.

The square became a slaughterhouse. Blood sheeted the cobblestones, slicking everything crimson. Beings slipped in entrails, falling into the snapping maws of the devils. Eyes were gouged, skulls shattered, throats opened in fountains of red. Children shrieked for their mothers only to be torn from their arms.

The air reeked of copper, bile and burning flesh as Lucifer sent fire into a cluster of survivors. They convulsed in the flames, skin blistering, flesh sloughing from bone as their screams merged into a single, hellish wail.

When the last cries died, silence lay heavy. The square was carpeted in butchered bodies, guts unravelled, heads caved in, skin hanging from bone. The few who lived huddled in alleys, blank-eyed and broken, their sanity shredded.

Lucifer, dripping gore, clawed a hole in reality. The vortex swirled with blood-red light. "Come, my son," he growled.

Lucigon stepped through first, soaked to the wings. Lucifer lingered just long enough to admire the carnage. *It's been so long since I've been able to do this with someone.* Then, he followed into the abyss.

Bastion

Chapter 13

Xania stirred at first light; her sleepless night had relented as fatigue set in. Rubbing her eyes, she looked around for Bastion. He was nowhere to be seen amongst the group of native beings. They were all busy packing up their belongings for the next leg of their journey. She had to ask three individuals before she got an answer; Bastion had set off early as he would be slower over the rocks ahead, and time was running out.

Xania smiled a thank you, and set off after him, collecting her utility belt on the way.

Her pace, although not as fast as sShearon, would have made him proud. She bounded and leapt over rocks and boulders. She stopped just once to cool down, standing with her boots on in a small stream, while she filled her water bag for the onward journey.

After a short rest, she set off again, towards the looming moon hanging on the horizon. Without warning, Xania was knocked off her feet by an enormous earthquake. The rocks and boulders all shook and moved, some split in half, while smaller ones were crushed in the violent quake. Twice she had to get back on her feet after being thrown down, once, nearly twisting an ankle. Suddenly, she heard a squeal.

"Bastion?" she said to herself, then shouted out, "BASTION?" before setting off at full sprint towards his voice and whimpers. The after quakes now seemingly not affecting her, it was like she was merely running on the wind. Traversing more rock formations, Xania came across a large boulder that had been split in half. A small crack, the size of her fist, emanated light from the wildflowers below, like rays of sunshine.

Bastion's plea for help echoed from under her feet.

"Bastion are you down there?" questioned Xania, shouting into the void.

"Xania?" came the voice of a relieved Bastion, "I'm trapped down here."

"Are you alright?" asked Xania as she lay on the boulder and peered down into the small crevice.

"The earth shake," echoed Bastion's voice, "the floor opened up and I fell in. But then the rock closed, trapping me," he said in a worried voice.

"Can you see another way out?" asked Xania feeling a little desperate.

"I... I don't know," replied Bastion. The small, cramped space that he had fallen into seemed to be all blocked, up was his only way of escape. Xania could see through the cracks, that some light bearing flowers had also fallen in with Bastion and were giving off a warm glow. *At least he's not trapped in the dark.*

Xania sighed and looked around for anything that could help, but there was nothing, and no one around. She knew it would be quite a while before the rest of the Qippoz would arrive, but even then, what could they do? Looking closer at the newly split boulder, she noticed some small hairline fractures running deep to the edges. *If I can just break some more off, maybe Bastion can squeeze out,* Xania thought to herself. So, she shoved her sais into the fractures, and with all her weight, she jumped up and down on the handles, hoping to open a gap between the fractures. The only outcome was Xania got more and more frustrated with every jump and stamp. She let out her frustration with numerous loud screams, the louder her scream the harder she stomped. The ground rumbled under her feet and the boulder shook, cracking under pressure. With a thunderous crash, the boulder exploded open. Xania moved quickly, and without words she jumped into the space where Bastion was and picked him up. He curled into a ball leaving his spikes flat. Xania took two steps forward, put one foot on the side of the rock and pushed off, up and towards the opposite side wall. Another well placed foot on the side wall, and she pushed off again, this time reaching for the top of the crevice. She managed to push Bastion onto the ground, where he rolled away, as she grabbed the ledge and pulled herself up. She lay there, on her back panting and gasping for air.

Bastion appeared over her and looked down, a grateful smile on his face, "Thank you, Xania. I will remember this day."

Xania sat up and leant back on her elbows, she smiled, still breathing heavily, "It was lucky there was another earthquake, and I could pull you out!" she said.

Bastion outstretched his paw for Xania to grab hold of, "There was no earth shake," he said, "the rock just trembled and broke apart."

Xania grabbed his paw, and he pulled her to her feet. "Did you not feel it?" she asked as she nodded a thank you for his help.

"I'm sorry," said Bastion, "but it was only this rock which moved," he said, pointing to the area they had just escaped from.

"Oh!" Xania exclaimed. *Was it me, did I cause the earth shake?* Xania thought it was best to change the subject, "Where are your possessions? I'll carry them for you!"

Bastion looked down into the gap near their feet, "I'm afraid they are lost down there."

"Oh, I'm sorry," replied Xania.

Bastion shook his head, "Don't be. Rather they be lost, than I be lost!"

Xania laughed, "You're right about that," she said.

"Do you care to keep this old Qippoz company on my journey?" asked Bastion.

"I would be honoured," replied Xania, and the pair set off again. Xania towards the Calling and Bastion towards the red man.

It took the rest of the rotation before all the other Qippoz had caught up with them and had exchanged stories of their journey so far.

In the distance, a great field lay open and flat. Nearly covered in Qippoz and a few other species. By now, the gravity had become much stronger, and Xania could feel it trying to pull her into the ground. The Qippoz didn't seem to be affected by the extra gravity, but it was certainly having its effect on the flora. All the tree trunks and branches along their route had broken off or snapped and fell to the floor with thunderous crashes. Even the sparse flowers and grasses had wilted and were now all doubled over, under their own weight.

"There he is, there's the red man, I see him," shouted the voice of a young Qippoz riding high on their parents' head. Xania quickly looked in the direction the Qippoz pup had pointed. She was already taller than all the Qippoz, which gave Xania a clear sight. If she narrowed her eyes, she could only just make him out at this distance. With his red skin set amongst the green sky, green foliage and mostly green beings, he was quite distinctive.

Xania turned to Bastion. "I have to go now. I will try and make things right," she said to him.

"I understand," Bastion nodded as he touched her arm gently, "I hope to see you again."

Xania smiled again, "So do I, Bastion."

"Keep safe," he shouted after her, as she sprinted off to face the devil. The closer she got, the slower she could proceed due to the throng of beings, all bustling to get closer to the red man. Abruptly, there was a loud boom, and a shockwave rattled through the air. Xania looked up to see a transport craft decelerating. Its jets bursting gas downwards, creating a lot of turbulence. The crowd started to cheer. Before Xania could even get near the front, the vehicle landed on a platform, behind the devil. Two small thrusters were left burning as the main engines were cut. The thrusters gave off small yellow and red flames, one either side of the devil.

It can't be, Xania thought to herself, *can Lucifer's fire now power space craft?* She shook her head, clearing her thoughts and got back on track, pushing her way forward.

Loudspeakers nestled on the ground, started to crackle, "My friends, I am here to save you, my name is Sauriel, but you can call me, The Red Man!" The devil paused for the cheers and whoops to die down.

Xania sighed, knowing she would have to listen to his lies. But she carried on, making her way through the crowd. She overheard some complaining about her pushing and shoving, cheating her way to the front, just so she could be saved first, but she didn't have the time to answer anyone.

"I will take you all, I promise," said the devil, his booming voice coming out from the low speakers. Xania heard a slight cackle, the type only a devil could make. "As you know, I can only take a thousand of you at a time, but we shall return," he said.

A boarding ramp lowered and a wave of green Qippoz surged forward to enter the transport vessel. "I will be back soon, for the rest of you," said the devil with a grin, "you shall all be together!" The devil finished with his arms outstretched, embracing the adorations from the crowd. Xania managed to reach the platform and jumped up onto it. She faced the devil, her back to the crowd.

"Your deceit ends here, Sauriel!" said Xania.

Sauriel froze, shock flashing across his face. He steadied himself, then spoke into the live microphone. "You're here to oppose me?" he asked.

"I'm here to kill you, for all the suffering you have put upon these beings," Xania said with distaste, and she pulled out her sais. The devil took a couple of steps closer to Xania, but suddenly stopped, as he caught the smell of her on the wind.

"Cydarion," he spat, before turning off the microphone.

"Yes," Xania sneered, "and your time is over."

Sauriel, thinking quickly, turned the microphone back on, "So, you've come here to kill me, just for helping these poor creatures?"

Some of the crowd started to mock Xania.

"You are destroying their home and killing them. You did it to Gomorrah first, and now you're doing it to Sodom," said Xania, raising her voice above the noise of the crowd.

The devil smiled, "Really? What proof do you have of this?" he asked.

Xania paused, there was no answer to this, or any proof, just a gut feeling, and gut feelings in Cydarions have never been wrong. So far. The crowd started jeering and shouting at her. She changed the subject. "Where are you taking them?" she asked, her hands gripping tighter around the handles of her sais.

"To join the others," Sauriel said, then looked at the crowd, "Isn't that right?' he asked them.

"Yeah, and where is that?" Xania snapped back.

The devil took a couple of steps backwards, then spoke again to the crowd. "Is it fair that I'm trying to help you, but *she*," he pointed to Xania, "she wants to keep you here, so you all perish and die!" The crowd roared with anger, and it was then, that Xania realised she was totally outnumbered.

A klaxon sounded from the transport ship, warning of an imminent take off. The devil looked back at the ship and nodded, then made his final move. He addressed the crowd again, "Friends, are you going to let this female stop you from your destiny? Or are you going to rise up and stop her?" The crowd roared again and started chanting. The devil dropped the microphone near a speaker. The resulting feedback on the speaker system gave off in an ear-splitting screech, which only angered to locals even more.

Xania strode toward the devil, but a clawed paw lashed at her ankle, sending her crashing to the floor, knocking her out cold.

The ash laden planet of Gomorrah

Chapter 14

Xania soon came around, but her senses were all over the place. There was a voice in her head, a sense of falling, and pressure pressing down on top of her.

Then, it started to clear, the pressure was from the thrusters of the transport ship taking off. *Damn,* she had missed her opportunity with the devil.

The falling sensation was her being dragged by her feet into the angry crowd. She kicked and stomped on anything that was touching her until she was free again, to stand up and get to a place of safety.

The voice in her head came again.

"Kid, are you there?"

Xania cleared the fog from her head. "NYK!" she shouted with surprise.

"Don't sound too surprised, you called me here," said Nyk from the cockpit of the Starlady, orbiting in space above the fragile planet of Sodom.

"Nyk, it's so good to hear you, do you have enough fire power to destroy that moon?" asked Xania, hopeful.

"Yeeaaah... Theksun mentioned something like that, but given the situation, there's nothing I can do," Nyk replied.

Xania looked up to the sky. "What do you mean?" she asked. She fought her way from the platform while fending off the angry locals, and away from all the outstretched arms of the jeering crowd.

"The only way I could destroy that moon, is to use Lucy," said Nyk.

"Well do it then!" snapped Xania, fearing for the inhabitants of this planet.

"It's not that simple," he said, "if I use Lucy, then that moon will break up into a thousand pieces, each and every one of them will fall down onto your planet. With the added effect of the radiation, that Lucy would cause. That planet would soon be unlivable. It's not something we can do, without consequences," explained Nyk.

And there are those consequences! Xania thought. "What can we do?" she asked.

"I don't know," he whispered.

"If we leave, that moon will come crashing down and wipe out everyone!"

"Yes," replied Nyk begrudgingly.

"Then we need to save them!" shouted Xania. Some of the Qippoz had climbed onto the platform and started to run towards Xania with sticks.

"Xania, you need to get out of there!" said Nyk.

"I am," she shouted back, as she started running towards a gap in the crowd. Pushing and shoving at anyone who came towards her. "But we need to save them," she said again.

"We can't," said Nyk quietly, torment in his voice.

"WE HAVE TO!" Xania shouted. She was now running through the crowd, which started thining out on the outer fringes of the congregation.

"We can't risk the citadel, and we don't have transport for everyone," admitted Nyk.

"If we leave them here, they'll all die," said a frustrated Xania, scanning the skies again.

There was a pause.

"Xania, there's a vessel on my scope, coming from your location."

"Track it," she said.

"It's just expelled something... green?" said Nyk, "What was that?"

Xania didn't answer. She heard Nyk tap some buttons on his console and then whisper to himself before speaking.

"Xania, they're beings! That ship has just jettisoned beings, directly into space!"

Xania collapsed to her knees, gasping for breath, her pursuers too far behind to notice. "He's just killed them," she whispered, trying to hold back tears. Sauriel's words rang in her ears, "To join the others!" he had said.

"Nyk, he's just killing them, one group at a time." Then the realisation dawned on her; *innocent souls are more powerful to Lucifer. Those who accept their fate, just aren't enough for him to achieve his goal, he needs their innocence.*

"Xania, you're literally between a falling rock and a hard place. You need to get out of there," said Nyk sharply.

Xania sighed, ignoring his last words, "Nyk, take out the devil's ship. I'm not letting him kill anyone else," she said.

"Are you sure?" asked Nyk.

"Yes, he's not coming back here, now that he's seen me, his only option is to escape, to run," she said.

"You're right," replied Nyk, "he's priming his light drive."

Xania heard the flick of switches as Nyk set up the targeting computer. Then, as she looked up into the dark green sky, she saw a flash of light as the transport ship was destroyed, her Calling faded away.

"Time to go home, kid," said Nyk quietly in Xania's ear.

"We can save them!" Xania snapped back.

"Xania, there's nothing we can do," admitted Nyk, his voice nearly cracking.

"If we leave them here, they'll all die!" Xania pleaded again.

"How would you even do that?" he asked, knowing there was no other option.

"It's your call, Nyk," offered Xania.

There was a pause, before a weak voice echoed in her ear, "Xania, get out of there."

Xania buried her face in her hands and screamed. "Argh!"

A massive shockwave shook the ground, so violent that Xania and every Qip-poz all fell to the ground.

"Xania?" Nyk shouted down his comms, "Xania, if you're still there, you need to get out, now! The whole planet has cracked open like a volcano."

Xania looked up again and saw the moon grow increasingly larger. *It's accelerating!* "I can't just leave them," Xania shouted back into the sky, as ash and debris started to fall, blocking out nearly all the remaining light.

"Xania, what would Jodrell tell you to do?" asked Nyk, getting increasingly desperate for her safety.

Through ash laden tears, Xania replied, "He'd say, you can save more by saving yourself."

There was a pause, "I'll see you back at the citadel, kid. I've to stop by Orn Scaffle and pick up Pace."

Without replying, Xania removed the comm device from her ear. A look of determination etched in her face, and she whispered, "That's not what my mother would say!" Xania stood up, wiped her face with a sleeve, and scanned the area for Bastion.

The moon filled the whole sky, plunging the world into near darkness. With the gravity increasing, most of the Qippoz were now affected and were giving up on life. They sat down to accept their fate. Some prayed, some held their loved ones close, while others just wandered around aimlessly, all struggling to breath in the thick ashen air. It took Xania nearly thirty fractions before finding Bastion, he was one of the ones praying. She quickly explained what had transpired, and that her actual plan had failed.

"As far as I can see, I only have one option left," she confided in him. Bastion looked at her with a questioning look. Xania smiled, "I can't take you all back to our citadel, it is forbidden. But I may be able to take you somewhere else," she whispered.

"Somewhere else? Is that allowed?" asked Bastion, his spikes collecting ash between the spines.

Xania looked around, as if someone could be listening, "No, but if you don't tell, neither will I," she said, then added quietly, "that's if it works."

"If what works?" asked Bastion, under a laboured breath.

"Open a portal to another world. That is against the rules, I think," she shrugged, "it's not exactly a specific rule, in writing," she said.

"And, this new world, are we allowed to live?" asked Bastion, worried. "If we are still going to die, we would rather do it here, on our home world," he said soberly.

Xania nodded, "It's a sanctuary moon, for the planet Neacho. No sentient species live there, but it's full of flora and fauna. I used to train there as a kid." She smiled as a small memory flashed across her mind.

Bastion coughed, "Are you sure it's safe?"

"As much as nature is safe," she said with a shrug.

"It does sound perfect, but why didn't you mention it before?" Bastion asked.

"Well..." Xania hesitated, "It's not something we've ever done before, and..." She bit her lip, this time she looked away, as though ashamed, "I didn't think of it."

There was another earthquake, large enough to make every Qippoz squeal. "Maybe it's time?" Bastion suggested.

Xania nodded in agreement and uttered the words. A yellow spiral opened in front of her and grew. She peered in and smiled. She remembered this place all too well. She turned back to Bastion and gestured for him to walk through.

"My dear, I will be the last of us to go through. We need to get the others through first," he said.

And so, they spent the next two and a half sections convincing others to go through the portal, while spreading the message to anyone that would listen. It was obvious by now that their time on Sodom was at an end. Most of the crowd had made their way to their new home world, apprehensive but excited for a new start, after rotations of impending doom. Some stubborn Qippoz stayed where they were, thinking paradise lived on the other side of destruction.

Xania, now talking through her sleeve for filtration, offered to walk Bastion through to his new home.

Bastion took her hand and they both crossed through. Once on the other side, Bastion stopped and looked back. Although the air was much more breathable here, he still had tears in his eyes. He slumped down and Xania sat beside him.

"I'm sorry I couldn't save your home," said Xania.

Without averting his gaze, Bastion patted her hand and said, "Home is where your family is, and my family is here, in a new home." He turned to Xania, "That is thanks to you. You saved us all." He paused and Xania took in the peaceful surroundings. "I used to pray to your God too," said Bastion eventually.

Xania looked confused, "Used to?" she asked.

Bastion smiled, "Yes, but I see now that we were wrong. It is you who saved us, not him."

"Whoa," Xania said, her hands up in protest. "I am doing God's work; it was him who sent me to you."

"I see," said Bastion, then he thought for a fraction longer. "Would it be acceptable to have a day of celebration, on your behalf?" he mused.

"That would be an honour," said Xania, a tear crept down her cheek.

Through the portal, the devastation could be seen as the moon started to crash into the planet. Strange things started to happen; rocks were being both crushed and thrown up in the air at the same time. Bastion looked away, not wanting to see anymore. Xania closed the portal and relished breathing in the fresh air.

She looked at Bastion, "Are you alright?"

He smiled back at her, "We survived, which means we can go forward. That's what counts," said the brave Qippoz.

"Come on," Xania said as she got to her feet, "let me show you around this area."

***

Xania spent two further rotations with Bastion and his extended family, teaching them all she knew about the area. But soon, it was time to return to the citadel and report back to Bork. She said her goodbyes to Bastion and his family and opened a portal.

Except Xania didn't go straight back to El' Azar, she uttered the name, 'Gomorrah.'

The planet she stepped onto was a dark desolate place. The air was thick with dust, barely any light penetrated the ash filled skies. Not a whisper of wind to blow away the floating debris hanging in the air. A dry earth taste filled her mouth, and Xania had to immediately hold her breath. Undoing the red ribbon in her hair, she folded it and placed it across her mouth. She held it in place with one hand and looked around. Everything was covered in dust and ash; she had never seen so many shades of grey and black. There was no Calling, no direction, no wind and no... sound. No sound at all, it was a deathly, eerie silence. A shudder ran through her body. Looking down, the soft debris came up to her shins. The gravity seemed to be a lot lighter that Sodom, *at least I've got that going for me,* she thought to herself.

She set off, toward an unknown destination. Trudging forward, the dirt and ash clung to every inch of her. She put in her comms earpiece and flicked it on, immediately having to pull it out again, "Static!" she winced into the red mouth covering. It was getting damp on the inside, from her hot breath. She tried the comms again, this time, holding it a hands width away from her ear. *So much static,* she thought, scanning all the channels, every one of them feeding back the same result. Her comms were dead. "Talking of dead," she said to herself, she had just spotted a group of large beasts, all huddled together against an old outbuilding, all of them dead. As she got closer, she realised it wasn't an old building, it had merely collapsed on top of the beasts. The whole scene was covered in grey ash. The more she made her way across the land, the more unfortunate animals she came across. All dead from suffocation, having laid down and accepted their fate, nowhere left to run.

She had an idea, not knowing what would happen, she opened another portal. Again, uttering the same name 'Gomorrah.'

It worked! She had portaled to another part of the planet. Another first. But there was little to celebrate; all she saw was the same grey colour and so much destruction. Three more times she portaled, each just like the first. No colour, no wind, and no life.

Xania heard a sound. Not loud, but a dry gurgle sound, like the last breath of a hunted animal. She ran over and dug into be debris. Feeling for anything, she placed a hand on what felt organic and heaved it to the surface. She looked directly into the face of a forlorn being. Its face was all crusted with dirt and tears. Xania couldn't make out the true shape of this being, but its eyes flickered open. Xania cleared out its mouth, the being barely registering Xania was even there. It tried inhaling a shallow breath, but a louder cough came out, and then a moan.

"Can you breathe?" asked Xania, trying to shield it from the falling ash.

"Zolon!" came a coughed reply.

"Zolon? What's Zolon?" asked Xania. She wished she had thought ahead and brought some water on this visit. Knowing that if she went back for some, there would be a slim to zero percent chance of coming back to the same place.

"Zolon!" the voice croaked again.

Xania looked around for help, not necessarily for anyone, but just for an idea of what to do. But before she could even reply, its body went limp in her arms. Xania dropped her head and closed her eyes. "How many more?" she asked herself, tears filling her eyes. A lone tear escaped her eye. It ran down her nose, pooling at the tip before dripping off and splashing onto the beings' forehead. She was about to lay the body back down, when a faint glow surrounded the body. The light gathered around the teardrop and turned into an orb, which then shot up into the sky. Xania watched it for as long as she could before having to look away, the ash falling into her eyes making more tears appear.

"Huh!" she said, then a thought came to her. She searched the area for more bodies and came across four more, each one already passed away. Nevertheless, she dropped a tear onto each of their heads, but each tear just fizzled and hissed, like water hitting a hot frying pan.

Hiss

Hiss

Hiss

Hiss

Xania stopped; she realised their souls were gone. Gone to Lucifer, and not by choice. "At least I saved one," she said with little comfort.

While she portaled many more times, looking for more beings, nothing came to fruition. There were plenty of bodies, just none left alive. She knew it was time to leave when she started vomiting, the fine particles of ash having built up on her makeshift mask.

Xania left Gomorrah, a grave planet. She shuddered to think how many had died here, their souls ripped from innocent bodies, all for the sake of one man's power. She felt sick again, just by thinking about it. She knew she would have to get medical aid when she got back to the citadel, but it was nothing compared to what these poor beings had gone through.

Xania said a prayer for the lost souls and dying planet, before coughing her way back home.

Her mind was conflicted with what story she should tell Bork, the actual truth, or the thing she should have done? But, as she walked into Bork's office, his warming smile made the decision for her. She would tell the truth, no matter the consequences.

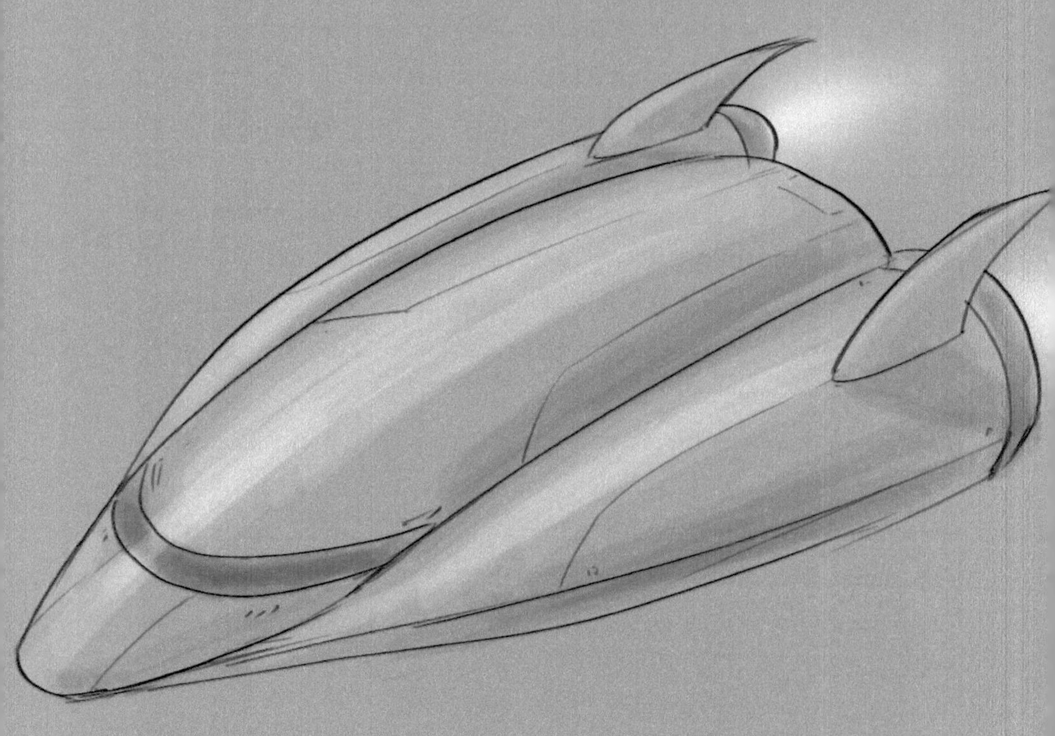

The Starlady

Chapter 15

"So, how did it go?" Nyk asked, as Pace settled into the co-pilots seat of the Starlady.

Pace let out a pleasing sigh, as the massage seat started its work. He closed his eyes, trying to relax some more.

"Well?" Nyk asked, shaking his head and flicking a few switches, then pulling on the control stick. His backside melted into the seat as the acceleration took hold.

"Oh," answered Pace, then shrugged, "Not a lot."

"Not a lot? You've been on Tantolv for five rotations, you must know something," Nyk said, exasperated.

"Okay," Pace smiled, pushing his shoulders into the moving massage coils of the chair. "I went to see Suclond Tory, find out what he knows. It turns out that he doesn't actually know as much as he purports to know. But he did put me onto an officer at the industrial yards, Phomaine Jerr. She had heard of some kind of spaceship being developed. It was privately funded, but pretty hush hush. She suggested I try the technical department, as they have access to the blueprints of all ships patented." Pace paused and scanned the cockpit, "Where's my red liquor?" he asked.

"Oh, it's back in its storage hatch," said Nyk, "I thought I may have been in a situation earlier, so I stowed it. You do know that stuff is sticky if it gets on the console!" he said.

Pace laughed, "Fair enough," he said as he got up to retrieve the bottle. He poured himself a glass and settled back into the massage chair. He raised his glass to Nyk, who nodded, and took a large sip. "Ahh!" he exclaimed with a smile.

"And?" Nyk asked, setting course for home and letting go of the controls. He relaxed back into the chair too and swivelled towards Pace.

"That is some good stuff," Pace said, smiling at his red stained glass, "Yeah, well, it turns out that there isn't a ship that has been patented. Not one that has the capability of moving a planet, at least," he said.

"So, it was a dead end?"

"Maybe not!" replied Pace, "There wasn't a ship, but there was some new tech that came through. Nuclear magnetism!"

Nyk frowned, "Nuclear magnetism, what's that?"

"To get that information, my friend, cost me a lot of credits," said Pace with a little chuckle. "Anyway, it turns out that nuclear magnetism is so powerful, it could crumple a whole industrial city, easily."

Nyk was astounded, "A new weapon?" he asked.

"That was my thinking too," said Pace, "until someone pointed out that the blueprints were wrong. They had the polarity inverted!"

Nyk looked confused.

"Magnets either attract, or..." Pace said.

"Repel?" Nyk answered.

"You got it. This nuclear magnet was designed to repel. To knock over a city, away from the magnet. Completely flattening it," Pace explained.

"Shit!" expressed Nyk.

Pace nodded his agreement.

"But that's not enough to move a planet," said Nyk.

"No, it's not," said Pace dryly, "Enough of them, theoretically, could repel a planet. Providing their own mass was either greater and travelling at the same speed, or a smaller planet travelling at a greater speed," answered Pace.

Nyk looked confused again, "So, if I fitted a nuclear magnet to the Starlady, I could move a planet?" he asked.

"Depending on its size and your velocity, it's a possibility," agreed Pace.

"That sounds like great information!" said Nyk, "Why did you say not really?"

"Because pal," said Pace, "as far as anyone is aware, no one has built a single unit, let alone enough to move a planet. They simply don't think it's practical," he shrugged, "I mean, why move a planet? It's much easier to move *to* another planet."

"So, what happens next?" asked Nyk.

"It may be time to visit Emperor Kethlu," replied Pace.

"The Emperor?" Nyk repeated, a little shocked at his mention, "I don't think that is a good idea."

Pace looked at Nyk, "Do you have a better idea?" he asked.

"No, but still..."

"Anyway, we have to deal with the Callings first," said Pace.

Nyk nodded in agreement, "We should take a Storous with us," offered Nyk. "On the next Calling, that is."

Pace thought about it for a fraction, then agreed, "Do you have anyone in mind?" he asked.

"Holan," replied Nyk, "I think he would do well. Plus, he is always asking me if he can join us on a Calling."

"Sure," Pace nodded. "What could go wrong?" he said as he closed his eyes and fell asleep.

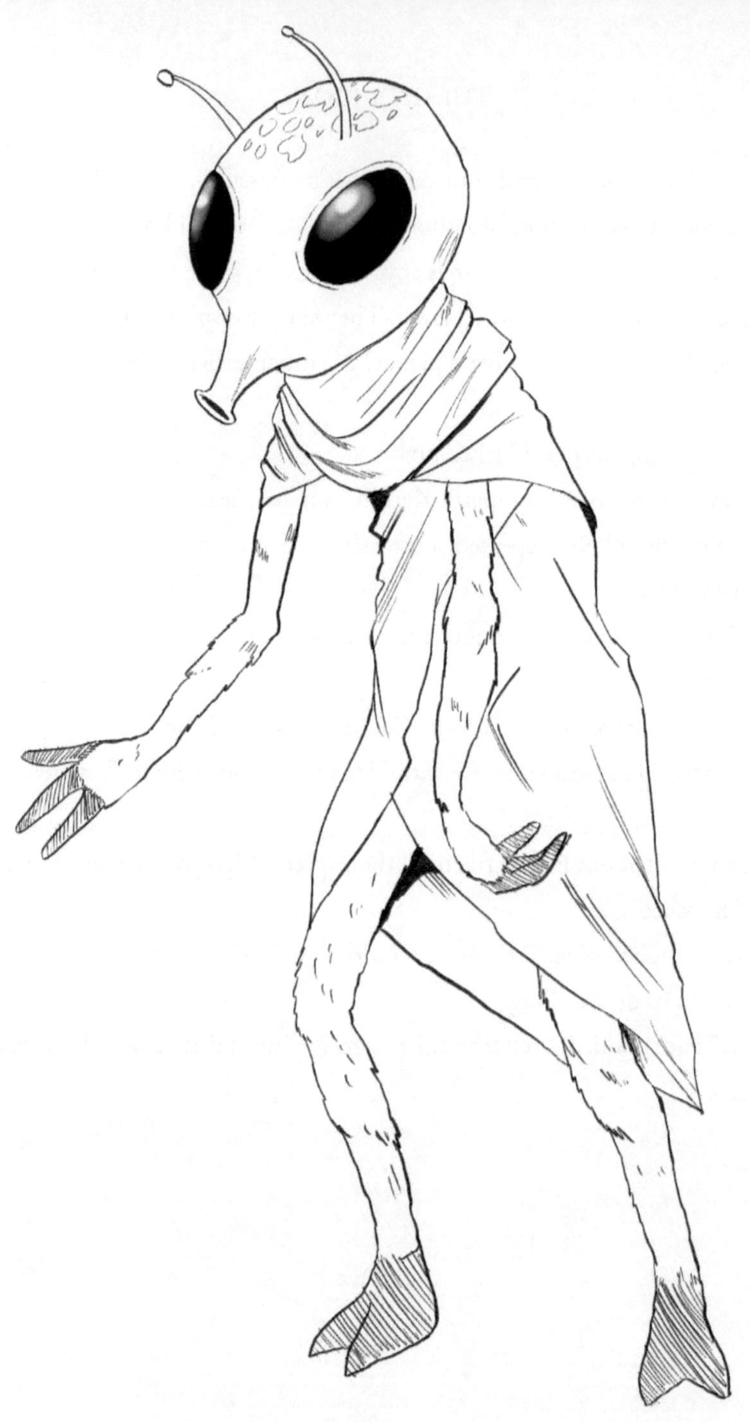

Daemich Petrovski

Chapter 16

"It can't be true," said Xania between sniffs. Her face was puffy, and her cheeks glistened from the tears pouring down her face, her eyes were red raw. She shook her head, unable to comprehend the words Kee had just told her.

Kee too, had tears in his large eyes and a hole the size of a planet in his heart. He had lost his life partner, and nothing anyone could do or say could ever change that. He felt that he couldn't pray for Swift, because the only thing he could pray for was Swifts return. But God didn't do that, he wasn't even sure if God could do it. If he had prayed, it would be for a selfish reason, and praying wasn't about being selfish. So, he accepted the pain it caused him. He didn't want the pain of course, but he accepted it. For him, it was a reminder of how much he loved his partner, the more pain he felt, the more love he had lost. In a small way he hoped his pain would never leave, but he knew, eventually it would. Right now, he wished he could take Xania's pain away from her. He never wanted to upset her, but he knew he had to be the one to tell her.

He had passed a message to her, via a resident, to meet him in the Tranquil Gardens. They had their favourite spot, underneath a weeping Elt tree. Its branches gently cascaded, like a crashing wave, down to the floor. A bench was hidden inside the foliage, unable to be seen by passers-by, but gave a perfect vantage point to look upon the grounds from within. Cool fresh air circulated around the tree. The stone bench was a tribute to the fallen firsts, and had been there a very long time, way before the weeping Elt tree had ever germinated. Xania hadn't known that the bench was here, even though she had lived in the Citadel for nearly twenty cycles. Both Kee and Swift had shown her their secret place, and all three regularly met here, away from the rest of the world and it's troubles.

Kee put his arm around her and held her tight. "I wish it wasn't," he said softly.

Xania's hands went up and covered her face, "It's all my fault," she whispered.

"Why would you say that?" asked Kee, in the same hushed tone.

"If it wasn't for me, you wouldn't have been exiled in the first place. Then, selfishly, I asked you to come back, and now he's gone!" She burst into tears again.

"No, no, no," said Kee. "None of that is your fault my dear. Being exiled was just the way it was back then. And I tell you; we would do it all again. It was the right thing to do!"

Xania nodded, the words hitting close to home.

"But," Kee carried on, "you asking us to come back was the best thing that ever happened to us. Swift told me himself. The last cycle that we have spent here, with you, have been so happy. We wouldn't change it. Swift went the way he always wanted to, guiding others into the light."

Xania turned to Kee. "He was happy?" she asked, her words barely comprehensible and a small bubble of saliva formed at the corner of her mouth.

Kee smiled, "Yes, he truly was." He let silence fill the air before stating, "We'll be having a service for him in ten rotations, on Dusorf. I'd like it very much if you could be there."

Xania looked puzzled. "Of course I'll be there, why wouldn't I?" she asked.

"I don't expect anything from anyone," replied Kee, "It is purely their own decision, as you know, everyone mourns in their own way."

Xania nodded knowingly and said, "Why Dusorf, and not here in the citadel with the other Cydarions?"

Kee patted Xania on her knee, "When we lived on Dusorf, we thought about our deaths and had decided to be buried there. We purchased a small plot, just for us two, overlooking an untouched landscape, the shores of the ocean off in the distance."

"It sounds peaceful," Xania said.

"It is," said Kee, "I'll show you."

"I'd like that," said Xania, then she gazed off into the distance, before looking down.

"What is it?" Kee asked.

Xania hesitated, "It's nothing, it can wait," she said.

Kee studied Xania's face, "It's a Calling, isn't it?" he asked.

Xania nodded, and without looking up, replied, "It's not as important as this... to me." She whispered the last two words.

Kee recoiled slightly, "Not as important?" he said, "Callings are the things that Swift lived for. He would be the first one to tell you to go. Death is permanent, life isn't. You must fight for the souls that can't fight for themselves. Xania, we are the lucky ones, we get to help the less fortunate."

"But I don't want to miss the service!" Xania protested.

Kee held up his hands, "I promise you won't miss it. I'll leave directions for you. Koách and I will be waiting for you when you get there," he answered.

"Koách!" Xania gasped, putting her hand to her mouth, "I was too caught up in my own grief, I forgot about Koách."

Kee replied, "It's okay, Koách understands death a lot more than you or I. Although, I wish that wasn't true," he added.

After a few more words, Xania walked off, ready for her next Calling. She was angry and wanted to take it all out on the next red devil she came across!

***

Xania, Beau and Daemich all fell out of the portal. They were expecting to step onto solid ground but instead found themselves falling through the air. They splashed down into a body of salty water.

"Urgh! I wasn't expecting that, mmm," shouted Daemich between mouthfuls of water.

Beau treaded water, to keep her head above the water line and looked around, to get her bearings. "I can't see land in any direction. But the Calling is that way," she said. Her hand just breaking the water's surface to point directly in front of her.

"I know," replied Xania sharply. She had already started swimming in the direction Beau had pointed.

Beau let out a huff and swore under her breath, then set off swimming to catch up with Xania.

"I'll be right behind you, mmm," shouted Daemich.

Beau was the first to feel the bottom. The ground was still submerged, but at least it was solid. Clambering out the water and onto a shelf, she instinctively reached her hand back to Xania.

Xania slapped it away, "I don't need your help!" she snapped.

"I do, mmm," gurgled Daemich, who was struggling to get out the water. Beau leaned over, grabbed his arm and hauled him onto the ledge. "You're a lot stronger than you look, mmm," he said. He stood at 16.3 decimetres tall, a skinny bipedal frame. Two thin legs, covered in course hair. At their ends, two hooves on each leg. A wet tunic now clung to his body, tracing the frail outline of his body. Equally skinny, two short arms finished with three thick digits on each hand. A largish round head that seemed to be out of place on the wiry body. Black round eyes and two stick like antennas adorned the top of his head. A retractable proboscis made up his mouth and breathing tube; he couldn't breathe and eat at the same time.

"You okay?" asked Beau.

"Yes, thank you, mmm," replied Daemich, clambering to his feet.

***

They walked on in silence, Xania still grieving and angry. *Why did it have to be her? Surely even God knows I hate her. Beau may have the others fooled, but she doesn't fool me. She caused Jodrell's death and stole his powers. They were meant for me.* She turned and scowled at Beau. *Look at her, acting all innocent. That red hair makes her a half devil, in my book. I don't think I could ever trust anyone like her.*

Sections later, they finally exited the water. The water had been receding for the last few kilometres, but it wasn't until they encountered another ridge and climbed out, that they were clear of the water.

Beau suggested they take a rest after the extra effort of walking through the water.

"I guess you can't keep up with the pace," said Xania, a bitterness in her voice.

Beau gave a heavy sigh, "Really? This is the first calling for Daemich, have you thought of him?" related Beau.

"I'll be alright, mmm," offered Daemich, rubbing his tired legs.

"You'll rest! We all will!" said Beau, shooting Xania a scornful look.

Xania stared back at Beau for a fraction, then said, "I'm going to check the surroundings," then walked off, muttering to herself.

"Is she alright, mmm?" asked Daemich, "She always seemed happy in the Citadel, but now, it's like she..."

"She'll be fine," interrupted Beau, "You can trust her," she offered.

"And you, are you okay, mmm?" Daemich asked.

"Don't you worry about me," Beau replied with a smile.

"But you and her..." Daemich stopped himself mid-sentence, when he noticed Beau glaring at him.

"We have history, something I'm not about to get into," said Beau.

He nodded an acknowledgement, and whispered, "I hope you sort it out, mmm."

Beau laid back on the flat rocky ground and looked up. Light grey filled the sky, darkening on the horizon. Blue clouds gave off a brightness, like spotlights in a gloomy room. A single red sun hung low in the sky.

If only Xania would listen to me instead of blaming me for the death of her father. I just know she would have done the same, in my position. She's the strongest Cydarion of all of us, she just doesn't see it. If she realised her potential, she could move planets. Beau laughed at the absurdity of the thought. *But she could be powerful. That's what you say, right Jodrell?* A sense of fulfilment overwhelmed her body, and she smiled. *She'll come around in her own time you say. Well, I'm not your typical patient gal. But you're the Master.*

"Mmm, can I ask you a question?" said Daemich, pulling Beau out of her musings.

"Sure, as long as it's not about Xania," said Beau.

"It's not, mmm," replied Daemich. "I was just wondering, when we portal to a new world, why are we so far away from the devils lair, mmm?"

Beau looked out across the expanse of terrain that lay ahead of them, then back to Storous Daemich. "Have you had enough travelling already? I can open a portal, and you can go back to the Citadel. There's no shame in that."

"Oh no, I'm looking forward to roaming this land, it looks perfect for my kind, mmm," said Daemich, he too looked across the terrain.

"Sorry, what was your question?" asked Beau.

"Why are we so far away from the devils lair, wouldn't it be easier to appear straight outside, so we deal with them and go home, ready for the next one, mmm."

Beau nodded, "Fair point, but honestly, I don't know. There are some theories that say, it's so we can get the lay of the land. Others say it's time to meditate and immerse yourself with the new surroundings. Bork thinks it's a good time to get to know the local species and their way of life. We do have to report everything back to him, and believe me, he's a sucker for details." Daemich nodded and listened intently as Beau carried on.

"Lucifer has identified what a Cydarion smells like, and he's passing that information onto his offspring somehow, and now, if we're not careful, they can start sniffing us out."

"But how does Lucifer know what a Cydarion smells like, if he's not supposed to get involved, mmm. Something about a pact with God, Drake told us in the classroom, mmm," said Daemich.

Beau scrunched her eyes shut, *Shit! I'm not going to explain how that was probably my fault.* When she opened them again, she saw Xania walking towards them. "That's a question for another time," she said.

"There's are a bunch of trees, just passed the horizon. We should rest there for the night!" Xania said, announcing her return. Beau and Daemich both agreed and set off again across the flat rocky landscape.

By the time they had reached the palm grove, yellow leaves were turning translucent as the sun set. Rushing water could be heard through the trees, and Beau investigated. It was a fast-flowing river, quite wide and quite calm.

"The Calling heads the same way as the river," Beau said to Daemich, returning to camp.

"The jagged rocks that follow the riverbank, is going to make it hard going," said Xania, "especially for Daemich. We should set off early."

Beau, glancing around, offered, "I can make us a raft, we can cruise down the river and save our energy."

"The Calling isn't supposed to be easy!" snapped Xania.

"What? Who said that?" said Beau.

Xania hesitated. "It'll never work, anyway!"

"You can just trust me," said Beau.

"That's just it, I don't, I'll never trust you!" said Xania.

"Fine, suit yourself," shrugged Beau casually, "I'm making one, it's up to you if you join us."

Xania just shook her head and looked at Daemich, "Get some sleep!" she said sharply.

Daemich looked uncomfortable and wasn't sure what to do. He had very little training, and although Xania had always been nice to him, it felt different now; strained. He wanted to ask Xania a question but didn't know she would react.

"Xania, what is a Calling like, I mean, how do you know when there is one, mmm?" he asked.

Xania took a breath before answering earnestly, "It's a feeling. It starts off as a whisper, a breeze in your ear. You focus on that noise. It comes across differently for each of us. Some only hear the wind; some hear their name being called. Others hear of what may become. Occasionally it can come in a dream. But if you get it, meditate on the noise, the voice or whatever you hear. The feeling will come over you and you'll know it's your time to go."

"How does the Calling work, mmm?" Daemich asked.

"Actually, we're not quite sure," Xania admitted, "but we think it's like God has a sense of where Lucifer is. And because the devils are Lucifers offspring, there is a trace of him on them. We are then drawn to them, like a magnet being attracted to a pole."

"Is it something I will learn, mmm?"

"Unfortunately, no," Xania said, putting another log on the campfire. "It starts just after you commit to the allegiance." She paused, reminiscing about the time she had spoken her allegiance. It all seemed so long ago. *Jodrell was proud of me that day.* She cleared her throat, "I'm sorry for snapping at you earlier, it's just..." Xania said out of the blue. "We lost Swift; he has joined the light."

"Swift?" Daemich asked himself, "Wasn't he close to you, mmm?"

"Yes, very close, in such a short time," Xania said, looking down at the ground. "I feel partially responsible too. If it wasn't for me, he wouldn't have come back."

Daemich frowned, unsure what Xania meant.

Xania explained, "Kee and Swift were expelled from the Cydarions, for saving me as a child."

"That sounds a bit harsh, who would do that, mmm?"

Xania took a deep breath before answering, "It was complicated."

"But expelled for saving someone, isn't that what we do, mmm?" said Daemich.

Xania grimaced, "The rules are different now," she said.

"Whoever was master could have made an exception, mmm."

Xania stayed quiet, not wanting to admit that it was her own father who had expelled her saviours.

After an uncomfortable silence, Daemich realised he wasn't going to get anymore answers tonight so he settled down for the night, still exhausted from all the swimming, something his species rarely did.

Beau had set about building a raft from various bits of branches and fallen trees. Palm leaves were laid out on top for a little comfort. When the leaves were shredded, they made for excellent bindings. Twin moons gave off enough light through the translucent treetops, for Beau to be able to finish building the raft by the water's edge. She fell asleep later by the dwindling fire.

***

Just after first light, Daemich gently woke up Beau, with a tap on her shoulder.

"I think Xania has already gone, mmm," he told her. Beau closed her eyes and sighed.

"I guess it's just me and you, then. We should get going too," said Beau, "We can eat on the way."

After making sure the campfire was out, Daemich helped Beau to launch the raft into the water and climbed aboard. "It works, mmm," he said, a little surprised.

Beau laughed, "Of course it works, and I reckon with this current, we'll be in front of Xania in no time!"

"It's not a competition, Beau, mmm," Daemich said.

"No, of course it's not," she said. "It definitely isn't," she muttered under her breath.

***

I was right, these jagged rocks are hard going, Xania thought to herself, *maybe I should've got on that raft?* She struggled to get over some parts. A few falls had left cuts and scratches on her legs and hands. Her trouser legs had been pulled up, to stop them getting snagged on the sharp rocks. It had passed mid rotation, before she heard the voices of Beau and Daemich echoing on the river below her. Xania stood atop a large, pointed rock and looked forward. "This isn't going to get any easier," she said shaking her head. Before her, lay kilometres of the same landscape, in all directions. She looked down to the river and sighed.

In the distance behind her she could see the vague shape of a raft with two people aboard. *Oh no, she's not helping me. I'm making this decision. I swear I'll stab her if she says anything!* Xania looked back at the impossible landscape that lay ahead of her.

"Fuck it!" she said, and set off down the rocks towards the river, leaping from one jagged point to another, all with the grace of a mountain cat. Reaching an overhanging edge, she waited before jumping off. Mid-air she pulled out her sai's. Landing feet first on the raft, startling Daemich enough that he almost fell overboard. Beau didn't flinch, but nodded at the sai's,

"Are they supposed to scare me?" she pulled a large hunting knife from her boot.

"Xania, it's good to see you again, mmm," said Daemich quickly, trying to diffuse the situation. Xania smiled at him before replacing the sai's back into her thigh holders.

"I thought you didn't trust me?" smirked Beau, also putting away her knife.

"I don't!" snapped Xania, "I never have! You stole my heritage; you took everything from me!"

"This again? I didn't steal anything!" shouted Beau.

"You took him from me!" snapped Xania.

Beau stood up level with her. "From what I've read, Jodrell could've put me on my ass, anytime he wanted. He didn't. He chose to do what he did, I didn't ask for this! But here I am, babysitting you! From what I do know, you and I have had just about the same number of Callings..."

"I was a Cydarion before you!" interrupted Xania.

"And I was a bounty hunter before this!" snapped Beau, "What were you, a child! And from my point of view, you're still acting like one! Either be helpful or get off this raft!" shouted Beau. "I've had enough of your animosity towards me. I'm doing what your father wanted me to do; I'm keeping that promise!"

Xania slumped down on the palm leaves, a scowl on her face. She knew there was nowhere else she could go at this moment. *Say his name again and see what happens!*

***

She's impossible! thought Beau, *Jodrell, you wanted me to look out for her, but she's making things difficult. You're much wiser than I realised and I'm sorry for what happened, but I did it for the right reasons. You understood that from the beginning. I wish you were here now.* A warmth surrounded her body, and she knew Jodrell was listening. She held onto that warmth for as long as she could.

The silence soon got unbearable, and Beau decided to break the tension, "Storous Daemich, why don't you tell Xania that story you told me earlier?" She smiled, trying to put him at ease.

Daemich looked from Beau to Xania, not sure what to do.

Xania smiled at him with a little nod. "It's okay," she said.

"Okay," said Daemich, a little too excited to make things better. "Suon, the place I'm from used to be a peaceful, tranquil place, mmm. We didn't have possessions or even a home, mmm. We wandered our world, went where we wanted, when we wanted, mmm. The whole place was a woodland paradise, trees and fields everywhere, mmm. There were open plains where we could run around, as fast and as free as we wanted, mmm. Life was simple," he said, "not that we were simple, mmm. We had education, history and botany mainly, mmm. We didn't need sciences or maths, mmm.

"One season, a group of strangers arrived, and all of a sudden, we were being hunted, mmm. Our species got to the point of near extinction, mmm. Thankfully, a peace-loving race took pity on us, mmm. They helped a few families escape and gave us a place to stay in their own vast lands, mmm." Daemich looked sad, his eyes averted to the water. "Our families soon realised that it was all for those beings' amusement, mmm. We were their wild pets, mmm.

"Yes, they may have saved us from extinction by ruthless hunters, but they had no compassion or remorse for what they were doing, mmm. Our new home wasn't the same, mmm. We were separated from our tribes, and things didn't seem right, mmm. My family didn't want a life of containment for me, mmm. A few families got together when I was born, and kept us hidden, mmm. Me and thirteen others, mmm. They educated us the best they could, without any resources, mmm. Eventually they found a way to sneak us out of that compound, mmm. We stayed in various prayer houses, gaining more education, mmm. The idea was simple, educate us to the point where we could come up with a way of saving our species, mmm. We were all supposed to be free, to roam our home world, mmm. Most of my friends joined the scientific community, I'm not sure what they were hoping to achieve, mmm. Some started a freedom army and went back to hunt the hunters, mmm. I never heard from them again, mmm." He paused, remembering his lost friends.

"The prayer house offered me an opportunity, one that I couldn't turn down, mmm. The chance to become a Cydarion, mmm. As you are probably aware, they were asked to put forward anyone they think would make a good candidate, mmm. I volunteered, not for retribution, but if I can save any species, whether my own or not, then that is the right thing to do, mmm. I'm just glad to be able to have the opportunity to do that, mmm. If I can save the less fortunate, then, that is worth a sacrifice, mmm." He smiled with pride, he knew he was doing the right thing.

"That's very nice of you to share your story, Daemich, thank you for telling us. I'm sure you'll make a fine Cydarion," said Xania.

"I hope to be master one day, mmm," he said, still excited.

"Master? Oh, erm, well that takes a lot of dedication and cycles of Callings," said Xania

"I know, but I'm committed for the long term, mmm," Daemich said proudly.

"Good for you," said Xania, "I hope things work out for you, I shall follow your progress."

Another tense bout of silence lasted for the next two sections as the raft whipped steadily down the river.

"Rapids!" Xania shouted out of nowhere.

"I see them," said Beau.

"Well do something then!" snapped Xania.

"What do you want me to do?" Beau shouted back. "There's no way around them. We have to go straight through the middle. Hold on tight," she said. The noise of the rapids nearly drowned out her own voice.

The raft dropped down a gradient and increased its speed. Beau dug the makeshift paddle into the water and pulled furiously, trying to veer away from an approaching rock. With a bump, it scraped by, into a constricted flow. The raft bounced from side to side along the high walls, knocking all three of them onto their backs. Beau quickly jumped back up and shouted,

"Stroke!"

Xania and Daemich both grabbed makeshift paddles and began furiously paddling.

The raft headed straight to a whirlpool. The front end of the raft swirled around the whirlpool, while the rear end got caught and was dragged down. The front lifted out of the water.

"Keep paddling!" shouted a panicked Beau. With a mighty effort from all three of them, the raft broke free of the whirlpool, the front-end came slamming down onto the white waters. Daemich bounced from the raft and fell into the turbulent waters. Xania and Beau both rushed to the edge of the raft, reaching out for him. The raft, now unbalanced, flipped over, throwing the two females into the river. They each fought their own battles against the raging waters, as they were swept away, downstream. Fighting to stay alive between certain drowning or being crushed against the rocks. The raft smashed to pieces on sharp rocks, right in front of them. Beau managed to get one foot onto the riverbed and pushed off, just missing the splintered pieces of wood. Slowly, the rapids eased, and the waters calmed. Both Xania and Beau clung to pieces of the floating wood and rested their torsos over. They were exhausted, their legs dangling in the water. Both searched for any sign of Daemich.

By nightfall they had drifted onto a small beach and the relative safety of land. They both recited a prayer for Daemich, on their own. Neither one of them spoke to the other. Then, absolutely exhausted, and with the stars as their blanket, they fell asleep.

***

Xania rose, fury burning in her chest as the moons faded from the morning sky. She searched for Daemich, praying it had been a dream, but the riverbank was empty. Her eyes fell on Beau, stirring awake.

Without warning, Xania drove a kick into her ribs.

"Oof!" Beau gasped, clutching her side.

"You killed him!" Xania roared, slamming another kick. This time, Beau caught her ankle, twisting hard and sending Xania crashing to the ground. She rolled up, teeth bared, and charged. Her knee shot for Beau's stomach, blocked. Her fist cut the air, dodged.

"That raft was dangerous!" Xania spat, raining blows. "I told you!"

"It wasn't!" Beau shouted, her own temper sparking. "It was fine, you got on it yourself!"

Two of Xania's punches connected, snapping Beau's head back. "I knew you couldn't protect him!"

Beau's front kick drove into Xania's chest, hurling her into the shallows. Water splashed. Beau stepped in after her. "How did *that* feel?" she taunted.

Xania sprung up, eyes blazing. "I SHOULD HAVE YOUR POWERS!" Each word landed with a strike.

"Jodrell gave them to me for a reason. I can't just throw them away!" Beau blocked furiously.

"I WANT HIM BACK!" Xania screamed. The river shuddered, its waters surging higher.

"I know!" Beau shouted, straining to hold her off.

"Phos didn't have to die either!" Xania's voice cracked, grief spilling through rage.

Beau hesitated, noticing the river's sudden rise.

"ALL THE LIES! MY PARENTS' SACRIFICE!" Xania's kicks battered Beau to her knees.

"Xania, stop!" Beau pleaded.

"Swift was banished because of me, and now he's dead!" Xania's whole body shook. The river clawed at them, waist-deep now, thrashing with unnatural force.

"This war with Lucifer, we're losing!" she cried, fists still hammering.

"Xania, get out of the water!" Beau backed toward the bank, fighting the current.

"AND YOU - ALWAYS PERFECT!" Xania's tears streamed, her voice breaking. "FIGHT ME!"

"No," Beau said flatly.

Xania's scream tore the sky, one word, all her fury, grief, and despair condensed into it.

"ARGH!"

The river exploded upward and wrenched her away.

Beau froze at the bank, watching as the current hurled Xania into a jagged rock midstream. Water crushed her against it, pinning her like an insect beneath glass. Xania's gaze found Beau's-pleading desperate.

Beau's jaw tightened. She turned.

And walked away.

Behind her, the river swallowed Xania's screams, until there was nothing left but the roar of the water. Xania's world went black.

Beau and Xania

Chapter 17

"Xania, grab my arm!" Beau shouted, herself struggling to keep her head above the water line. She had gone back upstream and jumped into the dangerous waters.

"Take my arm as I come past you," Beau said again, "my momentum should pull you away from the rocks!" Beau saw Xania's head flop to one side. She carried on shouting, "Xania, you have to do as I say. You've got this! We can do it!" There was no response from Xania. Beau tried shouting again, over the sound of the rushing water, one final tine and at full volume, "XANIA, I NEED YOUR HELP!"

Xania looked up. She saw Beau in the water, her outstretched arm coming towards her. With every last bit of strength she had left, Xania reached out and grabbed it. Xania felt her arm jerk in its socket, as Beau tugged, trying to use her weight to free Xania. Beau made herself as big as possible under the water, hoping the current would grab onto her. She gripped tighter onto Xania, before both of them were pulled free from the rock, like a mollusc from its shell. Xania disappeared under the water as their grip was ripped apart. Beau instinctively, turned and kicked with her legs, diving down into the waters. She felt around and managed to grab Xania by the waist, then kicked and clambered them both to the surface. The raging waters started to calm. Beau swam to the shore and dragged Xania to the emerging embankment. Xania was unconscious. Beau laid her on her back and administered Cardiopulmonary Resuscitation, talking to her the whole time.

Xania coughed up some water and gasped for air, she rolled onto her side. Beau collapsed onto her back at the side of Xania. They both lay in the mud, exhausted.

Xania's breathing slowly returned to normal. The water receded, back to its original serene level. Neither of them wanting to be the first to speak, they both lay on their backs, convalescing.

After a little time, Beau pointed at something in the sky. A dark cloud rapidly coming towards them.

She suddenly realised what it was. "MOVE!" she shouted, as she rolled to her left, Xania rolling to her right. Just as a volley of arrows came raining down into the ground where they lay, merely one snap ago. They both got to their feet but stayed low.

"Head for the trees over there," Xania said pointing inland, "I'm not going back in the water."

Beau nodded, "Good call."

Keeping low as they ran towards the trees, more arrows landed, sporadically in the open ground and tall grass. They reached the safety of the trees and caught their breath again. Xania dropped to her knees due to exhaustion.

Peering from behind a tree, Beau pointed, "They're over there, on the brow of that hill."

"I've got an idea," said Xania catching her breath and getting to her feet. Beau gave her a questioning look.

Xania smiled. "Trust me," she said walking off, away from the water and the open land. She headed behind the group that were firing upon them. Beau huffed and followed. The two of them went deeper into the trees until they were parallel with their attackers.

"Follow my lead," whispered Xania.

"Don't do anything stupid," Beau retorted.

They sprinted out from the cover of the trees, and approached a group of attackers, from behind. Twenty hairless bodies stood in two rows of ten. Their light blue skin, easy to disappear amongst the rolling green hills behind them. One man with a full head of hair and short beard stood in front of the small army. A long spear in one hand and a khopesh in the other.

The men stepped back in shock, at the arrival of two strangers right behind them. Xania walked to the front, hoping to speak with the leader. She motioned for Beau to stay at the back. Beau followed Xania's plan without knowing what it was. She trusted Xania with her life. The bearded leader, only moved to raise his hand and stop the men firing their arrows at such a short distance. "What are you doing on our lands?" asked the leader.

"We are just passing through, we mean you no harm," said Xania calmly.

"You have no permission! You seek us out and ask for safe passage or we seek you and take your life," beamed the man, a loud cheer erupted from the soldiers behind him.

"Okay," asked Xania hopefully, "Can we pass through?"

The leader shook his head, "It's too late, our law says that you must go through me first. If I win, you go no further. If you win," he paused to laugh, "my men will let you pass."

"I won't kill you!" stated Xania.

The man gave a hearty laugh, "I am Tholeton the fifth, my family is undefeated in three ages."

"Well, Tholeton, if you want to keep your undefeated title, I suggest you just let us pass," said Xania more seriously.

The two lines of soldiers started to chant, "Fight! fight!"

"No more talking, prepare to die," said Tholeton. He tightened his grip on the khopesh and lowered his spear.

Xania pulled out her sai's, knelt down, and stabbed them into the ground, in an act of peace. Slowly standing up, she offered, "Before you kill me, she'll kill all of you!" Xania nodded towards Beau but kept her eyes on Tholeton.

Tholeton looked at Beau, then at his men. Their bows ready to be drawn.

Beau looked a little worried, "Xania, I don't have my blasters!" she gave a little shrug.

Xania said, "You've got this. *We* can do it!" she then glanced at Beau, "I need your help."

Beau smiled, realising Xania had listened to her. She snapped her fingers and her eyes lit up, electric blue.

Tholeton crossed the distance between himself and Xania quicker than she had expected. Xania had to jump out of the way, leaving her sai's in the ground. *Shit, that hadn't gone according to plan,* she thought to herself. A jab of his spear just missed her torso, the khopesh sliced down through the air where she had moved to. Ducking below the blade, Xania threw a glance at Beau, who had just been watching.

"Oh yeah," Beau remembered. Blue sparks spat between her fingers, and she sent a bolt of lightning across both rows of soldiers, making them all collapse in pain and convulse on the ground. The air turned as blue as the clouds, distracting Tholeton. Xania took her chance and dove at his legs, toppling him over. His head hit the ground with a thud, a cloud of red dust fell from his hair and beard. Then, in one swift move, she grabbed both sais and jumped on top of Tholeton, straddling his torso. He had only managed to get his bearings, as Xania slammed both sais down by his wrists. The sais' guards pinning his arms down to the ground, both the weapons still in his hands.

"Do you want to renegotiate now?" asked Xania. Beau stopped her lightning barrage.

"What, what's going on?" asked Tholeton, seemingly coming out of a daze.

"It looks like you're coming out of a spell," said Xania triumphantly.

"Spell, what spell?" Tholeton asked.

"How did you know he was under a spell?" asked Beau, curiously walking up to Xania.

"You were under the spell of a devil, I have just released you," Xania said, she turned to Beau and replied, "I saw the red dust in his hair. It's an old way of manipulating a subject."

"You saw that from back at the trees?" ask Beau.

"Well, not exactly," admitted Xania.

"So that wasn't part of the plan?" asked Beau.

"No, not that bit," Xania said sheepishly.

"And you leaving your weapons in the ground, I know that wasn't part of the plan either!" said Beau.

"Well, no, that neither. Actually, none of it went to plan!" laughed Xania. Beau laughed too. Tholeton wriggled in his restraints.

"Oh, sorry," Xania said, removing the sai's that pinned him down, and climbed off him. The soldiers slowly got to their feet, holding their heads and rubbing their aching muscles.

"I'm sorry," offered Tholeton, "this isn't our usual welcome," he said.

Beau asked, "Is your village close by, we're happy to explain everything to you."

Tholeton looked between the two Cydarions, then nodded, "Yes, this way." He pointed to the horizon and led them off, over the hills. The army followed behind, struggling to get their joints moving again.

Later, at the village camp, Tholeton, Beau and Xania had to hold the village chief down and clean his hair and full beard of all the dust. He resisted until it had all gone.

Between nutritious mouthfuls of broth that was offered to them, the Cydarions explained the reason why they were there. They asked what they could do to help.

"We ask of nothing, but to rid this place of evil," replied Chief Soldue, the leader of this tribe.

"We shall do what we can," offered Xania honestly.

"If I may ask, how did this start?" asked Beau.

"About half an age ago there was an earth rumbling. It was like the whole ground expanded and then suddenly popped, like a water bubble would do. Everyone fell over, but this red dust stayed in the air. At first it was difficult to breathe without a Polunth rat skin. But that was when things started to change, our minds were altered, we didn't have control anymore, all we wanted to do was kill. Not each other," Soldue confirmed, "but our neighbours. So, we came up with new laws that would accept that. The other tribes were doing the same too."

He had a realisation, "In fact, they still are, they wouldn't know that their minds have been poisoned. We need to stop them!"

"It's probably best that you don't. Just keep away from them until this is over." Xania said.

"How do we know if you've succeeded?" asked the chief.

Xania smiled, "Everything will go back to how it was."

"And if you don't succeed?" the chief asked earnestly.

Both Beau and Xania went quiet for a fraction, before Beau spoke, "Then all is lost. We are your last hope."

"Then we should revel you!" offered the chief.

"We don't deserve that!" said Xania.

"Not yet, anyway," chimed Beau.

Chief Soldue smiled, "Then enjoy your last days, yes?"

"Do you mean our last rotations with you, or last rotations alive?" asked Xania.

"Is it not the same?" said Chief Soldue.

Beau shrugged, "What do we have to lose?" she said.

"Well, he may be right," agreed Xania.

Chief Soldue stood up and announced a revelry at sunset. The rest of the village cheered and set about preparations.

Music and dancing enthralled the evening. All the food had been consumed but the fermented berry wine was still flowing.

"C'mon," said a slightly drunk Xania to Beau, "have a dance, this music is intoxicating."

Beau, who could hold her drink a lot better, accepted the invitation, only if it was to keep the peace. The two danced and had fun with the locals late into the night.

After the music had stopped, the pair sat down by the glowing embers of the fire. Most of the village had already sloped off to bed.

Beau turned to Xania. "You know we work better together than against each other. What do you say we bury our issues here?"

Xania hesitated "Then tell me, why risk your life to save me? Back in the water?"

"Didn't even think about it," Beau said. "Like it or not, we're on the same side. You may not like me, but I'll always have your back."

Shame cut through Xania.

Beau offered her hand. "Truce?"

Xania shook her head, "Not a handshake." She grabbed Beau and pulled her into a crushing hug, long overdue, fierce, then softening. Beau felt Xania's breath on her neck, a shiver racing through her. They lingered, faces close, smiles breaking. Xania closed her eyes. Beau followed-then kissed her.

The world tilted, Beau's knees weakened before she wrenched herself back, breath ragged. They held onto each other anyway, unsure, suspended in the moment.

"I didn't know you were..." Xania whispered.

"I thought you were," Beau blurted.

"No."

"Shit." Beau turned away.

Xania caught her hand. "Don't. It was... nice. Just in the moment."

Beau cursed again, shame in her eyes.

"Bury it," Xania said quickly. "With the rest of our issues."

Beau gave a crooked smile "I'd like that."

They sat by the fire, watching sparks dance.

"Jodrell didn't pick me because I was perfect," Beau said quietly. "He picked me because I was. broken. Flawed. I have to work on myself."

"He still picked you," Xania muttered, tracing circles in the dust. "I spent my whole life trying to be perfect for him."

"You don't get it. He picked you too. Always. You don't need sparks or gimmicks." Beau flicked a crackle of blue lightning from her fingertips. "You're enough as you are. Truth is... I'm jealous. You're so fucking natural, its nauseating!"

Xania laughed softly.

"You think *I'm* strong? *You* could level this place with a sneeze. That's real power."

"I don't have any powers," Xania said, frowning.

Beau pressed a hand to her chest. "When Jodrell gave me mine, he left a piece of himself. He whispers sometimes. Not words; more like a presence. He's still watching over you. Waiting for you to wake up to what you are."

Xania's eyes filled. "He's alive? Can I speak to him?"

"It doesn't work like that. But he's proud of you. That much I know."

"What power? I don't feel anything."

"Are you serious? Back in the water, you made the tide rise with your emotions. The moment you calmed down, it dropped."

Xania stared into the flames. "Nyk..."

Beau tilted her head. "Nyk?"

"The day of Phos's funeral-on the cliffs. He told me to let go. I did. The wind answered. He asked if it was me."

Beau's eyes widened. "So... wind too?"

Xania gave a helpless laugh., "I don't control anything."

"Try."

"Try what?"

"Control the wind."

"That's ridiculous."

"Want me to punch you first?" Beau teased. Both laughed.

"Then Beau smirked. "Fine. Jodrell says, 'Just try your best.'"

"No he didn't!"

"Okay, that was me. But still... try."

Xania sighed, closed her eyes, and lifted her hand. Nothing. Then... fire roared skyward, a column of flame twisting into the night.

Beau stumbled back. "Holy shit, that was you?"

Xania opened her eyes, baffled. "I didn't feel the wind."

"You just threw a fireball into the sky. That'll come in handy," Beau said with a shaky laugh.

Xania froze. "Water. Wind. Fire..." Her voice fell to a whisper. "Bey Norcia."

"The first Cydarion?" Beau asked.

"The only one to command all the elements," Xania breathed.

Beau exhaled. "Looks like you've got work to do."

"I don't even know where to start."

"Maybe where it always begins... with emotion," said Beau.

Xania turned to her. "Will you help me?"

Beau smiled, steady now. "Always. But first, sleep."

Holan Plege

Chapter 18

Nyk was in the kitchens of the Citadel finishing his breakfast with the residents, when he felt the Calling. He'd had a good night's sleep with no disturbances from the voices in his head and he was looking forward to some more peace with Crown Claw, now that it had hatched. He never understood how the little bird could clear his mind of everything, but he gladly accepted it, and cherished all time that they got to spend together. He'd been bonding so much with the small bird, it would be hard for him to take a few rotations away. He looked out of the window, through the kitchen gardens, across the open hill and focused on the small farmhouse in the distance. *I'll be back soon little one, and when you're ready, we'll fly together.* He paused for fraction longer, then set off down the corridors to collect Holan for his first Calling.

"Yesss!" Holan exclaimed, as he punched the air with his paw, his long rabbit ears flapped above his head.

Nyk smiled, "Don't be too excited, it's not a vacation. And definitely don't let Pace see you do that. He's still not sure if you Storous' should be going on the Callings yet. You're not fully prepared."

"I can handle anything," said Holan.

"I'm sure you can, just keep the enthusiasm down. Come on, we best get going."

"Nyk," said Holan, on the walk towards the portal room. "I've been told by someone, that the Cydarions are a cult, or some secret religion that only go to war."

Nyk laughed, "We are definitely not a cult."

"That's what a cult would say," said Holan with a laugh.

"Who told you these things?" asked Nyk.

Holan shrugged. "It's just what I picked up from my home planet."

"Huh!" said Nyk. "We're not a cult; we wouldn't stop you from leaving. But neither are we a religion. We don't tell you how to live, what you should be doing and how you should do it. Sure, we have rules and pledge an allegiance to God, but that is about having faith. Faith in yourself, faith in each other and faith in God. He doesn't ask for anything except acceptance. Let him into your heart, feel his love, his warmth, and you will feel an overpowering sense that you can do anything. He is always around, although at times, you may feel he has deserted you, he hasn't. He lets you stand up for yourself, gives you the courage to do it all by yourself. He is the voice inside your head, saying, 'You can do this.' You don't want him to do things for you, that would make you reliant on others. He's just there as support. Yes, you may fail, maybe multiple times, and yet he won't step in. Why? Because he believes in you, he has faith in you. He is still by your side, willing you on, to try again. Just have faith in yourself to do the right thing."

Holan nodded as though he understood what Nyk was saying.

As they got closer to the portal room, Nyk started to hear noises, when suddenly, there was a loud explosion and Nyk dived to the floor, covering his head.

He looked up and saw Holan just standing there, looking baffled. "You didn't hear that?" Nyk said.

"Hear what?" said Holan, "you just jumped onto the floor."

The corridor was quiet again, and Nyk got to his feet. "The explosion," he said. "You didn't hear it, with them ears?"

Holan shook his head, "There's been no sounds at all."

Nyk stayed quiet, *I definitely heard something, and it was close.*

As they carried on towards the portal room, Nyk could still hear noises. It wasn't until they entered the room that Nyk realised the noises were coming through the portal, although Holan swore he couldn't hear anything.

It wasn't long before Pace entered the portal room, taping away on a data pad. Nyk gave Pace a quiet nod when Holan blurted out,

"Master Pace, I've got all my rations in my pockets." Holan patted the pockets of his jumpsuit to prove they were all there.

Nyk had noticed a vein throbbing just above Paces left temple, *this isn't good.*

When Pace didn't react to Holan, the young Storous tried again, "Master Pace, I'm all ready to go. And look, I don't even have a weapon." He beamed with joy.

Pace got angry and nearly threw the data pad across the floor. "HOLAN! Why are you telling me this? It is your duty to carry your own rations on every Calling. You never rely on anyone else."

"But..."

"This isn't a reward moment, you won't get affirmation from me, for doing the bare minimum. And you certainly won't be carrying any weapons, until *I* deem you suitable," said Pace.

Nyk saw Holan withdraw into himself, and he had to say something. "Pace!" he said sharply, "are you okay?"

Paces eye flicked between Holan and Nyk before letting out a big sigh. He pinched the bridge of his nose. "I'm sorry, I've got a lot on my plate at the moment."

"Maybe you should stay here for this one," said Nyk.

Pace looked at the green swirling portal, "No, I need to get out of this place, clear my head a bit."

"I know what you mean," said Nyk

Pace looked at Holan and gave a half smile, "Are you ready?"

Holan nodded and all three of them stepped through their portal, emerging on the other side, onto a muddy and slippery road. Suddenly an explosion erupted nearby, thunderous bangs were heard in all directions. As they were getting their bearings, something whistled past Nyks ear and he flinched. Pace was about to laugh, when he suddenly came to the realisation of what it was.

"Get down!" he yelled, as he jumped behind a low bush and lay down flat, scanning the area. Nyk was only half a snap behind him, Holan right by his side.

"What the...?"

"Shush," Pace interrupted, with a finger on his lips. He nodded towards a derelict building about half a kilometre away and gestured to make their way there. Pace moved first, crawling on his stomach and knees nearly all the way. Nyk and Holan followed in the same manner. Holan had to fold his ears flat against his head to stop them from sticking up. Entering the building Pace finally stood up, just as Nyk and Holan arrived.

"Look at these boots! They're ruined now," Pace said, very annoyed. He tried to scrape the mud off on the corner wall.

"Dress for the crawling not for the Calling?" Nyk offered as a joke. A smug look on his face as he waved a combat boot under his nose. Holan laughed

"Give it a rest," Pace said, clearly a little distraught.

Nyk quickly changed the subject, "That doesn't sound like blaster fire," he said pointing outside of the building.

Pace nodded in agreement, "It's not, it must be much older."

"You mean, like a miniature blast projectile?" asked Nyk, "I've read about them."

Pace feigned surprise, "You read?"

Nyk laughed. "Real funny! How's them boots of yours?"

Pace stared at Nyk for a snap, then responded, "No, it's older, probably gunpowder projectiles. Nasty things. We don't come across them very often, very barbaric. Those weapons are actually worth quite a lot, to the right buyer," he said.

"Well, you'd know!" smirked Nyk.

"If *we* were still in that trade, *we'd* be able to make a small fortune from them," replied Pace. "Especially at the auctions on Stiil Boe. There's a huge market for these antiques."

Nyk was a little surprised. "Well, maybe we could just ..." he suggested with a little shrug.

Holan's mouth dropped open, his eyes flicked between the two Cydarions and his pupils dilated at the thought.

"That's not our Calling. We have a bigger issue to deal with," snapped back Pace.

"I know, it was just a suggestion," said Nyk.

Holan let out a sad moan.

"Hmmm, but you may have a point," Pace conceded, "Although, we do need to focus on the present situation. Maybe we could come back at quieter time and have a look around," wondered Pace, "For now, we shouldn't use our technology in this place."

"Yes Master," Nyk smirked, looking across to Holan. Pace just smiled and shook his head. He still hadn't gotten used to being called Master. Even with all the new recruits, he still felt he had a lot more to learn himself. Although he had been elected Master Cydarion over a cycle ago, he was still finding his feet. So much had change in the timeframe, he was struggling to keep it all together. The buildings, the finances, the new students, all that and the exponential threat of Lucifer increasing his attacks on different worlds. There were no manuals or guidebooks to help him do his job, and he was getting exhausted.

Pace rummaged around the old building and found some dirty, used bandages. Handing them to Holan he said, "You should wrap these around your head, hide those ears of yours."

"What do you mean?" asked an offended Holan, "What's wrong with my ears?"

"There's nothing wrong with your ears, it's these people," said Pace. "If they're still using gunpowder projectiles, then they're a primitive species. Meaning, they haven't ever seen another sentient species. So, you need to cover up and not freak them out."

Holan huffed the whole time he covered his head with the dirty bandages. "They should get used to other species," he mumbled to himself. "I'd make sure of that!"

"Oh, and maybe keep your paws in your pockets too," Pace shrugged, "just in case."

Holan slunk his paws into his jacket pocket with a loud sigh and turned his back, still grumbling to himself.

The three of them waited a while longer, until the explosions and projectiles had eased, before making their way out of the ruined building and crossing some crater covered fields. An eerie silence covered the land between rounds of gunfire. Field after field they walked.

Darkness fell, as fast as the temperature, and soon, they had to settle in a small copse of pine trees for the night. The fallen pine needles making for a comfortable bed. Pace had ruled against a fire, for fear of giving away their position. Instead, they just ate some of their supply rations cold. Nyk and Pace spoke quietly into the night, about their old weapon trading days, laughing about the scrape they got into on Violet Capri. Holan hung on every word. He was taking in as much information as he could, filling his brain up with so many questions, before all three of them settled down for some sleep.

Holan saw himself at the head of an army, thundering into the void. The ground split wide, and from the chasm rose a gate of searing light. As he neared it, a voice filled the abyss, rhythmic and eternal:

"Two worlds burn beneath the sky,

For one to live, one must die.

Choose the flame you'll let expire,

Or both shall drown within the fire."

The rhyme struck deep, every syllable echoing in his marrow. He reached toward the gate... and woke, shuddering, slick with sweat. The words clung to him like chains, their meaning too vast, too terrible to deny. His kind had always known their dreams, their meanings woven clear as threads of fate. But this one... this one terrified him.

Holan rose and slipped away from the camp. Nyk and Pace slept on, unaware of the destiny gnawing at his chest. At the edge of the copse, he sank down and gazed outward. The night was alive with fire. Missiles screamed across the black sky, bursts of light clawed at the horizon, the earth shuddered with the fury of war. Yet as he watched, an unnatural calm wrapped itself around him, the stillness of a man who had glimpsed the end and accepted its approach. He repeated the words that had been burned into his brain: "For one to live... one must die."

Holan stayed there for most of the night, embracing the calmness. It wasn't until a section before the sun rose that Holan made his way back to the pine needle bed and fell asleep, this time without the tormented images.

Nyk and Pace woke just before sunrise and meditated for a section, before waking a grumpy Holan. The bombs and mortar explosions were still going, throughout the night. After a small morning rations pack, the Cydarions and Holan ventured out of the copse and crossed over more mud-covered fields.

"You know, I didn't sleep much," said Nyk, "the bombs, the earth shaking, the explosions. I couldn't tell if it was in my head or out there." He pointed to the horizon as he made his confession.

"Me neither," admitted Holan.

"Oh, it's definitely out there, buddy," said Pace, replying to Nyk. "It was just about nonstop," he said, ignoring Holan.

"Yeah, I know, but there's other things in here..." Nyk tapped his head.

"Look, there's someone over there," Pace interrupted, gesturing to a small wall off to their left, "we should talk to them."

"Sure," Nyk said with a heavy sigh. "I'll take point. You and Holan stay behind that wall and cover me." Pace agreed, while Holan kept quiet and kicked the carcass of a dead animal. Nyk approached the being slowly and cautiously, hands up in surrender, "Friend or foe?" he asked.

It was a young-looking human, with jet black hair chewing on some spice. He wore a dark olive-grey military uniform, matching trousers, shirt and jacket, and a small helmet that covered his short hair. He was squatting by a low wall, checking his weapon.

"Friend, are you lost?" he asked.

"Not exactly," said Nyk, "We're looking for someone."

"We?" the soldier questioned, looking around.

"Pace?" Nyk shouted.

Pace and Holan walked out from behind the wall and up to Nyk. The soldier gripped tight onto his weapon.

"Hey man, whereabouts, are we?" Pace asked politely. The soldier looked Pace up and down, before standing up and replying, in a not so polite manner.

"Well, you're certainly in the wroong place, neegro!" came a long-drawled reply from the soldier.

"It's not by choice, my friend. More of a necessity," Pace said with a smile.

The soldier in front of him stood up to his full height, still a half decimetre smaller than Pace. A badge on his jacket showed his name as Smith. His attitude was far higher than his height. "Listen here neegro! Nobody wants you herree. Fact, that's maybe one gooood thing Hitler said, 'get rid 'o' those niggers!'" The man spat on the ground in front of Pace.

Pace took a step closer to the man named Smith. "Do we have a problem here?"

"Yeah, we do! I don't like yous niggers!" scorned Private Smith.

Understanding Private Smiths tone, Pace responded, "Just because we come from different places, it doesn't mean you should hate." Pace gave a polite grin.

"You can go back to the fucking jungle as far as I'm concerned, we don't need you to win this war!" Smith said, spitting on the ground.

"Well, I come from Strectar One, which is far from a jungle, I can assure you. But I really do think you need my help," said Pace.

Private Smith took a step closer to Pace, their chests nearly touching. "Look, I suggest yous fuck off outta my sight!" said Smith.

Nyk stepped up and pushed both the men apart. Looking at Smith, he said, "You got a problem with him, means you've got a problem with me!" he said thumbing between himself and Pace.

Smith looked at Pace, but nodded in Nyk's direction, still chewing on some spice. "That your Master?"

"Actually," Nyk retorted, "he's my Master."

"Private!" a voice came out of nowhere, "who are you talking to?"

"A couple 'o' fellas, who are in the wrooong place, sir." Private Smith shouted back, without taking his eyes off Pace. Pace was about to speak again, when a stocky man, smoking a herb stick appeared in his peripheral vision. He was the same height as Nyk but with a more weathered face. His name badge said Colonel Crisk.

"Can I help you?" Colonel Crisk asked politely.

Pace smirked at Private Smith and then addressed the Colonel. "Thank you, Colonel, we have a certain... mission."

"I ain't heard of no mission in my area," said Colonel Crisk bluntly.

"It's a need-to-know basis, I'm afraid," offered Pace.

Private Smith snorted, "Yeah, send the niggers in first!" he laughed.

"Private, stand down!" snapped Colonel Crisk. Private Smith relaxed a little and kept quiet.

Pace continued, "It's about two or three rotations in that direction." Pace held up his hand and pointed beyond the horizon of the morning sun.

Colonel Crisk looked surprised as he followed Pace's gesture. "What mission is *that*?" he asked, his face in a grimace.

Nyk stepped in. "It's to get rid of the devil from this place," he said, cutting to the chase.

"Ha," scoffed Colonel Crisk, "We've been trying to stop Hitler for the last six years, my friend. But if you three think you can make the difference, go ahead. You're heading in the right direction, to Berlin, straight into the lion's den. What *is* your mission?" he asked again.

"Walk right into the lion's mouth and..." Nyk looked at Holan before changing his tone, "convince him to stop."

Both Colonel Crisk and Private Smith both let out a hearty laugh.

Private Smith, still laughing, turned to Pace and said, "He don't like your kind!"

"Private, stand down! I won't tolerate any racism in my platoon!"

"Yes sir," replied Private Smith, looking down to the ground.

The Colonel then turned back to Pace. "We can't offer any help, but we can cover you. We have our own mission." He paused and furrowed his brow, "You guys don't seem like the military kind, what regiment are you from?"

Nyk was thinking of something to say when Pace answered, "Probably best you don't know, but we are on your side my friend. We will finish this for you," Pace nodded with a smile, "Just have some faith."

"Praise the lord," the Colonel shouted, then looked the three newcomers up and down. "Say, where's your weapons?"

Pace smiled back warmly. "They just slow us down, we'll be alright," he said.

Colonel Crisk looked a little wary. "Well, you fight your way, and I'll fight mine; this weapon is my life." He tapped the butt of his rifle that was slung over his shoulder.

Nyk leaned in, close to the Colonel and whispered, "The one with the biggest stick, doesn't always win."

The colonel looked a little confused, "Riiight! Anyway, as I said, we can cover you as far as the tree line over there." The Colonel pointed past the wall to a small woodland area where most of the trees had already been destroyed.

"Thank you, Colonel, we appreciate it," thanked Pace.

Private Smith thought to himself, *If that nigger gets in front of me, I got a bullet waiting for him.*

Nyk immediately turned to the Private, his face serious, "What did you just say?"

The Private was taken aback, "Uh, nu, nuthun!" he stuttered.

Nyk took a step closer, their noses nearly touching, "I heard what you said, do you care to repeat it?" Nyk asked.

"I, I, I din't say nuthun," stammered Private Smith, his breathing matching his heartbeat.

Holan bit his lip and smiled.

"Hey, hey, hey!" shouted Colonel Crisk, stepping between both of them. He pushed the men apart. Pace did likewise and placed a hand on Nyk's chest.

The Colonel turned to Nyk. "He didn't say anything, let it go mate."

Nyk looked at Pace, who nodded in agreement before letting out a huff and relaxing his shoulders.

"Come on, we should get going," Pace said to Nyk, who in return, gave a nod of acceptance and stepped away.

Straightening his uniform jacket, Private Smith had a thought: *Yeah, you and your negro get outta here!*

Nyk spun on his heals and punched the private, square on the jaw, knocking him to the floor in a heap of pain. The Colonel immediately brought his gun up and pointed it at Nyk.

Holan's eyes blazed with a sharp intensity, a thrill sparking through him.

"Whoa, whoa, whoa," Pace shouted, as he stepped between the gun and Nyk, his back to the muzzle. "What's going on man?" he asked.

Nyk was confused by Paces actions. "You heard that, you all heard what he just said." *It wasn't just the voices in my head.*

"Nyk, no one said anything, and we're all right here!" Pace said, gesturing around.

The Colonel lowered his gun. "I suggest you three get going, NOW! The fight is over there," he cocked his head towards the woodland area, "not right here, with each other."

"I agree with you Sir," Pace said, not taking his eyes of Nyk, "We'll be on the move now." Nyk stood there, open mouthed and confused. Pace took his shoulder and guided him away. "Come on, mind back on the job Nyk," Pace said softly. The two Cydarions walked away from the skirmish. Pace looked back and nodded at the Colonel. Holan fell in line behind them, not saying a word. After a good few strides, and well out of earshot of Colonel Crisk, Pace asked Nyk, "What the hell was that?"

"You heard him, right? He was disrespecting you," said Nyk.

"Nah man, he didn't say a word."

Nyk looked at Holan, who shook his head. "What?" Nyk whispered to himself.

"Nyk, what's got into you?"

"I don't know, I..."

"You could've gotten us killed. We're here to save them, not start a fight with them," said Pace.

"I know, I know," said Nyk, "but I keep hearing these voices in my head. I don't know what's real."

"Well, you need to figure it out, and quick," said Pace, "I need you to focus on the Calling." Nyk didn't reply. "Nyk!" Pace repeated, louder this time.

Nyk shook his head, trying to clear the confusion from his mind. "I'm good, I'm good," he lied, nodding at Pace.

"Riiight," Pace said, not sure if what he was hearing was actually true. "We need to make for them trees. The Colonel is covering us until we get there. But also keep an eye out, which means, stay focused!" said Pace with conviction.

Nyk tried to focus his mind to the dangerous situation they were in.

Firing suddenly erupted from behind them, passing to their right. That was their signal to get moving quicker. The three of them set off with the speed of a hunting grass cat. Over a couple of small, ruined walls, through shelled craters and over splintered trees before reaching the sanctuary of the woodland area. The firing, now off in the distance, quietened. The trees got thicker the further they ventured into it, and the less exposed they were.

Nyk walked on in silence, while Holan spoke to Pace, asking all sorts of questions. "What was it like to be a weapons dealer? How many demons have you killed? Which weapons are the most effective against a demon? What was Lucifer like when you met him?"

Pace either ignored, scoffed or disregarded every one of Holan's questions, until he asked about something that stopped Pace in his tracks.

"How do we portal through time?"

Pace turned to look at Holan, "Where have you heard that?"

Holan smiled, finally getting a reaction out of Pace. "I read about it," he said, "when I was helping Bork in the archives."

"Forget what you read, it's dangerous."

"Why would it be dangerous?" wondered Holan.

Pace frowned. "Have you ever played with the timeline?" he asked.

Holan shook his head, his long ears shaking lose from underneath the bandages as his head twisted. "No, I don't know how to."

"Good," said Pace curtly. "No one should mess with the timeline." He paused to take a long breath, calming himself down. "Look, we don't know how changing something in the past would affect the future, the present or even our past. It could wipe out a whole species, change the order of things on a certain planet or many planets. Think about how many planets have interacted with each other for millennia. It could only take for one of them species not to survive Lucifers wrath, to drastically alter history. Imagine a placid peace-loving planet, it's sentients not there anymore. Other war mongering species would face no opposition, they'd either overrun many planets or go to war with others."

"But how do we know we're not in the past now?" asked Holan.

"God doesn't play with the timeline," said Pace.

"But what if Lucifer has? Wouldn't God send us back there too?"

He may have a point there. "Holan, *you* don't play with the timeline. When we get back, you show me these books, and I'll keep them safe personally."

"That's not fair," said Holan, "I thought the archives were for everyone to gain knowledge from?"

Pace sighed. "If anyone went back in time, without Gods approval, everything could change, you and I may not exist, the Cydarions may not have even started yet. All of the worlds that we've helped over the course of our existence, they would have been left helpless. In fact, they still could be. This fight is far from over. It's going to take all of us to stop that from becoming a reality. It's not just you and the planet you are visiting that are at stake, but the future of every planet in their galaxy."

Holan finished hiding his ears back under the bandages. "But what if the opposite is also true," said Holan, "we go back in time and save more beings?"

"What if you don't though, what if you don't save anyone, but it costs more lives? Is that a risk you are willing to take?" said Pace. "We are not gods who can make that decision."

Holan went quiet, thinking about the statement.

"I suggest your time would be better used if you could walk and meditate at the same time," said Pace, shutting down their conversation. *So many questions, and in the middle of a battlefield too.* Pace sighed. *Time travel through portals isn't something we should be doing. Only God can see the bigger picture... but what if he's wrong?* Pace shook the doubt from his mind and caught up with Nyk.

Pace and Nyk didn't do any meditation, they were too busy listening for anyone or anything in the vicinity that could pose a threat. It had been a long time since they had been in an actual war situation, and they knew they had to keep their wits about them. As they edged towards the far end of the forest, they saw a small town ahead of them, in the distance.

"That looks to be a good place to stay for the night," suggested Pace, "if we can find some shelter. I've got a feeling that it may be a cold one tonight."

Nyk nodded in agreement. "With a warm fire, some cold mead and maybe some company?" Nyk said with a smile.

"Now that would be a nice change," Pace said chuckling. First, they had to get across some open ground and over a small bridge before the entrance to the town. Pace walked on first, Holan and Nyk followed in single file. They got barely fifty metres from the stone bridge, when a couple of shots rang out, hitting the ground in front of them. All three of them jumped into a crater for cover. The shots kept coming, infrequently, but still there.

"Those shots are terrible, they're not even on target," said Pace.

"Isn't that a good thing?" said Holan.

"That gives me an idea," said Nyk, "do you remember our first meeting?"

"You mean, when you tried to kill me?" scoffed Pace.

"After that." Nyk laughed.

"You're going to call the Starlady, here?" asked Pace, then laughed. "That would confuse them."

A small yelp of excitement came from Holan. The two Cydarions looked at him.

"No, the comms won't work from here," said Nyk. "I'm talking about those Topains. I just talked nicely to them." Nyk was about to stand up, when Pace pulled him back down.

"You know they nearly killed you too!" he said.

"That's right, nearly! But they didn't, did they?" said Nyk, this time standing up quicker.

"Nearly?" Holan questioned, "that doesn't sound good! I don't think I like this plan."

"Neither do I," admitted Pace.

Nyk took a step towards the firing. Some pot shots pinged and whizzed around him, but he didn't flinch. Hands held up by his shoulders, he shouted out,

"Hey guys, you shouldn't be shooting at us, we're on the same side."

The sporadic firing ceased, and a shouted reply came from behind a large mound of dirt, "Vho are you?"

"We're one of you, but we're not from around these parts, we're lost. My friend has been injured and needs medical assistance," Nyk said, using the bandages around Holan's head as an excuse. Nyk carried on walking, slowly making his way forward.

There was a long pause. "Ve haf orters to schoot anyone komingkt zis vay!" came the wobbly, slightly high-pitched voice. Nyk wondered if it was the voice of a female.

"Surely you don't want to shoot one of your own?" said Nyk, "Especially someone that is injured, that isn't the way to fight a war." He was so close to the pile of dirt now, there was no turning back, just a few more decimetres and he could face them. From the gunshots, he had deduced that there were three of them.

Nyk had thought of a plan; with a surprise move, he could take two of them down, the third would have to make a quick decision. Fight, flight or fright. Two out of three outcomes are good. *The third is still a good chance, if he's quick enough.*

"Ve are Hitler's youzz, ve are ze future uff ze fazzerlent!" shouted back a young voice.

Nyk appeared from around the mound, about to make his move, when he came face to face with three young boys, each holding a rifle. Nyk nearly froze. *No, no, it can't be.*

Three boys, each wearing a long-sleeved brown shirt, and a red armband depicting a black hooked cross. Dark brown shorts and oversized black boots. They all had fair hair, trimmed short. The first boy was surprised at Nyks appearance but lifted his weapon up and pointed it straight at Nyk. The second boy jumped and dropped his gun into the dirt. The third boy didn't know what to do. He just kept looking between the two other boys, his rifle nonchalantly waving at the ground. Nyk was prepared to take down a couple of soldiers, but three boys had him stumped.

"Son of a... You're just kids!" he said.

The first boy still had his rifle pointing at Nyk, but now, it was shaking in his trembling hands.

"Stop right zere, back away!" the boy said, unsure of his own words.

Nyk closed his eyes and sighed, "Go home kid, all of you, this isn't the place for you!" As he finished his last word, he reached out, grabbed the gun by its barrel and yanked it out of the boy's weak grip. The quick move surprised the boy and all he could do was grab for the handle. The boy stumbled forward a couple of steps and fell into Nyk. The other two boys gasped. *I have to save you, all of you. If I can't, then there's no need for me to be here.*

Instinctively, Nyk threw the gun away and wrapped an arm around the boy. The young teen felt a little squashed against Nyk's muscled body, but he didn't move. A warm embrace flowed through the child. Unexpectedly the boy gripped Nyk back and burst into tears. Nyk placed his free hand softly onto the boy's head and held him close. Tears welling in his own eyes.

"Pace, you're all clear," Nyk called back, his voice almost trembling. He held tight on to the boy. The other two boys were standing still, rooted to the spot, when Pace and Holan arrived. Pace let out a huge sigh of disappointment when he saw the young soldiers.

"There's no need for this," he said to no one in particular. The first boy let go of Nyk and backed off, wiping his tears away with the back of a hand. Pace looked at the third boy, obviously the youngest of all three, who was still waving the gun at the ground.

"Put that gun down, son. You won't need it anymore," he said in a warm tone. The boy promptly dropped the weapon like it was a hot iron, but didn't know what he should do next.

"Do you want a hug too?" Nyk asked, his arms open wide. The young boy nodded, then ran into the arms of Nyk.

Holan stood there in bewilderment, "Why are children fighting a war?" he asked. As soon as he finished speaking, the second boy must have realised he wasn't speaking a language he recognised.

The boy pointed and started to shout, "Chew, Chew, Chew!"

Pace rushed over to the boy, "No, no, it's okay, he's one of us. He just has a head injury, he's delirious, no one knows what he's saying!" Pace then shot a look to Holan, warning him to keep his mouth shut for now.

"Maybe you kids should just go home, stay safe. I promise all this will be over very soon," said Nyk. The youngest boy let go of Nyk, nodded sheepishly, and went to collect his gun.

"Ah, no. You all leave your weapons here," said Pace, "you won't need them again." The three boys walked off, over the bridge and down the street. They never looked back.

Nyk shook his head. "That's not normal!" he said, rubbing his temple.

Pace sighed, picking up the weapons, "How do guns like these end up in the wrong hands?" he asked rhetorically, looking over the primitive deadly weapon.

Holan had a question. "Master Pace, didn't you sell weapons? Surely you sold them to the wrong people too?" he asked.

"Huh," nodded Pace. "Ask me about it when we get back, this isn't the place for that discussion," he curtly replied. Holan made a mental note to bring up the subject again.

"Come on," Nyk said, "let's see what's in this town, it's getting late."

"Hang on," said Pace, "we need to hide the weapons. Anyone could pick them up again." The three of them each took up a rifle, and started to dig in the dirt, using the barrel as a tool. It was tougher than it looked, the ground was nearly frozen solid. Eventually, there was a small ditch, just large enough for the three rifles, and they were each placed inside. Dirt and rocks were then kicked over the burial, until it was all covered. Pace looked down at his boots again and shook his head with a sigh.

Nyk laughed, "You'll have a hard time cleaning them now!"

"They're going in the incinerator when we get home," said Pace.

They walked over the bridge, in the direction of the town. The sunlight started to fade as they reached the first of the pot marked buildings.

"Master Pace," said Holan, "I'm sorry for speaking earlier. I had forgotten what Drake had taught me in the classroom."

"Which was?" Pace asked.

"He said that not all beings speak basic and that we may not understand each other's languages. But after we pledge allegiance to God, his light would give us the ability to understand any language, but it would also make our own voice heard in their language."

"So, you are actually listening then," said Pace, giving Holan a sideways glance. "But you are correct, that's why it's risky having you here."

Holan let out a huff and wrapped his arms around his body. He looked up towards the setting sun, "The rotations here are quite short," he said.

"There's a lot of variances on different worlds. Just accept them and keep moving forward," offered Pace as a response, not really in the mood to deal with Holan's quizzical nature.

Most of the streets were deserted or blocked with the rubble of fallen buildings. The one or two people that they did see, ignored them. They had enough to worry about, to even think about getting involved with three strangers coming into town.

Turning a corner, the street opened up into a large square, with a tall municipal building on the far side. Holan looked to his left and gagged, nearly throwing up in his mouth, quickly turning away. Nyk spun around to see what Holan had reacted to and was also repulsed by the sight. A large, crudely made set of gallows, stood in front of a library building. Five bodies hung on ropes by their necks. It looked like a whole family. The smallest, barely younger than the boys with the rifles, swayed in the breeze. Birds pecked at their exposed skin, stripping rotting flesh from the bone. Their feet having been chewed off by ravenous, homeless dogs.

"It's like they're fighting themselves," said an exasperated Nyk.

Pace just closed his eyes and whispered a short prayer for the deceased.

"Come on, let's get away from this place," said Pace, trying not to make an issue out of it in front of their young Storous.

"That building looks empty," Nyk said, after they had well and truly passed the town square. He pointed to a small, two storey dwelling, the front door only hanging on by the bottom hinge.

Having checked out the small complex, they settled in a front room with a fireplace. Nyk stacked some small kindling onto the grate in the fireplace, the larger pieces of wood, resting on top. Dry wood was found out the back, in a small bunker.

"I've been thinking," said Pace, "it's probably best to send Holan back to the Citadel." He shook his head and walked up to behind Nyk, whispering "This Calling, he's not ready for it."

Nyk nodded slowly, "I agree. There's too much evil here, and it's only getting stronger the closer we get to its lair."

Holan overheard everything and was outraged, "But, but I don't want to go, I want to fight that demon, I want to kill it." He pretended to stab something with an imaginary knife.

Both Pace and Nyk turned to face him.

"Have you not learned anything from Drake? Or even Nyk and I?" asked Pace. "We don't come here seeking vengeance!" he said, raising his voice.

"But look what we've seen, children running around with weapons. A family killed by being hung in public, why?" He shrugged. "Are these people really too scared of the authorities, to cut the bodies down and give them their proper send off? Or not brave enough to stand up to them?" shouted Holan.

Pace was surprised at Holan's words, but argued back, "You think that we see all this," he did a circle motion above his head, "and want to do nothing about it? We, Cydarions, don't do this for retribution, anger, vengeance, revenge, or any other reason you want to call it, just to get back at someone or something. We do this out of compassion, for the love of all beings! We don't go in there, guns blazing looking for a final showdown, hoping to come out the victor! We should go in there wanting to know, to understand why the devil is doing what they're doing!"

"But they're just evil, they enjoy bringing suffering and death. All so Lucifer can become more powerful. He needs to be stopped!" retorted Holan.

Pace was dumbfounded.

Nyk took over the conversation in a more soothing tone. "Don't you think that a devil should have the choice to repent?" he asked. "If they could see the error of their ways," he shrugged, "Maybe from a different perspective, they may change their ways, don't you think *that* is worth a chance?"

"IT'S KILLING ALL THESE BEINGS, WHY SHOULD THEY GET TO LIVE ONE MORE ROTATION? THEY DON'T DESERVE IT!" shouted Holan.

Nyk calmly said, "I'm sorry, but that's not faith, that's revenge. We don't work like that. Everyone deserves a second chance, to change, to see the light, don't you think?" he asked again.

"NO!" exclaimed Holan. "Sometimes, beings are past redemption, they don't deserve to live anymore! Besides, every report that I've read, the devil is killed by a Cydarion. What is it that you are so scared of now?"

"Who appointed you judge?" snapped Pace.

"God did!" said Holan, with a smirk.

"ENOUGH!" screamed Pace. "You're going back, we don't need you here!" Pace then opened a portal back to the Citadel. The green dot grew, swirling its emerald light all around the room.

"I'm sorry Holan," said Nyk, "but it's time you went back home. This place is getting too dangerous." He pointed to the portal. "We'll talk when we get back."

Holan let out a sharp sigh. "It's always later with you two. You never tell me anything, treat me like a hatchling. I'm sick of it!"

He ripped the bandages from his head; his ears snapped upright; one bent at the tip. "This isn't what I expected. I wanted action, but all you do is dodge it. Back home you were legends, heroes. Here? You're just a bunch of poltroons." His voice cut like a blade. "I'll do this my way... or not at all."

With a vicious kick, he sent a wooden chair clattering across the room. Then, without another word, he stormed through the portal, his middle claw raised in defiance-the last thing they saw before the green swirl collapsed into nothing.

Pace went to shout something back at Holan, but Nyk stopped him. "Not cool, Pace."

Pace sighed heavily and sat down. He placed his head in his hands, "I know, I know," he said, "but I'm responsible for him, for all of them, and I brought him into this!"

"It's not just your fault," Nyk said, "we're both responsible for him while he's here. Probably me more so. You have master duties to take care of, that's enough responsibility. Plus, I was the one who suggested for him to join us."

"Yeah, I know," said Pace, nodding in his hands, "you're right. I'm sure we can sort it out later. We need to concentrate on this place, it doesn't seem right. Something is off," he said.

Nyk went quiet as he finished building a fire and then struggled to light it with an old box of matches.

"Having trouble there?" Pace asked, creeping up behind Nyk, making him jump.

"I think the sticks are wet," said Nyk, shaking the box.

"Here, let me," offered Pace. Nyk moved out the way and held out his hand, the matches sitting in his palm. Pace took the matches in one hand, then with his other, he cast a small green ball of energy into the fireplace. Immediately, the wood erupted into a glowing fire.

Nyk was shocked. "You sat there, watching me struggle to light the fire, when you can do that? How long have you been able to do it?" asked a bemused Nyk.

Pace shrugged, "I've been practicing," he smirked, "looks like I'm getting better too."

"Huh!" exclaimed Nyk, "I thought we didn't have any secrets?" Then felt immediately guilty, so he changed the subject. "Hey, while you've got them, take a look at the box of fire sticks," Nyk said nodding to Pace's hand.

Pace was curious and looked down at the small box in his hand. "Oh, well that is interesting!" he said, reading the label out loud, "Lucifers matches." He laughed and mockingly said, "The light bringer?" Nyk laughed too.

They both settled in front of the fire for the night and chewed on some ration sticks.

"You know, I feel bad for Holan," said Nyk, "I should have paid him more attention."

"It's not your fault," said Pace, "I shouldn't have brought him here, that's on me," he accepted. "Maybe we're bringing the Storous' into our war too early. They are not ready for this type of conflict yet."

"Ready for this type of conflict?" Nyk questioned. "Pace, no-one is ever ready for this," he said pointing outside the window.

Pace sighed, "You're right. But Holan, he just has so many questions."

"He's just curious, he wants to learn. That's a good thing," said Nyk.

"That boy is going to cause trouble."

"He's not a child; you should encourage such an inquisitive mind."

"I don't know, I just feel he's going to cause me to question everything."

"So, this is about you?"

"No, it's just..." Pace shrugged, "I don't know, maybe his destiny isn't with us."

"Holan isn't the child he looks," said Nyk.

"Are you disagreeing with my decision?" asked Pace defensively.

"No, not at all," said Nyk, "It was the right call. I just think... I don't know, I'm confused all the time. I have so much conflict in my brain, it's hurting me."

"Yeah, me too buddy," said Pace, "me too."

"Yeah, but still..."

The silence hung in the air until they both fell asleep. Nyk, long after Pace.

The split mountain

Chapter 19

Beau and Xania were both shaken awake by a deep rumbling along the ground. They quickly found their footing, before falling over, as the whole earth dropped away from them.

"Is this you?" Beau joked at Xania, as they both got back on their feet. Her smile soon wore off when she realised the red dust was still in the air. The villagers all ran around in a panic.

"I'm going to check on the Chief and Tholeton. Xania, try and use your wind power," Beau shouted over all the chaos, as she ran off.

Xania ran out of the hut and planted her feet, she stood still, slowing her breathing and concentrated. The hairs on the back of her neck tickled as a light breeze blew past. She stretched her arms out to the side and opened her palms. Feeling the wind pick up, she mentally encouraged it. The noise changed from a whisper to a whistle, as the wind sped past, battering the wooden huts. It was working, the air was clearing.

Beau got Tholeton, the Chief, and anyone else with hair, to stand outside. Barely able to stand up straight, they had to lean into the wind, as their hair and beards flapped around. The red dust got dislodged from every follicle. No more dust flew through the village when Beau put her hand on Xania's shoulder, to let her know to stop. When Xania opened her eyes, the wind had stopped, and all was calm. Chief Soldue walked up to Xania and thanked her again.

"We have to get going," said Beau, "we need to stop this devil."

"We shall escort you through our lands," offered Tholeton.

"That's very kind of you, but we don't need..."

"Thank you, we accept," Beau interrupted, then turned to Xania and said quietly, "We can work on your powers, while they keep a look out for any danger." Xania agreed, and they were soon on their way.

A squad of men, all armed with bows and arrows. Tholeton at the front, being directed by the Cydarions, set off towards the Calling.

***

"The path that we are walking, only leads to one place." Tholeton shouted behind him, after sections of walking.

"Which is where?" asked Beau.

"The split mountain," he replied.

"Well, that sounds like our kind of place," said Beau sarcastically.

"We can't go past the first ridgeline, it is forbidden," said Tholeton.

"That's ok, it's our fight, you've done enough for us," thanked Beau. She turned to Xania, "How's the training going?"

"I'm not sure, I think I need a reason for it to work. It's not a party trick I can do when I want," Xania said.

"It's still early yet," encouraged Beau, "just have some faith."

Reaching the ridge line, the soldiers came to a halt. Tholeton offered to stay until Beau and Xania had returned, but it the Cydarions suggested that the soldiers go back to their village and wait. They both watched as all the men marched back down the pathway to the lower ground.

Beau and Xania had just gotten over the first ridge and rounded the corner, when they saw the split mountain. The tall black mountain stood like a shadow against the red sky. A split ran vertical, straight down the centre of the mountain, virtually breaking it in half. A red glow emanated from the fissure.

"This looks like the right place," said Xania, "are you ready?"

"I am, let's do this," said Beau, with determination.

It took them another couple of sections of scaling the steep mountain side before they found an entrance to the devils' lair. As they crept inside, they felt the heat radiating from the rock walls of the tunnels. They headed slowly inwards, towards the centre. The heat growing in intensity with every step. They could hear the cackles of laughter, faint at first but getting louder the deeper they ventured into the mountain. Rounding a sharp corner they saw a devil in front of them, and they froze against a dark wall. The devil was peering deep into the crevice filled with fire, burning inside the split mountain. Except, he didn't look like a devil. He looked exactly like Chief Soldue, but only half the size, standing at only eleven decimetres tall. A large head of hair and the bushy unkempt white beard. Skinny legs and wiry arms. If it wasn't for his red skin, they would have thought they were seeing things.

Beau stepped out from the darkened corridor. "Well, what the devil do we have here?" she said, mockingly. Xania stayed hidden. The devil jumped in surprise, nearly slipping from the edge and falling into the fire filled crevice.

"Who are you?" he snapped, as he turned towards Beau. He then noticed her red hair, and added, "Ah, you're one of mine." He laughed, a smug self-satisfying laugh. Beau noticed his gaze fall on her hair. Realising that the devil thought her red hair was due to his red dust of control.

"I'm here for you!" Beau said cryptically.

"Oh, you want to mate with this fine specimen?" he asked. "Let me introduce myself, my name is Furcas, I am a knight of the infernal realm. All this land you see around you is controlled by me." Furcas took a step closer to Beau. In one hand he held a long stick with two points at the end, like a fork. His other hand extended out to her, a limp wrist dangling his fingers. Beau wasn't sure if he wanted to shake her hand or have her kiss the back of his. Repulsed at the thought of her lips being near him, she chose the former. Grabbing his hand with both of hers, she summoned her magic. Blue lightning coursed through his body, inducing him to convulsions and uncontrollable movements.

Beau shouted to Xania, "Finish him!"

Xania ran over, one sai withdrawn from its holster, and up in the air ready to strike. Furcas saw the threat coming, and with a painful movement, he raised the fork above his head and dropped it. The fork hit the solid rock and vibrated. The prongs sending out a high-pitched screech, echoing throughout the cavern. Xania stopped running and fell to the floor, her hands covered her ears. Beau's lightning dissipated as she too, fell on the floor in pain, covering her ears. Furcas quickly gathered up his fork and struck it again on the ground, renewing the high-pitched screech. Laughing, he ran off into the mountain tunnels. As the high-pitched screech faded into the distance, Xania and Beau slowly regained their senses.

Beau got to her feet. "Son of a..."

"Listen!" interrupted Xania. The two of them stood still, the silence now being penetrated by a deep roar echoing through the mountain. From below them, hot air rose from the crevice and started to fill the cavern.

"Let's move!" Xania shouted, and they both ran after Furcas.

A thunderous roar bellowed out from below. Then, in front of them, climbing out of the fiery crevice, emerged a green dragon.

"That's not normal," stated Xania, "any ideas?"

Beau shrugged. "Kill it?"

"Thanks for that wisdom!" replied Xania. The dragon spotted the Cydarions and let out a jet of fire from its mouth. Xania and Beau both leapt to their left. The only safe place at the time.

"Down that tunnel," Beau said, pointing to one side. They both scrambled to their feet and sprinted into the tunnel, just as another jet of fire scorched the ground on where they had just stood. They ran away from the dragon, towards a feint light in the distance. Getting closer to the light, they realised it was an opening. Reaching it, they skidded to a stop and looked down. Sharp rocks jutting upwards were the only things to be seen.

"That dragon will be right behind us," Xania stated.

"I know, but this opening, there's probably a star ship here somewhere," said Beau.

There was a down draft of wind from outside the entrance.

"Probably for that," Xania said, pointing passed Beau, towards the green dragon, slowly flapping its wings and descending to their level. It was too late to run back into the tunnel, as the dragon opened its mouth, fire building up inside. Beau closed her eyes and waited for the inevitable.

Fire exploded towards them, just as a whistling came through the tunnel. A strong wind blew straight passed the Cydarions and met the fierce flames. Stopping them from reaching its target. Beau opened her eyes, expecting to have been burnt by now. She realised Xania was saving them both by controlling the wind. Beau's eye turned electric blue, and her hair stood on end, as she summoned all the power she could muster. She sent a continuous streak of lightning through the fire and into the dragons' mouth. Its head started to shake, its eyes bulged, then exploded, extinguishing the flames. One wing twitched and stopped beating. The dragon fell, twisting and turning all the way down. It landed with a squelch on the sharp rocks below, impaling its body. The head hit another sharp rock and exploded. A ball of flames erupted, and the smoke rose high into the sky. The Cydarions peered over the edge.

"We work well together," said Xania.

"There's still that devil to deal with yet," said Beau. With caution, they headed back into the mountain and again, followed the Calling. Soon coming across him again, they kept out of sight. He had his back to them and was waving the fork over the crevice, muttering in devilish.

"He's still got that fork," whispered Beau, "We need to get it from him before he can make that noise again."

"You could always flirt with him," Xania said sarcastically.

Beau didn't rise to the bait. "Can you disable his hand?"

Xania slowly pulled a sai from her belt and twisted it in her hand, "Not a problem."

As they both stepped out from the darkness, Xania aimed and threw her sai. It flew straight as an arrow, knuckle first and smashed into the hand of Furcas. A crack of broken bones was heard, and Furcas let out an almighty scream. Releasing his grip on the fork, it fell to the ground, the handle hitting first. It bounced, levelling itself up horizontally and hit the floor again landing on the edge of the crevice, its prongs hanging over the chasm.

Furcas turned to see what had happened and stumbled over his forked weapon, kicking it into the abyss. It clanged and clattered all the way down, the high-pitched screech fading as it fell deeper and deeper.

"No!" shouted Furcas. "What have you done?"

"Give up Furball, you're done," said Beau.

"It's Furcas! And you don't understand," he said, "my fork will set off an eruption, that only my beloved Valdemar could control!" Furcas' expression changed, "But you just killed him!"

"That dragon was your pet?" mocked Beau. Furcas made a run for it, back into the shadows. Xania and Beau both looked at each other and sighed. A scuffling noise was heard, and out from the shadows, emerged Furcas atop a small pale animal. Standing at only six decimetres high, Furcas had to lift his feet off the floor to stop them being dragged along. He kicked the animal on its rear, and it galloped away. Except, the galloping was not much faster than walking pace.

Beau burst out laughing. "What's this, a comedy?" Xania laughed too. But both were soon silenced, as the whole mountain rumbled and shook. Spits of fire and lava boiled up the crevice. Another tremble, more violent this time, knocked Beau and Xania off their feet. Furcas fell off his stead, the animal carried on without him. Furcas climbed to his feet, and looked back at the Cydarions, snarling. A large blob of lava burst up from the crevice and landed on top of him, burying Furcas under molten rock.

Beau blinked. "Okay, I didn't see that coming."

"We need to get out of here," said Xania.

"Follow that animal, it looks like he knows the way," said Beau.

"Hopefully it's the right way," Xania added. They circled the magma Furcas was now buried under.

"You think he's gone?" asked Beau looking down.

"Yep, the Calling has stopped."

"Huh, I never noticed," said Beau.

They ran after the animal, using the walls to stop themselves from falling over amid the worsening quakes and rumbles. Lava started erupting from the top of the split mountain, just as the animal led the girls down a stone stairway, carved into the side of the rock. Reaching the bottom of the mountain, they found the path back to Chief Soldue's village. The mountain soon far behind them, spewing smoke high into the air, lava oozing out from its broken side.

The villagers welcomed the two back into their homes, and Chief Soldue called a meeting of all the elders, Xania and Beau being their special guests.

The Cydarions explained that Furcas and his dragon had been contaminating the red dirt with black magic, it was a way older devils used to control their subjects. It took too long for Lucifer to teach this method now, so now they use different ways to achieve a similar outcome.

Furcas was one of the old ones, probably been here for cycles. He made his home in the volcano. Using his fork and Valdemar, he stoked the fire. But instead of the lava blowing up through the inside of the volcano, and out, he redirected the energy back underground, making the ground burp and covering everyone in the red dust.

"We are sorry for wrecking the mountain," Xania said apologetically.

"No, this is a good thing," replied Chief Soldue. "We have a prophecy. When the broken mountain heals itself, our world will heal itself," he said smiling.

"Erm, I think we blew it up though," said Beau.

"Again, you are wrong," he said. "My scouts tell me that the lava is filling the cracks in the mountain side, and when it cools, it will be healed. Not only have you saved us, but you have also fulfilled our prophecy. We will be forever thankful to you." He bowed his head out of respect. Xania and Beau felt a little embarrassed. "We will also send two people to each of the other villages, to explain about this red dust and give word about the mountain. This will be an era of peace." There was a pause and Chief Soldue looked to the ground. "Also, the one that fell from the sky with you..."

"Daemich?" Beau jumped in.

"Yes, this, Daemich," Chief Soldue said, "Our soldiers found his body, washed up by the shore."

Xania gasped. The Chief put his hand on hers. "We have buried him with our soldiers; he is at peace now!" he said.

"Can you show us?" asked Beau.

"Of course, please follow me," said the Chief. He exited the village meeting and took the Cydarions to the soldiers' burial square. Xania and Beau both knelt and said their respective prayers. Beau quickly wiped away a tear.

"We should we take his body back with us," said Xania. "We do have a place for fallen Cydarions."

Beau shook her head. "He wasn't a Cydarion, he was still a Storous, they don't get the same burial rights." Beau looked around, then spoke directly to Xania, "Look around you, Xania, what do you see?"

Xania took a look around. "The graves of soldiers?" she questioned.

"Yes, he was our soldier. What else do you see?" asked Beau.

Xania looked again, not seeing anything different. She looked up, down and all around, then shrugged. "Just empty land," she said.

Beau smiled and nodded. "That's what he wanted, to run around, free of any burden."

Xania's jaw started to tremble, "He got his wish," she said, before falling to her knees and crying.

Beau bent down beside Xania and put an arm around her. "He's at peace now."

Xania shook her head and mumbled, "Anyone who looks out for me, dies."

Beau was confused, "What do you mean?"

"My parents died to protect me, then Phos and Jodrell both died, and now Swift is gone."

"Swift is dead?" asked Beau, "When?"

"I found out just before coming here," sobbed Xania.

"Shit! That's why you were in a bad mood," said Beau, "Why didn't you say anything?" Xania looked at Beau apologetically. "Oh yeah, the you and me thing."

Xania looked down at the ground and her posture loosened. "Hey, that stuff is in the past. You and me, we're good," said Beau.

Xania rested her head against Beau's shoulder as she slowly stopped crying. "Why are we sent on these never-ending Callings, one after another, after another?" she wondered.

"To save each planet from..."

"Lucifers offspring," Xania finished. "But there's got to be more to it than that though. I mean, why not send us to Lucifer himself and finish him. End all the suffering?"

"I guess that is the bigger question," said Beau. "You know, Daemich asked me a similar question after we got here. Maybe it's time we found out?" Xania nodded an agreement. "Besides, if it wasn't for this Calling, this wouldn't have happened." Beau squeezed Xania's shoulders tight.

Xania smiled, "I guess each Calling has its own purpose."

"Exactly!" said Beau, "We just have to figure out what that purpose is." She stood up and extended her arm to pull Xania to her feet. "Come on, we need to get home." Suggesting that they should work on honing their powers, whenever they can.

Xania and Beau both said their goodbyes to the villagers, vowing to come back every cycle, to pay their respects to Daemich, and to keep in touch with the village.

Xania opened a portal before they both walked into the green haze and disappeared.

Klein Marzhens church

Chapter 20

Nyk was awoken by Pace poking at the remaining embers in the fireplace, the sun had just poked its light through a gap in the window coverings. A cup of hot herbed water was waiting for him on a small side table. He looked at it.

"How long have you been awake?" he asked.

"A while, I fell asleep just about straight away. I had such a good rest. What about you?" Pace asked, more out of reaction than of meaning.

Nyk hesitated. "Erm, yeah. Me too," he lied.

"Well drink up buddy, we've got some walking to do."

Nyk took a deep breath. "Pace, can we talk?" he asked nervously. *I have to say something; I can't go on like this.*

"Sure, what's up?" said Pace, a look of concern on his face.

Nyk swallowed hard, his palms became clammy, and he had to put a hand on his knee to stop it from shaking. "I, I keep thinking..."

Suddenly there was a crash by the back door and Pace jumped up, looking out the window.

"Yeah, keep that thought buddy. I think we should get moving, now."

Nyk nearly cried, he had to dig his fingernails into his thighs before swallowing his emotions. He nodded to himself. *It can wait.* He finished his brew and collected his things, before stepping into the cool brisk morning air.

As they made their way through the small town, a sweet smell came wafting from a side street, catching their attention. They both sniffed at the air and turned towards each other.

"That smells good, wanna check it out?" offered Pace.

A smiling Nyk nodded in agreement. "Yep, I sure do."

They turned into the side street and came across a small outlet. The windows were boarded up, but a line of people, queued outside the doorway.

Pace snorted, "Looks like we're not the only ones who have found this place."

The queue of five people quickly went down to two. More people had joined behind them, although every one of them eyed the Cydarions suspiciously. Nyk, noticing this, whispered to Pace,

"Is it my hair? Does it look a mess?"

Pace burst out laughing, enough to make the people in front of them turn around and give them a look of disgust. No one else cracked a smile. The two stayed quiet until they reached the front of the queue.

"Two of your baked goods, please," Pace asked the baker politely.

The baker looked a little confused. "Able schtrutel?" he asked. Pace didn't know what that was, but nodded enthusiastically, enough to satisfy the baker. The baker promptly handed over two apple strudels, wrapped separately in newspaper. Pace went to pay but assumed that this dated planet wouldn't accept intergalactic credits yet. The only other form of currency he had were small strips of gold. So, he handed a strip over the baker, who looked at it for a fraction, even bit into it, then tried to return it to Pace.

"I cannot accebt zis. It iss too much. I haffe nien change," said the baker. Nyk had already taken a bite out of the pastry. Pace wrapped both his hands around the bakers open palm and gently closed it, keeping the gold strip inside.

"It is for you, heck, get everyone in this queue whatever they want. It would be enough, right?" Pace said warmly. A look of astonishment crossed the bakers face, and he slowly started to nod.

"Ja, ja," he said, beaming with joy. Then shouted to the rest of the queue, that their ration books were not needed today. There was a small eruption of joy in the shop as Nyk and Pace walked away, happily eating an apple strudel.

"This is really good," said Nyk between mouthfuls of the pastry

Pace nodded, "Drake would love this." The pair finished eating as they exited the town and walked down a dusty road, open farmland sprawled out on either side.

Every now and again, they had to take cover from the air vehicles passing overhead, occasionally dropping explosive devices. It took their wits and resolve to make good progress during the rotation.

As the temperature started to drop again, Pace pointed ahead, slightly to the left. "Look, there's a shaft of light," he shrugged, "maybe we should head there? I feel it will be a safe place to rest for the night."

Nyk agreed and suggested taking a path off the road, which seemed to head straight towards the shaft of light, and another small village.

A further quarter section of walking, they found themselves in front of an old house of prayer.

Pace smiled. "Nice solid building," he said.

"Let's see if anyone's home."

The surrounding grass that covered the church grounds lay home to various weathered tombstones. Nyk read a few of them solemnly, he could almost hear their long-lost voices. The main building was made from solid stone, with a slate pitched roof. The entrance held a bell tower and some sort of clock face, that neither of them understood. The main section of the building was wide bodied, with a few coloured windows. The rear wall had a semi-circular apse to finish off the building. Pace cautiously tried the front door, it was unlocked. Slowly, he pushed the one of the wooden doors open, until there was enough room for them to step inside. It seemed empty. Thanking their lucky stars, they lit a couple of candles with the Lucifer matches they had kept, and meditated by the altar.

They didn't know how long they were meditating for, before they were alerted to a noise behind them. They sprung to their feet and spun around. An older human with greying hair and a matching moustache, stood in the doorway. He wore a black cassock with black thin-soled shoes.

"Don't be afraid," said Pace, holding his hands up to the stranger.

The man stepped forward and answered, "I am nicht afraid," he said, "How kan I help you?" he asked.

"Oh, we just needed a place to rest our heads a while, we won't be any bother," Pace replied honestly.

"Zzat iss nicht vhy you are here, iss it?" questioned the man.

"Erm, I'm sorry," questioned Pace, "what do you mean?" He glanced at Nyk, who just shrugged.

The man in black, took a few steps closer, then paused, "May I?" he asked, gesturing to the pathway in front of him.

"Please, yes," Pace nodded, feeling at ease.

The man moved, slowly walking and talking. "Mein name iss Heinrich, I am ze priest here." Soon, he was stood in front of Pace and held out his hand.

Pace nodded and held out his own hand. "Pleased to meet you Heinrich," he said, as they shook hands. Pace introduced themselves, "I am Pace, and this is Nyk," he said, gesturing beside him.

Heinrich stared straight into Pace's eyes without flinching. Nyk took up the conversation, "Heinrich, it's very nice to meet you," he said, "we are travellers, a long way from here. We're just looking for somewhere safe to rest. Would that be okay?" he asked.

The priest clapped his hands together in excitement, "Of kourse you kan, but nicht in here, it gets kold. Come mitt me, mein vife has made fegetable schtew. It vould be our honour if you schtayed for dinner," Heinrich offered.

Pace smiled and looked at Nyk, who nodded enthusiastically, even rubbing his belly to show hunger. The two of them followed Heinrich out of the stone building and into a smaller two storey stone dwelling just outside the church grounds. They got introduced to Heinrichs wife and all of them sat down around a small wooden dining table. Heinrich gave grace, before everyone heartily ate all their food. Nyk said that it was one of the best stews he had ever tasted. Even though he knew it to be a lie. The meal was very watered-down vegetables, but he appreciated the effort more than the taste in these trying times.

After the table was cleared away by Heinrichs wife, she stayed in the kitchen to clean up.

Pace started the conversation again, "Heinrich, do you mind me asking, why do you keep staring into my eyes? You did it when we met, and you've been doing it all mealtime."

"Oh, I'm sorry, I did nicht intendz fur you to be uncomfortable," said Heinrich.

"Not uncomfortable," Pace said, "I just wondered." He shrugged and gave a smile.

"I see your light," said Heinrich slowly, "You vere sent here, vasn't you?" he said. Pace glanced at Nyk, who in turn just looked back at Pace, expressionless.

Pace looked back to Heinrich. "Erm, I'm not sure what you mean," he replied.

"God sent you!" stated Heinrich. "I speak to him too," he admitted, then made the sign of a cross on his body and blessed himself.

Pace sat back in his chair, and cryptically asked, "Why would you think that?"

"I vas vriding out mein sermon fur ze next serfice, zhen I heart a foice. It said to me, 'And zus you schall greet him: Peace be to you, undt peace be to your house, undt peace be to all zat you haf. Samuel ferse twenty-fife khapter six.' It vas zhen I got an ofervelmingkt urge to enter ze khurch. Ven I saw you; I knew it vas a sign!" explain Heinrich.

"It does sound like the words we would say," agreed Pace.

"Vere are you from?" Heinrich asked straight out.

Pace wasn't sure whether to be honest or not, but Nyk was more straight forward, "A small moon plant called El' Azar. We are Cydarions," he said.

"Zydarions? Aliens?" asked the priest. Pace had noticed something sitting on the side counter, a bottle of liquid, called Whiskey. He made an assumption that it was alcohol, so he got up, collected three glasses and poured each of them a drink. All of them had downed one small shot before Heinrich's wife came out of the kitchen and announced she was going to bed. Waiting until she had left the room, Pace poured another round of drinks.

The conversation started up again and both Nyk and Pace regaled Heinrich with some history of the Cydarions, as well as their own recent skirmishes. The priest hung on every word, but to Paces' surprise, he was less interested in alien species and their worlds, than he was about working with God. Heinrich admitted, that being a Cydarion was not something he could do himself, even when he was younger and healthier.

"I prefer to spread ze vort uff God, nicht spill ze blood," he said.

Nyk nodded in understanding the older man's preference. "I feel the same way, sometimes," he admitted.

Pace asked a question, "So, Heinrich, why do *you* think we are here?"

"To banisch ze defil, aren't you?" answered Heinrich with a little smug grin.

Pace nodded. "Yes, but why is there a war out there?" he asked, pointing at a blank wall, adorned with only a wooden cross.

Heinrich explained, "Ven Hitler kame to power, he vanted to make Germany great again. An all-powerful, all konqferingkt Germany! At first ve all vent along mitt it. Zen, he persecuted ze chews, a vhole race! He vanted to exterminate zem all. Zen, he infaded Polent, claimingkt ze lent to be rightfully German. Next it vas Denmark, Norway, Belgium, zze list goes on. It vas awful. Mein two boys got sent to fight zis var, his var!" He went quiet and swallowed hard.

Taking another sip of Whiskey, he spoke quietly, "Zey von't be komingk home!" He wiped away two tears. "I only allow meinself two tears, ein fur each uff mein boys." He stopped to compose himself from breathing hard before carrying on. "I kan't affort a tear fur efery person lost to zis var. I pray efery night fur all zis to schtop!" He looked at Pace, "Mein prayer has been answered, nein?" Heinrich asked.

Pace smiled and placed a hand on top of Heinrich's. "We shall do what we can," he said.

"Fery vell," said Heinrich with a smile. He paused for a thought, "It iss time I vent to bed. Pleaze make yourselfes komfortable. I vill be up at ze krack uff dawn, I bid you farewell."

They all said a goodnight and settled down for a well-deserved rest. Again, Nyk couldn't settle, his mind was playing tricks on him. The sun was nearly up before Nyk finally fell asleep, mentally exhausted.

Russian bridge blockade

Chapter 21

By the time Pace had woken Nyk, there was a pot of tea on the dining table, along with a hard-boiled egg and one slice of bread each.

"This, all this is very kind of you Heinrich, you didn't have to do anything," said a thankful Pace.

After breakfast and some small talk, the Cydarions bade their farewells. "There's a long road ahead," said Nyk. Heinrich nodded and offered to pray for them.

As Nyk and Pace exited the property, Heinrich wondered, "May I ask ein more zingkt? How do you do zis, time after time?"

Pace turned back to face Heinrich. "How do you get through this war, with everything that's going on and everything you know, how do *you* get through it?" he asked back.

"Mein faizz, Master Pace, mein faizz gets me zrough, day after day," answered Heinrich.

Pace placed his hands gently onto Heinrichs shoulders and looked him in the eyes one last time. "Faith," said Pace, "We have faith too, faith in God, faith in each other and faith in you, my friend. You're a good man Heinrich, look after yourself." With that, Pace turned and followed Nyk out of the village.

It wasn't long before they were immersed in the countryside again, staying just off the muddy roadways. Despite a few setbacks, of the military kind, the Cydarions made good progress before the sun was too high. Eventually they arrived at a man-made waterway with no way across except for an arched stone bridge, occupied by military personnel. All dressed in olive-green, long-sleeved jackets with red collars, matching trousers and calf length boots. A slewed hat and a brown leather utility belt. As the two approached the roadblock, a youngish man held up a hand for them to stop.

"Vare are uh goeeng?" demanded the man, stepping closer to Nyk. Close enough that Nyk could smell his bad breath. A name tag said, Dorokhov!

"Hey man, we're just going for a nice walk," said Nyk.

"Vhy?" snapped Dorokhov, in the same angry tone.

"Why not?" Nyk said with a shrug.

"Not audzhorized, no papers! Go back!" demanded Dorokhov. Nyk took a step closer, but the soldier brought his gun up.

Nyk quickly backed off, but his smile never wavered. He gave Pace a smirk, that told the Master, 'I've got this.'

Pace mumbled under his breath, "I hope you do buddy; I hope you do." He had noticed a small barrier blocking their way. But the barrier was the least of their problems: Six more soldiers with guns. Although, they seemed more interested in playing cards on an upturned wooden box and smoking a small white stick, than to bother with a couple of strangers. He knew he would normally be able to take on a situation like this, with Nyk, and their usual weapons. But this was a different place and time. *Play by the rules Pace,* he told himself. Then he spotted something that made him whistle in appreciation. Two armoured vehicles with tracks on either side rolling up the bridge. They were painted the same olive green as the soldier's uniforms, with a swivel turret, containing a considerable barrel at nearly fifty decimetres in length. *That could do some damage,* he thought to himself. He also ran through several scenarios in his head, of how to get out of here if he had to.

Option one, take on the guards, head on, at full speed. *Only* if he got the shout from Nyk, except that wouldn't be fair, him taking on six while Nyk only had the one to deal with.

Option two, accept defeat and walk away. Try to find another way across the water further up. Although we could be faced with the same situation. That's common warfare, control your bridges.

Option three, jump off the bridge into the water and swim for the other side. But that would give the soldiers too much time to fire at us or just pick us up from the shore.

Option four, walk away, wait until dark, and then swim quietly across. That would be the least desirable of the options. A cold swim is not appealing.

Which brought him back to the unfair option one. He tensed his body and surveyed the area, looking for any little detail which could help. He was ready to make his move.

"Pace, c'mon, they're letting us through," said Nyk. Pace came out of his thoughts with a shake of his head. The barrier lifted and Nyk motioned for Pace to get moving. As soon as he caught up with Nyk, he had to ask,

"How did you...?"

Nyk cut him off, "Smile, nod and walk on," he said through a gritted teeth smile. Pace smiled and nodded to all the guards too, not knowing what was happening. But he did admit that it was a lot easier than any of the scenarios he had thought of.

They kept walking until the soldiers, bridge and armoured vehicles were all out of sight, although their smiles had diminished as soon as they had passed the last guard.

Pace turned to Nyk, "So, how did you get us through that one?" he asked, clearly impressed.

Nyk laughed to himself. "You haven't noticed?" he said.

Pace looked Nyk up and down, then shook his head, "Nope, care to elaborate?"

Nyk pulled up a trouser leg, exposing a military grade boot running up his calf.

"You swapped your boots?" Pace asked in disbelief.

Nyk nodded. "Yep, these are made out of Kirza," he said.

"What's kirza?" asked Pace.

"I've no idea," said Nyk with a laugh.

Pace laughed too. "So, swapping your boots for a shittier boot, they just let us through?"

"Um, not exactly," said Nyk, "we bartered and eventually settled on an exchange."

"What kind of exchange Nyk?" asked Pace, a little worried.

"Erm, they wanted seven German women, bought to them," said Nyk.

"What?"

"Don't worry, we're not doing that!" said Nyk, "I had to give him my chronometer as a deposit. He thinks it's a western watch, whatever that means."

"So, basically you swapped boots because you liked them and then gave them your chronometer, which makes no sense on this planet, as a bribe?" said Pace.

"Um, yeah," Nyk snorted, and they both laughed.

The laughing didn't last long, for further into the city they walked, the more they were faced with the absolute destruction of rows upon rows of buildings. The vague carcasses of homes and shops stood dormant, their roofs caved in, the windows smashed, and their frames broken. There were no animals in sight, not even a bird.

"This is much worse than the villages we have already passed through," said Nyk.

"The evil, it's feeling much stronger than I've experienced before," said Pace. "As for the Calling, we're not that far away."

A distant noise grew louder and louder, soon changing into a growl, the growl turned into individual engines above them. Flying machines, dropping explosives!

"Find cover!" Pace shouted, as soon as he realised what they were. They both moved for cover. Nyk crouched down and hid under a steel beam on one side of the road, whilst Pace jumped down a nearby small chute at ground level. The bombs were dropped, and explosions rattled the ground. The two Cydarions feared for their lives. After what felt like sections, the noise faded, and the vibrations settled. The buildings had stopped collapsing, and all was quiet again.

Nyk emerged first, looking around in disbelief, *so much destruction*. He had to dust himself down. With no one else around, he started calling out for Pace. They located each other, and Nyk had to clear some rubble away from the chute that Pace had jumped into. Nyk realised exactly what Pace had taken refuge in,

"You sly hound," Nyk said with a laugh, "I thought I was the one who liked a tankard of mead?"

"Very funny Nyk, now help me outta here," said Pace, offering up his hand.

Before long they were walking through more deserted streets, the destruction of the buildings getting worse. The debris on the roads had been swept to the sides, like a snowplough. Piles of rubble, that were once people's homes, were now completely destroyed.

The sun had started to set, but the Cydarions made the decision not to stop. To carry on to the end, tonight.

"Can you smell that?" asked Nyk.

"Yep, maybe a sewage line is broken?" offered Pace. A few more streets of walking and the smell only got worse. Nyk started to gag.

"It's awful, that's no sewage line, Pace," said Nyk. By the end of the next street, they saw it, something that immediately burned straight into their memories, a memory they'd rather not have.

Bodies, human bodies. By the hundreds of them. The further walked, the more bodies they came across. Every one of them, disformed, disfigured or desecrated. Some, reaching out in the throes of life, some holding younglings, or just each other. All of them had been killed, their innocent lives gone. The decay and wretchedness were overwhelming. Nyk was ashamed, feeling as though all this was somehow his fault.

Pace was like a radar, "The Calling is this way," he said pointing slightly to the right.

"Do you not see what's around you?" said Nyk.

Pace, a little taken aback by Nyks accusation, replied, "Of course I do! But what do you want me to do? Raise the dead? I can't do that. What I can do, is keep focused and hopefully stop anymore of this from happening. But I do need your help."

"Right, right, I get it. I'm with you," agreed Nyk, "let's keep going!" He nodded, his mind not fully focused. By now the sun had fully set, but the sound of warfare relentlessly carried on

The Cydarions unknowingly walked right into a gunfight. Pace suggested that they get off the streets if they can. They found a building with access to the roof, and made their way slowly across some rooftops, the ones that were still standing, to avoid the deadly bullets. Eventually they had to climb back down the ruined walls, luckily behind the defending army.

Pace pointed across to a courtyard. "See that entrance? That's our lair. Are you ready for this?" he asked Nyk.

Nyk nodded. "What's your plan for getting across there?" Nyk asked, referring to four soldiers patrolling the area.

"Stick to my side," offered Pace. They both stepped into the open, immediately a voice called out to them, from their right.

"Halt!"

Adolf Hitler

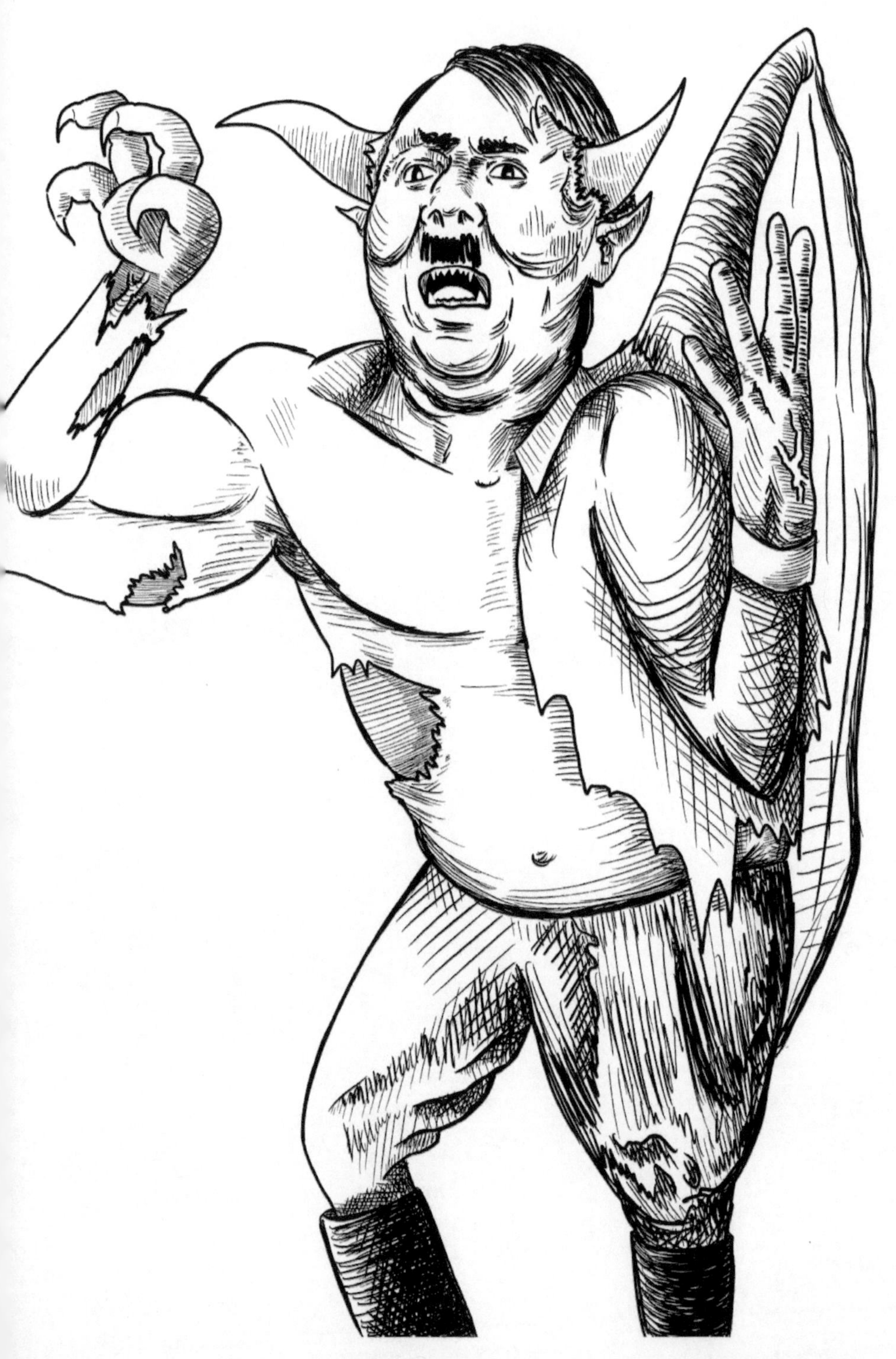

Chapter 22

"Ignore them," whispered Pace, although he did increase his speed, Nyk stayed close by his side.

"Stop!" shouted the voice again. The Cydarions didn't look over in that direction. Pace flicked his right wrist, a black bracelet sprung to life, and a translucent blue shield flashed on. Covering the height of Pace and Nyk, its energy emanating from the wrist band. At that exact moment, a volley of bullets rang out and impacted the blue shield, its hue flickered with every ricochet.

"I didn't think we were to use our technology here?" said Nyk.

"Needs must!" answered Pace, as they quickly entered into the walled garden. The firing ceased as soon as they entered that courtyard and Pace deactivated the shield. Looking across, they saw a steel door, the entrance to the lair.

"What's your idea for this one?" asked Nyk, nodding towards the door, as they approached.

Pace pulled out his favourite weapon, his yonca fighting implement, and smiled knowingly. Muscle memory made Nyk try the door handle.

'CLICK,' it was open!

"You still wanna use that?" Nyk smirked, looking at the weapon in Pace's hand. Pace stowed the yonca fighting implement again, and they crept in, down some concrete steps, and into a small corridor. It was quiet as they followed the Calling, turning into the third room on the right, straight into two guards. Dark grey military uniforms with black lapels and badges that pronounced 'SS' on their chest. Nyk and Pace quickly and quietly, immobilised the surprised guards, leaving them unconscious in two chairs by a desk. Pace and Nyk burst through the next door, into a sitting room. The devil, in human form stood with a woman, by a long comfortable seat.

"Give yourself up, devil!" Pace said sternly.

"Nein!" replied Hitler.

"Vho iss zis?" asked the female.

"Ma'am, this person is not who you think he is, he is deceiving you," replied Nyk.

Pace threatened Hitler, "Release these people from your grasp, and you may survive!"

Hitler responded, all too quickly, "I am Ze Fuhrer, zese are mein people, undt zis iss mein lent. I vill nefer surrender. Nicht to ze allied powers, nicht to zem chews undt kertainly nicht to you!" he scoffed.

"Then we are left with no choice," said Nyk, pulling out his blaster and pointing it at Hitler. He spotted a three headed dog, lying dead on the floor, its drool of poison puddled underneath its muzzle. "You killed your own dog, why?" Nyk asked, exasperated.

Hitler started to turn into his natural red form, the grey uniform burning away in places, his pistol and belt dropped to the floor. A large, ugly, red beast now stood before the Cydarions. A disfigured face, nearly too grotesque to look upon. Broken horns on its head, dry, cracked red skin. Its jaw protruded past a flat nose. He had a strong body and two thick legs, ending in large claws that poked out from its ripped boots, scratching independently on the bare concrete floor.

The woman screamed at the sight of this hideous devil. The devil, in defence, raised his arms above his head, to attack Nyk, accidently knocking the woman to the ground.

"I am Asmodeus! Ruler of all this land," the devil shouted, his fake accent now gone.

"I think Lucifer will have something to say about that," said Pace.

"I am not scared of my own father; my armies could destroy him!" sneered Asmodeus. Before anyone could say another word, the female grabbed for the pistol and scrambled to her feet.

"Adolf, vhat happened. I lofed you!" she said. But just as the devil opened his mouth to answer, she flinched, and accidentally pulled the trigger. Asmodeus was shot in the mouth and fell to the floor. In fright, the woman dropped the gun and ran out of the room, past Nyk and Pace. They looked at each other in disbelief.

"What just happened?" asked Nyk. In the confusion, they missed Asmodeus scramble onto all fours, a dislocated jaw hanging from his face. He barged through the Cydarions, knocking them both to the ground.

They were soon back on their feet as they heard the scraping of claws on concrete, the devil was escaping up the steps.

"Shit!" Nyk exclaimed, both of them racing after the devil.

Asmodeus reached the top of the stairs and ran out into the darkness. He spotted the woman straight away, the human he had loved, in his own way, Eva. She was standing in a small crater, tears streaming down her face. Her arms stretched out wide, as though she was presenting herself as a target. He ran over and embraced her. She screamed again, still not recognising this devil, and tried to fight him off, but he was too strong.

Nyk and Pace arrived in the doorway witnessing the event.

"Let her go, Asmodeus, she has no part in this," shouted Pace, pulling out his weapon.

The devil relocated its jaw with a free hand and spoke, "Never! I shall prevail, it is you who has lost, I am the god here!" his anger rose, along with his body heat. A lick of flame erupted from his head. Eva screamed in pain as her skin started to burn, from the devil's tight grip on her.

Pace noticed, behind the devil, a projectile headed towards them. "Get down!" he said to Nyk. They both took cover behind the steel door, as the projectile exploded directly on impact with Asmodeus, creating a fireball. Burning liquid covered the devil and the seemingly innocent Eva. Asmodeus let out a spine-chilling scream. In his rage, the devil made things worse, producing more flames and heat. Instantly realising he was finished; the devil placed a clawed hand across Eva's screaming mouth and pulled her in tight. They were soon engulfed in a mass of flames, burning as hot as a furnace. Nyk and Pace kept their distance, covered by the steel door; there was nothing they could do now.

The fire eventually dissipated in the cool night air, and all that was left were unrecognizable ashes, the two bodies had burnt down beyond their bones.

"Damn, she didn't have to die!" said Nyk, as they inspected the pit. His words were no sooner out of his mouth when, a shock wave of white vapour exploded from the charred remains, spreading out in all directions. Nyk and Pace were knocked off their feet, the mist like substance expanded, penetrating everything in its path. Buildings, trees, machines and all life forms. It was the light of God being spread, the tyranny of one individual was over.

Nyk and Pace got to their feet. "Why did God take so long to bring us here?" Nyk asked in bewilderment.

Pace placed a hand on Nyk's shoulder. "We're in tough times Nyk, he has a lot to keep track of," he said, trying to reassure Nyk.

Nyk wasn't having it. "Don't you think this place would be flashing like a red fucking beacon to him?" he shouted, anger building. "Look how much destruction there is."

Pace didn't reply, no words would help right now.

"WHY?" Nyk screamed at God, into the dark sky above.

"Nyk, pray with me," Pace said.

"Here?" Nyk asked, a little stunned.

"Yes, and now," Pace replied slowly. With a huff, Nyk sat with Pace in the garden and let out a quiet prayer.

It did have the desired effect, Nyk slowly calmed down.

"I'm sure life on this planet will never be the same again," said Nyk, "at least the worst is over with." He let out a sigh.

"Is it?" Pace wondered, looking around.

Nyk opened a portal back home, then turned to Pace, "What do you mean?"

"I don't know," said Pace with a shrug, "I just feel that these beings will never learn their lesson. We may have to return." He nodded to himself. Pace stepped through the portal. Nyk inhaled sharply, the retched stench caught in his throat, and he closed his eyes. The images of hundreds of dead bodies occupied his mind, boys in uniforms protecting their town, public hangings, Holan disillusioned with everything, and an innocent woman burning to death. So many innocents! He opened his eyes, took two steps, and left that world behind.

The images stayed. The voices rose, sharper and closer, accusing him until they filled his skull. The portal slammed shut. Nyk blew past Pace, nearly taking him off his feet, and sprinted down the Citadel corridor towards his room, head bowed, tears burning behind his lids. "Get out," he chocked, over and over, a mantra against the noise.

He hit the door switch with the heel of his hand and slid inside. The room was a pocket of black; only the faint halo of a datapad painted the desk. He folded into a chair, sweat slicking down his neck, breaths coming in ragged, shallow bursts. His body started to rock on its own, a small, desperate motion. He let the voices agree with him, let them tear him down until his shoulders trembled.

When the rocking slowed, he reached for the G16 blaster. Cold metal met his palm like a promise. He brought the barrel to his mouth and bit down. Iron on tongue, the taste of danger. His hand shook as he found the charge switch and thumbed it. The sound of the small ignition click was tiny in the dark, but to Nyk, it sounded like the answer.

***

Pace raised his hand to knock on Nyk's door when a sound froze him: the sharp, electric hiss of a weapon charging. He knew that sound. Too well. It had haunted him since his days as a dealer, burned into his memory like shrapnel. No hesitation. He slammed the override, and the door hissed open.

Nyk sat slumped in the chair, a blaster wedged between his teeth, the ready-light pulsing red. His eyes flicked up-wide and broken, the eyes of a terrified child-before rolling back.

Pace lunged. He ripped the weapon free just as Nyk's finger clenched. The bolt spat upward, scorching past Nyk's cheek and burning a hole in the ceiling. The smell of charred ozone filled the room.

Nyk stared, stunned, trembling, still wearing that same frightened look.

Pace powered down the blaster with careful hands, prying it from Nyk's slick grip. His voice came soft, steady, as though speaking to a wounded animal. "Nyk... are you with me?"

Nyk's lips moved, barely a whisper. "Pace?"

"I'm here, buddy. I'm right here," Pace said, his own eyes wet now, voice breaking under the weight of it.

***

Nyk's head and shirt was soaked, but his mouth was dry. His voice came out as a rasp. "I... I... I..." he stammered, then collapsed forward into Pace's arms.

Pace caught him without thinking, wrapping him up, holding him tight. Not just to steady him, but to keep him from falling.

They stayed like that for a long time. No words. Just shaking shoulders and quiet sobs, clinging to each other like wreckage. Neither of them let go.

When they finally moved, it was awkward, slow. Nyk's legs were jelly. Pace guided him to the bed. Nyk broke again, and Pace just held him through the storm, whispering whatever comfort he could find.

Seventy fractions passed before Nyk's breathing evened enough for him to speak. "I'm sorry, I..."

"I'll stop you there," Pace said, cutting him off gently but firm. "You don't apologise. Not for this. Apologies are for mistakes. You didn't do anything wrong, my friend."

Nyk's gaze slid to the blaster on the floor by the chair.

"Oh no," Pace said quickly. "That isn't on you. None of this is."

Nyk sat up a little, taking slow breaths to calm his racing heart. The sweat, the tremor, even the dryness in his mouth began to fade. He gave a weak smile. "Thank you... my hero."

"Nyk," Pace said softly. "That wasn't heroics. That was me being almost too late. Too late to see what my best friend was going through. I could have lost you, man. Why didn't you ever say anything?"

"I tried," Nyk whispered.

Pace looked away, shame flickering in his eyes.

"I couldn't," Nyk stuttered, "There was never a right time. This anger... it's been with me since before we met."

"Tsera?" Pace asked quietly.

Nyk nodded. "That was the start. But it grew. I held it down when I had to. After Jodrell and Phos died, though, it... it got out of control. More and more worlds falling apart, and every day it felt like we were losing. Like I was losing." He tapped the side of his head. "I fight this battle every rotation, right here. And it didn't feel right to burden you guys with it."

"Not right?" Pace's voice cracked. "Nyk, that's why we're here. To save others, it's our calling."

"How can I save others when I can't even save myself?" Nyk whispered. "Look at me, I'm a fucking mess. And trust me, the inside's worse than the outside." He paused, staring at his hands. "I do feel like I was put here to help. But at what cost? My sanity? My life? I can't keep going like this." He reached out for the glass of water on his bedside table, his hand trembling as he took a slow sip.

"I have this cloud inside my head," Nyk said, voice low and rough. "A black cloud. Any time something good happens-anything-I feel it roll in and piss all over it. And then the questions start." His eyes went glassy, distant. "Why are you happy? What makes you think you deserve it? You saved one world from Lucifer, but what about the others? How do you live with yourself, knowing they're gone? Why do you deserve your life over theirs? You're not innocent. You never were."

Pace opened his mouth, but Nyk kept going, words spilling like a dam breaking. "You're a divine being, Nyk Cepler. You're no one. You won't be remembered.

You're taking up space someone better could fill. You're a drain. Everyone knows it. Just end it. Spare them the pain. Spare them from you." His voice cracked into a sob. "Do it. Do it now. It's the only way to save them all."

Pace's own eyes filled. He hadn't known the weight Nyk carried. "Let me help you," he said quietly.

Again, Nyk's gaze flickered to the blaster on the floor.

"Oh, hell no." Pace's voice snapped, sharp. "Real help. Living help. You're the glue that holds us together, Nyk. You don't even see it."

Nyk stared at the floor.

"You are," Pace insisted. "You keep me grounded when my ego runs wild. Xania adores you; she trains every day to be like you. She does impressions of you when you're not looking." Pace gave a small, sad smile. "You're her hero, Nyk. You don't have to save billions. You've already changed one life."

Nyk let out a little wet laugh and wiped his nose with his sleeve.

Pace pressed on. "You're the peacemaker between Beau and Xania. sShearon looks up to you like a big brother. Drake? You're his best drinking buddy, the only one who listens to his awful songs." Pace chuckled softly, then his tone hardened again. "And me. You save me every rotation. If you hadn't pulled me out of that marketplace, I wouldn't be here. I'd be dead. All this-us-exists because of you. Maybe we met for another reason, but I believe God put us together for this. You may not believe that, but I do."

Nyk blinked, ashamed. "I didn't know."

"I should be the one ashamed," Pace said, his voice thick. "For not seeing your pain."

"I hide it well," Nyk murmured.

"You don't have to. Not from me." Pace's hand tightened on his shoulder. "I won't judge you. I'll help you with anything. Anything. Just don't shut me out."

"I don't know if I can be helped," said Nyk honestly.

"Then we'll try," Pace replied.

"How?" Nyk asked, his voice small.

"Dok's rehabilitation service," Pace said. "He set it up on his world. Maybe they can help. It's a start."

Nyk sniffed, "I... I do want to live."

Pace smiled and pulled him close. "Then we'll do this together. For as long as it takes."

Nyk nodded. "I need Crown Claw with me. He keeps the voices at bay, somehow."

"I'll make sure you have him," said Pace. "Hell, I'll tie him to your shoulder if I have to."

Nyk chuckled, the sound faint but real.

***

Pace called for Dok on his commlink, and after explaining the situation to him in the corridor, the doctor gave Nyk a sedative to help him sleep.

"What do you suggest?" Pace asked.

"I'll take him to the rehabilitation centre. There, he'll be in good hands. They have non-intrusive methods for this sort of thing, so he should be diagnosed properly. Then an on-going plan will be figured out."

"Thank you, Dok," said Pace. "I'll go and get the Starlady ready for you, and here." Pace pulled out a small comms device. "Give this to Nyk when you get there. Tell him I'll talk or listen whenever he needs me."

Dok nodded and went into Nyk's room to collect some of his things.

Pace stuck his head into the room to see Nyk asleep. "Get well buddy, I don't know what I'd do if..." He bit his lip and took a long breath. He gave a quick nod to Dok before leaving for the hanger holding the Starlady.

Lucifers fall

Chapter 23

Lucifer found Lucigon in the main hall, ignoring all the freshly cooked food on the long wooden table. Lucigon was stood by the fireplace, one hand on the thick stone mantle surround, the other caressing the fire, like one would play with water. Lucifer stood in the doorway, smiling to himself. For several heartbeats he stayed there, admiring his son. Eventually, he moved forward, tracing a clawed finger along the solid wooden table. "You know, that's the original eternal flame," he said as he approached the fireplace.

Lucigon didn't look up, instead he kept his gaze on the intoxicating intrigue of the flames. "Why am I drawn to it, yet it doesn't burn me?" he asked, his hand lingering in the flames.

Lucifer stopped beside him and put his hand in the fire too. "It is our flame, if this was ever extinguished, that would make us mortal."

Lucigon looked at his father, then back into the flames. "Where is it from?"

Lucifer pulled out his hand; a flame burned brightly in his palm. "It's from the beginning. When my mother and father first met, they induced a spark. That spark turned into a flame. Soon after, my brother and I were born. The flame kept us company through the cold times, it kept us nourished and warm. Until we were big enough to look after ourselves. When God banished me, from my rightful place, he sent me down here with the flame." Lucifer paused, then said, almost to himself. "I guess it was his way of looking after me." Lucifer went quiet, staring into the fire. Three fractions passed.

"The eternal flame?" Lucigon asked again, interrupting the awkward silence. Lucifer flinched, as though coming out of a trance. He clenched his fist, extinguishing the flame. "Yes, the eternal flame, ahem." He cleared his throat. "I stayed by its side, again it nourished me, kept me warm in a place that was cold to me. I carried it with me for millennia. It wasn't long before I got angry, this time, flames erupted from my body. In God's rash decision to banish me, he sent the eternal flame and me down here together. This forged us as one. That fire now burns inside us, Lucigon.

"It took a while before I could control it, but ever since I could..." He snapped his fingers and flames appeared from his fingertips. "All creatures fear me."

"Can you teach me how to use it?" asked Lucigon.

"Of course," said Lucifer, "it's a part of you too. I put that spark in your mother's belly, you just have to access it."

Lucigon nodded and concentrated hard.

Lucifer laughed at Lucigon's expression. "You don't have to lay an egg. Let the anger burn through your body like a wildfire. Let it spread to your limbs. When you feel it at your hands, throw it like a knife."

Lucigon closed his eyes, the lies his mother whispering through his mind, lies that bound him, denied him his birthright, his power. A spark of rage lit inside him. He fed it with loathing for Lucifer, the murderer of his mother. The spark grew. Fire spread through his chest, hot and ravenous. He fanned it with darker thoughts, visions of happy worlds, innocent faces, and his hatred for them all. The blaze surged down his arms, searing through his veins until his fingertips burned.

He flicked his wrist. A fireball ripped free.

Lucifer shifted easily from its path, stone shattering where he had stood. Instead of fury, he smiled, pride glinting. Satisfaction curling at the edges of his mouth.

Lucigon's eyes snapped open. He grinned. Turning from his father, he unleashed a storm of fireballs. One struck the outer wall, blasting it open in a roar of flame and rubble. He stopped short, chest heaving. "Sorry," he muttered.

Lucifer's smile deepened, both approving and predatory. "That can be repaired. You've done well... for a first lesson." His gaze lingered, sharp as claws. "Yes.

Very well indeed." Then almost casually, he turned away. "Now," he said, voice silky with command, "it's time to eat."

The fire still tingled in Lucigon's veins as Lucifer led him toward the table. Smoke curled through the cracks of the shattered wall, but neither of them looked back. They sat across from each other, the table full of platters of roasted meat and bowls that steamed with unfamiliar stew. The smell was rich, cloying, laced with something metallic beneath the spice.

Lucigon hesitated. "What is this?"

Lucifer gestured to the spread with open arms, the smile never leaving his face. "Strength. Power. Family." His eyes gleamed. "The fuel of gods."

Lucigon shifted uncomfortably. The fire inside him still burned, urging him forward, urging him to take what was his. He reached for a piece of meat, charred and dripping, and tore into it. The taste was sweet at first, then bitter, wrong. His stomach turned, but he forced himself to swallow.

Lucifer watched, pleased. "Good," he said, voice low, almost tender. "Hunger is as important as rage. Feed it. Always feed it.

Lucigon swallowed again, his throat tight. He felt the fire answer the meal, growing hotter, sharper. He caught his father's gaze, those ancient eyes, proud and cruel, and realised the feast was no celebration.

It was binding.

***

After the hearty meal Lucifer and Lucigon sat in front of the large open fire, the flames danced in the dark room, its light flickering on the features of their faces. Small carcases lay strewn across the dining table behind them, discarded after having its flesh succulently stripped clean. Large bottles of red wine sat empty at one end of the table, while at the other end, a large candelabra silently melted away at its seven candles.

"Tell me about these Cydarions," asked Lucigon, his gaze not lifting from the fire. Lucifer look a sip of wine, he still enjoyed the taste, he just never got a buzz from the alcohol.

"God's army," Lucifer scoffed with air quotation marks. "They're insufferable. They need to be wiped out!"

"Why don't you find them and kill them?" Lucigon asked.

"I don't know where they are. Their world has been hidden from me, by him…" Lucifer nodded upwards, "my brother," he snarled. "Ever since the last time, he knows I would kill them without hesitation. It's his only way of trying to stop me."

"The last time?"

Lucifer smiled. "That, Lucigon, is a long story."

Lucigon nodded, knowing that would have to wait, for now. "What about when the Cydarions kill your demons? They leave their home then," he said.

Lucifer nodded. "Yes, they do, But I don't know which planet they would go to. I have subjects in over a thousand worlds at any one time, there's no way I can be at all of them."

"Don't your subjects ever fight back?"

Lucifer huffed. "Some do, most don't, they're cowards!" He took another sip of wine. "The ones that do fight, are weak and are easily killed, others are banished to the dark realm," said Lucifer.

"The dark realm?" asked Lucigon curiously.

"The dark realm…" Lucifer repeated, looking at a blank space on his left, as though he could see the dark realm itself. "Is a place out of time. My subjects are sent there but never return."

"Maybe they're killed too?"

"That's what I originally thought," answered Lucifer, "but I always feel when a subject of mine is killed, and those haven't been. They still live!"

"So, there's no way back for them?"

"I didn't think so," Lucifer admitted. Then he held up a finger. "But I've heard rumours about a Cydarion being there and escaping."

"If one of those Cydarions escaped, can't we go in and get them back?"

Lucifer smiled at the use of the word, 'we'. *He's accepting his destiny.* "Yes, that is one plan I'm working on."

"And the others?" Lucigon asked.

Lucifer smirked and took another sip of wine. "Here's what I want you to do…" Lucifer started, then spent the rest of the night going over his various plans of attack and retribution. Lucigon listened intently offering his own suggestions and advice. Lucifer was especially keen on one idea that was presented to him.

"It will be a great day in hell when that hidden planet of theirs burns. I hope God smells the smoke and tastes their ashes," said Lucifer, giddy with how his plans are coming together.

Lucigon laughed.

"You know, you should lead the fight on their world," suggested Lucifer.

"How will I know which ones are Cydarions?"

"Oh, you will smell them, I guarantee that," said Lucifer, "besides, do you plan on leaving anyone alive?" He raised a scorched eyebrow at Lucigon.

"Of course not, I want to taste those innocent souls most of all," Lucigon said, running his tongue over his young sharp teeth.

"You bring me victory, and I will show you my worth," offered Lucifer finishing his goblet of wine.

"I shall make you proud, father," Lucigon said.

"I know you will, my boy," replied Lucifer, his heart feeling…

Lucifer caught himself. "Now, it's time for rest, we still have a lot to organise, and a clear mind is essential."

Lucigon agreed, got up out of his seat and turned to walk, but stopped. He cocked his head to one side, looking at Lucifer up and down. Then asked in a low growl, "Why do you change your physique, to look like one of *them*?"

Lucifer never expected such a question, but it didn't surprise him. "That form," he stated, "is to blend in with other worlds. They are much more accommodating if they see a friendly face, this is my natural form."

Lucigon nodded and headed for the door, before stopping again. "You should embrace your true identity." He then sauntered out of the room, leaving Lucifer alone with the eternal fire, and his thoughts. He'd heard that phrase before, from Lucigon's mother. He cursed her for what she had done, and he cursed himself for killing her. At least she had raised Lucigon well, even if it wasn't *his* way. Lucigon had to learn the hard way about life, *but at least he's accepted his destiny.*

Lucifer closed his eyes and spoke within himself, *Soon, we shall take his throne and destroy him for his treacherous ways. Mother, I swear to you, I will make the universe peaceful again.*

***

Lucifer called Lucigon into the war room for a highly secret mission.

"Lucigon, Generals," Lucifer said, "soon, we will have *our* judgement day. The Cydarions have taken the bait, thanks to some good acting on Purah's behalf. They have taken the amulet back to their home world. What they don't know, is that it contains a location tag."

Lucigon grunted his approval.

"We, my friends are going to infiltrate their home and destroy the Cydarions, once and for all. Then there will be no one to stop me. I shall bring the peace and tranquillity to this universe, that we all desire."

A loud cheer erupted in the war room as Lucifers offspring congratulated him on the plan.

"Whiro, you shall lead the invasion," said Lucifer.

"It will be an honour, sire," Whiro replied.

"How many demons do you have?"

"As instructed, sire, I have all sixty-five demons ready to fight."

Lucifer nodded to himself, *Excellent, sixty-six of them will be enough.* "Whiro, pick one member to go first. Find a good place for everyone to gather, call them through..." Lucifer paused to build the tension, a grin forming on his face. "And then raise hell."

Another cheer erupted.

"Go and prepare, tell your army that if any one of them shows cowardice, they will face my wrath," said Lucifer.

"Yes sire, we shall be victorious," Whiro said, collecting his things.

"Make sure that you are."

Lucifer looked at Israfil. "Once we have established a foothold on their world, you shall give three blasts on the trumpet. That, my friends, will symbolise the time of judgement. The reign of the Cydarions will be over, and peace shall prevail. Israfil, I place that great honour on you. Let everyone know that it is *our* time. The Cydarions are finished."

"Where shall I be?" asked Lucigon.

"You, Lucigon, will be pivotal in this fight," said Lucifer. He pulled out two silver stars from a drawer on his desk, handing one to Lucigon, the other to Whiro. "Whiro, you shall place this device on the ground in front of the Cydarions and activate it. Lucigon will use his device to portal through from here."

"The Cydarions will quiver at his sight," said Whiro, grovelling.

"Lucigon, you shall decimate them all," said Lucifer.

"I'll start with their master, the others will fall easily," said Lucigon.

Lucifer nodded, then waved his hand. "Dismissed." Whiro bowed and backed away, out of the war room. Lucifer turned to the other generals, all waiting to be spoken to. "How is Project M.U.R.I.S. coming along?"

Kokabiel stepped forward. "Everything is on schedule; the test sites were a success."

"Excellent," said Lucifer. *It's a shame that I have to destroy the very planets that I created. But that's the price I'm willing to pay, so I alone can rule the universe.* He raised an eyebrow to Kokabiel. "Were there any survivors?" he asked.

"Our sources have reported that there were no survivors, sire," Kokabiel said.

"Well, that is good news," said Lucifer. He set his eyes on his son before pausing, the cogs in his mind ticking over. Finally, he said, "Lucigon, follow me," and then stormed out of the room.

The Soul Throne

Chapter 24

Lucigon pulled his eyes away from the data screen and watched his father walk away. He was soon only two paces behind Lucifer, making their way through the maze of rooms, twisting and turning around corridors, increasing speed. Lucigon ran behind his father, getting quicker and quicker, he didn't realise he could even move this fast, let alone the old man in front of him. They ran for nearly three full sections with no chatter, no conversation, just heavy breathing. Lucifer eventually slowed coming to a halt. Lucigon stopping by his side.

"This place," Lucifer gestured around him, "was one of the training camps. I had birthing pools, education rooms, dormitories, kitchens." He pointed to each area as they passed through their respective areas. "And here," Lucifer pointed to some iron bars, the gates being left open, "were the quarters for the workers that helped out around here. Some said they were prisoners!" He laughed to himself and shrugged, turning to face Lucigon. "They were free to leave at any time, I just required their soul, and they could be on their way. It was a simple choice," said Lucifer dryly. "But either they refused or preferred to work here. They got fed and had a place of belonging."

Lucigon peered through the bars, setting eyes upon rows of mattresses laying in the dirt. Solid walls on three sides going straight up, it was the bottom of a sinkhole. He looked back at Lucifer. "It looks...homely," he said without a hint of sarcasm.

Lucifer moved onto the next set of iron bars and knelt on the sandy floor. Scooping up a handful, he let it run through his long fingers. "This is where I lost this," he pointed to his broken horn. "I WAS ATTACKED IN MY OWN HOME!" he shouted, then took a breath. Calming down, he coolly said, "I killed their Master Cydarion, right here." He studied the iron bars, as though remembering the incident.

Lucigon sniffed a couple of times. "What is that smell?"

Lucifer deeply inhaled. "That, my boy, is the smell of a Cydarion."

"It's foul," grunted Lucigon.

"Yes, it is. But it will serve you well to remember it," offered Lucifer. Then he smiled. "I have one more thing to show you." He opened a portal and told Lucigon to enter. Lucifer followed behind.

This world around them was smothered in grey- still, lifeless, stripped of colour. Above, the sky writhed in endless black swirls, as though the void it-self were breathing. Shadows lashed down without warning, vast and formless, brushing so close they stirred the air. Screams and whispers rushed past, tangled together, grief and malice carried on a wind that seemed alive.

And there, at the heart of it all, stood a chair. Enormous. Defiant. Not a throne of majesty, but a cruel monument of iron and spikes. Its design promised agony more than rest, a seat forged to break rather than honour. It radiated power and revulsion in equal measure. An object both sacred and profane, daring them to draw nearer.

"What is this place?" Lucigon asked, looking around, then settling his gaze on Lucifer.

"This is my Soul Throne!" Lucifer said. He pointed to the sky and the swirling black mist. "They are all souls, waiting for me to consume them."

Lucigon looked wary. "Don't they just enter you, like on Darkit?" he asked.

Lucifer shook his head. "No, that only happens when you kill them yourself. When my subjects kill for me, the souls are delivered here, trapped in this atmos-phere. Here they stay until I am ready to receive them," he explained.

Lucigon stepped forward and took a seat on the soul throne. He looked around. "So, what now?"

Lucifer gently waved his hand. Immediately, a thousand needles erupted from the throne, driving into Lucigon's flesh. They punched through his neck and back, shredding his hamstrings and carved down his calves. Hot rivulets of blood spilled in sudden streams, soaking his skin, running into the grooves of the iron seat. His muscles seized under the assault, every nerve screaming as the chair claimed him.

He screamed out. "Argh! Mother of pain!" His face contorted in agony.

Lucifer smirked.

Lucigon's voice waned as the souls started to enter his body. His eyes grew large, and a smile grew.

"That's enough!" Lucifer said and waved his hand to retract the needles.

Lucigon's eyes fixed on Lucifer, and he waved his own hand. The needles pierced his skin again. "Ahh!" he said this time, his eyes rolling back into his head.

"How did you do that?" muttered Lucifer, then waved his hand.

Lucigon didn't even open his eyes, he just waved his hand, operating the needles again.

"Enough!" Lucifer's voice thundered. He surged forward, seizing Lucigon's arm and yanking hard. Lucigon braced, muscles straining, refusing to budge.

Lucifer's eyes narrowed. He clamped down on his son's wrist instead, this time with true force. Lucigon resisted again, but to Lucifer it was no more effort than tearing the wings from a Cerutile beetle. With a single violent flick, he ripped Lucigon from the throne and hurled him across the grey wasteland.

Lucigon crashed, rolled, and scrambled upright in one motion, fury blazing in his eyes.With a snarl, he launched himself straight back at his father.

Lucifer was ready. No longer playful, he caught Lucigon by the horns mid-charge, pivoted his body, and slammed the boy into the ash-strewn ground. The impact cracked the earth. He pressed his son's head down, pinning him like a beast. Lucigon writhed and thrashed beneath him, but the harder he struggled, the deeper Lucifer's grip drove him into the dirt.

"Stay down, until you calm down," whispered Lucifer into Lucigon's ear. Grunts and snorts were the only thing that came out of Lucigon's mouth.

"I didn't understand that..." said Lucifer, "but understand this. I am the only one who uses the throne, once we have taken power, you can have all the thrones you want. But this one is mine, understand?"

Lucigon roared, the sound muffled against the dirt, his claws raking trenches into the grey soil. His wings beat furiously, kicking up clouds of ash, but Lucifer's grip did not falter.

"Pathetic," Lucifer growled, forcing his son's face deeper into the ground. "All that fire, all that rage... you're nothing without control."

Lucigon's body shook, every muscle straining against his father's strength. His breath came ragged, hot with fury. A flicker of flame leaked from his mouth, searing the earth beneath his cheek.

Lucifer leaned in closer, his voice a whisper filled with venom. "You think power comes from hatred alone? No. Hatred is fuel. But discipline is the weapon."

With a sudden shove, he released him. Lucigon gasped and rolled onto his side, coughing up dust and blood. His chest heaved, eyes burning with defiance even through pain.

Lucifer's smile sharpened. "Good. Now that's settled, we eat."

"Maybe I'm not hungry," Lucigon snapped.

Lucifer's eyes burned, his voice cutting like a blade. "You *are* hungry." He flicked a hand, and a portal ripped open before them. "Through."

Lucigon hesitated, scanning the grey surround one last time. "What do you call this place?"

Lucifer chuckled, low and cruel. "You'll never know." With a shove, he forced his son through the portal and stepped in after him.

The grand hall welcomed them again, the feast waiting, untouched. Meats steaming, wine glowing like dark blood in crystal goblets.

"Sit," Lucifer ordered.

Lucigon sat.

"Eat."

His hand trembled as he reached for a slice of meat. The scent clawed at his hunger, and he obeyed.

Lucifer leaned back, watching, satisfied. "Good. You see, boy, whether you admit it or not, you do as I say. Always."

Lucigon met his father's gaze for a heartbeat, fire still flickering in his eyes. But the weight of it, ancient and merciless, crushed him. His defiance faltered. Slowly, he lowered his head in submission.

Lucifer's grin spread, cold and triumphant. "That's better," he murmured. "You're learning."

***

"What happened to the devil that defied you, wanting to rule by your side?" asked Lucigon. The feast now cleared away.

Lucifer looked at him, puzzled.

"The one who sent you that Master Cydarion," Lucigon said.

"Ah," replied Lucifer with a smile, "that was Azazel. I didn't punish him. I thought it was a good plan. But he should have told me of his intentions first. I would have gone along with it." He paused and looked sternly at Lucigon. "But not in my home! *This* is sacred."

Lucigon nodded with a snort. "I agree!"

"Anyway," Lucifer said, seemingly changing the subject, "Recently, I heard a rumour about a demon that had prematurely hatched, so I..." Lucifer paused, confusion written on Lucigon's face.

"I don't lay eggs, is that what you're wondering?" said Lucifer with a smile.

Lucigon nodded again, his expression not changing.

"Well, apparently, two of my demons decided to procreate and had a clutch of their own babies," Lucifer announced joyfully.

"And you're okay with that?" asked Lucigon.

Lucifer nodded. "Of course! It was a surprise to hear, but more of *my* kind, carrying out *my* work, is a good thing," he said. "So, Azazel was sent to raise it. It was his second chance."

"It sounds like you're getting weak," sneered Lucigon.

"There's more than violence, Lucigon. If I killed Azazel, what would it achieve? One less cunning demon and another infant to raise..."

"It would show the others that you are strong," Lucigon replied.

"On the contrary, I showed mercy and gave someone another chance, for having a good plan. That shows others that I am fair. Plus, it will encourage them to come up with their own plans too. I see that as a complete win. Don't you?" Lucifer smiled.

Lucigon grunted an acceptance but added, "I would have sliced its throat."

"Yes," sighed Lucifer, "and that is why I'm in charge here."

Lucigon bowed his head. "You are right, Lucifer."

Lucifer smiled. "Call me dad."

The Hydra

Chapter 25

Pace was awoken in the middle of the night. It was a Calling. He'd been awoken by a Calling before, but nothing as strong or as urgent as this. He didn't have time to choose his outfit, he just climbed into the first pair of trousers and shirt that he could find. Slipping on his boots and choosing a utility belt from the rack, he headed out the door. He always kept at least three utility belts ready; his main one, and a backup one in case of another Calling, before he had the chance to restock 'Mother.' The name he had given to this inanimate object, since it was that which provided him with everything he needed. The third utility belt was for any Storous who wasn't prepared for their adventure with two Cydarions. Pace liked to wear his utility belt low on one side of his hip, like the old-fashioned gunslinger he used to watch as a child. The holovids of 'The Lonesome Man,' was his favourite, after education, show. The show featured Billy Joe Thwaite as the space cowboy, going from planet to planet cleaning up villainous scum, one town at a time. Pace had always wanted to be Jake 'The Lonesome Man' Moran. Even as a child, he would carry a pair of toy blasters with him. Which he named, 'The Twins'. Nowadays, his go to weapon was his yonca fighting implement, an exquisite combination of technology and opulent styling. Its accompanying neural transmitter had been inserted into the soft tissue, behind his ear a long time ago.

Pace popped a menthol capsule into his mouth and bit down, crushing the shell and releasing the active agent within. Using his tongue to spread the paste all over his teeth, he let his saliva interact with it and foam up. The foam killed off any bacteria on his teeth and left them feeling like he had just finished at the dentist. He took a few gulps of liquid from a water flask and washed it all down, just as he reached the top steps of the armoury. Here, he kept his weapons, along with everyone else's, in their allotted spaces. One of his new rules, after being elected master, was that all new Storous' could understand and train with different weapons. Something he never practiced himself. Not that anyone was allowed to use his beloved yonca, but it was there for them to look at and study. Even if a student was brave enough to try and use it, the weapon wouldn't fire, as it was implanted with biometrics to keep it from falling into the wrong hands.

Collecting the weapon and his holo bracelet, he quickly marched off towards the Calling. A blue glow greeted Pace as he walked down the corridor and into the portal room. One blue portal was swirling between the solid wooden frames.

It wasn't long before he heard sShearon's foot slaps on the stone flooring, and he smiled. It had been so long since he and sShearon had been on a Calling together, he was looking forward to some time with his old friend.

Just as sShearon entered the room, the portal disappeared, along with the Calling.

"What happened?" asked sShearon.

Pace shook his head. "I don't know. It just stopped."

"Did you do anything?" sShearon asked.

"No," replied Pace. "The portal closed, and the Calling stopped."

sShearon frowned. "Doesss that mean?" he asked ominously.

"I'm not sure, I'd surmise that we're too late," Pace agreed.

"To sssave them?" asked sShearon.

Pace just nodded again and sighed.

"Perhapsss the devil left?" sShearon wondered.

"We'll never know," admitted Pace, looking to sShearon.

sShearon yawned, his mouth opened wide enough that Pace could nearly climb inside. Then Pace yawned. Seeing Pace yawn, made sShearon yawn again. Pace quickly turned away, not wanting this to carry on.

"You go back to bed, sShearon, it's late, get some rest," Pace offered.

sShearon nodded, stifling yet another yawn. "And you?" he asked.

"I'm going to wait here a while. I'll let you know if anything changes."

"You ssshould get sssome ressst too," said sShearon as he walked out of the room.

Pace didn't respond, he just walked around the back of the wooden portal frames and inspected them all. He didn't know what he was looking for, if anything, but he knew it wouldn't hurt to inspect the whole room. "Just in case," he said to himself.

After inspecting the whole room twice, and finding nothing, he slumped down on the cold stone floor, his back leaned against one wall, facing the portals. He sighed and tilted his head back, resting it softly on the hard surface. He glanced up and sighed again, closing his eyes. The roof above him was missing. It had been replaced by plastic sheeting to keep the rain out. Pace knew the roof had to be replaced; it was on his list of things to do. A list that was only growing longer and more stressful with each passing rotation. The stress of being a master was beginning to take its toll on his body and mind. His once dark black hair was starting to grey at the temples, and he was sure he had permanent bags under his eyes. Sometimes he found himself wishing for a Calling, just to get away from this Citadel and all off its problems. The place needed a full-time caretaker, someone who could dedicate their attention to the aging property without the distractions of the Callings.

Pace's eyes flickered open, as bright blue light filled the room. He had fallen asleep. He had to shield his eyes with the back of his hand until his pupils adjusted to the new lighting conditions. Pace felt the Calling come to him, subtle at first, but getting strong very quickly. He was now eager to get going but knew he had to at least wait until another Cydarion arrived. He listened out down the corridors and throughout the citadel for any sound of approaching footsteps. But there was nothing. The blue light shimmied with the swirls, almost like a blue circle of flames. It was a beautiful sight, unfortunately, it only appears when a world is faced with unstoppable evil.

He heard a faint sound, a shuffling, echoing from deep within the citadel. *Someone's coming,* he thought. Suddenly, the room was plunged into darkness, as the portal was extinguished. Pace spun around. "No!" The Calling had also left him. He smacked the wooden portal frame with his palm, like he was trying to make the portal come back on.

"What happened?" said Beau as she entered the room.

Pace spun back around with a start; he hadn't heard her arrive. "I don't know," he replied, "it just stopped."

"Not again," said Beau with a sigh.

Pace frowned. "Again?" he asked. He knew it had happened earlier to him and sShearon, but he doubted the Sanol would have told anybody else at this time of night.

"Yeah, it's happened to me three times already," said Beau. "There's not much we can do."

Pace sighed. "No, there isn't. But why are we getting the Calling's so late?"

Beau shrugged. "I guess there are a lot of places out there to look over," she suggested.

Pace just answered with a nod.

Another portal opened. Pace and Beau looked at each other.

"Shall we go?" asked Pace, gesturing to the portal.

"Or we could wait thirty fractions, see if it closes itself," Beau offered.

"I'd rather not waste time on this side."

"You're the master," said Beau.

Pace grimaced and walked through the portal, Beau, one step behind.

They entered a desolate landscape; dark grey covered every surface that wasn't plunged into darkness by the black clouds looming above.

Beau started to cough and gag, occasionally she had to spit on the floor.

"Sulphur!" Pace said between Beau's coughing fits. "That's what you're smelling and can taste. The air is thick with it." He looked around the landscape, twisting his neck hither and thither.

"It's gone," Beau said, regaining her breath. She wiped away spit and snot from her face with the back of her sleeve. "The Calling, it's gone," she repeated.

Pace stopped looking around and dropped his head. He didn't want to admit it, but it was the truth. The Calling had ceased and there seemed to be no living thing that they could see. He walked over to a fallen tree and wiped his hand across the bark. The settled ash was finger deep.

"Come on, let's get back," said Beau, "there's nothing we can do."

"But we might be able to do something here," Pace said.

"Like what, Pace?"

"I don't know," he replied. It seems to be the only thing he is saying recently. There was a time when he had an answer for everything or was at least able to find an answer. But now, he felt like he knew nothing, and everyone was looking to him for answers.

Beau opened a portal and waited for Pace. He eventually walked through without saying a word.

Beau took a big gulp of fresh air once she was back home.

"You go back to bed, Beau, I want to keep watch here," said Pace.

Beau paused, then nodded and left the room.

She returned within fifteen fractions with two chairs, and placed them down, next to each other, in front of the portals. She sat down on one and patted the other seat while smiling at Pace. He reluctantly sat down with an overly loud sigh.

A new portal opened right in front of them and Pace jumped back up.

"I'm not going yet," said Beau, then patted the seat again. "Let's talk first."

Pace grumbled but sat down again. "What makes you think I need to talk?" he asked.

Beau smiled. "It's a woman thing," she said.

Pace nodded; he knew not to argue.

"Hey," Beau said seriously, "I'm sorry to hear about Nyk, I know you guys are really close. How are things going?"

Pace exhaled slowly. "Thanks, it was a shock for sure. I spoke to him a few rotations ago at the rehabilitation clinic, and he seems to be doing much better now. He's got Crown Claw and the Starlady with him, said he'd come back if we needed him." Pace tapped the communication device on his wrist. "I call him when I can. But he's in the best hands now."

"And you?" said Beau, "How are you doing?" she asked earnestly.

Pace grimaced. "I'm doing okay. These battles are starting to take their toll on all of us," he admitted.

"We are training new Storous', hopefully that will ease the load," said Beau.

"That's what I'm worried about. I just don't feel that they are trained enough yet. They're all my responsibility. I must keep them safe until they are ready."

"I get that," said Beau with a slight nod.

They spoke for more than a whole section. No other Cydarions came for the Calling, and the portal was still open.

Beau nodded at the wooden structure. "Shall we?" she said.

Pace agreed. "Yeah, but it feels..."

"Different!" answered Beau, "like a Calling, but not like a Calling," she said.

"I guess we should find out," said Pace.

***

After nearly three rotations on their current Calling, Pace and Beau walked along a footpath beside a marshy lake, the edge of the waters lapping serenely onto the dirt track. Birds chirped happily in the trees above them. Pace stopped to admire the view, his shadow falling onto the murky waters at his feet. He took a deep breath of the fresh countryside air.

"This is the best part of a Calling," he said, "every world has a fresh smell to it."

"For me," said Beau, "it's the food. Trying the local delicacies, just makes it all worthwhile." She smiled. "That banquet we had last night in the royal hall was just..." she rolled her eyes, "to die for!"

Pace agreed. "There was so much food! I bet Drake would still be there now," he said with a laugh.

"Don't forget, we were also warned about this place," said Beau, then changed her voice to impersonate the messenger, "The path down to the cave is fraught with danger and monsters, you must be wary and tread lightly."

Pace laughed. "We should take heed though; they do know this place better than anyone."

Suddenly, almost as if on cue, something burst out of the water in front of them and blocked their path. A giant water snake rose up; its tail still submerged beneath the dark water as it thrashed from side to side. Wet glistening skin rippled as the beast writhed in the glaring sun. Five heads, all facing Pace and Beau, hissed and spat. The two had to dodge and weave to stay out of the way of its projectile liquid.

"Is this danger or monster?" Beau said.

"I don't think the two are mutually exclusive," said Pace.

Beau stood upright and faced one of the heads. "Excuse me, can we just get past?" she said trying to reason with it. Her reply came when one of the serpents' head lunged and snapped at her. But Beau was quicker and slipped out of the way. She pulled out her blasters and shot a couple of bolts into the serpent skull.

Almost immediately, its inflicted wounds healed up.

"What the?" uttered Pace, as he too had to dodge vicious strikes from the various heads. Some of the other heads were taking it in turns to lurch for him. He pulled out his yonca fighting implement and fired, hitting one neck of the beast. The wound took longer to heal than the head. He fired again, into the same wound and it opened even further. Beau noticed what was happening and shot continuously into the same area of a different neck.

The neck that Pace shot at exploded and the head fell off, landing right by Pace's feet. Just as another head landed at Beau's feet. The neck flailing around squirting its blood over the canopy of leaves, which then fizzed and melted away. A large drop splatted across a rock, sizzling upon contact, quickly eating its way through the solid stone.

"Be careful of the blood, Pace," shouted Beau, "It's acidic." She quickly manoeuvred to get a better shot to the next head.

"Will do," replied Pace, then added, "What the…" as he realised what was happening to the beast.

Where the heads had been shot off, two more grew in its place. Another head dropped by Beau's feet, and again, two more heads immediately grew back. Pace took a fourth head off, just for two more to grow back.

"We need a new tactic; this thing now has even more heads than when we started!" said Pace.

"I've got an idea, cover me," Beau replied. Pace moved to a defensive position to cover them both. Beau's eyes turned electric blue, and her fingers sparked with lightning. She charged herself up and stretched out her arms, sending the high voltage lightning from her hands into all the heads of this beast. Electricity leapt from head-to-head enveloping the creature in blue light. The beast slumped to the ground with a thud, its tail lay motionless in the water, the ripples decreasing.

"Good thinking," Pace said with a smile. He walked up to the creature and prodded it. Its body expanded and contracted, taking a large breath.

"It's still alive!" he shouted.

"I must have just stunned it," Beau said, "let's just get past, before it comes around." Beau moved cautiously around the beast's heads, making sure not to go near any of its lethal blood. Pace just climbed up and over the body, his foot slipping twice on the smooth reptile skin. He jumped down the other side and joined Beau on the footpath.

"We should pick up the pace a bit," he said, looking further up the track. "We don't want that creature to see us again. I get the feeling it was protecting something."

"Sure, that's probably the better option," agreed Beau.

Curious, Pace asked, "What was your other option?"

Beau smiled. "Use you as bait, while I follow the Calling." She laughed to herself.

"Huh!" remarked Pace, then set off running up the track.

"Yeah, I'll give you a head start," said Beau, before running after him.

***

As Beau reached the top of the long winding path, she came across a small waterfall. She took a refreshing drink and wiped her face, placing a cool wet hand on the back of her neck. Pace caught up with her and stuck his whole head underneath the waterfall.

"Ahh," he sighed, cooling his whole body down.

"You finally made it, old man," smirked Beau.

"It's my job ...to make you ...feel good," Pace said between heavy breaths. Beau giggled to herself. Pace soon caught his breath and turned to Beau. "When you've rested enough, come and find me." With that he followed the footpath, behind the waterfall, then stopped.

"You need another rest already?" laughed Beau, coming up behind him. "Wait, aren't these lairs supposed to have the eternal flame outside?" she said, looking around.

"Yep, they should," nodded Pace, "that's what I was thinking, but everything seems to be changing so much recently. I don't know what is normal anymore," he admitted.

"And since when do devils use monsters as protection?" asked Beau, rhetorically.

"Apart from Cerberus, never before," said Pace, shaking his head.

"The Calling is still this way though, yeah?" Beau questioned herself.

"Yeah, the Calling is still this way," said Pace, "but it's not as strong as it should be. Almost as if..."

"It's out of place?" Beau answered, surprising herself with the words coming out of her mouth.

"Yeah, yeah, yeah." Pace nodded in agreement, "Maybe you should be master?" he joked.

"Well, I am younger, and fitter." She laughed.

"You're definitely younger, yes," agreed Pace.

"Anyway," said Beau, "my head ain't that big," then gave a smirk. They both laughed.

Pace took a deep breath. "Let's go for it," he said.

"Why not."

Entering a cave system behind the waterfall, they realised the walls and floor were wet, even slippery at times. There was even the soft echo of running water coming from deeper within the cave. Stairs had been carved out of the rock, that had been worn down to leave deep indentations on every step. Pace looked at them, puzzled, taking in every detail. The further they descended into the cave the more they heard water, rushing like a stream. Moving more cautiously, they eventually got to the bottom of the stairs and stepped onto soft sand. A wide, flowing river lay before them. A small rowing boat was tied to a singular wooden post.

"Welcome, new travellers," said a voice from out of the darkness. Beau and Pace both reached for their weapons. A being stepping forward into the dim light. A small smile adorned his face, he held his hand out straight.

"My name is Charon. To cross this river, it will only cost one Obol." He smiled, then added, "Each."

"Is there a bridge?" asked Beau.

Charon laughed, "No one has ever asked me that before. But, no," he replied sternly.

Beau shrugged. "Worth a shot."

Pace bounced his eyebrows in agreement. "Do you take gold credits?" he asked Charon.

"I don't know that currency," Charon replied, "but you are welcome to wander these shores for a hundred cycles before I take you across, for free," offered Charon.

"What if I shoot you and take your boat?" Beau said, raising her blaster. Pace was soon beside her and placed a hand on the gun.

"Bork taught me, that words are better than weapons," said Pace.

Beau lowered her blaster, but replied, "Bork is an idiot."

Charon laughed again. "You cannot kill the dead."

"Fine," said Pace looking around, "it doesn't look too far, we'll swim!" He looked at Beau for approval, who nodded an agreement.

They both waded into the waters and started swimming, unable to see the other side from the water line.

Soon, Charon appeared beside the swimmers, rowing slowly, not even leaving a ripple on the waters. "Get in the skiff," he said to the two Cydarions.

"We don't have your coins," said Pace, between heavy breaths.

"I'll take you for free, conversation only," Charon offered.

Pace and Beau stopped swimming and treaded water.

"What's the catch?" Pace asked.

"No catch." He shook his head. "Only conversation," replied Charon

Pace and Beau glanced at each other, then climbed aboard the skiff.

"There's a long way to go my friends," said Charon.

"Uh huh," said Pace in response. "Why did you change your mind?" he asked.

"You shouldn't have survived the river Acheron, were you not mesmerized by it?" asked Charon.

"It's a river, why should I be mesmerized?" asked Pace.

"You should be able to see your sins, and relive your worst memories," replied Charon, keeping a steady stroke.

Beau sighed. "This seems like one of those times!" She nodded, not taking her eyes of Charon.

"You have an aura I've never felt before. Like you don't belong, yet you are here," muttered Charon.

"Death finally gets it," Beau said sarcastically. Pace laughed.

"Can you tell us anything about this place?" asked Pace respectfully.

Charon laughed at Beau. "I'm not death." Then he looked at Pace. "What would you like to know?" he asked.

"I mean, where are we, what's happening," asked Pace. "This is nothing like we've experienced before," he admitted.

"What do you mean, experienced before? You die only once," said Charon.

"I guess that depends on your point of view. We're very much alive, I assure you of that," said Beau with a laugh.

"Only the dead are allowed into the underworld," Charon said.

"Yet here we are," Pace gestured with his hands, still smiling.

"But... but I don't see how it's possible," mumbled a confused Charon.

"Magic," laughed Beau, blue electricity sparking at her fingertips.

Charon immediately stopped rowing and gasped. "Lightning! Zeus himself sent you!" he said in a terrified voice.

"Who?" asked Beau. "Nah, it's just me." She smiled, as she playfully threw lightning sparks from one hand to the other.

"You must be a god," he whispered.

Beau smiled and looked at Pace. "You hear that? I am a god, bow down before me," she said, laughing again.

"I ain't bowing down to anyone," said Pace, "but maybe you should stop that, you're scaring him."

Beau stopped producing the lighting, then winked at Charon, who continued rowing.

Pace asked again, "Where are we?"

Charon to Pace. "Oh yes, outside was the mortal realm, and now you're on your way to the underworld. You can only get there by crossing the Acheron River. On the other side you will find a passageway, there, a thousand steps will take you down to the court of Hades, where you will plead your case before him," replied Charon.

"Sounds like the devil to me," said Beau.

"I agree, but there's something different about this Place. Where are the fires, and where's the awful smell? I don't know, it's just not right," admitted Pace.

The skiff gently glided onto the soft sand on the far side of the river. "Well, we're here now, may as well check it out. That's what the Calling wants us to do, right?" asked Beau. All three of them climbed out of Charon's skiff. Pace straightened himself up, seemingly already dry, while Charon turned the vessel around, ready to set off back to the mortal realm.

"If you could stay here, for a while?" Pace asked Charon. "We shouldn't be long."

Charon agreed to stay around for these two strange beings. At least until there was another soul ready to cross the river.

"Come on, old man," Beau called behind her, as she set off down the steps. The passageway twisted downward, winding deeper into the earth.

"It should be getting hotter," Pace mumbled to himself.

Instead, a cold wind licked their faces as the tunnel opened into a cavernous hall. The air was damp, heavy, smelling of wet fur and mildew. At the far end, a sickly phosphorescent glow spilled across a jagged stone throne. A massive shadow stretched over it, motionless and immense.

Vermin skittered into cracks. The shadows along the walls writhed and seeped into the stone, dissolving into darkness.

A slow, deliberate shifting sound echoed through the chamber, like something vast stirring in its sleep. The glow brightened once, then settled, casting long fingers of light across the floor.

Pace's breath caught in his throat. Every instinct screamed. Something waited. Something watched.

The wind held its breath. The hall fell silent.

From the throne, a voice boomed...

Hades

Chapter 26

"Ah, we have a new guest," said the deep voice. It craned its neck forward and corrected itself, "make that, two guests." It said joyfully, "Come, come."

Pace and Beau looked at each other. They made their way towards the voice. "Be ready," Pace whispered.

"Uh-huh," said Beau, placing her hands behind her back.

"Welcome, travellers, I am Hades, ruler of the underworld. Tell me, what are your crimes?" Hades asked, his voice now soft and commanding.

Pace noticed that he was a tall man, even sitting on his throne, he commanded a presence. Thick long black hair and a full beard covered his facial features, except for his black eyes. A slender yet muscular frame. One hand holding a wooden staff with a two-pronged pitchfork at the top. The three headed dog of Cerberus lay by its feet, asleep. Neither of the three heads stirred as the Cydarions cautiously shuffled closer.

"We have committed no crimes here," said Pace.

"Really?" Hades laughed. "Then why are you here?"

"We're following a Calling, which has brought us to you," said Pace. "Our Callings always lead us to a devil, but you sir, are no devil." Beau gasped and muttered something to herself.

"I am not one of these, devils! I'm a god," said Hades. "The god of the under-world. I pass judgement on those who have sinned. When they die, up there." He pointed his pitchfork above him. "Their souls travel to me, down here by way of Charon. Did you meet him? Lovely fella, I should have him over for dinner sometime. Anyway, their souls end up in front of me and explain their sins. I pass my judgement onto them." Hades paused. "I do not kill anyone, especially the innocent. But who is truly innocent these days?" said Hades.

"If I may ask, how do you have a Cerberus?" questioned Pace.

Hades laughed, bent over and rubbed the belly of the three headed hound laying by his feet. "This one? I've had him since he was a pup, the son of Typhon and Echidna. He guards the gates of my underworld."

"I was under the impression that only demons had them," Pace replied.

"Ah, well, you're not wrong there," Hades said with a smirk. "Lucifer took a liking to him and offered to purchase him."

Pace was stunned. "You know Lucifer?" he asked soberly.

"Oh yes, he and I go way back," said Hades. "I couldn't just give up my best friend, here. But then, he popped out his own puppy just for Lucifer. Imagine that!" Hades laughed. "In fact, that gave Lucifer the idea for parthenogenesis, so now every now and again, one of his offspring's come down here to purchase their very own Cerberus."

"Pace, your mouth is wide open," said Beau whispering in his ear.

Pace shook his head clear. "Is Lucifer here now?" he asked, slightly worried and definitely not ready for that fight again.

Hades shook his head. "No, Lucifer isn't here..." Pace relaxed, his shoulders untensing. A bead of sweat trickled down his cold face. "But his offspring is," Hades finished. He gestured towards a dark doorway.

Pace spun towards it and pulled out his yonca fighting implement, the device starting to glow. Beau drew her two blasters and levelled them into the darkness. A tall, dark red figure appeared in the doorway, nearly covering the entrance. Slowly it stepped into the light, it was a devil. Its hands held up in surrender.

Hades stood up, his full height on display, and boomed at the Cydarions. "Put away your magic weapons!" His voice then mellowed. "You will not need them here," he said.

"I'm here in peace," said the devil.

"You don't know the meaning of the word," scoffed Beau.

"PUT THEM AWAY!" Hades shouted.

"If it's all the same with you, we'll keep them right here," said Pace.

"Urgh," replied Hades, then picked up his pitchfork and waved it at the Cydarions. Immediately, Pace and Beau's weapons slipped from their hand, wrenched away by a will not their own.

"This is neutral ground," said Hades. "There shall be no fighting here."

"Hades," Pace turned to face the ruler of the underworld. "Do you know who they are? What they're capable of?" asked Pace.

"I know Lucifer's struggle better than anyone," Hades said coldly. "Tell me, do you even know the full story?"

"I know enough," nodded Pace, "these devils cannot be trusted."

"Well strangers," said Hades with a smirk. "I have a very good relationship with Lucifer, and his kin. Not once has any of them betrayed me. But you, a stranger, wander into my realm and propose what I should do?" His started to raise again.

"He's got a point," said Beau quietly.

Hades exhaled and sat back down.

The devil took two more steps closer; it's hands no longer held up.

"*I* called you here, *I* manipulated your Calling," the devil said.

"How?" asked Beau directly.

"That," said the devil, "I'm not at liberty to say."

"Then what do you want?" Pace asked, picking up his weapon and storing it back on his belt. Beau did likewise, but her fingers hovered over the blaster grips.

"I was hoping the one called sShearon would come," the devil said.

"sShearon?" said Pace. "How do you know him, and what do you want with him?"

"sShearon made a pact with me, I have come to collect what is owed."

"Oh, I like the sound of this," said Hades.

"What pact?"

"A long time ago sShearon came to the Dark Realm, where I was. He spent quite a while there, and together we made a pact. I would show him how to get back to the time he came from if he would come back and free me. He promised, on his life, that he would return, but he never has. I came asking for that debt to be paid."

"If you can't escape the Dark Realm, how are you here?" asked Beau.

"Oh, I can answer that one," said Hades excitedly. "This is not your realm, and neither is it the Dark Realm. We are between the two realms, hence, the middle ground."

"I can visit here, just like you can, but I cannot go any further," said the devil.

"Hmm." Pace mumbled to himself.

"What's stopping us just leaving you here and not telling sShearon?" asked Beau.

"Don't Cydarions vow to stand by their word?" asked the devil. Pace pinched the bridge of his nose and gave a heavy sigh.

"Shit!" exclaimed Beau, then whispered under her breath, "I asked for that one."

Hades laughed hard. "I like this one," he said, pointing at Beau.

Beau looked at Hades. "You heard that?" she questioned.

"I hear everything in my realm," said Hades. Beau just smirked to herself and thought of something, hoping Hades couldn't also read minds.

"Okay," Pace sighed. "What's your name? All I can promise is that I will speak to sShearon about you," offered Pace.

"My name is Vassago, and I shall be waiting here to challenge him," the devil replied.

Pace sighed again and nodded. Vassago then faded back into the shadows.

Hades clapped his hands together. "I'm glad that is all sorted, I look forward to seeing those two in a fight." he said.

Pace looked confused. "I thought this was neutral ground, no fighting here?"

"It's his realm, he calls the shots," said Beau.

"Ho, ho, ho, I do like this girl," said Hades. "Red hair and a belly of fire." Beau blushed a little. "Here," Hades said, holding out a bowl in front of him. "Have some Pomegranate seeds."

"Thanks," said Beau, and went to take some.

Pace grabbed her arm and shook his head. "No."

"Very well, next time," shrugged Hades with a wink to Beau.

"Hades, you said you know the full story of Lucifers struggle, what did you mean by that?" asked Pace.

"Oh, that was such a long time ago," said Hades with a wave of his hand.

"Do you know about the Cydarions too?" Pace asked.

"I know the Cydarions are trying to stop Lucifers birthright," said Hades.

"Birthright? What do you mean?"

"Lucifers birthright, to be at your god's side.

Beau laughed. "At Gods side? Lucifer just wants to rule the heavens," she scoffed.

"He wanted to rule the heavens, with his brother. But..." Hades shrugged. "There was a falling out and he was cast down, made to live in the mortal world."

"His brother?" said Pace.

"Oh, you didn't know?" Hades laughed. "You've been serving your god all this time, not knowing the truth." He laughed again, louder this time.

Pace grimaced. "We fight to stop all the unnecessary killings that are done in Lucifers name."

"So just kill Lucifer, then everything will stop," Hades said nonchalantly. "Seems simple to me," he added.

"Lucifer can't be killed, he's immortal," said Beau.

"Anyone can be killed, with the right instrument," snapped Hades.

Pace looked up, a glimmer of hope in his eyes. "What instrument would kill Lucifer?"

"The Flaming Sword, of course," said Hades.

"Holy shit!" whispered Beau.

"What's the Flaming Sword?" Pace asked.

Hades sighed. "So many questions." He started to look around, an indication that he was getting bored of their conversation.

"Just this last one," said Pace, "then we'll be on our way."

Hades sagged, his voice edged with defeat. "Fine! When your God cast Lucifer from Heaven, he forged the Flaming Sword. A weapon meant to end Lucifer should he ever sway beings to his side. But that blade has been lost for an eternity."

Pace leaned forward. "Why would Lucifer seek it?"

Hades snarled, fury flashing across his face. "Because it can kill your God as well!" his voice thundered through the chamber. "Now... leave!"

Pace understood his time with Hades was up, so he nodded a thank you and turned away. Beau smiled and waved goodbye, following Pace back up the cold stone steps.

"Well, that wasn't normal," said Beau.

Paced laughed. "You're right about that."

"What are we going to do?"

"We need to find that sword!" said Pace. Beau grabbed his arm and turned him to face her,

"About sShearon?"

"Oh, we should have a meeting about that," said Pace. "We're always at least two steps behind every move they make."

Beau nodded in agreement, then looked over Pace's shoulder. "Looks like our yacht has arrived."

Charon had returned to collect them. Pace climbed into the skiff and Beau followed, steadying herself with a hand on Charon's shoulder. Then she stopped cold. In the endless dark, a light bloomed, gentle at first, then swelling, radiant, as if some hidden star had pierced the void. Her body trembled, overcome, every nerve alight with something vast and unearthly. And then blackness. Silence.

"Beau, Beau?" Pace said, gently shaking her until she responded to him.

"Sorry, what?" she said, feeling a little groggy.

"We need to get going," said Pace gesturing ahead. Beau looked up. It was the path going back up to the waterfall. She looked around, confused.

"How did we get here?" she asked.

"Are you alright? You seem a little out of it, ever since we got in the skiff."

"I, I saw..." She shook her head, forcing the image to a memory. "I think I'm just tired. Come on, we've got a lot of work to do."

The pair got to the top entrance of the cave and Pace took a moment to look around.

"What's up?" asked Beau.

"So, this place is neutral." He nodded to himself. "Bork will love this story," he said, then opened a portal.

Beau gave a cheeky smile and stepped through. "Gods before Masters!" she said, playing with electricity on her fingertips.

Pace rubbed his greying temples and followed her through.

Phlax Klophopaik

Chapter 27

"Whoa, what happened in here? said Phlax, as he entered the portal room for the first time. The room still had the plastoid covering rather than a finished roof and the walls had not been fully rebuilt yet.

"There was an incident," said Qútú, walking right behind the Storous. "But nothing you need to worry about. Are you all set for your first Calling?" he asked.

"Oh yes," said Phlax excitedly. Phlax was a descendant of the Cornuium and humanoid breeding program. The outcome was a new strand of DNA. They looked mostly humanoid, but with an extra wide mouth and a small nose. Instead of hair, they grew two horns that curved over their scalp and back around under their ears, ears that pointed outwards. They were known as placid beings with a high moral standing.

"I have all the rations we were told to pack, in here," said Phlax, tapping the utility belt hanging around his waist. "Drake has given us some great advice."

"That's good to hear," said Qútú, "I wish I had a mentor when I was young. Things were a lot different for me."

"Did you always want to be a Cydarion too?"

Qútú chuckled. "No, I had never heard of the Cydarions, until a cycle ago, when Beau contacted me."

"So, you knew Beau before joining?" asked Phlax. "I've met her a few times, she's funny!"

"Yes, we've worked together previously," said Qútú.

"You were a bounty hunter? Cool."

"I've had many jobs, Bounty Hunter, Bodyguard, Special Forces." Qútú shrugged. "Amongst other things."

I feel safer already, thought Phlax.

Just then, Theksun entered the portal room. He said a curt hello to Qútú and Phlax.

Qútú put an arm around Phlax. "Phlax, have you met Theksun before?" his free hand gestured toward the new arrival.

"Only briefly," said Phlax. "When he gave a talk in Drake's classroom. Although he had to leave before we could ask him any questions about his tattoos."

"I don't like talking about myself," said Theksun. "But I'm sure we'll get along, just fine." He smiled.

Phlax smiled back.

"Well, that sounds cosy," Qútú said sarcastically, as he walked over to number two portal. He moved his hand in a sweeping gesture toward the open portal. "Shall we? We've a demon to stop."

Theksun looked at Phlax. "Are you ready for this?" he asked.

Phlax patted his utility belt one more time and gave a great big smile. "I'm ready," he said.

Then, in single file, they all walked through the portal.

***

Theksun, Phlax and Qútú stood in the middle of a harvested field on an unknown planet. The portal closed behind them. Beneath their feet the crops had been pulled out from the ground. The soil, dry and arid. The air was warm, and a breeze blew into their faces. They heard a crackling noise behind them, and turned around to see a wall of flames, leaping skyward. All three of them took a step back. The faint smell of smoke wafted towards Theksun and Phlax.

Phlax coughed once. "I hope we're not going that way," he said.

"I agree," said Qútú, shielding his forehead from some heat. His red fluid eyes moved like waves in bottle.

Theksun stared at the flames.

"I feel the Calling in that direction," said Qútú, pointing in the opposite direction of the fire.

Oh good! I'm glad we don't have to go through the fire, thought Phlax. "Look," he said, kneeling in the dirt. "Track marks. We could follow them while we come up with a plan?"

"Good thinking, Storous," replied Theksun, eventually looking away from the fire. "You've been taught well." The three of them turned their backs on the slow approaching fire and followed the track marks. The fire got smaller in the ever-increasing distance. They passed through more empty fields of dried out produce. Tall thin trees grew along the edges. They walked for a whole rotation, not seeing another being, animal or even an insect, everything was just dry and brittle.

The two bright blue suns began getting low in the white sky by the time Qútú had picked a spot to camp for the night. He sat alone to meditate. Theksun and Phlax finished their rations quietly and lay back to stare at the emerging stars. An orange glow on the horizon constantly reminded them of the fire they had walked away from.

"So, what's your story?" Phlax asked Theksun out of the blue.

The tattooed body of Theksun stayed still, his hands interlocked behind his head as he looked at Phlax. "Story?" he asked, tilting his head as though not understanding the question.

"Yeah, your background, I've not been on a Calling before, and I want to know all about the guys I'm spending time with. What did you do before becoming a Cydarion?" Phlax asked.

"Oh, my story," mumbled Theksun, his gaze drifting off into the distant fiery glow.

There was a fraction of silence before Phlax started up again. "Well?" he urged, "How bad can it be?"

Theksun sat up slowly, his arms holding his torso up, and looked at Phlax directly in the eyes. "How bad can it be?" he repeated, a clear distaste for the question. He shook his head and whispered. "I killed my wife and son. I stood there and watched them both burn to death." He turned away; his voice rising. "Every night I hear their screams when I close my eyes, and every night I'm still standing there, listening to their cries for help, calling out my name!"

Phlax was stunned into silence.

"Is that it?" Theksun thumped the ground. "Is that what you wanted to know?"

Phlax flinched and cowered. "I, I, I'm sorry," he said, regretting that he ever asked the question. He swallowed hard. "Maybe I should just get some sleep," he said. "I'm very sorry for asking." His hands shook.

Theksun let out a hefty sigh and shook his head. "No, I'm sorry I got angry with you. I was out of order. The flames, they just..."

Phlax didn't feel any more at ease. "Okay," he replied quietly. At least the shakes were not so noticeable now.

"I don't really want to talk about my past, it can't be changed," said Theksun, his voice now calm. "But the future hasn't been recorded yet. It's what we do in the present that counts. Phlax..." Theksun paused. "Can I give you one piece of advice?"

"Erm, yeah?" Phlax mumbled, not sure what other response to give.

"Every morning you wake up, say to yourself, what I do today defines *me*!"

Phlax nodded. "I understand, thank you. I still think I should sleep now," he said, still wary of Theksun.

Theksun mumbled something to himself as the two of them settled down for the night. Phlax never taking his eyes off Theksun, who now had now turned onto his side.

"I didn't mean to scare you, young Storous. You are quite safe with me. I promise to protect you," said Theksun over his shoulder.

Phlax wondered if Theksun could see behind him. The words only eased Phlax a little, but he still waited until Theksun was sound asleep before closing his own eyes. One hand firmly clenched on his Alfont dagger. Just in case.

***

A section of meditation after the first sun had risen, had the Cydarions and their neophyte thinking clearly, before setting off towards the Calling. Phlax was noticeably always behind Theksun. After nearly a rotation of walking, in the distance, a slow-moving band was seen, and the warriors made their way towards them. Getting closer from the rear, they saw it was a group of sleighs. Wide bases with items stacked high atop. The runners of the sleighs were made from young tree trunks, thin, but strong enough to skim the dried ground. Cattle beasts were pulling the sleighs. The beasts had two long skinny legs; a large oval body covered in down. Its short neck held a small head with a flat nose, and a mouth that was good for grazing with two forward looking eyes. Qútú had noticed, that the further they travelled, the richer the soil became. The group seemed to be travelling in single file. Qútú explained to Phlax that it's so back members have an easier time using the same track marks. A shout came from the front of the group to cease and set up. Qútú and Theksun was impressed with the efficiency at which the sleighs were unloaded, and a small village of low yurts were set up in a circle. The off-worlders approached the village with smiles on their faces and a greeting on their lips.

Many of the women and children ran inside their accommodation, while the men picked up anything they could find and followed them through the village. One being walked towards them, with neither a weapon nor a smile.

"Travellers, how can we help you?" The voice wasn't warm and welcoming.

Qútú was the first to speak. "Hello friends," he said, taking a step closer to the native. The native moved back, one step.

"Do not fear, we are here to help you," said Qútú with a smile. The native stopped moving and stood their ground. Qútú took another step closer and gently placed one large hand on the native's shoulder. Immediately, a sense of warmth ran over the native's body and the acceptance of God, entered its heart. A smile entered its face.

Phlax was shocked.

"I am Ginfriffes, the matriarch," the native said, bowing to the newcomers.

"It is a pleasure to meet you Ginfriffes. I am Qútú, this is Theksun and Phlax," he said gesturing to his two companions. "How did you know we were travellers?" Qútú asked.

"You are not one of us, we alone live on this ring," Ginfriffes said, speaking of the planet.

"Ah," Qútú said with a smile. "You are correct, we're travellers, but we are here for a reason."

The natives raised their weapons again. Qútú quickly explained that they were there to help their people and not to take anything from them.

The beings slightly resembled a Hyena, with two hind legs and two longer arms at the front. Their shoulders being higher than their waist, with a gentle, sloping back. The back legs had paws, but the front arms had three opposable thick fingers. Their skulls were wider than they were tall. Often standing on their hind legs, their exposed skin showed off a spotted pattern, each one unique. A strip of fur cascaded down their backs, from the ears to the tail.

The Cydarions were soon invited to stay for a meal before dark, which they gratefully accepted.

***

"Qútú, how did you do that thing earlier?" asked Phlax.

Qútú looked confused. "What thing?"

"When you put your hand on the shoulder of Ginfriffes. I saw an energy pass between you and her. What was it?"

"Oh, that," Qútú said with a smile. "I was passing on God's acceptance. She then understood his light."

"Wow," exclaimed Phlax. "Can all Cydarions do that? Drake hasn't mentioned it yet."

"No, unfortunately not," said Qútú. "Only I can."

"That's a shame. How did you know you could do it?"

"I didn't. During my first Calling, on Muncia, sShearon and I were having difficulty convincing a local that we were sent by God to help them. So, I put a hand on their shoulder; to let them know I wasn't a threat. That's when I felt God's light pass through my body and into theirs. It took a fraction for them to register what had happened, but when they did, they were humbled and grateful." Qútú looked down at his hands. "I have the power of God in my hands." Then he laughed uncontrollably.

Phlax laughed too. "Do you use it every time?" he asked, although he had to wait until Qútú had stopped laughing before he got an answer.

"No, not always. Sometimes you can't get close enough, or it just isn't needed."

Phlax nodded. *That would be so cool.*

"*You* may get given a special gift from God, when you take the pledge of allegiance," said Qútú.

"I hope so," said Phlax. "But either way, I just want to be the best Cydarion I can be."

Qútú smiled again. "That's the right attitude. I'm sure you'll be brave."

"Thank you. Oh, it looks like dinner is ready," said Phlax, pointing toward the bowls of paste being laid out.

The meal, which comprised of simple vegetables and cold water, made into a paste, didn't look appetising to Phlax.

Qútú is lucky to have those gasses and nutrients fed into him through that jawbone. At least he doesn't have to smell or eat this stuff. Phlax glanced across at Theksun, who was obviously enjoying the meal. *Always try something once, Drake advised us.* He plucked up the courage and took his first mouthful. *Mmm, it's not bad.* He finished the meal in silence while he watched some younglings play in the fields.

After the meal was over, Phlax decided to ask Ginfriffes a question. "Why don't you cook the vegetables in the water and make a tasty stew?" he said, trying to be helpful.

"We don't use fire, we are mesmerized by it," Ginfriffes replied. "It draws us in and engulfs us. So, we stay away."

"Then we must tell you, there is a large fire about, a rotation from here, and with this dried ground, it's possible the fire could spread here," warned Theksun.

Ginfriffes nodded. "Yes, the fire is inevitable. You see it is all part of this ecosystem," she said. "We have four seasons. Destruction, Birth, Growth and Life. Destruction is the fire; it burns up everything in its path. It fertilises the earth and releases the burnt seeds, trees as well as the grasses," Ginfriffes explained.

"After the fire comes the rain, the season of Birth. The water puts out the fires, feeds life into the seeds and creates our watering holes. This is followed by Growth. The suns shine, and all the vegetation shoots up. Good, fertilized land with water and two suns, make things grow very quickly. The season of Life is this one, the one everything lives in. We stay in harmony with the planet. We only hunt twice a cycle and use every part of the kill. Not just for food, it's hide is used for repairing our yurts. The bones are made into utensils and tools. The skull of the animal is used as a bowl for water and the shoulder blades as plates. Ligaments are stretched out and used for our bows, smaller bones are used as the arrows. We crush its backbone into a powder and mix it with the muscles and sinew to feed our farmed animals. They also get to graze the freshly grown crops." Ginfriffes paused to take a gulp of water. "We move every thirty rotations, to stay in front of Destruction, harvesting the crops as we get to them. Some of our young adult's travel to Birth, to collect the fresh water."

"It sounds like a very peaceful life," said Qútú.

"It was, until the burning man arrived," replied Ginfriffes.

"The burning man?" Theksun questioned, almost too quickly.

Ginfriffes nodded. "We don't know when he arrived, but he's been luring the water carriers into the fire, killing them. It's devastating our population, and we don't know what to do, we still need water."

"Have you tried to defeat him?" asked an eager Phlax. Theksun nudged Phlax and gave him a questioning look.

Ginfriffes smiled and answered. "You must be a young one too. I'm sorry, I'm not familiar with your species: We don't get many visitors." Her eyes gazed into Qútú's pulsing red pupils.

Theksun threw his arm around Phlax and squeezed him. "Yeah, he's still learning." Then he looked at Phlax. "How would they fight a man of fire?" Theksun asked. Phlax was still a little wary of Theksun and was afraid to upset him.

"With...." Phlax paused. "Oh, yeah," he said, as he suddenly realised what Ginfriffes had mentioned about being mesmerized by fire.

"We shall do what we can for you," offered Qútú genuinely.

Both the suns were soon setting, and without any fires to cast light, the village soon succumbed to the dark. Theksun said his farewells and found an empty spot of land to lay out, for a night under the stars. Before Qútú could do the same, Phlax indicated that he wanted to say something, but waited until Theksun was out of earshot.

"Master, can I ask you something?" Phlax asked.

"Of course," Qútú replied, the red in his eyes stopped moving and enlarged as he listened. "What is it?" Qútú had picked up that Phlax was starting to feel uncomfortable. He put his hand onto the shoulder of Phlax. "It would serve you well as a Cydarion, to ask all questions, especially the difficult ones."

Phlax nodded and swallowed hard before asking his question. "Erm, it's about Theksun," he whispered. Qútú didn't respond, his eyes just pulsed like a heartbeat, listening to the young Phlax.

"Well, he, he... he said he killed his wife and child; he watched them burn to death and didn't do anything. I don't know why he is a Cydarion, I don't think we can trust him," Phlax blurted out, all in one sentence.

Qútú let out a loud sigh. "What else did he tell you?"

"Nothing! That's why I'm afraid of him," said Phlax nervously looking around.

Qútú smiled, his pupils started to sway. "First of all, you can completely trust him. That should go without saying, Storous," His pupils narrowed to a dot to emphasise the point. "But he was only testing you, to see how you would react. Probably with this reaction, you've just failed." He laughed quietly.

Phlax let out a huge gasp of air that he didn't realise he had been holding. "Oh, thank you, I thought it was all true, he was so convincing."

"Oh, it's all true," Qútú said, closely watching the reaction of Phlax. A reaction that was priceless to Qútú.

The eyes of Phlax bulged in their sockets, his pupils dilated to the full diameter of his eyeballs and his mouth dropped open, seemingly to the floor. A little rasp was heard from his backside.

Qútú chuckled at the sight. "Phlax, you questioning a Cydarion, means you're questioning Master Pace. Is that what's happening here?" asked Qútú, with a stern look.

"Err, no, no. Not at all. I'm just... I don't know," stuttered Phlax, not knowing what to say.

Qútú relaxed. "I'm only joking, you should question things, especially when your soul tells you to. Question me whenever you want, even Master Pace... within reason," he added.

Phlax looked more confused than ever. Qútú carried on. "It is your role as a Cydarion to question everything, but also, you must have a lot of faith. Our faith in others is strong, use that as *your* strength," he said.

Phlax nodded as he started to understand what Qútú was saying.

"As for Theksun, maybe he didn't mean to scare you, but he does carry his own demons."

"He did apologise straight after, said he would protect me," Phlax mentioned.

"There you go," Qútú said encouragingly. "You can trust him."

"So, everything he said was true?" asked Phlax.

Qútú nodded. "In a way," he said. "About three hundred cycles ago he was happily married. Had a young boy too, who was growing up strong. Theksun was so proud and would do anything for both of them. He said his boy had the good looks and smarts from his mother, the strength from God and his cheekiness from Theksun. For eight cycles they lived in happiness. One rotation, his wife received a visit from the mayor of the town. Apparently, the mayor and Theksun's wife used to court, when they were both in adult education. Well, since he was now the mayor, he decided he wanted her back. She refused and told him as such. Well, a few rotations later, Theksun returned home from work and the mayor was there, assaulting his wife. He did what anyone would do and forcibly removed the mayor, threatening to press charges. What Theksun didn't realise was that the planet enforcers were in the pocket of the mayor. Theksun, from then on, was constantly hassled by those planet enforcers. Later, arriving home after work, he saw that the mayor was waiting outside for him. The mayor's security personnel taunted him. When suddenly his house exploded. Theksun tried to run inside, but the security personnel grabbed him and wouldn't let go, no matter how hard he struggled. The mayor then taunted him.

"If I can't have her, no one will."

Phlax gasped, a look of shock covered his face.

Qútú carried on. "His house was on fire at this point. His wife and child had been tied up inside. He could hear their screams and tried in vain to rescue them, but it was to no avail. He was forced to watch his family and home burn to ash. He was threatened to stay away from the mayor. They only left after the last flame flickered out. Theksun ran into the smouldering building, only to find the ashes of everything, he couldn't distinguish between the bones or wood."

"But the fire wasn't his fault," said Phlax jumping in.

"I know. He even knows, but you can't stop someone blaming themselves for something. You see, he says it was his job to protect his family, and he failed," said Qútú. "Maybe you could be more diplomatic with your questions next time?" Qútú suggested.

Phlax nodded in agreement. "So how did he become a Cydarion?" Phlax asked genuinely.

"After the fire, he had no family to help him through the trauma, so, he wandered the city for cycles, homeless and tormented. Eventually the city took him in and had him evaluated, sending him to an institution for the mentally unstable. There he was kept for more than fifty cycles before being released. Now, because of the incident, which the mayor spun to his own advantage, he was elected the new Premier, by votes of sympathy. From there, he became head minister or something and totally forgot about Theksun. That was the only reason Theksun was released. Anyway, while Theksun was locked up, he found God. By the time he left, he had a plan. He had decided to face his nemesis, one on one. The day he was released, he made his way to the minister's office. Each and every security personnel were disabled by Theksun along the way. Obviously, the minister was surprised to see him and feared for his life. Theksun reached into his pocket, the minister had expected to be killed and started to beg for mercy. Theksun pulled out a well-worn book of God, the one he had read while being locked up. He had read it cover to cover, non-stop. Theksun slammed it on the desk, looked directly into the minister's eyes and said to him, "I forgive you." Theksun then walked away. He wasn't seen again for nearly two hundred cycles," said Qútú.

"Two hundred cycles? What was he doing?" asked Phlax.

"Theksun went on a spiritual journey. He won't say exactly where he went, but during that time, he found the high priestess of Shendu and became enlightened. They called him 'Karoto', which means enlightened one. That was where he got his tattoos. Each animal represents his awareness of the elements. Air, water, and fire. His body being the earth. After that he left to spread peace and faith. Nyk crossed paths with Theksun and listened to what he had to say."

"He's been through so much," said Phlax. "I shouldn't have judged him."

"Not everyone is as they seem on the outside," agreed Qútú. "Now, it is time for us both to get some rest. Oh, and Phlax?"

"Yes?"

"You can read all of that in the record archives. Maybe you should visit there... from time to time," said Qútú.

"Yes master," said an ashamed Phlax, as he got up and went off to find a suitable place to sleep.

Ginfriffes

Chapter 28

T he whole village was awake at first light and got busy readying the sleighs for another rotation of travel. Qútú, Theksun and Phlax were invited to ride on Ginfriffes' sleigh, all of whom willingly accepted. They talked the whole journey about their lives and other planets. Ginfriffes explained that this was not their home planet.

"Our ancestors had arrived on this ring planet, a millennia ago. At that time, there were an abundance of animals here. But, after cycles of constant hunting, they had virtually hunted the animals to extinction. Eventually, they realised what they had done and had to change their ways. The ancestors turned to farming to protect the animals and we were able to survive as a species." She paused for a brief time. "We have a prophecy, Qútú," Ginfriffes said. "When our species have ended all mutation wars, they will come for us."

"Mutation wars?" Qútú asked.

Ginfriffes nodded and explained further. "Our ancestors were picked for this mission because of their pure unaltered DNA. On our home world, the clans were constantly at war with each other. Each side mutated themselves, by genetically altering their DNA, to gain a weaponised advantage. A group of scientists got together and came up with a plan to save our original DNA. Sending a select group off to a faraway planet and stay there until they collected us. Then we can return to a peaceful home. One where we can settle and finally rest. Any information that was brought here from our home world was destroyed; fire consumed their travel ship within the first cycle. Our people had tried to put the fires out, but many were lost. They had to live in harmony with the planet. We now know that is the natural order of the planet."

Qútú didn't say anything, his pupils stopped pulsing, his black voids stared straight ahead.

Phlax broke the silence. "Were your ancestors not afraid of the fire back then?" he asked.

Ginfriffes smiled. "No, they were the brave ones. They left their home world to save our species, knowing that they would never see their home again. They weren't afraid of anything. But, over the long cycles, we had grown wary of the destruction and power of fire, vowing to never use it. Now we can't even look at fire without being drawn to it."

The red in Qútú's eyes returned and started to pulse again. He turned to Theksun and whispered something. Theksun, in return, gave a sorrowful nod.

"Ginfriffes, we have something to tell you, and it won't be easy to hear," said Qútú.

Ginfriffes looked at Qútú, a little confused. "What is it?" she asked.

"Theksun and I have visited your home planet, Huet," replied Qútú. The jaws of both Phlax and Ginfriffes dropped wide open.

"You've been to their home planet? What happened?" asked Phlax, after a fraction of silence.

Phlax was ignored.

"Huet?" Ginfriffes repeated, wrinkling her forehead. It was more of a question to herself.

Qútú nodded. "Your prophecy was true; they *were* looking for you."

"That's great," exclaimed Phlax, with a little cheer.

"Were... Qútú, you said, they *were* looking for us." Theksun placed an arm around Ginfriffes.

"Yes," Qútú said, the red in his eyes moving very slowly. "We were there about half a cycle ago, one of our first Callings together. Your people were dying out; there were no younglings left."

Ginfriffes looked down, watching the ground slowly disappear underneath the sleigh. "They did it then," she nodded. "They finally killed themselves," whispered Ginfriffes. The noise of daily life carried on around her. She thought for a while before speaking again, her voice along with her spirit, broken. "We weren't sent here just to return home at a later time, restoring our species. Our ancestors were cowards. Instead of making things right, they ran away." A snarl appeared on her face, and she pulled up the sleigh, coming to a stop. She jumped to the ground and started digging at the earth using her hands and feet. "You cowards, you cowards." She repeated, over and over.

The other sleighs all came to a halt and looked on, watching the actions of Ginfriffes.

"What is she doing?" asked Phlax.

"It seems she is angry at her ancestors and wants to get at them," replied Theksun.

"But why is she digging?" wondered Phlax.

"Everything returns to the earth eventually," said Theksun.

Qútú jumped down from the sleigh to speak with Ginfriffes. "I think you have misunderstood me, my friend. They didn't kill themselves," Qútú said. Ginfriffes stopped digging and looked up at Qútú, her head tilted to one side. Qútú sat down in the dirt beside the matriarch.

"Our Calling there was because of a devil. We got to know your people; they explained that the wars had ended over two hundred cycles ago and that they now had peace. They did send scouting parties out to look for you. They never forgot about you. *Their* prophecy foretold, of a set of brave male and females, who had set out across the stars, to save your species. When the time was right, and peace covered the planet, Huet, they would search for their saviours. That is you, Ginfriffes," Qútú said. "They *were* still dying out, but not by war of their own making. They couldn't reproduce. Fifty-seven cycles, and they hadn't produced any young."

Ginfriffes looked deflated, she was finding all this difficult to hear.

"Theksun and I got to the devil's lair, but it was empty, he had already left. We found evidence of a red poison which had been released into the water table. The poison killed the reproduction cells in their bodies. It wasn't detected until it was too late. I am sorry, there is nothing we could have done. They made the decision to stop the search for their saviours. Knowing that if they brought you home, it would only doom your whole species." Qútú paused. "Ginfriffes, you are the last surviving members of your species," he said with compassion.

There was a fraction of silence before Ginfriffes spoke. "But we too, are dying out, we don't know how to stop it," she said.

"That is why we are here," smiled Qútú. "We shall do what we can for you."

"It's a miracle you found us," said Ginfriffes.

"It was Gods will," nodded Qútú.

***

During pre-dark dinner, Ginfriffes, along with the help of the Cydarions, re-counted to the whole village, the story of their planet and its demise.

"What can you do against the fire man," asked one villager to Theksun.

"We shall do whatever we can to help you," answered Theksun. "We will fight until the end for you, if necessary."

One villager stood up tall. "I shall fight with you!" he proudly announced.

"No!" snapped Ginfriffes, before anyone else could reply. "Donfriffes, you are my only son, I cannot let you take that risk," she said.

Donfriffes had to say something. "I can't sit here and watch these good strangers fight for us, for our lives, our species, and not feel any guilt. You taught me to stand up for myself and do the right thing. Well, this is it! These people..." He pointed at the Cydarions. "Have brought us news of our home world. Something no one else has ever done. Telling us that we are the only survivors. *I will fight*! Not against our own brothers and sisters, like our ancestors once did, but *for* us; for the survival of our species!"

"How can you even face the burning man without being mesmerized?" asked Ginfriffes.

Qútú's eyes glowed red.

Donfriffes looked down at the ground. "I don't know. But I..., *We* must do something," he replied, stamping a foot into the ground to emphasise his point.

Ginfriffes opened her mouth, but another younger villager raised his head. "I will fight too!" he shouted.

"And I," shouted another.

"Me too," called a young female, who came and stood by Donfriffes.

He nuzzled her neck. "You don't have to do this," Donfriffes said to the female.

"I do." said the female. "I want our family to survive." It took a fraction for Donfriffes to realise exactly what she meant. But when he did, he licked her ear and placed his hand on top of hers.

Four more villagers of various ages agreed to fight and make a stand.

Ginfriffes' posture sank. "I fear this could be the end," she said, voice cracking.

"I may have a plan," Qútú said, his eyes returning to a swishing motion. "But first, I need to know everything you can tell me about the burning man."

"Of course," replied Ginfriffes. Everyone who was willing to fight moved into a smaller circle and a plan was discussed.

By the time the villagers had dispersed, a plan had been formulated. And, for the first time in a long while, the villagers all went to sleep with hope in their hearts.

As Phlax was settling down for his rest, he heard a type of grunting, just outside of camp. The dried brown foliage rustling with movement. Phlax got up, wondering if he should wake Qútú or Theksun. He made his decision. Grabbing his Alfont dagger, he made his way over towards the noise. To his surprise he found a young villager crying. Phlax made some rustling of his own, so as to not spook the young one.

"Are you okay?" Phlax asked, hiding his dagger. The young villager saw him and stopped her crying.

She sniffed. "Yes, I'll be fine," she said.

"I don't like to see anyone upset," Phlax said, sitting down in the dried foliage, not too close to the villager.

She sniffed again. "You're one of the new strangers, aren't you?" asked the female.

Phlax smiled. "Yes, I am, we're here to help you," he said proudly. "I'm Phlax," he gestured to himself.

The female came closer and sat down opposite of Phlax. "I'm Jogille," she said quietly.

"It's nice to meet you, Jogille. But why are you crying?" Phlax asked out of concern.

"Oh, you heard that?" Jogille said, a little embarrassed.

"Oh, it's okay," Phlax reassured Jogille. "You're allowed to be upset, you've heard a lot of information recently, and none of it was good. I'm sorry about that," he said looking down to his feet as he spoke.

Jogille shook her head. "It's not that!" she exclaimed, her demeanour was defeated and standoffish.

He looked at her. "You want to fight, don't you?" said Phlax, assessing her posture.

"Yes!" yelped Jogille. "But they think I'm not old enough."

"I understand," said Phlax. "You want to protect your family."

Jogille nodded. "My two brothers were killed by the burning man. I want revenge, I want to kill him, I want to rip him apart with my teeth!" she said in anger.

"Revenge is not the way," said Phlax calmly.

"But that's all I want!"

"Please, sit with me," Phlax said patting the ground next to him. Jogille looked at him, before slowly moving and sitting down by his side. "Now," said Phlax, transitioning to a meditative state. "Relax. Don't think about revenge, just let God into your heart."

Jogille followed Phlax and closed her eyes.

The pair sat, quiet and motionless for half a section.

"Do you feel him?" asked Phlax eventually, hopeful that Jogille had had a change of heart.

"No," replied Jogille.

Phlax smiled. "That's okay, you don't have to feel him. You've let him in. I can assure you; he is there."

"Is he supposed to tell me what to do?"

"No, he never tells you what to do. Sometimes he'll guide you, sometimes he'll correct you. Other times he'll leave you alone. It is always *your* decision," explained Phlax.

"If it's my decision, why are my parents saying no?"

Phlax chuckled. "What does your heart really say?"

Jogille thought about the question and looked deep within herself. "It says to look after everyone," she replied.

Phlax nodded. "That doesn't mean you have to fight. With the strongest villagers going off to fight, your people will need a guardian. Could you be that guardian?" he asked.

"Yes," snapped Jogille. "I can look after all of us!"

"I believe you can," said Phlax with a smile. "Just have some faith." Jogille pranced around in circles at the thought of being a protector. "Even guardians need their rest," said Phlax, getting to his feet.

"Thank you, stranger," said Jogille. "For showing me my own path." With that, she bounded off. Phlax made his way back to his own sleeping spot, pleased with himself for being a real Cydarion, if only in training.

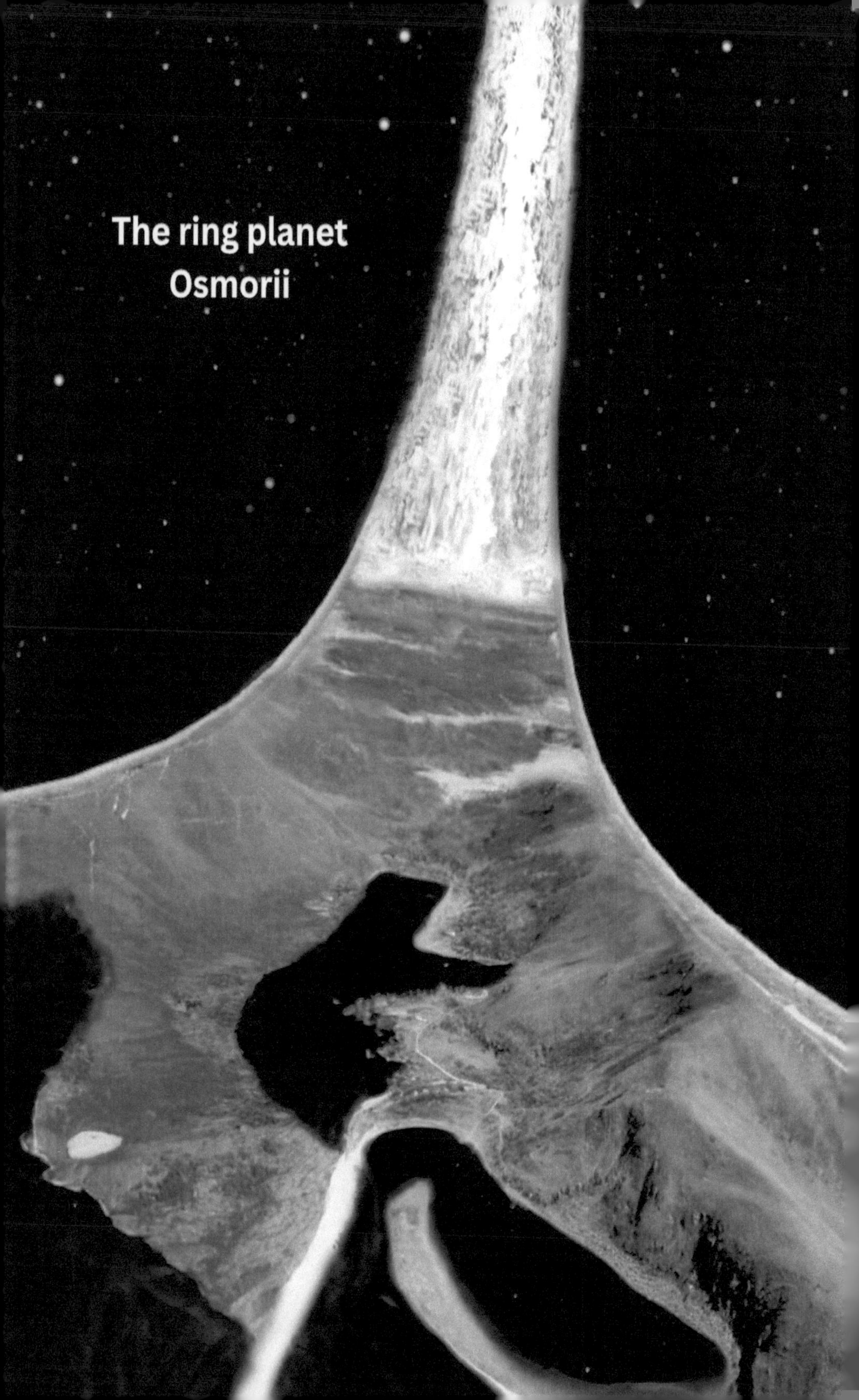
The ring planet
Osmorii

Chapter 29

As the second sun rose, Phlax and Theksun climbed atop two of the large, farmed beasts. Jogille ran up to Phlax and said, "Be careful out there. Don't worry about the village, I'll make sure we're safe." She gave a little yelp and ran off.

"What was that all about?" Theksun asked.

Phlax smiled. "She found her faith," he replied. Theksun gave an approving nod. On masse, the village pack set off across the fields, the two beasts bounding after them.

Qútú turned to Ginfriffes. "Farewell my friend," he said before running after the group, soon catching up with his two companions. They travelled fast for four and a half rotations, only stopping for water and sleep. By mid-rotation on the fifth, they had reached the season of Birth. Gone was the heat of the blazing suns, and a welcome cool breeze blew onto their faces. The air smelled fresh and clean, refreshing. The ground got wetter the further into the season they travelled. Ash from the Destruction season covered the ground in a thin crust that crunched under every footstep.

"We must be careful from here," said Donfriffes to the group, "we've never seen the burning man this far out, but we need to be wary nonetheless."

"I agree," said Qútú. "If any of you see fire, inform me."

They carried on forward, along a narrow pathway. A great lake either side of them, spreading out as far as the eye could see. The rain penetrated the Cydarions clothes, soaking them, until they were just useless garments. Two full rotations of walking and constant vigilance got the group to the halfway point of the season. It was also the heaviest rain they had encountered. Settling down together in one circle, sentries took it in turn staying awake, watching over the others. The rest, for all of them, was tumultuous: The rain pounded on the waters relentlessly as storm clouds thundered above them. Little sleep was had that night, for their minds were filled with apprehension.

The following rotation, with new light barely peeking through the dark clouds, they set off again, Qútú leading the way. For some, they knew it could be their last rotation alive. Phlax commented to Theksun that he had never seen a more determined group march toward their fears.

"They make me proud to know such fine spirits," said Theksun.

A further half rotation of marching, before an orange hue was spotted on the horizon.

"Not far until we start seeing the flames," said Theksun.

The group was called to a halt.

"Donfriffes, you keep everyone here. Look out over the horizon and wait for our signal," said Qútú. The pack nodded in agreement. Qútú, Theksun and Phlax went ahead on foot, following the Calling. Flames appeared, small at first, growing larger as they approached the Destruction season. A mix of smoke and damp air filled the lungs of Phlax, who gave out a loud cough.

"This is close enough," said Qútú as he looked at Theksun. Theksun unwrapped his tunic, exposing his tattooed torso, and knelt with one knee on the ground. Extending his left hand to contact the ground he recited a spiritual verse. His eyes rolled into his head and his body stiffened. The outline of the tattooed Echidna started to glow white, and his skin bubbled. The shape of the animal formed, and jumped from his arm to the ground. The Echidna sniffed the air and looked at Qútú, before running off into the flames.

"That's so cool," exclaimed Phlax. "I've never seen him actually do it before."

"It is impressive, isn't it?" agreed Qútú. "Your job is to look after his body, here," he said.

"What happens if he doesn't come back to his body?" asked Phlax.

"If Theksun's soul doesn't return to his body for sustenance, both vessels would wither away. It takes a lot of energy for him to project his soul to an element," said Qútú.

***

Theksun, now as an Echidna, scurried through the ash laden floor of a smouldering forest, his nose twitching in all directions. His little ears only picking up the sound of fire cracking and spitting. The heat getting more intense as he made his way deeper into the flames. The Calling drew Theksun to the fire's edge. Through the flickering heat, he caught sight of the devil crouched in a circle of flames, gnawing on a charred branch. The devils head snapped up, eyes locking onto the Echidna-just as Theksun's paw cracked a dry twig. He froze, nose twitching.

"What's this?" the devil muttered, rising to his feet. His tail dragged across the ash as he tossed aside the half-eaten bark and strode closer.

"You don't look native. But I'll take you nonetheless." Flames flared in his palms as he bent to snatch the Echidna. Theksun sprang first, spines flaring as he curled into a ball and hurled himself at the devil's hand.

"Argh!" The devil staggered back, five quills buried deep in his palm. Snarling, he ripped them free and snapped them in his fist.

Theksun scurried, weaving in zigzags through the flames, but the devil gave chase, fire erupting from his body. His rage carried him further than he realised, until he overtook the Echidna. Ignoring the pain, he clamped both hands around the thrashing creature and lifted it high, a cruel grin splitting his elongated face.

"Grrr, you beast!" he roared, tearing spines out one by one as the Echidna shrieked.

So focused was he on his prize that he didn't see Qútú Charge. A swift kick slammed into the devil's gut, forcing him to hurl Theksun aside. The Echidna's screech tore through the firestorm.

Fuelled by pain, the devil snapped upright, backhanding Qútú to the ground. Without pausing to fight, he bolted toward the season of Birth, fiery footprints searing the damp ash.

Theksun crawled from the blaze, spines torn, body trembling. Whimpering, the Echidna dragged itself up his arm, clinging to him and slumped into place. The animal melted into his skin and Theksun was reanimated. He gulped in some air and glanced around. He was a little disorientated, before suddenly realising Phlax was missing.

"Phlax?" he shouted, scanning the area. A sonic boom vibrated through his body. He shouted again, louder this time, "PHLAX?"

***

From a safe distance, Phlax had seen the devil attack Theksun and heard his cry of pain.

"Nooo!" Phlax screamed, and ran to help Theksun, without thinking about his own safety. Jumping over burning bushes and embers falling like snowflakes, he looked for the injured Echidna.

The devil sent fireballs into the forest, which exploded all around Phlax, branches creaked and cracked above him. One bough split in two and came crashing down on top of Phlax. It knocked him down pinning him to the ground. He saw the flames creeping closer, as he blacked out.

The sonic boom rattled Phlax back to consciousness, the flames had scorched the side of his face. He screamed in pain, and tried to move, but the thick, dense bough was too heavy for him to lift. He only just heard his name being called, but still dizzy, he tried to shout, "Theksun." The name only coming out as a mutter. He swallowed and tried again, "Theksun, HELP!"

***

Qútú shook his head clear, admonishing himself for not doing enough, and got to his feet. He ran after the devil. The devil threw fireballs back towards Qútú. Although he managed to dodge every one of them, they did slow him down.

The devil kept on running, the heat from his body turned the rain into steam. Qútú stopped running and pulled out the E-whip, from his utility belt, along with a sonic pellet. Throwing the pellet high into the air, he depressed the two thumb switches on the E-whip, and it whirred to life. Qútú arched his arm back, and flicked the whip up into the air, the shaft staying firm in his grip. A long-tapered whip unravelled from the handle, a glowing yellow ball of energy on the end. The energy ball located the sonic pellet, smashing straight through it.

Crack, BOOM!

A sonic wave exploded out in all directions. The trees that were on fire behind him, rustled and swayed, some of the flames extinguished.

Donfriffes and his group instantly looked up, toward the loud sound. "That's the signal!" he growled. Then, right on time, the burning man appeared in the distance, running towards them. A few deep growls were given and the group set off, bounding toward the devil.

Donfriffes and his clan sprinted towards the devil like a hunting party. Trying their hardest not to be mesmerised by the flames. They kept their eyes on the devil, soon surrounding him. Snarling and snapping every time the devil tried to reach out and grab a villager. Their instinct was to head into the flames, but their shear will, stopped them from approaching. Qútú quickly arrived, his E-whip still in hand.

"Devil, give yourself up, we will tolerate you no more!" the Cydarion exclaimed.

"Never!" shouted the devil, "I *shall* please my father."

"You only get one chance to…"

The devil spun around. He kept spinning and spinning, faster and faster. This was something the Cydarion had never seen before. The spinning caused a wet tornado of ash. With the devils' exponential heat added, the ash dried and ignited. He started a fire tornado. Qútú flicked his E-whip at the devil, but it was ineffective, only bouncing back from the tornado. Qútú had to move quickly to stop himself being hit by the rebounding energy ball. The village clan also backed off, trying to avert their eyes. Except for one, Donfriffes. He snarled, looked at the mother of his unborn pup, and leapt into the fire. Qútú gasped. The smell of singed fur filled the air. Growls and screams echoed all around them. The fire tornado slowed to a stop, the rain extinguishing the fire. When the air cleared, Donfriffes lay on the ground, the devil on top of him, dead. Donfriffes breathed his last breath, as his jaws released from the devils' shoulder. The rest of the clan didn't hesitate, they all pounced, ripping the devil to pieces, limb from limb, flesh from torso, its bones crunching in powerful jaws. Within three frenzied fractions, there was nothing left of the devil, all flesh and bone had been consumed.

"That's not the way *we* work," Qútú said to the clan.

"It's the way *we* work," exclaimed a villager with a snarl.

Qútú sighed. "I understand, but *we* could have given him a chance."

The bloodlust soon drained from the villagers' thirst. One villager addressed Qútú. "We're sorry, but it's in our nature."

Qútú bowed. "Lupianous, I apologise, it really was your call," the Cydarion said.

"Please do not bow, it is us, who should bow to you," Lupianous said. The rest of the clan then followed her lead and lay their forearms down, raising their backsides.

"Make your way back to your families," Qútú said.

"Where are the other travellers?" Lupianous asked.

"I shall find them, you have done enough," replied Qútú honestly.

"We can't do that," said Lupianous. "*We* travelled as a clan; *we* go home as a clan."

Qútú smiled. "Thank you."

***

Theksun had heard a child's cry for help, coming from inside the flames. He froze to the spot; awful memories flashed through his mind.

A blood curdling scream brought Theksun out of his tormented memory. He had to act quickly. Wiping the tears from his eyes, he ran into the burning forest, towards the trapped Phlax. He found him, flailing on the ground, trapped, unable to extinguish the approaching flames. At great danger to himself, Theksun tried to clear away any flammables around Phlax. Just then, the bough stopped smouldering and burst into flames. Theksun wasted no time, he started to recite the spiritual verse.

"No!" Phlax shouted, grabbing Theksun's leg, a look of desperation in his eyes.

"Trust me," Theksun said, looking back into his eyes, and started again with the spiritual verse. The flames starting to burn Phlax, and he yelled out again. Theksun's eyes rolled back into his head and the outline of the tattooed Echidna started to glow white, the skin bubbling until the shape of in Echidna started to form. He stopped mid-verse and, with the raised tattoo on his arm, he pushed his body onto the flaming bough and lifted it. It was barely off the ground, but enough for Phlax to claw his body free.

"Theksun," Phlax shouted, pulling the Cydarion out of his spiritual trance. Theksun's eyes came back into position and his tattoo settled down. He looked down at the burnt disfigured face of Phlax. Without speaking, he scooped up the young Storous, and ran out of the flames into the rain, both of them collapsing into the sodden ash.

It didn't take long before Theksun and Phlax were located.

"We shall carry the young one back to the village," offered Lupianous.

Theksun shook his head. "No, Phlax is injured, I shall take him back to the Citadel, he needs medical attention."

Qútú agreed. "Tell Bork, I'll be back later. I will travel back to the village and speak with Ginfriffes," he said.

Theksun acknowledged Qútú, then opened a portal to the Citadel and walked through, an unconscious Phlax, draped in his arms.

It only took four rotations of running before the clan reached the village and an explanation was given of the occurred events. A small celebration was held the following rotation in honour of Donfriffes.

"I am sorry for your loss," said Qútú to Ginfriffes. "Donfriffes showed good spirit. He should make you proud."

Ginfriffes smiled a little. "Thank you, we shall carry his name with our ancestors. He was as brave as they were."

"I hear you have a grandpup on the way?" Qútú said.

"Yes," Ginfriffes nodded. "He shall know who his father really was," she said.

Qútú was a little surprised. "You know it'll be a boy?" he asked.

"Of course," Ginfriffes said. "A mother always knows."

Qútú smiled and bowed. "We used to have a similar saying on my home world," he said.

Qútú pulled a locator from his utility belt and thumbed it on. The screen flared, and a single appeared. "Gruonia?" His voiced cracked. "That's... my galaxy." His chest tightened, eyes fixed on the glow. Red pupils throbbed like pounding drums as the numbers spun. One by one, the columns locked into place, each digit pulling him closer to the truth, until the final coordinates settled, unmistakably, in his home.

He looked to the sky, searching. "Hmmm," he said, before hitting the 'save location' button. He turned the device off and replaced it back in its pouch.

Qútú promised Ginfriffes he would return. With supplies, a ship and the coordinates of Huet. He would bring the knowledge to test and purify the waters, so they could begin anew on their homeworld. At last, after his farewell, Qútú stepped through the portal, certain their prophecy was finally within reach.

Snow beast

Chapter 30

Crisp white snow blanketed the ground, unmarked and untouched. The air was fresh and clean, the sky a dark blue, with the occasional white fluffy cloud. One white sun hung low in the sky, too far away from the planet for its heat to warm up the surface. The two Cydarions, Dok and sShearon, looked around; there was nothing that could be seen, except for the covering of white snow.

A loud roar suddenly echoed across the sky. Dok and sShearon spun around to face the portal. Only a melted line of snow now stood where it was once active. Beyond that, two hundred meters away, three large animals sneered and chomped at the air, their noses sniffing the air for the scent of the two intruders onto their land. One stared at Dok directly and let out a mighty roar. A large grey wolflike creature bared its needle like teeth. A bony plate covered the top of the skull. Its hunter's eyes had locked onto its prey. Folding back two large sonar ears, it set off at a gallop towards Dok.

"I don't think it'sss a welcoming party," said sShearon.

Dok unstrapped his blaster planted his feet wide, extended his claws, and shot a couple of rounds. The first bolt hit the approaching animal on the bony plate, which just deflected the round. The second round missed completely, but the third hit it directly in the chest. A small explosion ripped open the chest cavity and the animal fell to the floor; black blood oozed from its gaping wound. A second animal set off racing towards him. Dok fired again, aiming for the chest area, but every time the blaster bolt got close, the animal ducked its head, meeting the blaster bolt with its bony shield, and deflected it.

"It had watched and learned," Dok whispered to himself.

He holstered his gun and dropped to all fours, muscles coiled, claws tearing through the snow as he charged the incoming beast. Both leapt at once, snarls ripping the air. The hostile's paw slashed at his head. Dok blocked it with his left and drive his right into its shoulder, claws sinking deep. The creature shrieked as pain surged through its body.

Using its momentum, Dok twisted, swinging onto its back like a rider mounting a wild steed. He inhaled once, then sank his canines into its neck. Veins, tendon and bone, all shredded in a single crushing bite. The vertebrae snapped, and the beast collapsed, sliding lifeless across the ice.

Dok was climbing off when sShearon hissed, "Dok, there'sss another one!"

A third predator prowled the edge of the clearing, pacing, head low, eyes locked.

"Maybe it'll leave," Dok muttered, though he knew better.

"It doesssn't look like it," sShearon answered flatly.

The creature charged. Dok sighed, dropped to all fours, and surged forward to meet it. They collided mid-air, claws flashing, teeth snapping. The beast ducked his grapple, letting him sail past. It's tail cracked across his face like a whip, blood spattering the snow as he tumbled hard, ungraceful for his species.

"They are learning," he growled, forcing himself upright.

The predator wheeled, then lunged again. Dok bounded to meet it, but at the last instant he cut his leap short, dropping low to the ice. Sliding onto his back, he drew the grappling gun, aimed up, and fired. The hook tore through the beast's belly, bursting from its spine. Bone shards fanned outward in a wet spray. The animal was dead before it struck the ground.

Breathing hard, Dok stood, ripped the grapple free, and scrubbed the wire clean in the snow before winding back into place.

"You're very good at combat," said sShearon, impressed with the display.

"A lifetime of war teaches you many things, sShearon. I don't wish that on anyone," Dok said ruefully.

sShearon nodded in agreement, then changed the subject. "There isssn't much out here, maybe we ssshould get going?" Dok agreed, after looking back at the three fallen animals and shaking his head.

They set off towards the Calling.

***

They had walked for nearly a full rotation before seeing anything more than white snow and dark blue skies.

"There," pointed Dok, slightly to his left. "There's a rocky outcrop; it may be a good place to rest for the night. It's going to get cold out here."

"You can have sssome of my sssecretionsss, if you're cold?" offered sShearon. "I'll keep you warm."

Dok looked at sShearon, and the oils he was producing to keep warm. "Thank you, but I think it would stick to my hair too much."

Finding a gap between the rocks, they squeezed their bodies in tight and lay back, watching the sky. It quickly turned from dark blue to purple and finally black, as the sun quickly set. No moon reflected its light, and only one star hung visible in the still blackness of space.

"I've never ssseen only one ssstar in the sssky before," said sShearon.

"What do you think it means?"

"I'm not sssure," replied sShearon. "Maybe we're at the edge of the universsse?"

"Is that possible, is there an edge?"

"I don't know that either," said sShearon. "But I bet Phosss would. He knew a lot about the ssstarsss."

"You were close with Phos?" asked Dok.

"Yesss, very much ssso. I sssspent a lot of time with him. He had the innocence of a youngling but the wisssdom of sssomeone who had been around for a long time, which of courssse, he had. I enjoyed lissstening to hisss ssstoriesss and watching how excited he got when retelling them. It wasss almossst asss though he wasss reliving them, for the firssst time."

"Would you tell me one of his stories, I'd like to know more about him, other than what I've read," asked Dok.

sShearon thought for a fraction, then replied, "My favourite ssstory wasss when he travelled to a living planet, I forget the name, but he could communicate with it." sShearon paused, but Dok nodded to continue. sShearon then regaled the story with as much detail as he could remember.

Before long it was time to rest.

sShearon turned his head slightly and began licking the rocks.

Dok looked over, his eyesight working well in the dark. "sShearon, why are you licking the rock?"

"Slurp, it's tasssty," sShearon replied. "There are a lot of mineralsss and water in the rock, it'sss good for you. Slurp."

Dok was puzzled but intrigued, he put out his spiky papillated tongue and tentatively licked the rock. It was cold and damp, then he started getting a taste of something sweet, tangy, metallic and salty. He took another lick, more of the same. Another lick and another. Soon, both the Cydarions were laid back-to-back, licking the adjacent rocks and drifting off into a deep sleep.

***

It had been a cold frozen night and sShearon and Dok were finally glad to feel the little warmth that the low rising sun offered. After eating from their ration packs and stretching, they set off again towards the Calling.

sShearon kept looking at Dok with a curiosity.

Eventually Dok had to say something. "Are you okay?"

"Your face," sShearon said. "I thought you had a fresssh wound?"

"Yes," said Dok, his paw went up to his face to feel the open wound. "I don't feel anything," he said, a little confused.

"There isssn't anything," confirmed sShearon. "Not even a ssscar!"

Dok was even more confused. "How can that be?"

sShearon shrugged. "Maybe it'sss in the air, it'sss good for you?"

"I've not heard of that before," replied Dok.

"There'sss a lot of thingsss we don't know," said sShearon.

"That's true," agreed Dok. "I'll take it as a blessing."

"Good way to think," nodded sShearon.

For a further half rotation, the two walked across the barren, windswept, snow-covered land, no sign of life anywhere and no change on the horizon. Traversing snow drifts and broken ice crevices, then back to flat land.

They talked about the lack of creatures, sentient or otherwise, but could not figure out why there was nothing and no one. Sometime in the late rotation, they started to see something in the distance. A cluster of trees, not many, about a dozen or so, all growing close to each other in a circle.

"It'sss not a natural formation," said sShearon. "Maybe they were planted for a reassson?"

"I agree, but we should take advantage of the shelter for the night. We may be able to get out of this wind," said Dok. As they approached the trees, something else appeared on the horizon in front of them. It was flat and hazy, a low building, but very wide, silhouetted against the disappearing white sun. Dok squinted to get a better look, but the glare was too bright. Behind the building, a mountain, barely visible through the low clouds, protruded high into the sky.

"There may be life inside that building," he said pointing towards it.

sShearon, who had wandered into the trees, shouted back. "Dok, come take a look."

"It'sss giving off heat like a thermo ssstick," said sShearon when Dok arrived.

Dok came up to the tree and touched it with a mighty paw, then, in a move that surprised sShearon, he hugged the tree. Dok's face lit up as the heat penetrated his body, warming his cold joints. sShearon shrugged and joined Dok on the other side of the tree. He hugged it, like a long-lost friend. They both stayed there until their whole bodies had warmed up, feeling more relaxed.

"Even with all this wood, we don't need to make a fire to keep us warm," said Dok.

"Phosss would have liked to sssee thisss," hissed sShearon with a smile. "And thisss on the ground," he added. With the tree heat radiating around them, the snowfall hadn't settled, it had just melted seeping into the ground. The resulting flora was vibrant and colourful, so many beautiful flowers. A noise, off in the distance got their attention. It was a transportation ship leaving the flat wide building and shooting off into space.

"At leassst we know there isss life," said sShearon. Dok agreed before he extended his claws and climbed the tree, his claws sinking into the soft warm bark. Finally, he settled onto one of the thick branches, surrounded by the warmth, and closed his eyes. sShearon jumped up onto a low hanging limb, one that could support his weight, and was also soon asleep.

By the time Dok had stirred from his comfortable sleep, sShearon was already awake and sitting up higher in the tree.

"There hasss been sssome activity at that building," sShearon said, when Dok joined him.

"What kind of activity?"

"Animalsss mainly, off to the right, but sssome beingsss, queuing to get in on the left. No vehiclesss, they have all walked."

"Has anyone come out?" Dok asked.

"Not while I've been watching, no," answered sShearon.

"Okay, well, let's go and find out," said Dok, and he sprung down from the tree with grace.

They made it to an entrance just as another group arrived. There were three guards on the door, all with auto load blaster rifles and wearing grey featureless uniforms, with black boots and a strange diamond shaped hat. Dok went through first following the crowd, it was unusually quiet. The guards seized Dok's weapons, 'For safe keeping," one of the guards had said.

A guard lined up his gun, and pointed it at sShearon,

"Animals go in the other door!" he loudly stated.

sShearon looked at the rifle, then at the guard. "If I sssee any, I ssshall let them know!" he said with a smile. The guard looked puzzled and wasn't sure what to do, until another guard whispered something in his ear. The gun was lowered with a grunt, and the guard walked away. sShearon moved on with the rest of the crowd until they got to an open room. A large fireplace sat at each end of the room; a fire burning fiercely in each one. Most of the crowd gathered around the fires to keep warm and started to chat amongst themselves, the Cydarions decided to join them.

"I don't recall seeing any smoke from outside," said Dok, nodding towards a fireplace. There was a loud clank as the outside doors closed, echoing through the room. More guards entered the room and stood in a line at the entrance. The lights went out and one lone spotlight appeared in the centre of the room. From out of nowhere, appeared a woman who seemed to glide into the spotlight. A long flowing red gown with gold stitching that looked to hover across the floor. A pale face appeared under the light. Piercing yellow eyes and thick, dark wavy hair stood out on this beautiful looking woman. Yet, it was her presence that captivated everyone, she clapped her hands once, and the whole room fell silent, so quiet, you could hear a rodent clean its whiskers. Dok looked over at the fire, still burning brightly.

"Curious, the fire isn't making any noise either," he whispered.

"Welcome," the woman called, her voice warm, almost too warm. "I am Lady Abaddon, Countess of Sheol. You know your world, Bilvuum, is dying. The meteor struck half a cycle ago, nudging your planet from its path. Now the cold deepens, and life here will end." She smiled, the expression delicate, practiced. "My family once came here during the warm seasons. Because of that, and my generosity... I have chosen to help you. All of you. Even your beasts."

The crowd erupted with cheers. *Our Saviour!* someone cried. sShearon caught the faintest flush on Lady Abaddon's cheeks... or was it a mask slipping?

"Something's wrong," Dok muttered.

Lady Abaddon lifted a hand for silence. "Yes, I can save you. But not alone. I have the resources. I need your strength. Will you fight for survival?"

"We're with you Lady! What can we do?" a voice shouted.

Her smile sharpened. "The journey to another world is long. We cannot take everyone at once. Most must remain behind until my ship returns. Every two rotations we can make one trip. While you wait, this facility is yours. Or..."

With a hiss, a side door blew open. Snow howled in, stinging faces.

"You may choose to stay with your dying planet. Your chances of surviving another cycle are zero," Lady Abaddon said lightly. "But I won't stop you." She shrugged, waiting. Dok thought he glimpsed a sly curve at her lips.

No one moved toward the open door. A beat later it slammed shut, sealing the blizzard outside. Lady Abaddon dipped into a graceful bow, gestured to her guards, and sauntered out as if the room already belonged to her.

Murmurs broke the silence, rising to sharp chatter.

Dok leaned to sShearon. "I can't feel the Calling. What do we do?"

"Don't panic," sShearon hissed. "It vanissshed the moment we entered. Perhapsss we are meant to help thessse creaturesss."

Before Dok could reply, two doors opposite the entrance slid open. Faces peered through, hesitant. A guard's bark shattered their indecision.

"Move it! You heard the Lady. Find your quarters, you'll need the rest." His laugh was cruel, echoing off the stone.

The crowd shuffled through, Dok and sShearon among them, the guards herding close with rifles raised. Once the last had crossed, the great doors slammed behind. An electronic lock clunked into place.

They found themselves in a corridor stretching impossibly long in both directions. Figures drifted past without a glance, their eyes hollow, their movements mechanical. Dok and sShearon turned right, following the curve until the hall bent away. Small doorways lined the inner wall. Each opened onto the same scene: twelve bunks stacked in corners, four to a frame. Rooms of weary faces, blank stares, despair etched deep. Every set of eyes followed them, silent, as though already half-ghosts.

"This looks like an internment camp," said Dok.

"I think you're right, and we walked right in! I really can't figure out what we ssshould do," admitted sShearon.

"We should find a space and come up with a plan," offered Dok. They carried on walking, seemingly in a huge semi-circle before spotting a room with only a mother and two small children. The Cydarions nodded their greetings and sat down on one of the empty beds.

"Why are we here Dok?" sShearon asked.

"The Calling…" replied Dok with a questioning look.

"I know, but I mean, what are we to do here?"

Dok rubbed his forehead. "God sent us here for a reason," he offered.

"Ha! No one comes 'ere without a reason!" The woman said from out of nowhere.

sShearon turned to her. "Why do you think that?" he asked sincerely.

"Meteor that hit this planet, wasn't no accident," she said.

"What do you mean?" said Dok.

"Don't play dumb, everyone seen that holonews footage," she snapped.

"We're not from around here," said sShearon.

"Well, you're no travellers! No one comes 'ere no more. I bet you work for her; you're spies aint ya!" snapped the woman.

"No mam, I assure you we don't work for Lady Abaddon," said Dok.

"It'sss clear that you don't believe in Lady Abaddon, but do you believe in God?" asked sShearon.

"God?" said the woman. "Never 'eard of em."

"Let usss explain then," said sShearon. So, he and Dok explained all about being a Cydarion and working for God.

The woman wasn't at all impressed or even pleased. "I guess you're too late," she said. "There's no hope for us now!"

"You ssshould alwaysss have hope."

The woman just shook her head. "I've lived on this rock all me life, worked hard too, but what happened? Corruption, everyone's at it ain't they?"

Dok and sShearon had blank looks on their faces.

"You really don't know what I'm talking 'bout do ya?" said the woman.

"No, we don't. Pleassse tell usss," said sShearon.

The woman sighed in defeat. "Kliney, me name's Kliney." The woman said, "and these two." She pointed to her children. "Are Evie and Sindelino." She sighed again before explaining the situation.

"Three cycles ago we had a prosperous planet, everything thrived 'ere, we had some of the oldest vegetation in the universe. That itself attracted lots of tourists, people who want to study 'em, others just wanna be among 'em, thinking they 'ad magical healing powers, which 'course they don't, they're just plants," she said with a laugh.

"We used to get a lot of stargazers too, some professional, most amateurs. You see, being the edge of the universe an all, at night it gets dark, very dark, and they wanted to look past the edge of the universe. Well, these stargazers noticed that one of our local asteroids behaved differently. They saw it had changed direction ya see, only slightly, mind, but enough to do calculations. It was on course to collide with us, within a cycle. It was all over the newsreel footage. The government, *our* government, that was supposed to keep us safe, told everyone not to panic, it won't hit us, like. But the government lied to us, din't they? They built massive transport ships for themsens. The government used our credits to build transport ships, then left us 'ere! They just abandoned us ten rotations before it hit! Same with all them rich folk, they paid to get out of 'ere.

"When the meteor hit, it landed in the Umto ridges. It just about flattened the mountains; the impact did knock us out of orbit. Then it got colder, soon it'll be too cold to live 'ere. Some people prayed to their leaders, others killed themselves in despair, I mean, what else can we do? No one was coming to save us, all the food was running out, ain't no power either. It's like the beginning of time all over again. Half cycle ago, word got round that there was someone 'ere to save us. People walked for ten rotations to get 'ere. Lady Callous out there gives a great speech about saving us, then throws us in 'ere!"

"But isn't she here to help?" asked Dok.

"Nobody in 'ere believes that anymore," said Kliney.

"Why did you call her Lady Callousss?" asked sShearon.

"Huh, I guess you've not seen yet," said Kliney.

"Ssseen what?"

"The trials!" Kliney whispered, almost as though she shouldn't be mentioning it.

"The trials?" said Dok. "What are they?"

"You don't wanna know,"

"If you could tell usss, it may be easssier for usss to help you," said sShearon.

Kliney sighed and jabbed a finger threateningly at the Cydarions. "You're gunna find out soon enough, 'cos you'll be in 'em!"

Snow capped mountain

Chapter 31

"The trials," said Kliney. "Is just a sick way of getting us to play her games. I don't know exactly what goes on in them trials, but I seen people come out injured, lots of 'em. They don't like to talk about it though. Always a fresh group of players waiting for the next round though. I tried to join when I first got 'ere, but I wern't allowed to come back for my kids, if I'd won," she explained. "And they're too young to compete. So, now we're stuck 'ere."

"So, what happens to the losers?" asked Dok.

"Dunno, 'suppose they get to leave too," said Kliney. "I ain't ever seen any losers, not back in 'ere, any rate," she shrugged. "I guess the games should be easy, that's why there's always a queue."

"And what happens to the winners?" asked Dok.

Kliney shrugged. "They get to go up in that spaceship, first class I hear."

"We sssaw that take off earlier," said sShearon, looking at Dok.

"But we never 'eard anyfing back from them who've left. At first, we're all full of hope, but the longer we're here, the more we lose it."

"How long have you been in here?" asked sShearon.

Kliney shrugged again. "I stopped counting after sixty-three rotations. Not that we ever see the sun light in 'ere though."

"I really don't know why *we're* here," admitted sShearon, to Dok. "It doesssn't ssseem like a devil isss involved, maybe Lady Abaddon wantsss to help?" sShearon said positively.

"There may be more at stake here. We wouldn't have been sent here for no reason," said Dok.

"Maybe we ssshould take a look around?" suggested sShearon.

Dok agreed, and the two moved down the endless corridor, eyes scanning for anything unusual. Most of what they passed were identical dorms and a single food station that opened only once a day. But two doors broke the monotony, one at each end.

At one door, four guards stood watch. Through it, the latest 'contestants' were marched into the trials. The other had only two guards. That would be their entry point.

Dok's plan was simple" strike fast, strike hard. Claws out, he meant to tear them down before they could react. sShearon's approach was subtler. He released a piercing sonic yelp that rattled the air, aimed just wide of Dok. The guards reeled, clutching their heads.

Dok lunged. A blur of fur and paws, he smashed them to the floor and bound them tight with their own gun straps.

Without a word, the Cydarions slipped through the door and into a steep passage that tunneled into the ice. It ended in a vast hollow carved from frozen earth. An arena waiting in silence.

"It looksss like a lair," whispered sShearon.

"We need to be careful; this area doesn't feel the same. Wait... the Calling is starting again."

"I feel it too," said sShearon. "Thisss way," he pointed a claw to his right.

"This place is bigger than it looks," Dok muttered as they slipped through yet another maze of corridors and doors. At last, they came to another vast chamber.

Guards crowded the floor, rifles slung, while a raised platform loomed at the far wall. The Cydarions melted into the shadows and waited.

Lady abaddon appeared without warning. Her crimson cloak rippled as she crossed the hall, but with each step her form shifted-colours running, shapes twisting-until the woman was gone. In her place stood a devil. Neither Dok nor sShearon flinched.

The creature's voice carried across the room. It spoke of efficiency, urging the guards to spend less time tending prisoners and more time selecting contestants for the tournament.

"Make them desperate enough to beg for the transport ship," it concluded, a cruel smile cutting its face.

sShearon hissed, "We mussst get on that ssship. Find it out where they're taking them."

"I agree, we need to..." Dok froze. Footsteps. A guard was approaching.

Without another word, the two slipped back into the corridors, vanishing into Kliney's quarters before the patrol arrived.

"This whole place is just a ruse for Abaddon to have her sadistic fun," said Dok.

Kliney just shrugged. "What else can we do?" she asked.

"An uprisssing? A demonsssstration?" sShearon offered.

"An uprising?" Kliney scoffed. "With what? Half us are weak and starving, other half are too scared. Besides, they've got the guns, we don't even have a stick to defend ourselves. No it won't work." Kliney dismissed with a shake of her head.

As they spoke, frantic footsteps pounded down the corridor. A voice cried out, raw with desperation.

"Medic! I need a medic!"

Dok hesitate. He sprinted toward the sound. "I'm a medic, what's wrong?"

The figure whirled around. It was not a soldier, but a frail old ma, eyes wide with panic.

He replied, "Quick, this way. My son has a wound to his stomach, please help!"

Dok followed the old man into a room identical to Kliney's. On the bed lay a young man, writhing in agony, his clothes and the bare mattress beneath him soaked in blood.

Without hesitation, Dok tore the fabric away from the wound. From his utility belt he pulled a folded bandage, a vial of green powder, and a flask of water. He cleansed the gash quickly, then sprinkled the powder onto the raw flesh. The wound hissed faintly. Pressing a bandage over it, Dok leaned his heavy paw down to stem the bleeding.

"What happened?" he asked.

The patient still in pain replied, "I was in the trials, and doing well, when a blade came out of nowhere and got me good. I had to lay there while the trial continued. People had to step over me just to carry on." He gasped for a breath. "After the trials ended, I was taken to a room where my wound was stapled up. Then they sent me back here." He paused. "I think the staples have opened."

Dok nodded. "The staples have ruptured, but they didn't cauterize the wound, they just covered it up. No doctor should have done this," he said.

"No Doctor, it was one of the guards," said the young man, his pain starting to ease.

Dok growled.

"Ow, ow, ow,"

"It's okay," said Dok. "The powder is just to stop any more blood loss. You'll be bedridden for a while, until the wound heals completely. I'm afraid there won't be another trial for you."

"But I have to," said the patient. "It's the only way to get my family out of here." He winced. "To keep them safe."

The older man spoke, "Son, we don't need you to save us. Our time is coming to an end. You need to look after yourself."

"Ow, ow, ow," he protested again.

"Your father is right," said Dok. "You need to look after yourself, your family won't last if the strong die first."

"Ow, ow, ow. It's getting hot," said the patient, starting to squirm.

"Keep still, the powder freezes the blood vessels. Give them time to coagulate themselves. It's probably just cold for you," said Dok, applying a little more pressure to the wound.

The patient started wriggling more. "No, it's not pain or cold... it's just hot."

Dok frowned but placed his other paw on the patients' shoulder, pinning him to the bed to keep him still. Then Dok started to feel heat in his own paw. He looked down at his paw but saw nothing. Turning his paw over, he saw his pads and the wound, emanating heat. And, before his very eyes, he saw the wound close up on its own. The redness faded away, a thick scar emerging in its place.

"It's a miracle!" exclaimed the old man, looking upon his son.

Dok, now puzzled, had to ask, "How do you feel?"

The patient took some time to think, then said, "I feel good. No pain at all, the heat has gone."

Dok released his paw, and the patient sat up, looking at his own stomach.

"What did you do?" he asked.

"Nothing," replied Dok. "I just cauterised the blood vessels."

"Well, thank you doctor," said the old man, trying to give Dok an awkward hug. "You saved his life."

"I... I have to go," stuttered Dok. "I'll check on you later." He wandered back to Kliney's room in confusion and tried to explain to sShearon what had happened. All of a sudden, a loud siren wailed, and a voice echoed through loudspeakers positioned in the corridors.

"All volunteers for the trials, make your way to area C. The transport ship is waiting for you," the voice teased.

sShearon looked at Dok. "I'm getting on that ssship," he said.

Dok nodded. "Me too, we need to get to the bottom of this."

They bade their farewells to Kliney, and set off towards area C. sShearon shouted back to Kliney, "Don't forget what I told you!"

Area C was the single door with four guards that went down into the trials. An assorted group of about a hundred beings lined up to take part, there was a loud cheer as the door opened, and they all set off down the ramp. At the bottom they were greeted by more guards with guns, one of them stood on a box to address the crowd.

The overseer's voice rang out: "This trial has three parts. First, through those doors lies the main hall. Inside, each of you will find a ball. Hold onto it for thirty fractions. You may throw balls, but if one is thrown at you, you must catch it. Drop a ball at any time, you're out. End the trial without one, you're out."

Uneasy murmurs rippled through the crowd.

The doors slammed open. Contestants surged forward into a vast chamber. A hollow durasteel box, its floor etched with narrow grooves. Harsh white lights blazed from above, stabbing their eyes until they adjusted. Scattered across the floor were a hundred identical, lightweight aluminum spheres.

A red counter lit up: Thirty fractions.

Everyone grabbed a ball. The room fell into stillness, all waiting for the tick.

Everyone looked around at each other. Tensions were high. The timer had started and already showing twenty-seven fractions left.

Another fraction passed. Someone shouted,

"This is easy!" someone laughed. "We're all getting on that ship!" A cheer rose.

The clock flickered to twenty-six fractions left.

"I don't like thisss," sShearon hissed, eyes darting.

"Doesn't feel right," agreed Dok.

Twenty-five fractions.

The first scream tore the silence. A ball detonated, shredding its holder in a spray of blood and organs. Another sprouted spikes, tearing through its victim's hands. One sphere glowed red-hot, searing flesh to the bone.

Cries erupted as a ball shook violently, impossible to grip; another hissed and spat vapour, melting skin and blinding eyes. A sphere split apart, razor blades spinning out, severing fingers and wrists. Sparks arced from another, convulsing its victim until they dropped lifeless.

screams layered screams.

One sphere froze solid, fusing itself to raw skin. The holder tore free, leaving palms skinned to tendon and bone. Another crumbled to dust in it's victims hands. Relief flickered, then a shot cracked the walls, dropping them dead.

A tenth ball grew heavier and heavier until it crashed to the floor. A single thud sealed its fate.

Indiscreet holes in the walls flared open. Any contestant without a ball was gunned down where they stood.

The hall became a slaughterhouse, echoing the agony, gunfire, and the stench of burning flesh.

Twenty-four fractions.

The screams died down as the shock turned to realisation, that this wasn't a game. People started to panic and threw their balls to other beings. Both sShearon and Dok had balls thrown at them, but in turn, they had to throw a ball to someone else.

Twenty-three fractions.

The magnitude of the throwing increased with desperation.

Twenty-two fractions.

Most of the group slowed their throwing due to exhaustion and decide to keep their ball.

Twenty-one fractions.

Five or six people decided to swap balls, thinking they each would get a safe one.

Twenty fractions.

Another explosion started off the same series of incidents, limbs were lost, balls were dropped and shot rings out. More bodies fell to the floor. Panicked screaming ensued, and balls were quickly thrown again.

The screaming echoed again.

Nineteen fractions.

As the screaming died down, there was a click and a whir. The hiss of released air was heard and suddenly, four random square floor panels dropped away, two people fell to their deaths. sShearon looked to Dok, exasperated.

Dok returned the look.

"I don't know what we can do," said sShearon.

"We just have to survive, we can't save everyone," Dok said with a heavy heart.

Eighteen fractions.

Four more random floor panels dropped away, sending one other being to their death. Even more chaos now ensued, as some beings ran around the remaining floor, not trusting any square or each other.

Seventeen fractions.

Dok felt a slight click through his attuned body, and he leapt for another square, just as his own dropped away.

"Dok?" sShearon shouted.

"I'm okay," Dok said, after landing softly on his hind legs. "Be aware of any vibrations in the floor," he advised. sShearon looked down at his own square, only to be hit in the head with a ball. His reactions were quick as he managed to throw his own ball before catching the new one.

Sixteen Fractions.

Two beings on one square, fell, as their shared space disappeared beneath them. Three other, empty squares, fell away. And, in a last panicked attempt, balls were exchanged again.

Fifteen fractions.

Dok and sShearon both said a prayer.

All the open square floor tiles reappeared and settled into place.

The whole room fell silent as the time struck the halfway mark. No more floor panels fell away, no balls exploded, no more balls got heavy, none released anything or changed its temperature. Everyone breathed heavy, not trusting anything.

Fourteen fractions.

Still no movement. "Is it over?" someone shouted.

"No, look at the timer," came the reply.

"But nothing is happening," the first said.

"Why would you want it to?" said a third voice. To that, there was no reply.

Thirteen fractions

Everyone was on edge, the stresses fully on show, yet there was little movement, no more balls were exchanged. The only sound was heavy, panicked breathing.

Twelve fractions.

Out of sheer desperation, one being dropped their ball and ran towards the doors. Before they could get anywhere near the exit, a shot rang out, and their lifeless body fell to the floor.

Eleven fractions.

Whispering started between small groups. Their eyes sheepishly darting from one contestant to another. Others turned away and held their ball like a baby, close to their chest, as if protecting it.

Ten fractions.

Dok and sShearon prayed again.

The silence of the room was broken by an explosion, which started the chain reaction of nine more balls, harming the contestants. The screams were soon replaced with self-relief. One being who just lost their hands, writhed in agony on the ground.

Someone shouted, "Will you shut up! At least you're going to survive this, I may be the next one to die!"

"Hey, we're all in the same situation!" someone shouted.

Nine fractions.

The conversation was interrupted when a side panel opened, and a hundred more balls were released into the game. Balls bounced and rolled over people's feet; the noise was nearly deafening. Eventually coming to a rest. A look of bewilderment on everyone's face.

Eight fractions.

One being bent down to look at the balls.

"Leave them," someone whispered.

"It's a trap!" whispered another. Yet they didn't take heed. They picked up a new ball with one hand and gently placed the other ball down. Then slowly stood up and closed their eyes. The others held their breath, waiting for a shot to ring out.

Seven fractions.

More people decide to change their balls, swapping for the new ones on the ground, rather than throwing them to each other. Some changing many times, never confident with their decision.

Six fractions.

Whispered moans became louder, so many beings complained about their tired arms and that they needed a rest.

"What if we all put the balls down at the same time?" came one suggestion.

"They can't kill us all" replied another. Five of the beings, close together, decided to take the risk. Slowly, they all bent down, as though they were to be swapping balls, but as they stood up, their hands were empty. A smile crept across their faces. Several shots rang out, and all five bodies hit the floor at the same time, scattering balls in every direction.

The remaining contestants sighed.

Five fractions.

Dok and sShearon, closed their eyes, held their breath, and prayed again.

Nearly everyone had taken to holding out their balls at arm's length on the five-fraction mark. It was meaningless. An explosion still killed one, others still lost their limbs and some merely just dropped the ball and were shot dead. By now, there was only flinching from the surviving members. The brutality of it all, now becoming acceptable. People even sighed with relief as they were awarded a few more fractions of life.

Four fractions

Suddenly, all the lights went out. Panic resumed and people ran about, bumping into others, even knocking their own balls from their grip. Numerous shots rang out and more people fell.

"Stop moving!" growled Dok. "Keep still and keep safe." Both Dok's and sShearons eyes were suited to the dark and could see clearly.

Three fractions.

The red light from the countdown timer cast an eerie glow over the remaining contestants, everyone standing still.

Two fractions.

Dok counted how many had succumbed to injury or death, fifty-six. A doubt entered his head, *Could I have saved them?*

sShearon noticed that Dok wasn't concentrating and whispered sharply over to him. "Dok concentrate! Our sssurvival meansss their sssurvival!"

Dok's mind came back to the present, and he looked across at sShearon. "Thank you!"

One fraction.

"Is the game over after the time is up or will they go off again?" someone asked.

"The game is over, isn't it?" questioned another.

"Were the balls actually random or was someone watching us and setting them off on purpose?" asked a third.

"What does it matter?" said a fourth. "Just hold it until they say so.

Zero.

Nothing happened.

The timer had reached the end, and for another fifty snaps nothing happened, and no one moved, their hearts all raced.

The lights came back on, and a small door opened at the opposite end of the room from where they entered.

A voice came over the loudspeaker to address the survivors.

"Congratulations on passing the first part of this trial. You may need to decompress after your recent experience. Please make your way to the next room for a well-deserved rest." The speaker clicked off, and people dropped their balls, some carried them through, not trusting anyone. They made their way towards the small doorway, stepping over dead bodies and dismembered hands.

The next room was quite small for the number of beings entering it. A square space with durasteel walls and one other door to their left. A large rectangle box sat in the middle of the room and most beings took to sitting upon it. Mumblings between each other echoed around the room. Both Dok and sShearon went around and tried to check on everyone. The exit door was tried and even the one that they had entered through had already been sealed shut. Slowly, three or four beings started complaining about the shortness of breath.

"Yes, my chest is getting light," replied another. Someone started coughing, causing, in turn, others to cough too.

"I don't feel too good," said a voice, then a thump, as its body collapsed to the floor. By now everyone was either yawning or adjusting their jaw to release the build-up of pressure in their ears.

"I can't see, everything is going black!" someone shouted in a panicked voice. Even Dok had fallen onto all fours and was struggling to breathe, his fur standing on end,

"Too much oxygen," he laboured to say. He looked at sShearon, who didn't seem to be as affected as anyone else.

sShearon's gaze swept the sealed chamber, walls, floor, ceiling, no escape. Around him, bodies sagged and wheezed, some already collapsing. He knew then: if anyone was to act, it had to be him. He hurled his shoulder against the door, but the weight of the others around slowed him down. Snarling, he traced the seam with his claws and found a weakness: the lock.

He filled his lungs, jaw stretching wide, and let loose a focused sonic scream. The air itself shuddered. For long, punishing fractions nothing gave. Then the frame began to rattle, faint at first, then violently, until with a final shriek of metal, the door tore free.

Cold air howled in, sweet and sharp. The crowd gasped like drowning souls breaking the surface. Some vomited, others fainted. Dok staggered upright, gulping down breaths.

"Thank you, sShearon," he rasped.

While Dok tended the fallen, three desperate figures bolted through the doorway, only to be shoved back at gunpoint. Overhead, a loudspeaker crackled alive.

"Our apologies," a voice sneered. "A minor... malfunction in the air system." It broke into mocking laughter.

The guards gave no words, only sharp gestures and the nudge of rifles.

They marched up a steep corridor. Transplast doors groaned open, and the night struck them like a blade, pure air, cruel and cold. Ahead loomed a mountain, its peak swallowed by a shroud of fog. A narrow durasteel walkway stretched from the prison to its side, suspended high above the abyss.

The guards stepped back. The voice returned, low and metallic, crawling from hidden speakers.

"This is your final trial. Reach the summit, and your transport awaits... though it departs in six sections." The line went dead, leaving only the wind and the mountain's silent, watching face.

The climb started steep but manageable. Below him, the winding trail echoed with calls of encouragement as some tried to help the weaker along. After two sections, the path sharpened into a jagged climb. sShearon urged the lead group to wait and aid the stragglers. They grumbled at first but eventually agreed. When the main body caught up, a handful of the slowest pressed on stubbornly, refusing to pause.

Dok and sShearon passed around their dwindling rations. Water for the parched, protein tablets for the faint. The cold gnawed at them all, forcing the group onward before the freeze set in. Then, breaking the silence, another anouncement hissed from hidden speakers.

"Update on the transport ship," the voice chimed brightly. "Due to... unforseen circumstances, only half of you will be boarding. Our apologies! See you at the summit!"

The words hung in the frozen air.

"Where did that come from?" someone whispered.

"Inside the mountain," said another.

"I don't care where, it means we move faster," snapped one man, already climbing again.

A voice tried to stop him. "Wait! We need to work together!"

"Didn't you hear? Half of us are dead weight!" he spat.

"We'll reason with them, we'll all fit somehow," pleaded an optimist.

The man turned, face twisted. "Not me. Not today."

A kind hand touched his shoulder, urging calm. The man lashed out, boot connecting with a knee. Bone cracked. The victim staggered, slipped on loose rock, and tumbled to his death.

A gasp tore through the group. Then the panic broke.

Shoving, scrambling, cursing, bodies fought to surge ahead. The mountain path became chaos. Five more were lost, pushed screaming into the void.

Dok and sShearon roared for calm, but their voices were drowned in desperation. The climb was longer together. It was now survival, every soul for themselves.

"What ssshould we do?" sShearon ask Dok.

Dok looked up into the sky and at all the people still squabbling. Finally, back at sShearon. With a heavy heart, he said, "Their survival relies on our survival. We climb!"

sShearon nodded grimly, and they climbed breath steaming, fingers stiffening as the wind howled and bit into raw skin. Muscles cramped, progress slowed to a crawl.

CRACK!

A thunderous report split the night. High above, snow and stone broke loose. An avalanche thundered down, boulders hurtling like missiles in the storm Screams echoed as climbers tried to scatter, but there was nowhere to run.

sShearon moved without thought. Power surged through his legs as he bounded upward, two, three, four bodies at a time. His claws sinking into every fracture of stone. Even Dok, hardened as he was, stared in awe at the speed of him.

Reaching the highest climber just as the storm hit, sShearon braced himself against the mountain, dug his claws deep, and inhaled. Then let loose a sonic yelp, pitched high and unrelenting. Snow slammed into him, blinding, suffocating. He shifted frequency. The wall of white broke against his scream, bouncing away in great plumes. Rocks struck, but the wave sent them spinning outward, tumbling into the abyss. He held it until the last of the debris clattered harmlessly past.

Below, the survivor erupted into cheers of exhausted relief. sShearon had saved them all.

But as the echo of his cry faded, something else revealed itself, beneath the strippstone, the unmistakable gleam of metal.

Durasteel.

Frowning, sShearon pressed closer, narrowing his voice to a scalpel-thin frequency. Layer by layer, the false rock crumbled away until seams of riveted plating shone in the faint star light. Not welded. Riveted.

He began to strike it.

Bang. Bang. Bang.

The sound carried through the mountain, shaking loose more snow below.

Dok scrambled up beside him, eyes wide. "You saved us," he said, still catching his breath. Then he froze at the sight of the exposed sheeting. "What is this?"

sShearon's lips curled back in a grimace. "Thisss mountain..." he rasped. He clawed at the metal and pointed. "It isssn't real. Look."

Dok understood what sShearon was doing. "Here, let me try."

sShearon leant back as Dok drove a heavy paw into the durasteel. The metal groaned and creased. Three more strikes and a gap split open. Hooking his claws into the seam, Dok wrenched the panel free. Rivets popped one by one until the mountain itself seemed to peel apart.

"That'sss a new twissst," sShearon said, peering into the hollow darkness beyond.

Dok's ears flicked. "I'm starting to realise we shouldn't underestimate this devil. But now what?"

"I'm going in," sShearon said, his tone low and certain. Then, with a pause, "Maybe you ssstay with the group?"

Dok extended a paw. sShearon clasped it firmly.

"Good luck, my friend," Dok said.

"Do what you mussst," sShearon replied. Their foreheads touched: a brief, wordless vow.

"You too, I'll see you soon," Dok whispered with quiet hope.

Without another word, sShearon slipped into the dark gap, swallowed by the hollow mountain. Dok huffed out a breath, then turned back to the climb. Ahead of him, nearly thirty figures fought upward, claws and hands scrabbling desperately. If he lingered, he'd fall behind. And that meant death.

He bared his claws and surged forward, bounding upward with raw strength. The mountain shredded beneath his grip as he clawed for purchase, muscles burning, lungs searing.

Then, there was a scream.

Dok's head snapped up. A climber lost their footing, tumbling into the void.

He launched himself sideways, tearing across the cliff face, claws gouging sparks from the rock. Timing it to the heartbeat, he swung his arm out, snaring the falling climber's collar. His claws punched through fabric and flesh, but he held fast. With a guttural roar, he heaved the body back to the rock wall.

The shaken climber clung to the stone, eyes wide with terror.

"Th... thank you... you saved my life. How can I repay you?"

Dok expelled a sharp breath, his voice like stone.

"Climb."

And he did, bounding upward again, his great body carving a furious path toward the summit.

Space station Omega

Chapter 32

The air was icy, stabbing at his lungs like knives. The oxygen level decreased, and quick shallow breaths did nothing to ease that pain. Two or three figures stopped to catch their breath, their thin clothing whipping around in the wind.

"I need to rest," one said.

"Just a few fractions," agreed another.

Dok noticed and scrambled his way over to them, shoving his face into theirs, he bared his teeth, snarling. "Keep moving," he growled. "You'll die if you keep still." The climbers trembled at the sight of Dok's teeth and immediately started to climb.

He looked around at the other climbers. Twenty-two above him and twenty-six below, the others were level but still climbing. His heart felt heavy, knowing there's nothing he could do to save the people below. They were climbing to their deaths. *I have to finish this.* Against, every fibre of his body telling him to go down and help, he sniffed, turned his back on them and started to climb. A tear rolled down his cheek and froze to his chin. He couldn't miss that transport ship. Lactic acid built up in his muscles, and even with the pain becoming more intense, he sped up. The last few rotations would have been in vain if he didn't make it.

He finally got above the clouds and could see the top. A small transport ship hovered on the peak, its boarding ramp lowered, already accepting exhausted passengers. A few more reaches, and a final spring, before he touched the flat peak and finally stood on the rocky mountain top. A guard walked over to him and nodded in the direction of the transport ship.

"Get in," he said.

"Where's the other ship?" Dok asked, referring to the larger ship that he saw a few rotations ago.

"That's the cargo ship, this one is yours," the guard replied.

"You can take more passengers in that one."

"That's for cargo!" exclaimed the guard.

"But..."

The guard thumbed off the safety switch and lifted his blaster rifle up to Dok's torso,

"Get in the ship!" he ordered again.

Dok bared his teeth and stepped forward, the muzzle of the rifle pressed into his chest.

"You can save more!" Dok roared.

The guard flinched. A couple of blaster shots rang out, echoing around the mountain. Dok didn't move, staring straight at the guard. Footsteps approached Dok from behind and another muzzle prodded into his back.

"We got a problem here?" the new guard asked.

The first guards mouth trembled. "This guy w... w... wants..."

"I don't care what he wants, the transport is leaving now, either with him or without. It's his choice."

Dok looked from the first guard to the ship and back again, grunted, and swiped at the rifle, knocking it to the ground.

He walked over to the ship and up the boarding ramp, pausing briefly to look back at the mountain and the struggling climbers, then sat down in the transport ship. He closed his eyes and prayed for them. A shudder ran through the ship as the thrusters ignited, then it lifted, smooth, relentless, up into the black.

The intercom crackled. "Congratulations. You have survived all three trials. We are en-route to Space Station Omega. Get comfortable, it will be a long journey."

Dok opened his eyes and scanned the cabin. Only twenty-seven remained. No guards. The cockpit sealed.

The survivors looked broken, clothes torn, faces hollow, eyes fixed on nothing. *They don't belong here*, Dok thought. *None of us do. We're just clinging to life.*

A man wept openly, confessing he'd abandoned his wife and child on the planet. Others lowered their heads in grim silence; the same shame reflected in their eyes. No one spoke.

Then a sharp gasp. A young woman, close to Xania's age, clutched her arm, her skin flushed with panic. Her chest heaved, beath torn. She rocked in her seat, trembling.

Dok crossed the cabin at once and dropped to a crouch before her.

"My arm," she said, through short breaths. "I think it's broken. I fell as soon as I got the top. I'm worried they won't take me if I'm injured."

Dok nodded and shrugged. "They haven't said they won't accept anyone," he reassured her. She smiled at him, then winced again and shifted uncomfortably in her seat.

"Here," said Dok. Holding out his paws, claws retracted. "Let me take a look at it, I'm a doctor." She let him examine her arm.

"I'm Fiengul," she said. Dok's eyes flicked up to hers and then back down to her arm.

"Nice to meet you, I'm Dok," he said.

"Dok?" she said. "As in doc Dok?"

Dok sighed, he'd heard that phrase so many times before. "Here." Dok handed Fiengul a tablet that he retrieved from his pouch. "This will help," he said. Fiengul smiled an acceptance and swallowed the pill. Dok sandwiched her arm between his paws to warm it up.

"It's tingling," she said. "And warming up."

Dok could feel her blood pressure rise, and it released a chemical that Dok was starting to smell. Her arm started to shake at the heat being produced. She tried to pull her arm out of Dok's paws, but suddenly, there was a click, and the heat dissipated.

"What was that?" she asked. Dok's mouth opened but no words came out. He removed his paws and looked at them. The glowing pads faded quickly. He took a sharp intake of breath.

"What is it?" Fiengul asked.

Dok looked back at her. "Nothing." He shook his head. "How do you feel?"

Fiengul took a fraction to answer, flexing her arm around and smiling. "It's great, that tablet, how did it fix my arm?" she asked.

Dok was a little dumbfounded. "That was just a pain killer you took," he said.

"Well, it worked," she said, still moving her arm around. "Thank you! How can I repay you?"

Dok patted her arm lightly. "You can help pray for those we left behind," he said solemnly.

"What's pray?"

Dok's pupils enlarged. "You don't know what a prayer is?" he asked.

"No."

"You think of God and speak to him. Ask him to look after others," said Dok.

"Okay," Fiengul replied. "But who is God?"

"You don't know God either?" he asked. Fiengul shook her head. "God is the being up there," he pointed upwards. "Who looks after all living things, he is responsible for everything."

"Where are you pointing?" she asked. "We're already in space. Anyway, no one looks after all living things, how could they?"

"He's in heaven, it's above the universe, he looks down on it," said Dok.

"He looks down on it, like we would look down on a small insect?" she asked.

"Yes, in a way," Dok replied. "But he cares for all."

"How?" she asked.

"What do you mean how? He created it all."

"How does he care for us all, I mean, of all the population on this planet, plus all the animals, adds up to a lot. Then multiply it by the planets in a galaxy, then multiply that by the galaxies, it's just incredulous that anyone can see it all," she wondered.

"I have to have faith," Dok said. "Faith that he exists, and that he can help you."

"What if he doesn't hear you? You know, all these beings asking for something, who does he listen to?" asked a being next to her, who had been listening.

"He hears all, he sees all, isn't that enough to believe?" asked Dok.

"You expect us to believe there is someone looking out for all of us, on every planet?"

"Yes," said Dok.

"Then why did he let my family die, on the way here, and in the trials?" one being asked angrily.

"He can't control everything; evil is at work here. Lucifer is on your world," said Dok.

"Sounds like this Lucifer is in charge," said another.

"I don't believe any of it," said a third.

"The only one in control here, is Abaddon!"

"Abaddon is Lucifer, at least one of his offspring," said Dok.

"Then she *is* helping us," said another.

Dok Spun around. "Don't any of you believe in God?" he shouted. There was a long pause.

"No!"

"Nope!"

"Nah!"

A lot of heads shook.

Dok closed his eyes and dropped his head in prayer. "Lord have mercy on these lost souls, for they know not what."

The rest of the journey was made in silence, some looked out the small view-ports but most looking anywhere else. *I need to find out what happens on that space station, and why they can't accept more beings. I must think of a plan to help everyone. I feel that this is a part of something bigger, but I just can't figure it out yet.* He closed his eyes and meditated.

Before long, Dok felt the slight shift of deceleration and took a glimpse out of the view port: A large horse-shoe shaped vessel, with booster rockets attached at right angles to the open ends. Its thrusters cut off as Dok's transport ship manoeuvred around to the bulbous back end and attempted to dock. There was a slight bump and thud, followed by a clunk. A loud hiss of air echoed through the vessel as the air pressure equalised through the air locks. When the door unlocked and opened from the outside. In stepped three more guards.

"This is the Omega, your last home!" said one guard. "Make your way through to the decontamination chamber. There you will get clean clothes.

There were gasps of excitement between the passengers.

"Did you hear that?" said one passenger. "We're home!" A small cheer went up.

"Clean clothes too!" shouted another.

"I can't wait for the refresher," agreed a third. Dok thought he heard a little laugh from one of the guards as they followed the survivors through the airlock. Sterile, stainless-steel corridors led to a sizeable room at the end of a brightly lit corridor. The unmistakeable smell of disinfectant filled the air. The door slammed shut behind the last person and sealed with a click. Dok looked around. "No guards," he said to himself, and before he could have another thought, gas was released from ceiling nodules. Dok took a deep breath in, before the gas took over.

The whole room was soon filled with the thick gas, penetrating clothing, fur and lungs. Some beings started coughing and Dok heard a couple collapse to the floor. There was nothing he could do except wait and hope it would soon clear. He slipped into a meditative state and managed to slow his heart rate down. Suddenly, an extraction fan by the floor, clicked on and soon sucked out all the gas. Everyone had recovered back to their normal health when a wall slid open, and a set of new clothing items were revealed. Far from being on a clothes rack in a fashion store on Brunel IV, they were all grey and folded garments. All the same dreary material with matching canvas footwear.

"These are your new clothes." Came a voice over the speakers. "If you don't require clothes, do not take any, there are a limited amount." It seemed incredible to Dok, that everyone easily went along with everything without questioning any part of this process. They seemed happy to accept whatever this utopia held for them.

Everyone was to wear an electronic bracelet; it couldn't be removed. It was explained that they were just trackers and must be worn for their own safety. When everyone had changed, another door slid open at the opposite end of where they came in and an announcement came again.

"Follow the walkway to the end, and into the next room. There you will be issued your dorms." One or two people ran down the walkway, but most kept together, Dok following behind. The walkway extended ever a vast body of water, like a canal made from stainless-steel. The walkway had no safety rails, and most beings filed down to two across before making the walk. Four or five got close to the edge and Dok looked for a rescue plan if anyone fell in. There wasn't one, but luckily, everyone made it safely to the other side and into another room, the same design as the previous. Except this time there was someone standing in the room. It was a man, hairless and red faced, wearing the same outfit as everyone else, yet tattered and frayed. His gaze didn't shift from the floor, his expression conveyed defeat and exhaustion, but his words were quite friendly, rehearsed.

"Welcome new passengers," he said with a faked delight. "It is a pleasure to have you here. My name is Kalgol, and I will show you to your dorms." Then he turned and walked off before anyone could even ask a question. The mood was getting more and more apprehensive as the air started to exude an electrical odour. Four by four, everyone was shown a room and were told to stay inside until further notice. Dok entered a room with the last group. There was a plate of fresh produce on each of the four beds, all lined up against one wall, and while three of them got stuck into the food, Dok turned to Kalgol.

"What's going to happen next?"

Kalgol paused for a short while, then finally looked up. "I'm sorry," he replied. "I have a family, down there. I have to." Then he nodded to a camera at the end of the long corridor housing.

All at once, every door silently slid shut, and Dok was stood, staring at his reflection in the reinforced window panel of the door.

Lady Abaddon

Chapter 33

S Shearon dropped into a maze of steel supports, breath slow, senses sharp. Strange sounds pulsed from deep within the core. He moved toward them, climbing, slipping onto a narrow walkway. No guards. No movement. Only the hum of machinery.

Stairs led him down... and into hell.

Rows of cages stretched into darkness, crammed with emaciated creatures of every shape and colour. Needles pierced their skin, tubes leeching blood into the ceiling, rivers feeding the mountain itself. Their eyes followed him, too weak to move.

"A blood farm," sShearon hissed. A memory flashed... Steber, the rocky planet, but Drake had burned that farm to the ground. Rage flared in him. He ripped out needles, one by one. Blood dripped to the floor. Some bodies collapsed. He froze, overwhelmed. Too many. He couldn't save them this way.

He followed the tubes deeper. Down. Around. Always down. Gravity doing the work, carrying oceans of blood into the heart of the mountain.

At the base he found it: three vast vats, chrome gleaming with red and blue liquid. Guards lounged nearby. One filled a vial from a spigot, holding it high.

"Drink up, boys. It makes us stronger."

They laughed and they drank.

sShearon's stomach turned. He killed to survive, to honour the animal. This—this was desecration. His vision went red.

He dropped among them with a scream. Blasters flashed, but his sonic yelp hurled bolts aside, slamming the guards to the ground. A shot pierced a vat. Blood gushed across the floor. sShearon became a blur of green. A claw across a throat. A tail crushing a skull. A leap that caved in a chest. He hurled the last guard into steel, a neck snapped, the vat buckled, and the room was drowned in blood.

The stench clung to him as he pushed deeper into the maze. Sadness pressed heavier with each step. The Calling urged him back, but he forced himself forward.

A door marked **INCINERATOR**.

He entered—and froze.

Guards laughed as they shovelled carcasses into the flames, feeding the furnace that powered the trials. He struck without sound. One guard crashed half into the fire, back snapping as his helmet melted in the heat. Another gasped for breath as sShearon crushed his windpipe. Helmet off—he was only a boy, younger than Xania. sShearon hesitated, then hurled him into the fire.

The guards gone, he faced the trolley of the dead. He could do nothing for them now. He turned away, following the Calling.

He retraced his steps back to a junction, and took the stairs, a plan formulating in his mind. A locked door to the main corridor. Carefully, he disabled the magnetic sensors with a ball bearing and slipped inside, heading straight to Kliney's room. He explained everything—the trials, Dok's fate, the blood farm, the guards' horrors. Kliney's eyes widened in shock, believing his words. He told her of his plan and helped to spread the message: the time for rebellion had come.

sShearon stood in the centre of the room, claws flexing, tail flicking like a metronome. Low murmurs rippled through the small crowd until his voice, like a wet, hissing blade, cut them off.

"I ssspeak to the oppresssed. That meansss you... all of you."

Uneasy glances. No one stepped forward. More bodies pressed into the corridor.

"You freeze in the dark. You ssstarve on rationsss. You endure their trialsss while Abaddon whisssspers hope." He spat on the floor. "Liesss. The trialsss aren't *for* you... they're to kill you. To feed her hunger."

People edged in. The corridor filled with curious faces and those who followed.

"Ssshe pledged unity but took your young. Vowed ssstrength, then drained you dry. You obey becaussse fear hasss clawsss in you. But look." His arm swept the room, slow and sure. "There are more of usss than there will ever be of them. They have gunsss. We have numbersss. Nothing can ssstop a determined crowd."

The crowd shuffled closer.

"It'sss hard to fight. You're afraid. I'm afraid." He struck his chest with a claw, a small, humane gesture. "Bravery is not the void of fear. It'sss what you do with it. Keep bowing to Abaddon'sss poissson, or rissse. Rissse with me. Rissse for your children. Rissse for breath."

Heads bowed, then lifted. Fists clenched. A murmur swelled into a low, hungry growl.

"You've ssseen the truth. They bleed the innocent. They drink the blood of animalsss. They burn bodiesss for power while you freeze." He leaned in; his voice dropped to a rasp. "And when they tire of you, they'll throw *you* into the fire."

"No!" A voice. Another. Then more.

sShearon raised his arms. "Then fight. Fight for freedom. Fight for your family. Fight for your livesss. No more cold. No more hunger. No more trials." He paused, letting the silence gather. "Ssstand with me, and together we will tear thisss place apart."

A guard stepped through the doorway, drawn by the clamour, blaster raised. "You, this way."

"No." sShearon's word was a challenge.

The guard advanced. A scuffle. A blaster clattered to the floor. A hand closed on a throat. Claws raked flesh. "Please, no," the guard choked. "I have family."

"Ssso did they." sShearon crushed the man's throat and tossed him aside.

The room exhaled as one. Gasps, then silence like a held breath.

"Did you sssee hisss face?" he demanded, looking over them. "Did you sssee the fear? They are not godsss. They are men, weak men, hiding behind gunsss. When confronted, they tremble. You? You are many. You are fire. You are ssstorm. Overwhelm them. Tear down their wallsss. Reclaim your world."

Murmurs became nods; whispers spread like kindling.

"You want freedom? Take it. Not tomorrow. Not after another trial. Now. For your familiesss. For your livesss."

The crowd roared. Fists rose. A chant broke free: "No more! No more! No more!"

A loud cheer erupted as the crowd dispersed to find weapons. sShearon didn't waste any time and he set off, the crowd growing stronger and louder as they went, their chant echoing through the building.

"No more! No more! No more!"

The crowd marched down the corridor, bursting through doors, meeting guards on the other side.

These guards opened fire, but the crowd still surged forward, anger in their eyes and fire in their bellies. The crowd, led by sShearon easily overpowered two guards blocking the main doors. Three more guards were swiftly dealt with, before the crowd burst through more doors. sShearon fell behind and he slipped away, leaving the crowd to fight their own battle.

He had to face off with Abaddon and do it alone. *That devil could trick any creature or being into doing her own bidding, anyone who didn't have God in their heart.* Following the Calling, until he rounded a corner and entered a room with ten guards, Abaddon sitting on her throne. The guards' helmets hit the floor with dull thuds. One by one, their gazes locked on Abaddon, drawn helplessly into eyes that churned and twisted, pulling at their very minds.

sShearon crept in, heading for Abaddon, when her eyes flickered back to normal. Her head exploded into a ball of flames, and she screamed at her guards, "Kill him!" Flames shot out of her mouth and a clawed finger pointed towards sShearon.

Suddenly, a loud roar burst into the room. The guards all raced forward, meeting the crowd streaming in. More guards joined in and there was carnage. Blood was spilt, a lot of blood.

sShearon made his way toward Abaddon. Flames extinguished, her eyes swirled.

"You don't have to fight me, Cydarion," she purred. "Join me. Rule beside me. Together, we can be gods."

He stepped closer, silent, eyes locked on hers.

She rose, moving with predatory grace. "Think of it, armies at your command. No more trials, no more hunger. Only power. Only worship.

Release your soul to me, and I will set you free."

For a heartbeat, it seemed he wavered. He leaned close, voice low: "I releassse…" He paused, eyes narrowing. "…nothing."

His claw whipped across her throat. Blood sprayed. Abaddon staggered, clutching her neck, eyes wide with disbelief.

"How dare you…" she choked, collapsing as life drained from her.

sShearon bent low, hissing. "Too much blood hasss been ssspilt. Yoursss isss the lassst."

Her last breath rattled. He pushed her aside.

Silence. Then a voice shouted:

"He's slain the devil!"

The crowd froze, then erupted in cheers. Even the freed guards stared, dazed.

sShearon sank to the floor, exhaustion catching him.

"You are free now," he rasped. "All of you."

A small voice piped up. "Thank you… for believing in us. We owe our lives to you."

sShearon smiled faintly. "Make the bessst of your life. And… do the right thing."

The crowd surged, fists raised, voices echoing: *No more! No more! No more!*

The trials were over. The oppressors defeated. And for the first time in a long time, the mountain, and the people within it, were free.

Ord
The Museum Curator

Chapter 34

Pace descended the transport ramp and joined the slow shuffle through planetary security. The scanner beeped twice at his sidearm, but he smiled at the guard as if to say *you really don't want to start this conversation.* They didn't.

Outside, the city of Calebro unfolded, full of all glass arcs and floating gardens, the skyline hummed with aerial trams that darted like silverfish. For a moment, Pace forgot why he was here.

"This is beautiful," he breathed. "Could retire here."

He laughed softly. *Retire.* What a dangerous word for a Cydarion. His knees had been filing complaints since the Final Skirmish of Thora, and his mind was worn thin from a century of saving people who couldn't remember his name a week later.

Jodrell, how did you manage this gig for a hundred and seventy-five cycles? he thought. *Probably with more alcohol and fewer morals.*

He *could* have opened a portal straight to his destination. But sometimes he liked pretending he was just a citizen, just another tired face on a transport, breathing recycled air and pretending to be normal.

He flicked open a holomap in his palm, followed glowing arrows through narrow streets, and stopped before a squat marble building framed in luminous script:

THE MUSEUM OF THE HOUSE OF PRAYER.

He frowned. "Catchy as a broken comm line," he muttered, and stepped inside.

The receptionist blinked twice at his credentials and waved him through. Pace wandered the halls, nodding at relics older than some stars. Tablets, ancient weapons, a half-melted idol from the First Expansion. *You could teach a dozen Cydarions something here,* he thought. *Assuming they could sit still for it.*

Then came the familiar sound of wet footsteps: *plap, plap, plap.*

"Mathter Pathe?" a voice chirped.

Pace turned to find a tall, birdlike being with white plumage and an expression of eternal optimism.

"Just Pace," he said, shaking the creature's offered wing. The feathers curled around his fingers like a handshake from a silk glove.

"I am Ord, curator of thith mutheum," the bird announced proudly.

"Nice to meet you, Ord. I trust you got my message?"

"Yeth. I did not think the Mathter himthelf would come."

"Well, you're in luck. I had nothing better to do than cross half a galaxy on a hunch."

Ord blinked, trying to decide if that was sarcasm. Pace smiled. "Is there somewhere private we can talk?"

"Of courthe. Thith way, pleathe."

The curator's office looked like a storage war between a library and a junkyard. Relics, crates, scrolls — and something that might've been a fossilized sandwich — competed for space.

"I'm looking for an artifact," Pace said. "Ancient, probably rusted. May or may not be a myth."

Ord cocked his feathered head. "Doeth it have a name?"

"The Flaming Sword."

Ord blinked again. "That ith... literal."

"Yep. I'm an optimist."

After a pause, Ord fluttered his wings. "No record of thuch a thing. But perhapth you can check our archiveth?"

"Music to my ears," Pace said. "Or possibly my doom."

The archive smelled of dust, wax, and the gentle despair of forgotten librarians. Candles guttered against a draft, throwing shadows like ghosts. Pace sat hunched over a book thicker than a hull plate.

***

Four rotations later, he'd sneezed eleven times and cursed more times than he can remember, finding nothing but mildew.

He slammed another tome shut. "I'm looking for a needle in a haystack. No—a sword in a galaxy."

From above, *plap plap plap* echoed again.

"Mathter Pathe!" Ord appeared, puffing proudly and holding a brown-bound ledger. "Thith might be it!"

Pace took it. "'Bill of Sales.' Riveting. Which page?"

"Thixty-eight."

Pace turned the page, squinting. "Rare metal fence post. Paid in... wow, that's a fortune."

Ord beamed. "Note the thquare by the entry."

"Let me guess... code?"

Ord produced another small book. "Croth-reference date."

Pace flipped pages, eyes widening as the translation aligned. "Purchased by... a Master Cydarion."

He froze. "Two hundred cycles ago... That could've been Jodrell's master."

"Would you like to thee the drawing?"

"There's a drawing?" Pace's grin returned. "You just became my favourite bird in the galaxy."

***

Procel burst into the dining hall where Lucifer and Lucigon were finishing their meal. The hall itself was vast. Obsidian pillars, chandeliers of molten iron, and a ceiling painted with the wars of creation. Flames flickered within the murals as if alive. The scent of brimstone and seared meat filled the air.

"Sire, sire, we have news!" Procel cried.

Lucigon's chair screeched as he turned, his expression already murderous. "What *of*?" he snapped, before Lucifer could speak.

Lucigon never liked being interrupted during a meal, especially not when he was almost enjoying it. Dining time, to him, was sacred: the one peaceful moment between endless war drills. He'd been locked in this fortress far too long. The training was mind-numbing. Even his perfect aim had begun to bore him. He needed blood. A new world. Perhaps a few terrified souls to remind him why he was alive.

Procel's eyes darted from Lucigon to Lucifer. The elder demon raised one hand, wordlessly permitting him to continue.

"The artefact you were searching for..." Procel stammered, then paused, expecting a question.

"Get on with it," growled Lucigon, wiping his mouth with the back of his forearm.

"Y-y-yes, my lord. The *Lahat Cherub* has been located." Another pause. "At least, it was... three hundred cycles ago."

Lucifer's gaze sharpened. He didn't move, but the shadows seemed to lean closer.

"We had to torture a Dotholmite to get the information, sire," said Procel quickly.

Lucigon slammed a clawed hand on the table. "So what? You're testing my patience. I'll gladly torture *you* if you don't get to the point."

Procel swallowed hard. "He was young, he still had another thousand cycles to live."

Lucigon pushed back his chair and stood abruptly. The air temperature spiked.

"Enough." Lucifer's voice was quiet but absolute. Lucigon froze mid-step.

"So, he died?" Lucifer asked, his tone controlled — though a small curl of smoke escaped the corner of his mouth.

"Yes..."

Lucigon sighed theatrically. "Mortals die too easily these days."

Lucifer ignored his son and inclined his head. "Very well. What did he say about the Cherub?"

Procel took a cautious step back from Lucigon. "He claimed that, in his youth, he saw something matching the description... on a planet called *Calebro*. That's all he remembered before... passing away."

Lucifer's eyes flared faintly, two red embers. "Procel," he said, voice soft as silk. "Are you growing *weak* on me?"

Procel straightened his back as if the words themselves were a whip. "No, sire, I..."

Lucigon's low growl drowned him out.

"That is all, sire," Procel finished quickly. "I bid you goodnight." He bowed and backed toward the door, closing it gently behind him, as if any noise might provoke instant death.

Lucifer exhaled, long and weary. "Lucigon," he said, rubbing his temple, "you can kill him in the morning. He's outlasted his usefulness."

Lucigon smiled, fangs flashing. "Why not now?"

"Because," Lucifer replied, eyes narrowing, "you need to learn *restraint* too."

Lucigon's grin widened. "I look forward to it."

Lucifer rose from the table, taking his goblet of black wine. "Do it at first light. We have somewhere else to be."

He moved to the hearth, a pit of eternal flame that devoured shadows instead of casting them, and stared into it thoughtfully.

Lucigon joined him, dragging his chair close. "This fire," he said, gazing into the shifting blaze, "it comforts me."

Lucifer smiled faintly. "Of course it does. It was the first thing I ever mastered."

He turned, eyes glinting like molten gold. "Tell me, do you know anything of this world... Calebro?"

Lucigon thought for a moment, then shook his head.

"Nor do I," said Lucifer. "Which means we tread carefully. If someone holds the Cherub, we may need to negotiate."

Lucigon frowned. "Negotiate? With *mortals*?"

Lucifer's gaze flicked sideways. "You do remember what the artefact *is*, don't you?"

Lucigon shrugged. "Some kind of weapon?"

Lucifer stood abruptly, the flames in the hearth rising with him. "That complacency will get you *killed!*"

Lucigon blinked. "But I thought we were immortal?"

Lucifer didn't answer. He walked out, his tail trailing sparks across the floor.

Lucigon remained seated, staring into the flames. They danced like serpents, whispering promises. His claws dug into the armrest. *I'm going to kill Procel before I settle for the night,* he thought, smiling at the idea.

***

Grey light filtered through the bloodstained windows of the war room, cutting through the smoky air. Lucifer stood by the holotable, a swirling red projection of the galaxy hovering above it.

"Did you do as instructed?" he asked, skipping pleasantries.

"Last night," Lucigon replied, bluntly.

Lucifer's eyes darkened. "I told you to wait."

"Why prolong a life already marked for death?" said Lucigon, unrepentant.

Lucifer exhaled slowly, disappointed. The sound like the crackle of a furnace. "It wasn't about him, Lucigon. It was about *you*." A pause. "But..." he conceded, "you have a point. Are you ready to go hunting?"

Lucigon's grin returned. "Always, Father. Here, let me."

He spread his arms, conjuring a swirling rift of crimson light. The smell of ozone and burning parchment filled the air.

Lucifer nodded with approval and stepped through. Lucigon followed a heartbeat later.

They emerged in a field of yellow grass, each blade shimmering like liquid metal. Above them, two suns burned, one gold, one pale blue. Ahead lay a sprawling city of glass towers and floating bridges, the distant hum of airships faint in the wind.

Lucifer inhaled. "Calebro," he murmured. "This place smells of fear and faith."

Lucigon grimaced.

"We start there," Lucifer said, pointing toward the city.

Moments later, their wings unfurled, great sheets of fire and flame, and they shot into the sky, twin shadows cutting through the morning dew.

Three sections and several killings later, Lucifer and Lucigon stood before the *Museum of the House of Prayer*.

"This place reeks," Lucigon said, nearly gagging.

"Breathe it in," Lucifer replied. "That's the scent of Cydarions. Their pride lingers longer than their bodies."

"They're here?" Lucigon asked, hopeful.

"I doubt it," Lucifer said, waving lazily at the civilians hurrying past. "But these trinkets of theirs, these relics, their smell clings to them. They consider themselves too important to be associated with lesser beings like these," said Lucifer, waving his hand at some passer-by.

"Every being is lesser than us, Father," Lucigon declared.

Lucifer smiled faintly. "You're a fast learner."

Lucigon almost smiled back. "Let's get this done. The smell's starting to make my nose itch."

They burst through the front doors.

"WHERE IS THE LAHAT CHERUB?" Lucifer boomed, his voice shaking the glass walls.

The terrified receptionist stammered but said nothing. Lucifer sighed and, with a flick of his hand, ripped her spine out in a clean, precise motion. She crumpled silently.

Screams filled the hall. Patrons fled, glass shattered, silent alarms flashed.

Lucigon grinned and started smashing every display he could find, relics scattering across the marble floor. "Nothing here!" he shouted.

"Whath going on here?" came a quivering voice. Ord appeared, feathers puffed, clutching a silver book.

"Who are you?" Lucigon demanded.

"I am Ord, curator of thith mutheum!" the bird declared, trembling.

"Ah," said Lucifer, stepping forward. "Then it's you who can help us."

"I will do no thuch thing," Ord said, bill wobbling. "Not until you thtop damaging the prithleth artefacth!"

Lucigon snarled and hurled a priceless vase through a window. "You are in no position to demand anything."

Ord let out a nervous quack.

"I'll ask *politely*," said Lucifer, his tone turning dangerously calm. "Where is the Lahat Cherub?"

Ord froze. His feathers ruffled.

"Ah," Lucifer said, smile fading. "So it *does* ring a bell." His eyes glowed crimson, and fire erupted from his crown. "WHERE. IS. IT?"

Ord squealed, dropped the book, then, in pure panic, scooped it up again and bolted.

Lucigon leapt forward, wings flaring, and landed in front of him. He grabbed the curator and lifted him off the ground, book and all.

"What do we have here?" Lucigon mused, bringing both close to his face.

"Ith nothing!" Ord stammered, and with desperate courage, he hurled the silver book away.

It clattered across the marble, straight into Pace's path.

***

Pace had busied himself putting away the mountain of books he had already scoured, fruitlessly, yet his excitement over this new find kept him moving. He'd previously assigned a few of the Storous to dig through the citadel's archives, alongside Bork and himself. This place was the only lead they'd uncovered, its records stretching well before the Cydarions, nearly to the dawn of written language. Finding anything was a colossal gamble, but a glimmer of hope shone through.

A thunderous crash above yanked him from his thoughts. Instinctively, he looked up. Stone and wood, nothing more. Then came the voices: unintelligible shouts at first, escalating with more crashing. He crept up the stairs, senses straining, until the unmistakable quacking of Ord cut through the din.

Pace sprinted the remaining steps and reached the main hall, blasters drawn. Ord had insisted the museum was peaceful, no weapons required, but Pace trusted his instincts over advice.

Peeking around a corner, he froze. A massive yellow-orange beast loomed, snarling, Ord clutched in one hand.

"Ith nothing, it ith jutht a thketch book," Ord said, just before the silver book clattered onto the floor ten steps away. *That must hold a sketch of the Flaming Sword,* Pace thought. *How do I grab it without being noticed?*

No choice remained. He stepped from behind the stone wall, levelling his blasters.

"Put him down," Pace commanded, advancing cautiously.

The beast fixed him with a glare. "Who are you?"

"Just a concerned citizen," he replied.

"He's a Cydarion," came a voice behind the beast. Pace's neck hairs rose as Lucifer stepped into view.

"What are you doing here, Lucifer? This is a house of peace," Pace demanded.

Lucifer scoffed. "There's never any peace. Even mortals fight amongst themselves; you don't need *my* help."

"That's your influence!" Pace shot back.

Lucifer shrugged. "Maybe, maybe not." Behind him, the beast shifted nervously. "Ah, yes. Let me introduce my son, Lucigon." He gestured toward the creature. "Lucigon, say hello to... the Cydarion."

Lucigon inhaled sharply, then hurled a fireball at Pace. It struck him mid-step, sending him crashing into the wall. He scrambled up, staggering, then dove behind a stone pillar as another fireball shrieked past, exploding against the wall. *There are two of them?*

"He stinks!" Lucigon sneered.

"Yes, unfortunately, they all do," Lucifer replied calmly.

From behind the pillar, Pace called out, "Lucifer, you don't do your own killing. Why are you here?"

"I'm looking for the Lahat Cherub," Lucifer said. "I heard it was here."

Pace took a measured breath and stepped from cover, hands raised. "We don't know what that is." One step brought him dangerously close to the silver book.

"This one seems to," Lucigon said, shaking Ord until feathers fell like ash.

"There's no need for that," Pace muttered, tripping slightly over the silver book and sending it skidding behind an archway. Lucigon didn't notice... but Lucifer did.

"Bring me that book," he demanded.

"Which book?" Pace feigned confusion, scanning the chaos of shattered glass and relics.

"The silver one. Or this pathetic being suffers," Lucifer said, gesturing at Ord.

Pace's mind raced. *Okay, okay... just keep him safe.* "Fine. Just put Ord down," he said.

"The book first," Lucigon snarled.

Pace retrieved it, flicking through the pages nonchalantly. "Lucifer, do we have a deal?"

"You have my word," Lucifer nodded.

"On three. One…" Pace scanned the remaining pages, "Two." There it was: a detailed sketch of the Flaming Sword. He memorized it, stepped from behind the pillar, and threw the book toward Lucifer. It landed short.

Lucigon crushed Ord in one hand, hurling his lifeless body at Pace with laughter.

Pace staggered, barely recovering before a fireball hit him again. Winded, he fired two blaster bolts at Lucifer's feet, vaporizing the silver book, then dove for cover.

Lucigon unleashed two more fireballs, the first one missed, but the other slammed into Pace's shoulder, spinning him across the floor. He rolled down stone steps, out of sight.

"WHERE IS THE CHERUB?" Lucifer roared, voice shaking the ceiling.

"It's safe. You'll never find it," Pace yelled back, unsure what he meant himself.

"You wouldn't even know how to ignite the sword!" Lucifer taunted.

Pace's mind raced. *We're after the same thing. Is he prepared to kill God?* He didn't know the sword's location, but he wouldn't let Lucifer find it first. At least he had a lead and the sketch committed to memory.

Lucifer turned to Lucigon. "Rip this place apart. He's lying."

"My pleasure," Lucigon said, grinning.

Pace had enough. He stepped fully into view, planted his feet, and shouted, "You'll have to go through me first."

Lucigon snorted. "I shall enjoy ripping the flesh from your bones," sending fireballs in a relentless barrage.

This time Pace was ready, parrying with his blasters, dodging most attacks. But then he saw it. Lucigon was absorbing every hit without flinching. *Immortal too, like Lucifer? Everything's changed.*

Artefacts, relics, treasures tens of thousands of cycles old shattered around him. He had only the two PL14s in his hands. Thinking fast, he aimed both at the central column, firing precision shots. Steel and concra chunks flew, the ceiling cracked above Lucigon and Lucifer.

The museum collapsed in a storm of dust and fire.

When the air cleared, Pace dragged Ord's crushed body from the rubble, opened a portal, and stepped through.

He emerged in a quiet harbour town under a violet dawn. Machinery hummed. The air smelled of salt and industry. Pace knelt beside Ord, setting him gently down.

"You were brave, my friend," he whispered. "Braver than most people I know."

He looked out at the sea, the horizon glimmering faintly. "I'll wait a while. Make sure the devils don't follow. Then I'll take you home."

The waves answered softly, and for the first time in weeks, Pace allowed himself to breathe. The weight of the universe resting heavily upon his shoulders.

Bork at his desk

Chapter 35

Holan was in a bad mood, and he let everyone in Drake's classroom know it. Although Holan was only a Storous, in the process of becoming a Cydarion, he felt the classroom activities were not for him, he needed more action. Drake, his teacher, had to admonish him numerous times for speaking out of line, until Holan finally snapped.

"I can't stand this anymore," he said, standing up, his chair scraping across the stone flooring. He grabbed his things and headed towards the door.

Alkira let out a loud gasp.

Holan stopped just short of the door and spun around. "You're all just as bad, you treat me like some adolescent! I'm middle aged for my species, and I deserve your respect!" He huffed and walked out the door. "I'm destined for more than this, I just know it," he muttered as he slammed the door behind him. He kicked the in frustration.

Taking a breath outside the room, he heard Alkira say, "Should I go after him?"

Holan scowled and stormed off. *I'm ready for more than this, I know I am. They all treat me like a child. Even our so-called Master Pace. He* scoffed, *Leader? He hardly knows what he's doing, let alone how to guide others. Even I could do better, I could... I would..."*

"Arghh!" Holan let out his frustration as he stormed through the corridors of the Citadel, unsure of where to go or what to do. He was conflicted. An itch that couldn't be scratched. Something constantly tugging at him.

Tears welled in his eyes, unable to let out his full anger. He kicked anything that was in his way.

"Argh," he constantly screamed, wiping away tears. His frustration had gotten the better of him and he felt he needed to do something drastic. But what?

Eventually Holan slumped to the ground somewhere in the Citadel, knees bent, his back against the wall and buried his face in his paws.

Bork appeared. "Master Holan, whatever is the matter? I heard some commotion and was curious."

Holan sniffed. his nose started to twitch as he removed his paws, "IT'S NOT FAIR!" he screamed.

"What isn't fair?"

"The way they treat me!"

"Whatever do you mean?" asked Bork.

Holan straightened his legs, the back of his knees slapping on the stone floor. "They treat me like a child," he said.

Bork stood up straight, almost authoritarian like. "To most, you are," Bork said flatly.

"Argh!" Holan let out another scream and pulled on his ears. "You're just like them! I'm middle aged for my species," he said. "I don't have as much time to accomplish my ambitions... unlike them." He paused and looked up at Bork. "Or you!" he added with malice. His nose twitched again.

Bork took the insult in his stride, calmly asking, "What are your ambitions?"

"I want to kill some devils, get the praise of being a saviour. We *are* God's henchmen, aren't we?"

Bork's eyes widened and he took a fraction to digest Holan's words. "Certainly not," he said. "We are no such thing. The Cydarion's are..."

"Sure we are," Holan cut in. "God wants us to kill. He opens a portal and points us in the right direction."

"Storous Holan," snapped Bork. "You are quite wrong. We gather information from other worlds, keeping documents regarding..."

"Why, what's the point?" Holan cut him off again. "God doesn't even read them; he has no interest. He doesn't even tell you to do that."

"Holan," snapped Bork. "That is blasphemous."

"No, it isn't," said Holan getting to his feet. "All he asks you to do is kill. That's what I was born to do, it's all I've ever known. Kill for a god, that's what my family taught me." He took a breath. "Take hunting, you kill. Need a sacrifice, you kill. Want to change the weather, you kill. Want a good harvest, you kill. Not happy with a government figure, you kill." Each sentence ended with a sharp smack of fist against paw, like an exclamation mark made of flesh an bone. He pointed to himself. "I got good at it. That's why you recruited me, right?" He raised his voice, "Well, let me do some goddamn killing!"

Bork, unsure of how to handle the situation, dropped onto all four and bared his teeth. "Holan, do not talk like that again."

"Oh, what are you going to do? Holan snapped back, "Write me a story?" He sniggered at his own words.

Bork growled loudly, then barked. "Holan! Go to your room and cool down!"

Holan smirked. "Who are you to tell me what to do? You're not even a Cydarion."

As they spoke, a neon purple glow lit up the end of the corridor.

Holan and Bork stopped arguing and turned to the light.

It was coming from the portal room. Holan hadn't realised where they were.

"What's that?" asked Holan.

"That colour isn't normal," said Bork. He turned back to Holan. "Let's go somewhere else," his voice low, calm.

Holan hesitated, he hadn't heard Bork, not properly. But he did hear the portal. *It's calling to me.*

His eyes transfixed on the light at the far end of the corridor. His mind flashed with a thousand memories. Through all the static one single memory stood out; Nyk advising him, 'Have faith in yourself, to do the right thing.'

"Please Holan, we should go somewhere else," Bork pleaded. "Some Cydarion's will need to use this corridor, we shouldn't get in their way."

Holan caught Bork's voice somewhere behind him: "Let's go somewhere else."

But only heard two words reached him. 'Somewhere else.'

He repeated them under his breath, nodding as if they were meant for him. Bork took it as agreement and disappeared deeper into the Citadel.

Holan turned the other way, toward the light. Toward his Calling. At the doorway he glanced back. Bork had stopped, panic flaring across his face, and was already racing towards him, teeth bared.

Holan hurried forward. The portal shimmered ahead, a violet pool in the air, standing apart from the three wooden frames.

"Master Holan, no!" Bork cried, voice breaking as he reached the threshold.

Holan smiled. "I can hear it," he whispered. "He needs my help."

Bork froze. "He? Who?"

Holan's gaze locked on the purple glow. "Lucifer... Lucifer needs me."

Bork staggered back, horror twisting his face. "Holan, don't move."

Holan's chest tightened, but his thought was steady; *This is my time.* He turned to Bork with a sorrow smile. please "I have to do this. It's the right thing."

"Holan,... no!"

He offered Bork one final nod, heavy with farewell, then stepped into the void. The portal flared, swallowing him whole. When it vanished, only silence remained.

***

Bork was in the record archives, waiting to talk with Pace, his nose was buried deep in an old accounts book, his half-moon reading glasses sat halfway down his muzzle. His right paw scrolled through a data pad while his left paw tapped out binary on the aged wooden desk.

"They suit you," said Pace, as he approached the desk.

Bork looked to his left and right before looking up and smiling, "Master Pace," he said, with a stifled yawn, "it's good to see you again."

"You too," Pace replied, walking around the desk and giving Bork a hug, while the records keeper was still seated. Pace pulled out another chair and sat down opposite.

"I said, they suit you," he repeated, pointing to Bork's new reading glasses.

"Oh, yes, thank you. It happens to most of us eventually," Bork mused.

"You know, there's a simple procedure to correct your vision. If you want to, we'll cover the costs," Pace offered.

"Oh, thank you, Master Pace. I appreciate the offer, but as a journalist, the glasses actually help," said Bork. Pace's quizzical look portrayed a question, so Bork carried on, "Most species identify glasses with being a trustworthy soul, so I am quite happy to wear them," Bork said with a warm smile.

Pace nodded, "Well I've never seen a devil in glasses!"

They both laughed, then Bork leaned closer to Pace and whispered, "They probably don't need glasses, because they can't read!" Bork let out a loud gruff.

Pace laughed at Bork's joke, nodding his agreement. "What was it you wanted to see me about?" he asked.

Bork went quiet, not knowing how to approach the subject, so, he just blurted out the words. "Holan has gone!"

Pace looked confused, "What does that mean?" he asked.

Bork looked down at the desk, "Holan has gone...I don't mean he's left the Cydarions, although, I guess he has..."

"Bork!" snapped Pace, "What do you mean?"

Bork exhaled, a defeated sigh, and explained, "He went into the portal room, I tried to stop him, but I couldn't. There was an open portal, and he stepped through. There was nothing I could do!"

"Where did he go?" asked Pace.

"I have no idea, it was a new place, not one he opened, but it closed behind him," replied Bork.

"Shit!" Pace said, putting his head in his hands.

"It was a different portal too. A purple one, but outside of the portal frames."

"What?"

"There was nothing I could have done Master Pace," said Bork.

Pace shook his head, "I'm out of my depth, Bork!" said Pace accepting his failures. He looked at the records keeper, who was staying silent. "It's all getting out of hand; we're losing more Callings than we're winning..." he paused. "Maybe I could call in a group of mercenaries that I know." He nodded to himself, "We could help them through the portals and..."

"That is isn't God's way," Bork interrupted.

Pace sighed and rubbed his temples, "I know, I know, I'm just thinking out loud, and with Nyk gone, I think..."

"Nyk's dead?" Bork asked, a shocked expression on his face.

Pace quickly realised that Bork didn't know about Nyk, and he held his hands up, "No, no, no, Nyk is still alive, he's just, erm, taking some personal time."

Bork made an '0' with his mouth before answering, "Is it his depression?" he asked in a whisper.

It was Paces' turn to be shocked, "You knew about that?"

"Pace, I'm a journalist, I can read people, plus I can smell their pheromones. Of course, I knew. He's spoken to me about certain things. I'm glad he's getting help," Bork said warmly, tapping a paw on the back of Paces hand.

"How did you know he was getting help?" asked Pace.

"You paused," said Bork, "you didn't know how to answer. I just put the pieces together."

Pace smiled, "You're a good journalist, Bork, and a better friend," he said.

Bork smiled back, "Thank you, Pace. What are you going to do about all the Callings?" he asked, getting back on topic.

"I don't know," replied Pace, "we really are on the losing side."

"Pace, this isn't about winning or losing. It's about faith," said Bork, "Are you losing yours?" He looked at Pace questioningly.

Pace's face went blank and he looked down, shuffling within his seat, unable to answer that question.

"You were chosen for a reason," said Bork.

Pace closed his eyes, as though bracing against a storm only he could hear. His breath left him in a slow, broken sigh, and when his eyes opened, they carried the shadow of something already lost.

He stepped from the room with the tread of a man walking to his fate.

To Bork, the weight on his shoulders was more than grief. It was a herald of ruin yet to come.

***

Pace scoured the portal room, tearing through every corner for any sign of Holan. Nothing. Just the cold hush of the stone and ache of absence. *Damn it, Holan... where did you go?*

His hands curled into fists. *I have to know, where are you?*

A vein throbbed, and he collapsed to the stone floor clutching his head, letting out an anguished cry.

He sat there for a while, thinking, before storming to his office, calling for a council meeting in three sections.

His office door shut with a thud that echoed louder than it should have. Pace leaned against it, every muscle trembling, the grief he had kept hidden spilling out now that no eyes were on him. Holan was gone, so was Daemich and Ord, Swift too, and maybe Nyk, his rock. Yet he was expected to lead.

He staggered to his desk, bracing himself on its ledge. His knees threatening to give way. For a moment he wanted to smash the datapads, crush the portals, and burn the whole Citadel down. Oh how he'd like that.

His hands balled into fists, shaking, then slammed once into the wood. The pain steadied him, barely.

They're looking to me, but I can't tell them the truth. He shook his head. *I can't let anyone else die. Not for me, not for God. This has to end.*

He pressed his palms into his eyes until stars flared behind the lids, forcing back tears. His chest heaved, but when he lowered his hands his face was cold, set. On the desk, he opened the Holo map.

Dok giving CPR

Chapter 36

Dok paced the length of his cell, claws tapping against the sterile floor. Too long confined. Too quiet. Something about this station was wrong — it thrummed with more power than it should, a constant vibration in his bones.

Without warning, the door hissed open. So did half the others along the corridor. A gust of recycled air brushed his fur.

"Move," barked a voice from beyond. Guards ushered them into another sterile corridor that curved left, toward the station's core, Dok guessed. The other half of the prisoners were likely marching the same route on the mirrored side. A door sealed behind them with a heavy clang, cutting off the guards.

Then came the voice from the loudspeaker, it was smooth, detached, the same one that had ordered their trials.

"Proceed when the doors open. Each of you will be assigned a worker. They will show you your new duties."

"What does that mean?" someone muttered.

"Probably ship maintenance," another said.

"I didn't come here to work," a third spat.

A disheartened voice added, "Haven't we been through enough already?"

The doors ahead hissed open. Warm, oily air rushed out to meet them. The smell hit next, a heavy mix of grease and sweat. A groan rippled through the crowd. Dok turned his head away, nostrils flaring.

"C'mon," shouted one hopeful being, "once we get this done, maybe we can explore the ship!"

Dok doubted it, but he followed the group inside. The doors sealed behind them, and another slab of metal descended from the ceiling, locking the way shut. The lights were dim, a sickly orange glow barely cutting the heat. Sweat dampened his fur.

Someone bolted into the dark. "I'm not waiting for you lot to get the best jobs!"

The rest hesitated, murmured, then drifted away in smaller groups until only Dok and a young woman remained.

"What's happening?" she asked.

"I don't know," Dok said, scanning the gloom. "Maybe wait. See what they…"

His bracelet vibrated. A surge of electricity tore through his body. He gritted his teeth, muscles tightening. Around him, screams erupted, dozens of voices writhing in agony. The woman collapsed, convulsing on the ground.

When the shock ended, Dok crouched beside her.

"They're not just tracking us," she gasped.

He lowered his head. "I'm sorry."

"You couldn't have known."

"Maybe we just do as we're told… for now." Dok rose and went in search of a worker.

The heat deepened the further he walked. He passed rows of beings, each bent to some grim mechanical rhythm. None smiled. None spoke.

"Hey, big guy," croaked a frail voice. Dok turned. An old man struggled with a heavy lever, his skin blistered and red, sores leaking across his scalp. His eyes were sunken but sharp.

Dok stepped forward. "Here, let me."

The man sagged with relief. "Thank you."

"Name's Dok."

"Eland," the man replied, breathless. He gestured toward a flickering panel. "See that green light? When it comes on, pull the lever and hold until it turns red. Then let go. It's steady work, you'll feel the rhythm soon enough."

Dok nodded, trying to ignore the stench of coolant and burned flesh. "What are we doing?"

"Cooling uranium cores. Drop them into the water before they melt. It keeps the reactors efficient."

"Efficient for what?"

Eland shrugged. "We're not told."

"How long have you been here?"

Eland exhaled softly. "Forty-three rotations."

Dok blinked. "You survived the trials?"

Eland caught his look and smiled faintly. "I was strong once, stronger than you, maybe. That's why they picked me."

"What happened?"

"Radiation," he said simply. "We all get it. The ones near the doors last longer. We don't."

Dok pulled the lever, watching pale steam rise as the rods sank into the cooling pool. "Ever refuse to work?"

Eland shook his head. "That would make things worse."

"Worse how?"

Eland coughed hard, spitting blood. He smeared it into the floor with a ragged shoe, embarrassed. When he spoke again, his voice was a rasp.

"If one of us refuses, they shock *everyone* in the group. Eventually, the others turn on you. There are no friends here, only survivors. And if you obey, you get extra food rations." He laughed once, bitterly. "To keep us strong."

Dok's grip on the lever tightened. "Has everyone accepted this?"

"Not all. There's always exile."

"Exile to where?"

Eland pointed vaguely toward the far end of the hall. "The other side. After a few rounds of torture first."

"Did that happen to you?"

He shook his head. "No. The one before me told me the story. I thought it couldn't happen to me."

Then the bracelets vibrated again. Electricity ripped through their bodies. Dok's muscles locked; he lost hold of the lever. The uranium rods plunged back into the water. Eland's back arched... then he fell, clutching his chest.

When the current stopped, Dok dropped to all fours. "Eland!" He lifted the frail man's hand. "Squeeze if you can hear me." Nothing. He pressed his ear to the man's chest. Silence. "No heartbeat," he muttered.

"Guards!" he roared, his voice echoing off the metal walls. The only answer was a blinking green light.

Dok looked from the light to the lever, then to the dead man's bracelet. "No," he growled.

He grabbed Eland's limp body, dragging it close. Wrapping his tail around the lever, he forced it up — keeping the rods suspended — and pressed his paw against Eland's chest.

"One, two..." He began compressions. "...twenty-seven, twenty-eight, twenty-nine..." Heat built beneath his paw. "Thirty!"

He hesitated, an instinct urging him to hold. His palm glowed faintly, warmth spreading into Eland's skin. The blisters on the man's arms began to shrink, sores closing over. His pallid skin flushed pink.

Dok's eyes widened. *What? Am I... healing him?*

He focused harder. A faint pulse stirred under his paw. First weak, then steady.

Eland's eyes snapped open. He gasped for air.

Dok sat back, stunned. The red light blinked on; his tail released the lever.

"What happened?" Eland rasped.

"You had a heart attack. I..." Dok faltered. "How do you feel?"

Eland flexed his fingers, blinked at his healed skin, and let out a trembling laugh. "I feel *good*. What did you do?"

"I... don't know."

"Well, whatever it was, thank you." He twisted his arms experimentally, a smile spreading. "No pain. None at all."

Dok nodded, pulling the lever again as the light turned green. "Rest, Eland. You've earned it."

Eland sat watching the miracle of his own hands, smiling like a child. For the first time since arriving, Dok smiled too.

The rest of the shift passed in silence. Eland slept, and Dok worked the lever alone, his mind racing.

Four sections later, the sealed door retracted and the double doors slid open. Relief workers shuffled in to replace them. The air felt heavier now, thick with heat and fatigue.

Eland stirred awake, his skin smooth and bright. "Time already?" he murmured, stretching.

Another worker took position at the lever — a hollow-eyed man with sagging skin and patches of missing hair.

"Crondal," Eland greeted, cheerful. "Good to see you again."

Crondal barely looked up. "Shift change," he muttered, voice flat.

Eland gestured to Dok. "This is Dok... saved my hide."

Crondal grunted, uninterested, and pulled the lever as the light flashed green.

"See you next shift," he said without emotion.

Eland and Dok stepped into the corridor.

"Eland, wait," Dok said quietly. "I need a favour."

Eland smiled. "After what you did for me? Name it."

"I need to reach the medical bay. If you fake another heart attack, I can use the chaos."

Eland's grin widened. "That all? Easy."

"Do it in the corridor, in front of the guards."

He winked. "You've got a plan?"

"The start of one."

Moments later, Eland clutched his chest and collapsed. The guards froze, unsure.

"Take us to the medical bay!" Dok barked, lifting Eland's limp body.

"You don't have one," a masked guard snapped.

"*You* do," Dok growled. "Help him and he'll live to work another day."

The guards exchanged glances. One shrugged, the other nodded.

"Move," said the first. "Everyone else, back to your rooms."

Dok followed, carrying Eland through a maze of steel corridors until they reached a small, sterile chamber. The smell of antiseptic stung his nose.

"Wait here," said the guard. "I'll get the medic." He left, locking the door behind him.

Eland cracked one eye open. "What's next?"

Dok placed a paw on his shoulder. "You've done enough."

"Like hell. We're in this together," Eland whispered fiercely.

Dok smiled faintly. "Then stay ready."

The door unlocked. A middle-aged Gethuul entered — pale-furred, tired eyes — and moved toward Eland.

Dok slipped behind him, pressed a paw to his shoulder, and drew a single claw to his throat.

"What is this place?" Dok growled.

The medic froze. "The... medical bay."

"The *station*. What is it?"

"The Omega?" the Gethuul stammered.

"Yes. What's its purpose?"

The medic hesitated. Dok pressed harder, a bead of blood forming.

"It's M.U.R.I.S.," he choked out.

"Say it," Dok ordered.

"Mass Uranium Repulsor In Space."

Dok frowned. "What does it *do*?"

"It moves large objects."

"How large?"

The medic swallowed. "A moon. Maybe larger."

Dok's eyes narrowed. "You can move planets?"

The Gethuul nodded nervously. "It's to *help* them, to correct orbits, prevent collisions. That's what we were told."

"You're destroying them!" Dok snarled. "You pushed one out of orbit by slamming another into it!"

"That can't be right," the medic said weakly. "We volunteered to *save* worlds."

"Volunteered?" Dok barked. "We were enslaved. Forced through trials just to end up here."

The medic blinked. "I thought you were all volunteers from the planet. Gratitude workers."

Dok's growl deepened. "We fought to *survive!* This was supposed to be refuge!"

Realisation flickered in the Gethuul's eyes. "What about the other operations?" he whispered.

Dok loomed over him. "What other operations?"

"I've helped with three already," the medic said, almost proud. "This is the fourth."

"You've destroyed *three planets*?" Dok roared. "How many more?"

"This is the last," the medic stammered. "Once the planet's stable, we abandon the prototype."

"How do you leave? There are no ships."

The medic froze, confusion dawning. "I... I don't know."

"Prototype," Dok repeated softly. "There are others?"

"Yes. Four times the power. Built after this one proved successful."

Dok's stomach twisted. "Big enough to move a *star*?"

"Or something denser," the medic whispered, as if realising it himself.

The truth hit them both like a shockwave. "What have we done?" the Gethuul whispered.

Then, suddenly, the light tugging in Dok's mind — the *Calling* — went silent. His eyes widened.

"sShearon," he breathed.

"Sorry?" the medic asked.

Dok released him and stepped back. "How do we stop this machine?"

"You can't," the medic said. "It only has forward thrust. We use planetary gravity to steer. Once set, there's no turning back."

Dok exhaled through his teeth. "Then I need to get off this thing."

"Me too," Eland said, leaping from the bed, alive and eager.

The medic gaped. "You're... you're alive?"

"Better than ever," Eland grinned.

The medic turned in confusion. "Then why..."

Thwack!

Dok's paw smashed across the Gethuul's head. The medic crumpled to the floor.

"I'm sorry," Dok murmured. "You can't come with me."

Eland's smile faded. "You used me... just to escape?"

"It's not like that," Dok said.

"You're no better than them!"

"No!" Dok's voice broke into a growl. "I can't save everyone."

"So you choose who lives? Like some kind of god?" Eland snapped.

"Argh!" Dok roared, the sound shaking the room. Eland stumbled back, terrified.

Dok's breath slowed. "Fine," he said at last. "I'll help you reach the shuttle. It'll take you planetside. That's all I can do."

"And the others?" Eland pressed.

Dok looked down. "I can't save them all."

"Maybe we can come back," Eland said, eyes bright with sudden hope. "Overpower the guards, launch a rescue..."

Dok didn't answer. He hit the emergency release. "Get back on the bed," he said.

The door slid open; two masked guards burst in. Dok moved first, a blur of fur and fury. He slammed one guard to the floor, kicked backward into the other, sending him crashing into the wall. One lay unconscious; the other gasped beneath him. Dok pressed down until ribs cracked.

He turned to Eland. "Put on a uniform. You'll have to pass as a guard."

Eland pulled on the armour and mask, trembling. "Thank you... for everything."

Dok nodded once. "Go."

The door sealed behind Eland. Dok sat on the bed for a long moment, listening to the faint hum of the reactor, the heart of a weapon masquerading as salvation. He whispered a short prayer for those he couldn't save, then stood.

A swirl of blue light formed before him, a portal. Head bowed, tail low, Dok stepped through and vanished.

***

Two rotations later, the prisoners overran the facility. The guards fell, one by one. Animals were released from their cages. Some bolted into the frozen wastes, others stayed, too weak to move. Those who remained were cared for, feeding them with what little they had.

sShearon watched the natives readjust to their new lives.

"What will you do now?" he asked Kliney.

"I'm aint sure," she said. "Some of 'em want to stay, turn this place into their home."

"But you're free," sShearon said softly.

Kliney smiled. "Free, yeah. But outside it's all ice 'n' death. In 'ere, at least, there's warmth. We'll wait..." She nodded to herself. "...for the others to return, take us to utopia."

sShearon blinked. "Dok..." he murmured. "I have to go."

Kliney frowned. "There's nowhere to go. It's frozen out there."

He raised a clawed hand, and a shimmering portal opened.

Her eyes widened. "You can *leave*... just like that?"

"Yesss," he said.

"And you could have left anytime?" she asked, disbelief and awe mixing in her voice.

He nodded.

"You stayed to fight, for us," she whispered.

"It wasss my honour," said sShearon.

Kliney hugged him tightly. "Thank you... for everything."

He returned the embrace. "I wisssh I could take you with me," he said.

"Oh no," she smiled. "I'll wait for the others. They'll come back for us."

sShearon hesitated, reading the fragile hope in her eyes. He couldn't shatter it. With a heavy heart, he stepped through the portal and vanished, leaving behind an ice-bound world filled with frozen dreams.

The record archives

Chapter 37

On the moon world of El' Azar, in a locked drawer on the third floor of the citadel's records tower, an amulet flashed. No sound. No vibration. Just a flash. Then stillness. The jewel returned to its dull, lifeless sheen.

A red spark bloomed in the centre of the room. It swelled, pulsed, and tore open a slit of molten air. From it stepped a devil—small, grotesque, his black skin slick with sweat that hissed when it struck the floorboards. He moved like smoke, soundless, until he reached the shelves. Then he raised one trembling claw. Fire burst from his hand, roaring across the room.

The records tower burned.

Flames swallowed shelves, scrolls, centuries of memory. Two residents screamed before the fire took their voices. Their ashes fell with the books.

The devil turned toward the portal and laughed.

"Come," he rasped.

One after another, more devils emerged—two squads of thirty and a smaller clutch of five. The heat welcomed them. Firelight painted their twisted faces as they basked in the glow, drinking in its fury. Without a word, they began to descend the spiral stairs.

At the base of the tower, their leader, Whiro, spread his arms. "Unleash fire and hell, my brothers!"

They obeyed. Most scattered through the citadel's halls, spewing fire, tearing down walls, hunting for the Cydarions. Whiro stayed behind. He crouched, gathering energy until his skin burned white-hot. Then he leapt outward in a starburst. A shockwave tore through the stone staircase, through three floors, and into the roof. The tower erupted. The citadel shuddered from its roots to its spires. Windows exploded. Foundations groaned. Every corridor shook.

The devils rampaged through the citadel, turning rooms to cinders and hunting anything that moved. The Cydarions were their prey. Their screams were music. Their deaths, an offering to their father, Lucifer.

Corridor after corridor fell in ruin behind them.

Pace sat at his desk in the master's study when the first tremor hit. He looked up from his data screen. The next one slammed harder—tenfold. The walls split, pictures crashed, glass burst. Roof tiles rained down.

He threw himself to the floor as shards of window glass knifed through the air. One long shard buried itself in his shoulder blade. He gritted his teeth, waited for the shaking to subside, then tore a sleeve from his shirt. Wrapping his hand, he pulled the shard free, slow and steady, hissing through his teeth. Blood slicked his back. He flexed once... still mobile.

Then a wind rose in the room. Papers swirled around him though the trees outside were still. A whisper rode the wind:

"Run."

Pace froze. He knew that voice.

"Phos?" he breathed.

"Run, Pace!"

That was no echo. His heart lurched. He bolted for the shattered door, glass crunching underfoot, and dove through just as the ceiling gave way behind him.

Outside, on the cliff-top gardens, he sprinted around the citadel's outer path, shouting for anyone who could hear him to evacuate.

Xania appeared, running uphill toward him.

"You okay?" he shouted.

"Are you?" she called back, eyes catching the blood on his back.

"It's nothing," he said. "Did you feel the quake?"

Xania shook her head. "Not the ground. My body."

He frowned but didn't ask.

They rounded the corner, and saw the records tower. A column of fire climbed the sky, then the whole tower blew apart in a single blast of stone and light.

"Bork!" Pace shouted, sprinting toward the collapse.

A second explosion thundered from below the tower. The shockwave slammed him off his feet, flinging him ten metres across the grass. He hit hard, rolled, and lay staring up at the smoke-streaked sky.

"Pace!" Xania's voice cut through the ringing in his ears. She reached him as he sat up, dazed. Her voice sounded distant, muffled.

"Can you hear me?" she asked.

He nodded. "What's... happening?" His own voice sounded underwater.

"We've got to get everyone out," she said.

He nodded again, slowly catching fragments of sound as his hearing returned. "Yeah. Agreed."

She helped him to his feet. Together they turned toward the citadel, and froze. Devils poured from a gaping wound in the wall, climbing, bounding, screeching into the open air.

"What the..." Pace started.

"How did they get here?" Xania whispered.

He clenched his jaw. "We need to stop them. Get the others. Protect the residents."

She nodded. "Where are your weapons?"

"In the armoury," he said grimly.

"Yours?"

"Same."

"Shit."

He tapped his comms device. *Nyk, we could use you right now.* Then turned to Xania: "I'll get to the armoury. You find survivors. Meet back here."

"Got it," she said, turning away.

"Don't get caught!" he shouted after her.

Through the smoke, fires burned in every wing of the citadel. Orange light flared behind the shattered windows. Pace's jaw tightened. *Lucigon... this has your stench all over it.*

He sprinted toward the kitchen entrance, one of the few areas untouched. Residents still fled through the gardens. He waved them onward. "Get clear! Hide anywhere... just go!"

The kitchen air was thick with heat. Not from ovens, these were fires deeper inside. He covered his mouth with his torn sleeve and pushed on through two corridors, breaking necks of devils who crossed his path. His anger sharpened him.

The armoury door hung off one hinge, the wall beside it cratered and blackened. He listened... no footsteps behind him, and descended the stone stairs. A faint scraping echoed below. Claws on stone.

At the control panel, he pressed his thumb to the pad. Lights flicked on. Then a thought struck. Instead of full illumination, he triggered a rapid strobe sequence. The room pulsed with blinding bursts and black gaps.

Blaster fire ripped through the flicker. Pace dove behind a heavy workbench. *Guess that answers that.*

He scanned the table: blades, tools, Xania's sais. He grabbed a knife, threw it blind across the floor. The devils fired at the sound. In that instant, Pace moved, crouching low between flashes, ghosting toward the next section.

A growl rolled through the dark.

"I can smell you, Cydarion." A sniff. "Come out where I can see you."

Pace stayed still, breath shallow. The rhythmic scrape of claws moved closer. He slipped toward the defence rack: his holo-bracelet lay there. Two steps away. Direct line of sight. No time.

He kicked off his boots, setting them at the far end of the table. When the lights died, he yelled, "I'm here!" and bolted the other way.

The lights returned. The devil fired at the boots, shredding them. Pace reached the bracelet, slid his hand in, powered it up; just as his hip slammed the table. He grunted. The devil turned, saw him, and opened fire.

The first bolt hit the holo-shield as it flared to life, blue light catching the blast. Pace charged. The devil fired again, but Pace didn't stop. They collided—shield to chest—and the stored energy released all at once.

The devil was hurled backward, torn apart by his own blaster's force. The rifle spun, struck the wall, and buried itself halfway through the stone.

Pace blinked, panting. "Didn't know it could do that." He swept the armoury for supplies, strapping on as many weapons as he could carry, and noticed a small square box, and grabbed it with a grin. "Hope this still works."

The ceiling cracked above him. A jagged line snaked through the stone.

"Move, move, move!"

He sprinted for the stairs. The dining hall collapsed behind him, stone and fire crashing into the armoury below. He didn't look back.

Through the kitchens again, he fired at anything red-eyed that moved. Three devils chased him into the corridor. He dropped a coin-shaped device from his belt and ran on. Twenty paces later, he stopped and turned.

One devil bent, picking up the coin. "Lose something, Cydarion?" it taunted.

Pace raised his wrist, showing the bracelet. "That one's for you."

He pressed the trigger. The coin imploded. A disc of energy flared outward, slicing all three devils clean through.

Pace smirked, turned, and sprinted into the open air; meeting Xania again on the grass.

The dead Cydarions return

Chapter 38

Xania's home was under siege. Flames licked the walls, snapping and curling upward like living serpents. Smoke choked the corridors, stinging her eyes, filling her lungs with a harsh, acrid taste. Heart hammering, she didn't pause. Instinct and training kicked in. A splintered plank became her weapon; an extension of her will. She swung, stabbed, and hacked with lethal precision. Devils fell, snarling, claws raking empty air where her strikes had landed. Room by room, she cleared the chaos, guiding terrified residents toward the open fields beyond. They stumbled through smoke and fire, coughing, hearts thudding, clinging to her every command.

In a quiet contemplation room, Theksun was cornered. Two devils closed in, teeth bared, claws raised. Sweat ran down his temple. He braced himself, but panic flickered in his eyes.

"Hey!" Xania's voice cut through the roar of the inferno. "Wanna make it a fair fight?"

One devil turned. A voice came from above, cold and sharp.

"Yes, let's!"

A massive devil dropped from the ceiling with a thunderous crash, shaking dust from the rafters. Four short legs, twice the size of the others, a mouth chattering with anticipation. Xania froze for the briefest instant. Her heart clenched. A third. She hadn't expected a third.

Flames danced along her splintered wood. "Fetch?" she taunted, letting a cruel, mocking grin slide across her face.

"I shall fetch your bones to my master!" it roared, voice bouncing off the walls.

Strange. Ridiculous. And yet—enough. Enough for her to plan. She darted backward, shouting, "Come and fetch!"

The giant lunged. Xania dropped low, pressing her hands into the stone floor with every ounce of strength she had. Cracks zig-zagged outward, spiderwebbing across the walls and ceiling. Dust rained down like snow. With a deafening crash, stone collapsed above the doorway, crushing the devil mid-leap. Its eyes widened in pleading, a scream caught in its throat before it exhaled its last breath.

"That was close," Xania muttered, wiping sweat and ash from her brow.

The smaller devils hesitated. Theksun didn't. He barrelled into one, shoulder smashing into the other, sending both crashing to the floor. He vaulted over the rubble, past Xania, murmuring a quick thanks.

Xania slammed her hands into another wall. The stone groaned and buckled, burying the remaining devils beneath debris. She didn't wait to see if it worked. She followed Theksun, guiding him toward Pace.

Beau came running from her parents' farmhouse, lungs burning, fear etched into every movement.

"You okay?" Xania called.

"Yeah… what happened?" Beau gasped.

"Devils," Xania replied, her voice tight, taste of smoke in her mouth.

"Fuck!" Beau cursed. "Who else is in there?"

Pace shook his head, panic visible in the tense line of his jaw. "Drake, the students, Bork, Kee, Dok, sShearon… I don't know who's left alive."

"I'm here," Kee said, voice quivering but steady, peeking from behind a boulder, eyes scanning the chaos.

"Drake will handle the students," Xania said firmly. "He's capable. Trust him."

"I hope you're right," Pace muttered, grimacing, scanning the horizon for movement.

"No one is down until we have proof," Beau said, locking eyes with each of them. Her hand shook slightly, but her tone carried authority.

"Right," Pace nodded.

"What's the plan?" Xania asked, eyes flicking toward the shattered building.

From the ruins poured a legion of devils. Forty-seven, lining up with uncanny precision, probably more hiding inside. The heat from the fires, the smell of sulfur, the crackle of burning timber: it all pressed down on them. A tense stand-off stretched across the open field, only broken by the occasional hiss of fireballs from the devils' claws.

A massive devil stepped forward, surveying the battlefield. Muscles tensed, eyes sharp as obsidian.

"Israfil, it is your time!"

A trumpet appeared in the hands of a devil who emerged from behind the debris.

"Shit," Pace muttered, unease twisting his features.

Beau squinted. "Bad music?"

Pace shook his head. "A prophecy. Three blasts. Marks the time of judgment—the beginning of the end."

Israfil lifted the trumpet. Three blasts echoed over the battlefield, bouncing off the distant hills. The devils roared in approval.

"They're going all out," Pace muttered, panic creeping into his voice. "We're not ready."

The devils surged, fireballs arcing across the battlefield. One crouched, claws digging deep into the soil, chanting in a guttural, reverberating rhythm.

"Get ready!" Pace shouted, firing at the incoming devils.

Horror struck Beau. "My parents..."

"No! We need you here!" Pace barked.

"They're my priority!" Beau snapped, lightning flashing at her fingertips, her voice trembling yet resolute.

Theksun stepped forward, eyes fierce. "I'll take them. You're more useful here."

Kee's eyes lit with determination. "We'll keep them safe," he said, jaw tight, muscles coiled.

Xania drew her Sais, blades glinting in the firelight. Every step was measured, every strike deadly. Pace zig-zagged across the battlefield, shooting, shouting, weaving between flames and debris. Beau nodded once to Theksun and Kee, then turned to face the devils. Lightning erupted from her hands, striking seven devils down in bursts of blinding energy. Dust and smoke swirled around her, flames reflecting in her eyes.

The chanting devil churned the ground violently. Skeletal hands burst through the soil, followed by skulls, limbs, and torsos. Nine figures clawed free, converging on the cemetery where the old Cydarions rested.

"It can't be," Pace muttered, eyes wide. "He's re-erecting the dead."

Jodrell emerged first, flesh decayed, beard stark against the ruin, fingernails twisted into claws. Hollow eye sockets stared with nothing inside.

"No!" Xania sank to her knees, trembling, tears streaking her ash-smudged face. Beau moved to shield her, placing a hand firmly on her shoulder.

The undead joined the devils, moving with eerie coordination.

"I can't!" Xania screamed, voice raw, echoing across the field.

A green light flashed from the portal room ruins. Qútú stepped into the chaos, immediately slammed down by a red wave of devils.

"Fuck!" Pace shouted, eyes wide.

Red bodies flew aside as Qútú rose, dust and blood coating him. One devil's head flew from a kick.

His E-whip snapped and cracked, severing undead Cydarion limbs with surgical precision. Purah, the devil of the undead, directed six devils to surround him, claws glinting in the firelight.

"Stop!" Xania shouted, panic and desperation in her tone.

"It is necessary," Qútú said, voice cold, emotionless. "They feel nothing."

The metallic star on the ground unfolded like a mechanical flower, points plunging into the earth. Yellow light bloomed, slowly turning red. From it emerged a massive devil, fire and shadow coiling around him.

The devils knelt in unison, a haunting, synchronized motion.

Lucigon had arrived.

Battle arena on Genesis Prime

Chapter 39

Lucigon rose to his full height and dominated the chaos like a dark peak. "WHERE IS THE MASTER?" His voice rolled across the field, deep and absolute.

Pace glanced at Xania and Beau and shook his head: hold back.

"I'M HERE!" Pace called, pushing himself upright.

Qútú didn't hesitate; he kept clearing the skeletal undead even as they reformed like bad memories.

"YOU? I will kill you first for what you did to Calebro," Lucigon thundered from across the grass.

"Sure, I've heard that before," Pace said, lips crooked.

"Not from me," Lucigon snarled, claws flexing.

"I'm not afraid of you," Pace shot back.

"You should be. I am your doom. I will erase the Cydarions, and then I will kill that God of yours." Lucigon's words carried the weight of promise and malice.

"No one kills God," Pace said, though the certainty trembled.

"That's exactly what he wants you to believe!" Lucigon surged forward.

Pace's yonca blasts flared, only to glance harmlessly off Lucigon's hide. A fireball slammed into the dirt at Pace's boots and hurled him backward. He rolled, scrambled up and fired again; bolts skittered off the demon's thick skin. Fireball after fireball hammered the ground around him.

His Holo-bracelet took the brunt; its blue glow warbled under the heat. "Shit!" Pace cursed, shaking it as if motion could coax life back into the device. I need another plan, his mind said, breathless. "You're Lucifer's kid, aren't you?" he called, buying time.

Lucigon laughed, a sound like stones grinding. "I am your new demi-god. Bow, and I may spare you."

"You're still a demon. Why should I believe you?" Pace kept moving, testing angles, watching for windups.

"You shouldn't. You'll die anyway!" Lucigon spat, and the air blossomed into flame. Pace darted, twisted. An explosive blast hit his side. He landed badly, felt the sickening pop along his wrist and a hot sting along his leg. The Holo-bracelet shattered like glass under impact; searing heat kissed through fabric.

A flicker of memory, *the square box,* shot through him like lightning.

"Lucigon... is that your name?" Pace called, ducking behind a jagged rock. "Can't hear very well with all this..." He let the words trail off on purpose.

"Yes. But you won't live long enough to say it twice," Lucigon snarled, advancing.

"Lucigon! Lucigon! Lucigon!" Pace jabbed the name out like a metronome and shrugged, the taunt buying him breath as he glanced at Beau and Xania, bloodied and surrounded. He needed a pivot.

Lucigon's roar rattled the grass and stamped the air.

"Fair fight?" Pace offered, stepping from cover with his arms lifted in a clear, ridiculous invitation. "You and me. Arena."

"I could finish you here," Lucigon said simply.

"You'll have an audience. Outsmart a Cydarion and they'll remember your name," Pace goaded, eyes flicking for the opening.

Lucigon snorted and barrelled forward.

Pace looked across the battlefield one final time, and shoved open a rippling portal. "Follow me to Genesis Prime," he called, and with a whispered prayer he stepped through.

Lucigon answered with a scream that split the sky and dove after him, just missing the portal.

***

When Pace hit the arena sand it felt cool and granular between his toes, the small, ordinary detail grounding him. A thunderous roar and a screaming raptor made him spin just in time to see a four-legged behemoth thunder past, its hide like layered armour. A flying reptile, wings beating like clumsy sails, dove for his head. Pace smiled, this was providence. He pulled the small box from his pocket, thumbed the dial to max, then flung it hard. The casing cracked open on the grit and a high, piercing tone shredded the air. Pain lanced through his skull; he clapped hands over his ears and shoved through a second portal, back toward El' Azar as a red whirlpool of light yawned open.

***

Lucigon slammed through expecting Pace. The piercing tone shredded his senses; for the first beat he staggered, disoriented. The two beasts fighting in the arena turned, fury redirected. The heavy, horned beast charged and struck Lucigon full, launching him into the sand. The flying reptile screeched and slashed at his back, tearing orange flesh with serrated talons. He beat his wings, tried to lift, but the horned beast's flank cracked into him and a horn ripped through the wing membrane.

Pain ate through him like a living thing.

He rolled to his back, clawed the sand, and with the third screech he lashed out—hooking his talons around the reptile's torso and biting its skull. Bone crunched under his jaws. He tore the wings free, flung the carcass away; blood slicked his claws and chest. The horned brute charged once more; Lucigon vaulted onto its back, digging a blade of a claw deep between armour plates. The beast bucked and flailed; Lucigon was thrown clear but landed on steady legs. He spotted a small box at his heel and crushed it under a stomping foot. The piercing tone died and his head cleared enough to think.

A slow trickle of black blood marked one of the beast's legs; wounded, it was slower but made unpredictably dangerous strikes. Lucigon timed it, slashed through tendon and joint, and the creature folded, flailing. He poured a continuous stream of fire into the thrashing body until ash rose. The crowd roared like hungry wolves; their cheers weren't for justice, only spectacle. The adulation warmed him briefly, then cooled as duty scraped at his mind. He remembered the mission. He opened a portal and left the arena's heat behind.

***

Back on El' Azar, Pace re-joined the chaos, adrenaline slamming through him. Xania and Beau fought with ragged breath; Qútú was a blur of precise strikes, mowing down skeletal ranks. But Lucigon returned faster than anyone expected, his scream driving a hush through the battlefield.

Lucigon found Pace and hurled a fireball with the calm of inevitability. It detonated at Pace's feet and threw him sideways into a hulking rock. A rib fractured under the impact; breath tunnelled out of him in a single, pain-shredded gasp. He coughed, tasted copper, lungs burning. He tried to rise, to force the world into sense, but each movement drew knives under his skin. Blazes smashed at him again and again; every landing knocked more air from his chest.

Pace's limbs slowed. He could hear the distant grunts and clashes but they were muffled, as if the battlefield were now underwater. Beau, Xania, Qútú were still fighting, still bleeding, still brave.

Lucigon walked over with the slow certainty of a predator whose kill is already named. His hand closed on Pace's throat like an iron vice and pulled him upright until Pace's head was tipped back, neck exposed.

Pace's heart hammered. He tasted smoke and iron and something like peace. His breath came shallow, jagged. He folded his hands almost without meaning and whispered, "Peace be with God."

Lucigon's claw flexed above the whisper as if the world held its breath.

The citadel in ruins

Chapter 40

Lucigon snorted. "Foolish mortal. I am the higher being here."

Thunder cracked above them, a shockwave tearing through the air.

A silver streak ripped across the sky, slowing as it turned, shaping into a sleek, wedge-shaped craft.

Pace's grin was forced. "Looks like my friend's higher than you," he said, but his voice wavered.

The Starlady, Nyk's luxury warship, dropped its nose, panels sliding open to expose glowing cannons.

TARGET ACQUIRED flashed across the console. Nyk grinned.

Lucigon scoffed and raised his arm.

Nyk fired.

A storm of blaster fire hammered Lucigon's chest just as his claw slashed for Pace's throat. The impact launched him backward, cracking, body tumbling. His strike still caught Pace, leaving a gory gash.

Pace gasped, face scraping against the dirt. Blood stung his eyes. He coughed, clawing desperately at the ground to push himself up.

The Starlady's barrels glowed white-hot, steam hissing in the humid air.

Lucigon clawed upright, rage blazing. Fireballs tore into the sky, scorching Nyk's weaving ship.

The undead Cydarions rose again almost as fast as Qútú cut them down.

"Nyk, go for Purah... he's the key!" Qútú shouted, his chest heaving, lungs burning from exhaustion.

"Purah's here?" Nyk scanned the chaos and spotted him. "If I hit him, I'll level the whole citadel," he said to himself.

"Whatever it takes!" Qútú yelled, E-whip snapping through bone and dust.

Then a faint, raspy voice cut through the comm, Pace. "Do it!" he wheezed, each syllable a struggle.

Lucigon turned toward the Cydarion women.

Nyk locked onto the devils guarding Purah. Blasters roared, driving them against a crumbling wall. They conjured fire, forming a blazing shield.

Nyk tapped the targeting screen. A twin-tubed missile dropped free, engines flaring. It soared high, straight past the devils. Two laughed at the near miss.

So did Nyk. The missile arced back and screamed into the wall behind them. The explosion folded both corner towers inward, crushing all seven.

Qútú's next whip strike missed; yet every undead around him dropped. He turned, saw the wreckage, and grinned.

"Nice work!" he shouted toward the ship.

Nyk nodded, unseen.

Lucigon came from behind, smashing Xania into the ground. She didn't move.

"Xania!" Qútú yelled, too far to reach her.

Beau's lightning sparked, throwing Lucigon back in spasms.

"Get up!" she screamed at Xania.

A devil blindsided Beau, knocking her flat. The lightning died. Lucigon steadied himself and closed in.

Xania's eyes flickered open. Pain lanced through her body, but anger kept her awake.

She pressed her palms into the dirt. The ground cracked and split open into a vast chasm. Devils fell screaming. Lucigon leapt clear before Xania released her grip, sealing the rift and crushing the rest.

She staggered to her feet and ran for Beau.

Beau tried to rise, but another devil stomped her hand. Cracks snapped through her bones. She collapsed, sparks fading.

Lucigon landed beside her and kicked her over.

"Take your last breath, bitch," he growled, foot rising.

Beau looked up. Through the firestorm she saw the T13 shuttle glinting high above: her family's ship. They made it.

A smile touched her lips. "Nothing left to lose," she whispered, summoning one last surge of lightning.

Xania planted her feet and unleashed a wall of wind. Devils tumbled, bodies slamming into Lucigon. Beau's bolt hit his leg, shaking him.

The gale caught his wings and hurled him into the sky, spinning out of control.

Xania sprinted to Beau, helping her up.

Far down the hill, Lucigon dragged himself upright and roared, guttural, un-natural.

Pace's heart hammered, chest heaving, vision swimming. His voice cracked as he rasped into the comm. "Nyk... pick everyone up... we're... we're done..."

He collapsed into the churned grass, trembling, shaking with exhaustion and dread.

The Starlady swept low, ramp open. Beau and Xania climbed aboard, beaten but alive. Qútú followed, exhausted.

In the cockpit, Xania froze, not the silhouette she expected. The pilot turned, grinning. "Hey, kid." Crown Claw perched on his shoulder.

It *was* Nyk.

"Turn us around," Xania ordered. "Low pass over the demons."

"This ship's on its last legs," Nyk warned.

"Shields?"

"Only in space; the graviton field..."

"Just do it!" she snapped.

Beau limped in behind her. "Trust her," she said through clenched teeth.

Qútú slumped into the co-pilot seat, merely shaking his head.

Nyk sighed. "She better know what she's doing." He spun the Starlady and dove toward the devils. Fireballs streaked up; the nose cone glowed red.

Xania stepped onto the ramp, wind whipping her hair. She raised her arms.

A hurricane blasted from her hands, sweeping the devils off their feet and over the cliff into the black sea.

Beau joined her, lightning sparking from her one good hand. Together, wind and lightning purged the cliffside.

***

Lucigon watched from afar. "He never told me they had powers, this changes everything," he snarled. "We may have lost this battle, but the war is ours."

He tore open a portal and stepped through, leaving ruin behind.

***

The last of the devils either fell into the waters below or leapt to their deaths. The citadel lay in ruins, its grandeur shattered. Only one room remained standing, defiant amidst the rubble.

Pace sank to his knees, body shaking, every muscle screaming. His chest heaved; the sting of Lucigon's claw burned like fire on his cheek. A wave of panic rolled over him. "How... how are we supposed to deal with this?" he whispered, voice cracking. Salt stung his eyes.

The Starlady landed softly on the grass, boarding ramp hissing open. Beau and Xania stepped down, faces streaked with dirt and sweat, each limping but alive. Nyk followed, calm as ever, his presence grounding them.

Qútú remained on the ramp, legs dangling over the edge. His eyes, black, stared out to sea, unseeing.

"Are you coming?" Nyk asked.

"No," Qútú replied, voice low. "I need... to process this... alone."

Nyk placed a hand on Qútú's shoulder. "We wouldn't be here if it weren't for you."

Qútú didn't respond, his gaze fixed on the horizon beyond the ruined citadel.

Pace watched the Starlady's ramp. He stumbled toward it, shaking, hands gripping Nyk's arm as if it could anchor him against the storm inside. "You... okay?" he asked, voice raw.

Nyk smiled faintly. "I am. Gone through a lot, but I'm here."

Pace blinked at Nyk's new buzz cut. "They didn't do electro-therapy, did they?"

"No," Nyk chuckled. "Helped me... in other ways."

Beau grinned. "It's badass. Suits the smile."

Xania pointed, approving. "I like it."

Pace's eyes drifted to Qútú, his chest tightened. "He's alright?"

"He'll be fine," Nyk said. "He just... needs space."

They turned toward the citadel. Flames hissed, smoke curling into the sky. Only one room remained intact. Pace shook, voice tight with desperation. "Where do we even start?"

"We rebuild," Xania said firmly.

Pace's breath rattled. "There's more devils out there. We can't keep up. This... this is too much. We're done. Lucifer beat us. It's in God's hands now."

Xania's eyes blazed. "No. We fight. We keep fighting."

"You saw what happened," Pace said, voice low. "We barely survived. Many didn't. Our home... it's gone."

"We'll rebuild," she insisted.

"How?" he shouted, voice breaking. "We don't have magic to fix anything!"

"Then we'll find another way," Xania shot back.

A roar shattered the silence behind them.

"What was that?" Nyk spun, blasters drawn.

Xania froze, hands rising.

"This is it," Pace whispered, trembling. "It's over... it's really over..."

Another roar, closer this time, rolling over the hill like thunder.

Beau stood with Qútú on the Starlady's ramp, eyes fixed ahead. She pointed.

Pace followed her gaze, a shiver ran up his spine. Shapes crested the ridge. One. Three. five. Then a sixth.

Drake. With five Storous'.

Pace's chest heaved, heart hammering. Relief, disbelief, exhaustion. His legs buckled and he sank to his knees.

Xania ran to meet them, checking each student. Nyk was already laughing, pulling them into hugs.

Drake reached Pace and lifted him, wrapping him in a bear hug.

"Oof... careful," Pace gasped. "Broken rib."

Drake grinned. "Then you might want that checked," he boomed.

"I thought you were gone," Pace said, glancing toward the ruined citadel.

"We would've been," Drake said lightly, "if not for an old friend."

"You heard Phos too?"

Drake nodded. "And Bork knew an escape route..."

"Bork was with you?"

"Of course. We were coming to help, but he stayed behind to cover us..."

"That roar, that was you?"

Drake laughed. "Spotted Grace hound battle cry. Learned it as a youngling. Supposed to terrify the enemy."

"Well, it worked," said Nyk.

Drake whistled a sharp signal. Moments later, Bork limped over the hill.

Pace's face lit up. "You're alive," he said as the records keeper arrived.

"Barely," Bork said, adjusting his fur.

Pace grinned weakly. "Sorry about the archives."

Bork smiled. "Most were backed up."

Before Pace could reply, Beau came running from the Starlady, disbelief bright in her eyes.

"My parents are safe!" she shouted. "They also got one hundred and thirty-two residents out before the collapse!"

"That's incredible," Nyk said, a smile breaking through.

Pace squeezed her shoulder. "You should see them... and get that hand checked."

Beau turned to Nyk. "Can I borrow your ship?"

"No," he said firmly.

"But he will fly you," suggested Xania.

Nyk smiled.

Beau smirked. "Deal."

A sharp green flash cut across the sky. Everyone froze. The light grew, twisting into a spiraling rift above the ruins.

"Portal," Qútú breathed.

Something burst through, landing hard on all fours. Dust billowed. When it cleared, Pace's heart leapt.

"Dok!"

The creature shook off debris and strode forward, nostrils flaring.

Pace gave him the short version: the battle, Lucigon's escape, the destruction.

Dok's ears flattened. "This is worse than I thought."

"You know something?" Xania asked.

"They have a weapon," Dok said darkly. "I've seen it. A ship. Massive. Powered by slaves. Nuclear magnets. Enough force to move..."

"We have a ship," Nyk interrupted, looking at Pace.

Pace stared, panic coiling anew. He bit his lip, blood ran again.

Dok turned, sniffing the air. His eyes narrowing at Beau's bandaged hand. "It's broken," he said.

Beau blinked. "Yeah?"

"I can smell it."

She pulled back slightly. "Creepy."

"May I?"

Beau hesitated. "You're the doc."

Dok cupped her hand between his paws. Heat shimmered. There was a sharp pop, then another. Beau winced, but didn't scream.

Moments later, Dok released her. "Better?"

Beau flexed her fingers. "You fixed it."

Pace stared, raw desperation etched across his face. "How?"

Dok shrugged. "It just... happens."

Pace's expression shifted. Panic, fear, hopelessness, all colliding. "Wait... Shearon was with you, wasn't he?"

"He was," Dok said. "We split up. He's not back?"

No one answered.

"He's alive," Dok said firmly. "I'd know if he wasn't."

Nyk exhaled. "Then we keep hoping."

"Dok," Pace said quietly, voice trembling, "this weapon, how can we stop it?"

"Not with what we have," Dok replied. "And there are more. Larger ones."

Pace ran a hand through his blood-matted hair. "Fantastic! Too many variables, too few of us."

He laughed once, it was short, bitter, and edged with panic. "Look at us. A handful of survivors against an immortal, his son, and now planet killers. How do we even fight that?"

He glared up at the darken sky, voice cracking. "When... when are you going to *do* something?!"

Thunder answered. The ground trembled.

A third of the cliff sheared away, sending half the of the citadel crashing into the sea below.

Pace threw his arms out, ragged, shaking. "Perfect! Just perfect!" His voice broke. "You watching this?!"

The others stood in silence. Even the wind had stopped.

"This is it," Pace whispered, voice raw. "The Cydarions are done. We fight only to survive now."

The young Storous's looked at him, pale and silent.

"You're giving up?" Xania's voice broke. "After everything? We still have more to give!"

"I won't risk another life," Pace said, calming his breath.

"You don't walk into a battle you'll lose," Dok warned.

Xania turned on him. "You do... you do if it's the right thing!"

Her voice echoed across the ruined shore. No one spoke.

Nyk scrunched his eyes in anguish, and breathed deep.

"I'll do it alone," she whispered.

Nyk stepped forward, pulled her close, kissed her forehead. "We're family. We stick together. But Pace is right. It's over."

Thunder rolled one last time, shaking the shore. The sea swallowed the last stone of the citadel, one room still holding strong. Nothing else remained but smoke and ruin.

Pace stood at the edge of the cliff, coat shirt, body trembling, the weight of failure pressing down. His voice was barely a whisper.

"Even God's given up..."

No one replied. Not Nyk. Not Xania. Not Beau or Qútú. No one.

They had nothing left to say.

The storm faded, leaving only the hiss of the receding tide.

Pace turned from the sea. "Let's go," he said, shaking.

One by one, they followed, broken silhouettes against the dying light.

Above them, the clouds split for a heartbeat, a single shaft of sunlight piercing through the smoke. It fell where the citadel had once stood... then vanished.

No one saw it.

The wind carried their footsteps into silence.

The universe no longer cared who won or lost.

It had already chosen its side.